A Son Comes HOME

A Son Comes
HOME

JOSEPH BENTZ

BETHANY HOUSE PUBLISHERS
MINNEAPOLIS, MINNESOTA 55438

Published by Bethany House Publishers
A Ministry of Bethany Fellowship International
11400 Hampshire Avenue South
Minneapolis, Minnesota 55438
www.bethanyhouse.com

Printed in the United States of America by
Bethany Press International, Minneapolis, Minnesota 55438

ISBN 0–7642–2207–4

To

Mom, Dad, and Debbie

JOSEPH BENTZ is a professor at Azuza Pacific University. He is the author of *Song of Fire* and numerous articles in magazines, newspapers, and scholarly journals. He holds degrees in English as well as a doctorate in American Literature from Purdue University. He and his wife have one son and make their home in Southern California.

Prologue

CHRIS

I wanted to kill my brother on the day he died. I think back to that with embarrassment now, and with guilt. At the moment his body was being crushed in a tangle of glass and steel, I was hurling his tools against the back of the garage door. I stood in the exact spot where his car should have been, imagining I was pelting him with wrenches and screwdrivers and hammers, denouncing him for his lies and betrayal as he begged me to stop.

David died on Culpepper Highway, a twisting, narrow road—not a highway at all—that slices through a wooded area west of Indianapolis. With almost no shoulder, the two lanes are barely wide enough for a single car. It twists through the woods in unpredictable directions, and yellow signs warning of elaborate curves dot the side of the road. The posted speed limit in some places is only fifteen miles per hour. It has not been resurfaced in decades, and the crumbling blacktop makes for a jarring ride even when driving at a snail's pace.

My brother did not drive it slowly. He liked the road for the same reason most people hate it: He said it was like a roller coaster except the danger was real. Culpepper Highway features two bridges so narrow, so old, and so damaged that only one car at a time can creep over them. The road and its bridges were the setting for most of the ghost stories I heard during my childhood, those tales of stranded cars on the bridge and mysterious murderers who popped out of nowhere to kill unsuspecting victims.

Culpepper's woods are so thick that tree branches hang in an ominous—some say beautiful—archway over the road. On the day of his death, David drove his restored 1953 Chevrolet Bel Air. He worked long hours as a mechanic, but even after being in the garage all day, David could still find the energy to come home and work late into the evening on one of his old cars. By age twenty-seven, he had restored eleven antique automobiles, and the '53 Bel Air was the only one he still owned.

The Bel Air was in perfect condition when David drove it away from our house that afternoon in July of 1992. Just that week he had waxed it, vacuumed the interior, scrubbed the whitewall tires, and polished the windows. He had wiped down the engine compartment and cleaned out the trunk. The car looked massive and indestructible by modern standards, with its bulky body, big rear fenders, imposing grille, and fender skirts. The dark metallic green top and pastel green bottom were striking and made the car impossible to ignore. I had ridden in it with David before, and everybody would stare as we drove by.

David liked driving his old cars on Culpepper Highway because he said it was one of the few roads that felt as old as the car itself. He hated taking the car out on the big freeways, with what he considered characterless modern cars zipping all around him. Dad had warned him many times about driving too fast on such a treacherous road. *"You've got to drive these old cars with a little respect. You can't go tearing around like they're some kind of brand-new sports car. You go too fast!"*

I don't think David thought of his driving as either slow or fast. He just wanted the car to feel a certain way when he was behind the wheel. "I need to know I'm really *driving* it," he would say. "What good is having the car if you're just going to poke along in it slow and straight down these neighborhood roads? Dad wants to park his cars in the garage and polish them. I want to *do* something with mine."

No one witnessed what David did on that bend on Culpepper Highway. The accident could be reconstructed only by examining the tire tracks and skid marks and the demolished car. David made it through one of the worst curves on the road, a turn so sharp it was nearly one hundred eighty degrees. Despite all the glaring warning signs, David likely drove the car two or three times the speed limit around that curve. There is no room for error on that part of the road. A driver who misjudges will skid over a gravel embankment and end up in the trees. David had driven that stretch countless times, sometimes with me in the car. On many nights since his death I have woken up haunted by the same dream: David and I hurtling around that bend together. I feel the car turning, my shoulder smashing against the door, but instead of straightening again, the car, in the surrealism of dreams, continues to spin, as if it has been picked up by a tornado. I feel the frightening loss of control of my body as it is tossed from side to side. I catch sight of David beside me. He is smiling! Then the bone-shattering thud of the car crashing to the ground, and I cannot catch my breath. I wake up gasping for air.

Once David had made it around the most dangerous section, he must have felt safe as his car started to straighten out again. But he was too far to the right. The Bel Air slid off the road, the right front and back wheels dropping perilously off the pavement and onto the rocky embankment, where they churned furiously as he tried to get the car back onto the road. He might have succeeded if he had been given a few more feet of clear ground, but instead, the car smashed head on into a tree, crushing my brother in a chaos of glass and metal.

A week later I visited the site where he had died and noticed how absurdly small and common the tree was that had killed him. I expected it to be shattered into kindling, but it stood resolute, barely scratched. My dad and I later went to see the husk of an automobile that had become David's tomb. My father ran his hand over the smashed hood and cried, as if he were stroking his dead son's head. It was almost impossible for us to believe David's death. He was so enormous in our minds that we were certain it would take more than a tree and an automobile to end his life.

David's death overpowered my grievances against him. I was justified in my anger toward him, for he had finally snared me in his trap of betrayal and deceit, but I had to swallow my rage whole. David's death transformed him, in the minds of everyone we knew, into my perfect brother. He was forever frozen in his youth, beauty, talent, and charisma, while in my family's eyes, I lived on as a pale reminder of him.

It had always been natural for my family to compare David and me, and his death only aggravated that tendency. Two years younger than David, I always felt like a smaller version of him. An inch shorter, a little slighter in build, a little less good-looking. We both had dark hair, dark eyebrows, and deep brown eyes that the women in our family coveted. Even at David's funeral, the comparisons did not stop. As we waited in the lobby of the funeral home, Aunt Shirley said to me, "David was so good-looking." Instead of leaving the comment there, she paused for a moment, looked at me, and said, "So are you, honey." Her comment annoyed me. Why should she mention me at all? I felt like saying, "So are you, Aunt Shirley."

After the funeral, I was lost in a whirlwind of grief and rage so powerful it tore at the relationship I valued most. David's scheming cost me Beth. Within two weeks of his death, she put off our engagement from Christmas to the following summer, a humiliating postponement, as if she were putting me on probation. Every day the temptation grew for me to escape Indiana. I had been living at home for the summer, and at the end of August I was to return to finish my Ph.D. at Purdue and to teach two freshman composition courses. However, I had another offer. Three of my university friends had invited me to Southern California, where they were teaching at a community college near Los Angeles.

One final catastrophe that summer persuaded me to accept their offer and flee. In the back of my parents' house, my father had built a two-and-a-half-car garage to make it easier for him and David to work on their cars. When I was home for the summers, I parked my car there. Dad had found that he could squeeze three cars in the garage if he parked one parallel to the back wall. The other two cars had to be driven in very close to the side of that car so the garage door could be closed.

That summer Dad had his most prized possession against the back wall—a '51 Chevy—which meant my car had to be just inches from his. I had told Dad, "I'm going to end up hitting your Chevy if you leave it like that."

"You won't if you know what's good for you" had been his reply.

A couple weeks after David's death, it happened. I had been out late and pulled into the driveway in a distracted haze, as was so often the case that summer. I pulled the car into the garage slowly while the door was still going up, and by the time the door reached the top, my car was only in three-fourths of the way. That night the door malfunctioned, as it did occasionally, and immediately started back down, poised to land on my car.

Suddenly emerging from my daze, I hit the accelerator too hard. The sound that followed was the heart-wrenching crumpling of metal on metal. I backed up in a panic and nearly slammed into the garage door. Then I sat motionless for a full thirty seconds, stunned, afraid to view what I had done to Dad's car.

Eventually I got the garage door open again, pulled my car out, and walked back inside to inspect the damage to Dad's favorite car. The fluorescent light above the workbench illuminated a caved-in front fender and passenger door. I put my hand on the dent and felt the perfectly polished paint crumble beneath my fingers. I ran my hand over the injury as tenderly as if it were the body of a child I had run over on the road. As bad as the damage looked to me, I knew it would look even worse to Dad. I knew that even if I paid to get the car fixed and made all the arrangements to have the work done, he would never be happy with it. To him it would always look damaged. No matter how perfectly repaired a door and fender might look to everyone else, Dad would see it as flawed and would declare that it was impossible to get everything matched just right.

A smashed antique car in my family was a disaster even in the best of times, but I felt certain that in the aftermath of David's death, it would take on huge significance for my father and would sever the frail cord that linked us. This would be yet another reminder of why David was the better son—he restored cars, while I destroyed them. Dad had already lapsed into silence since the funeral. We had never openly argued. Dad would never expend that much energy on me. He had simply turned away and shut me out.

It was daylight before I finally worked up the courage to go inside the house and confess to my Dad what had happened. He was sitting at the kitchen table, reading the paper and drinking a cup of coffee. I stated it as matter-of-factly as possible, not daring to stray from the words I had prepared and memorized. "You better come out to the garage. I crashed into the Chevy."

He ran out there immediately in his bathrobe, and I followed. The groan he let out as he first set eyes on the smashed car sent chills through me. I tried to detach myself from the scene. I tried to tell myself that in the long run, this accident might be a good thing. It would help me make the break with him that I had inevitably been heading toward.

Those first moments with him in the garage as he paced back and forth in front of the wreck, trembling in fury, were agonizing. His face and neck were so red, so throbbing with rage, that I half expected his head to burst wide open at any moment. Fortunately, it was an anger that did not engender many words. Instead he mumbled, "Just tear things up and leave the cleanup for somebody else. Never took care of other people's things. Just thought about yourself. Tear it up. What do you care?"

I didn't say a word to him, just stood silently like the idiot I had been labeled. Despite the tension that electrified the room, the fatigue from a sleepless night in the garage was weighing down on me, and my thoughts would not focus. I debated whether or not to tell him right then that I had decided to leave for California. I opened my mouth to stammer out an apology, but he saved me that torment by storming off to the house, leaving me alone in the garage, staring at a crumpled piece of metal.

Later that morning I planned my escape. My friends in California were still eager to have me visit, so I called a travel agent and booked a flight to Los Angeles for the next day. I called my boss at the magazine to tell him I was quitting earlier than expected. All this activity gave me a wonderful sense of relief. I was finally doing something instead of simply waiting for the next disaster to strike.

That night I said my good-byes. I told Beth that my trip was a much-needed vacation. She opposed the trip, mainly because one of my friends in California was a woman. She also thought I was wasting money that we should be saving for our future. I told her that as painful as it was to leave her, and even though I knew I couldn't afford it, I had to get away. My mother cried when I announced my trip at dinner that night, but my father said nothing. My seventeen-year-old sister, Robin, came to my room late that night to try to talk me out of leaving. She could not understand the problem between me and Dad.

"You never even argued!" she protested. "He'll get over you hitting the car."

I could not bear to tell her the real reason I had to get away from him: the unbearable knowledge that Dad believed if one of his sons had to die, it should have been me.

———————

I did not see my family again for two years, though that was not my intention. The poison that David had injected into my relationship with Beth continued its deadly work, and our conversations deteriorated from tense to nasty. I had planned to leave California after a week, but then it stretched to two, and my friend Rachel said she could get me a part-time teaching position for the fall semester that paid much better than what Purdue was offering. My friends Chad and Alan said I could continue to live with them and split the rent. Besides teaching, I could study for my exams and take them at Purdue in the spring. I took the job. I simply could not face going back to Indiana.

My plan was to go back for good at Christmas when the semester ended. That would leave plenty of time, I thought, to plan the wedding and make amends with everyone at home. Long before that, though, Beth became so disillusioned with me that she called the engagement off. I could almost hear David laughing in his grave. My father continued his cold silence, refusing my phone calls, so I stayed in California for Christmas, using lack of money as my excuse.

I taught for another semester in Los Angeles and, in May of 1993, returned to Purdue for four days to take my exams. I didn't tell my parents, a cheap little act of spite that I still regret. I tried to get together with Beth, but she did not want to see me.

I went back to Los Angeles to teach for a second year and to start the research for my dissertation. Beth cut off contact with me altogether, but I still talked to my family by phone. Mom and my sister, Robin, called most often, and now even Dad occasionally came on the line for a few minutes of polite conversation. Robin and Mom begged me to come home that second Christmas. They said Dad wanted me to come too, though he never asked me himself. By that time, I really was broke, so I settled in for another Christmas and another semester in L.A.

In April of 1994, Dad, who had had some minor heart trouble for several years, suffered a heart attack and was hospitalized for a few days at Methodist Hospital in Indianapolis. He told my mother that I was not to be informed until he was at home and out of danger. My mother called me anyway. Robin called me, too, several times, and pleaded with me to come home.

In a series of phone calls during the week after my father's heart attack, Mom methodically and insistently made her case for why I should come back for the summer. She said my father's condition was perilous and that he might not survive. She said she would not survive herself if she lost him so soon after losing David. I suspected she might have been exaggerating Dad's condition as a ploy to lure me home, but I couldn't be certain. What if he did die and all this hostility still lay between us?

Mom said my editor at the magazine had called and offered me my old position for the summer, with a fifteen percent raise and the chance at a permanent position if I wanted it. He had called me and made the same offer, but I tentatively turned him down. It was tempting, however, because I had no summer job lined up in Los Angeles.

Assuming that these arguments might not be enough to persuade me, Mom pressed her case on another front. She said Robin, of whom I had always been protective, was "spinning out of control," though she would not explain what she meant. Robin would not tell me anything either, but her evasiveness made me think Mom was at least partially right. "You've got to help me with her, Chris," Mom said. "You're the only one she'll listen to. If you don't do something now, it'll be too late. And if your dad knew what she was doing, it would kill him."

Mom unabashedly used Beth in her arsenal also. She said she had seen Beth at church and was sure Beth was still interested in me. According to her, Beth wanted to "clear the air" and "make things right."

"Did Beth say that to you?" I wanted to know.

"No, not in so many words, but I've talked to her a number of times and that is the distinct impression I got," Mom said.

"Well, I've talked to her a number of times too, and I got distinctly the opposite impression."

I tried to point out to my mother that Dad would not want me living at home all summer, that we would never get along. Of course, she had an answer for that too.

"He does want you here, Chris. He told me."

"He told you he wants me to come?"

She paused. "I told him I was going to try to get you to come, and he said that was fine."

"Well, that's different from wanting me to come. Would he tell me himself that I am welcome?"

"He wants you to come, Chris. Can't you see that? Don't make him grovel."

I laughed. "Only in our family would a direct expression of love or support be considered groveling."

Mom's tone sharpened. "He has as much pride as you do. That's the problem with both of you. You have the chance to work things out with him, and it may be your last chance. Don't destroy it just because the invitation isn't worded exactly the way you'd like."

I decided to go home.

I went back for Mom's reasons and for a few of my own. Leaving so suddenly two years earlier had left many things suspended, unfinished, frozen in time. My life was like a movie cut short in the last twenty minutes by a break in the film. I could go back and bring it all to a satisfying conclusion so that I could move on. With my father, I hoped merely to have some casual conversations—nothing deep, nothing that explored the depths of the problems in our relationship. The very point of the talks would be their ordinariness, to dispel the mystery of the silence that had stood as a barrier between us for so long.

Even though our relationship was dead, I couldn't get Beth out of my mind. I was convinced that if I saw her just once in an everyday situation—like walking across the foyer at church, where I was most likely to cross paths with her—the mystery that had held me to her would vanish in an instant, and I would be able to bury her in my mind.

Bill Adams, who had been one of my best friends since junior high, flew out to Los Angeles at the end of the school year, and after a week of vacation, we made the two-thousand-mile drive to Indiana. I had bought a car in L.A. after Bill had sold my car in Indiana the year before. Bill was the ideal friend to help me ease back into life in Indiana. We had gone to church and school together, and he had spent much of his teenage years at our house playing basketball and football and running around with me and David and our other friends. We were both in our midtwenties, but of all my friends from high school, Bill had changed the least. He had bushy blond hair and a huskiness from his football days. Our friendship was the kind where we could be apart for long stretches of time, but when we got back together, within fifteen minutes we were as close as we had been before. All across the country he played our old favorites—Billy Joel, Bruce Springsteen, Sting. He talked of girls we had dated and told me what had become of almost everyone we knew. He did everything he could to keep our trip lighthearted, but he knew I was apprehensive about returning.

The people I had left two years ago would have changed just as I had during that time. New layers of complexity would have been added, and it was possible that things would be even worse than I remembered.

I looked to Bill for encouragement, but he knew me too well to try to allay my fears with cheap reassurances. After hearing some of my doubts during the first five hundred miles of our journey, he finally brought me to silence by concluding, "You know, you're probably right. You're probably making a big mistake."

He was only joking, but I spent the next fifteen hundred miles dreading that what he said might be true.

CHRIS

$\mathcal{M}$y father never liked to talk about the past, but he made an exception when he worked on his '51 Chevy. The car seemed to coax stories out of him. As he stood in the garage, wiping the fenders with a white cloth or buffing the chrome until it shined, it was as if he were rubbing a genie's lamp, and out of that car would rise the secret moments of his early life, otherwise closed off to us.

As a teenager I would stand silently off to the side of the garage, trying not to break the spell, while Dad told of what it was like to buy his first car in high school, the pride it gave him to drive it around with his friends and to park in front of the school—one that didn't even have a parking lot in those days.

My grandfather, who had died when I was only three, came to life through my dad's fond recollections of the hours they had spent together working on the car. As the garage lights blazed over that black automobile and Dad tinkered with the engine or polished the hood, it was like staring into a crystal ball that revealed the real thing: my father, Jack LaRue. I wanted him to keep polishing, almost believing that if he rubbed hard enough, I would be able to not only imagine the stories but live them. I would be able to go back there with him and know what he knew, and we would be friends.

When I returned to my parents' house two years after my brother's death and saw the terrible condition of his '51 Chevy, I finally believed what my mother had hinted. My father was dying.

The first sign of his decline was to see his prized Chevy sitting out-side the garage at the back of the house. Dad had never left the car in the driveway—not even for a few hours! The dents I had made in the car two years before had been flawlessly repaired, but the car was spotted with dust, the whitewall tires were dingy, and the windows were streaked with dirt. Incredibly, around the bottom of the car there were actually a few spider webs with pieces of dead leaves and grass in them, as if Dad had cut the grass and just let the clippings fly up onto the car.

I parked in the driveway and walked around the Chevy, amazed. I kicked away some of the leaves that clung to the bottom of it.

Bill walked with me. "I forgot about this old car. Is this the one your dad had when you lived here, the one you ran into?"

"Yes, so don't remind me," I replied.

Bill did not understand the depth of meaning that accident still held for me. He walked over to where the crumpled metal had been repaired and ran his hand over it. As he touched it I winced, as if he were poking his fingers into an open wound.

"Can't even tell it's ever been hit," he said. "Did your dad ever let you drive this?"

"I have never driven one of Dad's cars."

Bill looked inside the car through the driver's side window. "Maybe he'll take us for a ride," he said.

"Dad must really be sick," I said.

"You haven't even seen him yet!"

"This car tells the story. Maybe Mom's right. Maybe he really is dying."

Bill let out a quick laugh of surprise. "Well, I'm glad people don't judge how I'm feeling by the way my car looks. They would have fig-ured I was dead a long time ago."

"You're not my dad. He would have left his own kids out here in the driveway sooner than he would have left this car."

"Oh, Chris, come on."

"You don't know him."

"What are you talking about?" countered Bill. "I practically grew up here."

"So did I," I murmured. "But not quite."

Bill looked toward the house and asked, "So how does it feel to be home?"

"My stomach is churning like a cement mixer."

"Excitement or dread?"

"Both." My insides had been twisting from the moment we got off the highway at the exit that led to our neighborhood. Our subdivision was in a slight valley, and when we descended that first hill, for me it was like plunging backward in time. Almost everything I saw contained memories, including the hill itself, which I had ridden up and down on my bike hundreds of times. We wound through the streets to my parents' home, passing one house after another that belonged to people we had gone to church with, kids I had grown up with, girls I had dated. Bill had spent a lot of time in our neighborhood too, and as we drove past these houses he would say things like, "Oh, isn't that where Kelly lived? Did you know she got married?" But I was in no condition to reminisce. Being thrown back into this once familiar place was so jarring that I needed to let it wash over me awhile before casual conversation could take place.

Our neighborhood was made up of mostly ranch-style homes built in the '60s and '70s. We had moved there when the houses were new and the trees were spindly things propped up with sticks and ropes. Now, after nearly thirty years, the trees and shrubs had grown so large around the homes that it seemed the neighborhood was gradually sinking into them and would one day disappear. As we rounded the final corner, my own redbrick house came into view, with everything about it looking as neat and precise as ever—the shrubbery around the front neatly trimmed, the black shutters recently painted, the lawn cut short and raked clean. Our four-bedroom home had started out with a two-car attached garage and a small patio in back, but over the years Dad had added a front porch, a second driveway to the back of the house, and his treasured backyard garage.

Now as Bill and I stood in the driveway looking at Dad's dirty car, I worried about this home that was familiar, yet totally new. I had experience dealing with Dad the perfectionist, but who was this man who let his car deteriorate in the driveway? I looked toward the house. The kitchen drapes were closed. The bedroom drapes were closed. The door to the attached garage was closed. Apparently no one was home. That surprised me, because we had called that morning and told them to expect us by dinnertime.

At my parents' house that meant six o'clock, and it was already almost six-thirty. We told Mom we would take them out to dinner, and that had seemed to relieve her. She had never been all that confident of her cooking, and she didn't want to be distracted with it on my first day back. I had asked Bill to join us for dinner, thinking his presence would keep dinner lighthearted and prevent any of us from delving into unpleasant issues immediately. I was relieved no one was home. It would give me time to get used to the place again, to prepare myself, and make the reunion as natural and pleasant as possible.

"Let's go on in," I said. "It looks like they're not home."

"Do you have a key?" he asked.

"Yes." But just that moment I heard someone fumbling at the door that opened into the attached garage. I looked over to see Mom in the window of the door, undoing the locks. Then I saw the corner of the kitchen drapes move slightly. Dad was watching us from inside.

Mom was crying even before she got across the driveway. She hugged me for a long time and cried words into my shirt I couldn't understand. Then she turned to Bill and hugged him too.

"We thought you'd never get here," said Mom.

"Just a half hour late after two thousand miles isn't too bad," I said. "Is Dad mad at us for being late?"

"He's fine," Mom said, turning to look at the door she had come through. "Look at you, Mr. California! So tanned. And your hair's so short. You're thin! Don't you eat out there?"

"I wanted to lose weight, Mom," I said. "Why do you have everything closed up? It looked like nobody was home."

"Oh, your dad doesn't like the drapes open anymore. Gets tired of the neighbors looking in."

"Neighbors? Why would they—" But I didn't finish because Mom's hands were fluttering through the air as if to wipe away my words before Dad arrived. He was locking up the doors behind him as he came. He slammed each one hard to make sure it was shut tight.

"We're starving here" were the first words my father said to me after my two-year absence.

Mom lost her smile, and her face took on a wary expression, as if she feared Dad might mar our first moments together by venting his irritation. Instead, he kept it mostly hidden and walked over to give me a quick hug, which was more than I had expected. Dad looked better than Mom's descriptions of him on the phone had made him sound. The only change I saw from two years before was that he looked a little more stooped and his hair looked thinner and whiter. Still, to me he appeared healthy and distinguished. Picture him out of his cotton polo shirt and in one of his dark suits, and he could be at the head of a conference table in a company boardroom: wise, serene, and on the verge of making some monumental decision. He was still employed by such a company, Maximilian Webber, but he had been on medical leave since the heart attack.

"You're looking good, Dad. I was led to believe you were in bad health."

"Yeah, they've started their death watch, but I'm gonna surprise 'em," he replied.

"Jack! Don't talk that way," my mother said in rebuke.

"And *you*, Mom. You look great!" I said, turning her way.

"Oh, please," she answered, glancing down in embarrassment.

"You do, and you know it. The rest of us look older every year, but even with all that's happened, you've barely changed in ten years."

"Remind me to make you an appointment with the eye doctor," she said. But she did look good. She had dyed her hair brown, and it was smoothly coiffed. She wore earrings and a gold necklace and a fashionable blouse and slacks. She had warned me on the telephone that she had temporarily failed in her determination to lose weight before I came back, but she looked fine to me. Mom was in her late fifties, and the only sign of aging since I had seen her two years before was a little more wrinkling on her neck and around her eyes. The rest of her face still had the brightness of a young woman.

To me, my parents' appearance corresponded well with their personalities. Dad had grown increasingly thin and gaunt as he aged, looking out from hard, inscrutable eyes. There was a preciseness about the creases of his pants and the shine of his shoes that was almost military— it said "keep your distance, maintain dignity above all." Mom was softer, shorter, plumper; her generous arms looking at any moment as if they were about to reach out and hug you.

Dad shook hands with Bill and then said to me, "We'll get your bags when we get back. I'm ready to eat."

––––––––––

We drove to the Cattle Country Steakhouse, Dad's favorite restaurant. For him, a steak dinner with a baked potato and salad and plenty of coffee was the only true meal. Everything else was sissy food. Robin was still at the mall where she worked at a women's clothing store. She was supposed to meet us around seven. I was glad Bill was along, because his presence put Dad on his best behavior. Dad was friendly and talkative, telling stories about being in the hospital with his heart attack.

"The part I hated the most was when they took my teeth away," he said. "I've never let anybody see me without my teeth. Just Helen."

"It's true," Mom agreed. "He has always been very particular about that."

Dad continued. "The first thing I did was make them give them back to me. I didn't understand what having a heart attack had to do with my teeth. They had no business—"

"Well, when he was unconscious, of course they—" my mother began.

". . . taking my teeth away." Dad finished his sentence, ignoring Mom's interruption. "And I never let anyone wash me. Not since I was a baby. I'd rather go dirty than have someone washing around on me."

"Even if it was a pretty nurse," Mom added. "He just didn't want them touching him."

"That and my hair," Dad said. "I always like to have my hair combed a certain way before I see people."

"Even if he's just going out to check the mail!"

"My hair was messed up the whole time I was in that hospital. With all those pillows, I just couldn't get it right. So there I'd be, people wanting to come and see me, and I wouldn't have any teeth, and I hadn't had a shower, and my hair was messed up."

"He was not a great patient," Mom said. "They got him out of there as soon as they could."

Robin came in not long after we sat down. She squealed in excitement when she first saw me, and Mom patted her arm to quiet her down. She hugged me and whooped a couple more times, not caring that people in the restaurant were staring. I was surprised by how much she had changed since I last had seen her. She looked more mature and appeared to have traded in the teenage rebellious look for a more sophisticated, though still daring, image. She wore a close-fitting black-and-red dress, and her hair was shorter and lighter than I remembered. She looked older than nineteen, certainly older than the sister I had left behind two years ago.

"You've grown up, haven't you, kid?" I said.

"Oh, please," she laughed. "Aren't I a little old for the speech about how much I've grown since you saw me last?" She turned to Bill, who had known her since she was a little girl, and gave him a friendly hug.

When we were all seated again, Robin grabbed my arm and cried, "I'm so glad you came home!"

"Keep your voice down, honey, please!" Mom said in a dramatic whisper.

Robin ignored her. "We've been needing something to liven things up around our house, haven't we, Dad?"

"You keep it pretty lively already, seems to me," he said.

Mom grimaced. "We're hoping you'll help us with this child, Chris. We're at the end of our rope."

Robin rolled her eyes and shook her head, then glanced around the restaurant and frowned disapprovingly at the saddles and ropes and paintings of Western landscapes that dominated the decor. The rest of us had ordered, but Robin grabbed a menu and breezed through it, barely looking at the words before she turned the pages. "You had to bring them to the steakhouse, didn't you, Dad? Couldn't go somewhere where you could get a healthy meal."

"Don't start in on me tonight," he said.

"Well, they don't serve anything I like here. I'll just get a salad."

Throughout the meal I was unable to get any hint of what Robin was doing that Mom thought would land her in trouble. That mystery would have to come out like they always did in our family—bit by painful bit. I knew she was hiding something, though. Ever since she was little, she always revealed her guilt by being incapable of sitting still or looking us straight in the face. That night Robin squirmed around in her slinky dress, barely looking at me when she spoke, filled with so much restless energy that she looked as if she would spring out of the seat at any moment and go flying around the room like an untied balloon. She smiled the whole time, but it wasn't the innocent, girlish smile I remembered. She had a coy, knowing look that told me her eyes had been opened to a great many things while I had been away. I wanted to get her alone and find out what was going on.

Mom kept her gaze steady on Robin, neither frowning nor smiling, as if to say, *You don't fool me.*

Robin tossed the menu aside and turned to me. "Everybody's dying to see you. People at church. People in the neighborhood. Beth."

"Beth knows I'm home?" I asked, trying to keep my voice free of the tremors of emotion that the mention of her name set off.

"Yeah," Robin said. "She and I have become friends. Have you talked to anybody yet?"

"No. I haven't had time."

"Aunt Dayle wants to throw a big picnic for you and invite all the relatives," Robin said.

"She doesn't need to do that."

"She wants to!" Robin insisted. "You're not gonna hide in your room this summer, Chris. We're going to have fun. We're going to have get-togethers and invite people over for dinner and go out and have a good time."

I was struck by how different her idea of this trip was from my own. She saw it as a homecoming, a joyous reunion. I had considered it only in terms of surviving without getting caught up in too many uncom-

fortable, emotional scenes—no fights with my dad, no painful con-
frontations with Beth.

Mom said, "When I saw Beth at church, I told her she'd have to
come over for dinner while you're home."

"Mom, please don't try to force Beth and me back together. It's not
going to happen."

Chided, Mom concentrated on cutting her steak for a moment.
"You were ready to spend your whole life with Beth. I don't see why
you can't sit through one dinner with her."

"Because we broke up!"

Robin rescued me from this uncomfortable topic by raising another
one. "Did Mom tell you Aunt Shirley is mad at her?"

"No," I said. "What's that all about?"

"Now, we're not going to get into that tonight," Mom said.

"Why not?" I asked. "You might as well tell me. Why drag things
out? It just makes it worse because I think of all these—"

"We are not going to ruin this evening by getting into that," Mom
interrupted, her face red, her eyes on the verge of tears. "This is Chris's
night. We are not going to get into all that ugliness. Now, that's it."

Everyone got quiet for a few moments. Robin turned to me,
shrugged, and gave a mischievous grin. "Aren't you glad to be home,
Chris?"

Mom shot her a disapproving glance but said nothing.

I wanted to ask Dad about the appalling condition of the '51 Chevy
without getting him all irritated. I thought that asking him while Bill
was still there keeping everyone polite would be the best way, so I
charged ahead. "I was surprised to see the old Chevy sitting out in the
driveway. I've never seen you leave it outside before."

"Well, the garage is pretty full right now," he said.

"The car's even dusty! It had cobwebs along the bottom, with leaves
and grass clippings stuck in them."

"Well, you'd better get out there and clean it up, then," Dad said,
his voice showing a slight quiver of annoyance.

"I wouldn't mind cleaning it up for you, if you don't mind me getting near it."

Dad did not respond at once. He stirred some sugar into the coffee
the waitress had just poured, then said, "With all that's happened, I've
kind of lost interest in that car the last couple years."

He didn't explain what he meant by "all that's happened," and I
didn't want to ask.

"Besides, I've been working on another one."

"What other one?" I asked.

"A 1938 Oldsmobile. It's like one I had when I was in high school."

"I'd like to see it," I said. "I wouldn't mind getting out there and helping you with it, if I wouldn't be in the way."

"That's all right with me," Dad said, "if Bobby doesn't mind."

"Who's Bobby?"

"The kid who's been helping me with this car."

"We know him from church," Mom said. "Your dad has been teaching him about restoring cars. He's a very nice boy. Kind of had a rough family background, but he likes Jack and seems very good at working on cars."

Robin said, "He's not a boy, Mother. He's in his twenties, almost Chris's age." She turned to Bill and me and complained, "She and Dad think anyone under thirty is a child."

Mom continued. "You might know him, Bill. He's in your line of work."

Bill was an insurance salesman, as were a number of other men in our church. Two prominent men on the church board, Jim White and Alan Ruiz, owned rival insurance companies and hired most of their employees from among our congregation.

"Is it Bobby McMahon?" Bill asked.

"That's right," Dad said. "He works for Jim White."

Bill worked for Alan Ruiz.

"I've met Bobby," Bill said. "I've heard Jim White's firm might be in some trouble. I hope Bobby's not involved."

"What do you mean?" Dad asked defensively. "Jim's been in business for years. He's been very successful."

"I don't know much about it," Bill said. "But there's some questionable investments they're involved in, from what I've heard."

"Well, I don't believe that," Dad said. "Sounds to me like the competition's getting jealous."

Bill shrugged and let it go.

Dad turned back to me and said, "Anyway, Bobby's coming over tomorrow, and we're going to do some work in the garage. You can come on out if you want to."

"Bobby's cute," Robin said playfully, as if this would help me decide whether or not I wanted to work on the car with him.

Mom shook her head and frowned.

"He's really good with cars. I wouldn't be surprised if I let him take those old cars off my hands someday," Dad said.

Astonished, I responded, "I never thought I'd hear you say that."

"Well," Dad said, "things change."

"Ha!" cried Robin, and Mom patted her arm to quiet her.

ROBIN

I have nothing to be ashamed of.

I am nineteen years old, a woman. I shouldn't have to explain myself to my family or get permission for everything I do.

So I'm secretly seeing someone. There's nothing wrong with that. We have our reasons for keeping it secret, one being that the man I'm seeing is not Brandon, who everybody thinks is my boyfriend.

Mom knows something's going on. She gives me that look all the time—the frown with the tilted head and sad eyes that says, "You're such a disappointment." But I don't want to rag on Mom too much. At least she hasn't gotten Daddy in on it. He's pretty oblivious.

But then Chris comes home and acts like he's surprised I'm not still carrying around dolls and playing tea party with my friends. At the steakhouse he gave me that same grade-school teacher scowl that Mom gives me.

I can just hear what they'll say if they figure out what I've been up to. "Oh, isn't that typical of her. She's always been that way." It'll be one more item to add to the list of things I'll be remembered for.

When I was six, I unpluggged the freezer and ruined all the meat.

I tried smoking when I was eight.

When I was a little older, I took twelve dollars from my mother's purse.

I drank beer when I was eleven.

The year I turned sixteen, Mom and Dad made a big fuss when I changed the color of my hair every month for seven months straight. What's wrong with changing the color of my hair? Just because Dad hasn't moved one hair on his head since he was ten years old doesn't mean I should wear my hair the same old boring way every day.

Sometimes it drives me nuts living with Mom and Dad. I'm so glad Chris is home. I screamed my head off when Mom told me he was finally coming. He's the only member of my family I've ever completely trusted. He's the only one who didn't think I was flaky or bizarre or lost or confused or whatever. Even David, who I got along with pretty well, thought I was a little weird. He tried to have rebellious streaks every once in a while himself, when he'd run off and do something stupid, but overall he was pretty conventional. He was a lot like Dad in that way. Just wanted to keep everything simple and low key. Give him a broken-down car and some tools, and he was happy. David was the typical big-brother type—strong and confident. Wanted me to think he had it all together. Wanted me to look up to him more than be his friend.

Chris is more like me. He doesn't have it all together, and he knows it. He's not afraid to say so either. That's one reason he and Dad don't get along. Dad thinks you should keep everything to yourself and not bother other people with it. He would never jump up and down and scream if he was happy. He would never pound the table in frustration. He would never dance around the room if a song came on the radio that he liked. When I did any of those things, Dad would tell me to quiet down, control myself, grow up. Chris would come and find out why I was screaming or pounding the table or dancing around. He might even join me.

I still get in trouble for turning up the stereo too loud in the house. I have to *feel* music. I have to be engulfed in it. I love to crank up the music, dance around the room, and then go spinning around through the whole house, singing and gyrating. Mom and Dad have been horrified by this, of course, the few times I've actually tried it when they were home. They thought I was acting like an idiot. Mom and Dad could never feel music like I do. To them, music is supposed to be nothing more than pleasant sounds in the background.

One day, the summer before David died, I walked into the house when Chris was the only one home. The house was shaking with music! Chris was in the living room dancing his head off. When he saw me walk in, he jumped on the couch and started dancing even more wildly! I threw down my purse and started dancing too. Neither of us said a word. We danced from one room to the next, riding the flow of the sound, our arms and legs flailing all over the place. We kept it up for half an hour, then collapsed on the floor laughing.

We let the music go until Dad walked in from the garage and yelled, "Shut that noise off!"

That should tell you something about the family I live in.

I think I have good reason for keeping a few things to myself.

CHRIS

$\mathcal{B}$ill helped me bring in my bags after dinner. We came through the garage and into the kitchen, then stopped while Mom fumbled to find the light. Being in that house again—where the biggest portion of my life had been spent—filled me with mixed feelings of nostalgia and pain. I was tempted to ask if we could wait in the kitchen until I got used to this room, and then go slowly into every other room and stand silently while I readjusted to the reality of the place.

When Mom got the light on and saw me looking around the kitchen instead of going straight back to my room, she started explaining, "We put that wallpaper on last year. I liked it better in the store. It seemed to go with the carpet. But in here it seems like the light hits it wrong. We'll probably change it again before long."

"It looks good," I said.

"It looks great!" Bill said, as if to make up for the halfheartedness of my response.

"Well, let's go on in," Dad said from behind us. "There's no need to stand out here." Mom had told me Dad tired easily, and when he turned toward the family room, he headed straight for the recliner and plopped into it with a sigh.

As we walked through the house, Mom ran around turning the lights on, as if to dispel the gloom.

"Do you keep the drapes closed all day now?" I asked her.

"Oh, if it's just the two of us sitting here, we . . ." She looked at

Dad and shrugged. "It doesn't seem that dark if you've been in the room all day. Let's go put your stuff in your room."

Dad stayed in his recliner while the rest of us went to my old bedroom. The furniture in the room was the same that had been there since before I was in high school. The beat-up chest of drawers, the twin bed, my little desk in the corner. None of my stuff was there, though, none of the posters and pictures and albums and books and magazines that had made the room feel it was mine, but that Mom had always seen as clutter. Mom had swept them all away, and this was a ghost of a room. I sat on the bed and let the memories wash over me. They weren't really memories so much as a tangle of contradictory feelings, little jolts of energy, rage, joy, love, obsession, and aspiration that had surged through me during the years I lived here. The room was so empty it seemed to echo. I could see the tracks of the vacuum cleaner in the carpet. Mom and Bill did not sit down. They looked ready to go back for a second load, but I could not rush.

"It feels strange to be back in this room again," I said.

"You remember this room, don't you?" Mom asked Bill.

"I sure do," he said. "I spent an awful lot of time in here."

"We still have some of Chris's games and stuff in the closet."

"You do?" I asked. "I thought you had thrown it all away."

"No. There's Monopoly and Clue and your chess set and a whole stack of albums."

"So tell me, Mom. Does Dad sit there in the dark all day long? You used to like it bright in the house. You wouldn't close the drapes until the last hint of daylight had vanished."

"Well, lately your dad prefers to keep the drapes closed. He said he gets tired of the neighbors trying to look in here all the time and see what we're doing."

"The neighbors can't see in here. And why would they want to?"

"I know. But there are kids that play around the neighborhood, and sometimes they come over in our yard. And . . . I don't know. I don't get it either. The fact is, your dad broods. He'll be all right at the beginning of the day—his old happy self, joking around—but then after he starts sitting in his recliner for a while, he gets gloomy. He won't tell me what he's thinking about or what's bothering him. He just wants to be left alone. Sometimes he'll sit there for several hours, not reading or watching TV or doing anything. He just sits and stares and looks upset."

Mom turned to Bill and explained, "That's not like him at all. He has never been a moody man. You know that. He used to always be cheerful, always full of energy, always ready to get up and go to work, work on the cars, cut the grass, or whatever he thought of to do. He's not the same. Not since David died. Not since Chris left."

Mom walked a step closer to me. "That's why I'm so glad you're back here for the summer, Chris. I need you to help him get out of this. It's not just his health problems. It's like he's finally so worn down by everything that he has given up." Her cheeks turned a little red, and her eyes got watery.

I didn't want her to start crying again, so I stood up and put my arm around her shoulder. "Don't worry, Mom. Dad's going to be fine. He looks much better than I expected."

"You don't know, though—" She broke away and headed out into the hallway. "Let's get your things before somebody steals them."

On our way down the hall, we passed David's room. Unlike all the other rooms in the house, the door to his room was closed. I couldn't resist opening the door and going inside. I flipped the light on. David's room was not empty or ghostlike as mine, which was odd, considering it was the room of someone who had died. Mom and Dad had not exactly made it a shrine to David, as some parents do who have lost a child. Mom, despite her grief, was still too much of a neatness fanatic to keep all of David's things exactly as they had been when he died. David's room had always been far messier than mine, and he hadn't cared what it looked like. His room had been a place to sleep and a place to get away from the rest of us when we were driving him crazy. He didn't really "live" in the room. He merely stopped off there for a few hours between the other things he was doing. Sleeping out on the living room couch would have been just as acceptable to David, except that it wouldn't have allowed him to shut himself off from the rest of us.

Mom had arranged David's room the way she wished it would have looked while he was alive. The bed was neatly made. There were no car keys, no change, no receipts, no chewing gum wrappers on the dresser. On the walls, which had held nothing when he was alive except for a few discount-store-quality pictures of ships, Mom had hung several photos of David standing next to the cars he had restored. I had seen most of these photographs before, when they were piled in a heap on David's dresser. Now Mom had them carefully matted and framed.

Bill walked around the room glancing at all the photos. "I had forgotten how many cars David worked on. Did he own all these?"

"No," Mom said. "Even those he owned for a while he eventually sold. It was the restoring he liked most, not the having. A few of them he got attached to, though. The '57 Chevy in the picture above the dresser was the car he loved more than any of the others. His dad had always wanted one of those ever since they were new, and he was always going on about how they were the best car ever built. David was so meticulous with it."

"It won an award." I pointed to a plaque on the opposite wall. "But he never owned that car. A guy paid him to restore it, then later David tried to buy it from him. But he wouldn't sell it."

"That guy done him dirty," Mom said. "He knew David had put more work into that car than what he had paid for. But the guy wouldn't sell it even when David offered a lot of money. I don't remember how much, but your dad said he was offering too much."

"So he gave up on getting it?" asked Bill.

"Yep," Mom answered. "He got himself another old car and started working on it night and day and never talked to that guy again."

I looked closely at the photo of David with the '57 Chevy. It was taken on the driveway. He was leaning casually against the driver's door of the blue-and-white car, wiping his hands with a towel. David's good looks were on the scruffy, rugged side: the shadow on his face heavy at the end of the day, his hairy arms flecked with oil, the hair on his head curly and windblown. He wore jeans and a T-shirt, both spotted with oil. He looked open and uncomplicated, just a guy who wanted to tinker with cars and not bother anybody. That's what Dad and most people thought of him, because that's how Dad was himself. David's dark eyebrows drew attention to his eyes, which were bright and innocent. The eyes gave him a look of boyish vulnerability that often made people think he was naïve and guileless. He carried himself with an air of success. I could never have copied his look for myself. When I didn't comb my hair or didn't shave for a couple days, I merely looked unkempt and dirty. The same look made David appear unpretentious and laid-back, his smile drawing you in, telling you to come on over and have a chat.

I was tempted to let the photo fool me. As I stared at him standing by that trophy of a car, his arms folded in contentment, his face beaming with that friendly smile, I wanted to go clap him on the back and say, "Good job, brother."

We had been close once. He had been my mentor and friend. But most of it had turned sour. I couldn't, like Mom and Dad, remember only the good things about him. As much as I loved him, I knew David to be the most deceitful, scheming, unprincipled person I had ever met. The longer I looked at his picture, the more I remembered, and the more I wanted to turn away. It was too late to make things right. Silence was my only option. We did not speak ill of David in this house.

Later that night Aunt Dayle, Mom's sister, called me. She was my favorite aunt, the most willing of all to tell the family gossip without restraint. I knew she would be more than happy to tell me about the mysterious rift between Mom and Shirley.

"I never thought you'd be crazy enough to come back to Indiana," she said to me in a greeting.

"Well, thanks a lot, Aunt Dayle. And here I thought you would welcome me back."

"Oh, I do, sweetie. I just think you're nuts, that's all. I'd go to California myself if I could be sure none of my family would follow me there."

"You shock me, Dayle," I said, though her tone of irreverence toward her family was as familiar to me as her voice itself.

"You're not shocked. You know what a bunch of bozos I raised." Aunt Dayle had five children, and a couple of them had caused her a great deal of heartache. "You were smart to take a break from this family. But I can't figure out why you kids keep coming back. I left home when I got married at seventeen, and believe me, I never looked back! But here you are in your late twenties and still a glutton for punishment. Some of my kids are the same way. I can't beat 'em off with a stick! Your brother was the same way when he was alive, wasn't he?"

"Yeah, David lived on his own several times, and so have I, but somehow we keep getting lured back. This is the last summer for me, though. Mom practically begged me to come."

"Well, she needs all the help she can get right now."

"I hear there's some turmoil in the family, but nobody will tell me what it is."

"Oh, just fussin'," she said. "Your mom won't tell you about it?"

"No, Aunt Dayle, nobody tells me anything."

"Well, I should probably keep my mouth shut too," she began, but her tone of eagerness contradicted her words.

"Come on," I coaxed, "you've always been the one person in this family willing to tell me the truth."

"Well," she drawled, "it's about Grandma and Grandpa, I can tell you that." She was referring to her parents, who were in their eighties and lived just outside Indianapolis in the house where Dayle and the others had been raised.

"What's wrong with Grandma and Grandpa?" I asked.

"Nothing that hasn't been wrong with them for the last twenty years. But it's getting so they're having trouble taking care of themselves in that house, and your mom thinks it's time for them to go to a retirement home or a nursing home. But your aunt Shirley says over her dead body will they go into a nursing home. They can come to live with her if it comes to that. Your mom and Shirley got into it one day, and your mom said it would never work for Grandma and Grandpa to live at Shirley's house because it's barely big enough for Shirley's own family. Shirley got all offended and said your mother was implying that her house wasn't good enough for their parents, and—well, you can imagine the rest of it. Off they went, trying to outdo each other on who cared more about Grandma and Grandpa. I guess Shirley accused your mom of not doing her part, and that got your mom riled up something fierce. Since then, your mom and Shirley haven't spoken to each other."

Shirley was Mom's younger sister. Dayle was the oldest at sixty, Mom, fifty-six, came next, then Shirley at fifty-three, Jackie at fifty-one, and Roger at forty-nine. Of all of them, Shirley was the most likely to be embroiled in whatever family dispute happened to be raging at the moment. She had fought with every one of her siblings at some point. Now it was Mom's turn.

"So what do you think Grandma and Grandpa should do? You must have some say in it too."

"Chris, honey, I have long since given up trying to persuade my parents to do *anything*. They can do what they want, and I'll help them if I can."

"What *do* they think?" I asked.

"Well, that's the thing!" she said. "Grandma and Grandpa don't know anything about all this! Your Mom and Shirley haven't bothered to ask their opinion."

"Are Grandma and Grandpa really having trouble taking care of themselves?"

"Oh, they muddle along. Every once in a while they do something crazy. Your grandma set the kitchen on fire about a month ago when she tried to dry a towel in the microwave, and it caught fire. Grandpa managed to put it out before it did much damage, and now Grandma has herself convinced the whole thing was Grandpa's fault. But Grandma has never quite gotten the hang of microwave ovens. She can't get it through her head that they're different from regular ovens."

"How old are they now, anyway?" I asked.

"Grandpa is eighty-four, and Grandma just turned eighty-two. They do get mixed up on their medicines, and that worries me some.

They either forget and take it twice, or else they don't take it at all. I bought them one of those pill organizers a while back, but they still get it all mixed up. I don't know, I figure as long as they don't burn the house down or kill themselves, we might as well leave them be. They're about as content as they can be considering how old they are and the condition they're in. Let's face it, they're not going to live forever no matter what we do."

"I think you're right," I said. "I doubt if they'd let Mom or Shirley pressure them into moving anyway."

"You got that right. I'm sorry you had to come home in the middle of a family feud. But what else is new? It's not going to stop me from having a big get-together for you. A big pot of chili. Playing Monopoly. Just like the old days. What do you think?"

"Sounds great! And you'll invite all the feuding parties?"

"Of course! Where else would the entertainment come from?"

Aunt Dayle's openness had always made her the peacemaker of the family. In situations where other family members would quietly harbor resentments, read subtle insults into one another's words, or refuse to speak for some period of time, Aunt Dayle would lay the whole problem out on the table without restraint. She would reveal every hurt feeling and unkind comment that had been made and not let anyone hide behind their shy bitterness. After she stirred everybody up in this way, she would do something lavish to bring them all back together, like throw a big family reunion with more food spread out on the card tables than a family two or three times as big as ours could eat, with endless games in the backyard that would keep the kids laughing and playing all day. She took it as her mission to keep the family together. She was not always successful. Sometimes her bluntness caused more offense than one of her dinners or gifts or visits could smooth over. In the end, though, her persistence usually won out, and the family would gather around her once more.

She was famous for her chili suppers. She would gather a bunch of us on a Saturday night, and all evening we would feast on her huge pot of chili, with crackers and sandwiches if we wanted them, and iced tea and usually pie or cake. While we ate we played Monopoly on a board so worn out that much of the printing had rubbed off. She had three Monopoly sets, and if there were enough people, we had three games going at once. Those chili nights were some of the most enjoyable evenings I remember ever spending with my relatives. Everyone seemed to loosen up in the atmosphere of the game, the good food, and Aunt Dayle's hospitality. We usually played until close to midnight, with everyone laughing and talking the whole time.

Aunt Dayle set my welcome-home chili supper for the next Saturday night, and she made me promise to persuade every member of my family to come.

———————

Given the miserable condition of the '51 Chevy that now rotted on the driveway, I was curious to see whether Dad had neglected his garage also. I got out there before he did the next night, when I was to help him and his friend Bobby work on the '38 Oldsmobile. It may sound strange, but I needed time to get used to each of the places that was part of the home I had grown up in. Each room, including Dad's garage, was so haunted by the past that I felt overwhelmed with memories—or at least the raw emotion associated with memories—the first time I stepped into each place. The feelings made conversation difficult for me, because instead of talking, I wanted to think and daydream and absorb the emotion.

Only the Chevy had been allowed to deteriorate. Dad's garage was as meticulously arranged as ever. Tools were not thrown haphazardly into a toolbox or left lying out on a workbench. Each tool hung on the wall in its own place in ascending order of size. It almost looked like a museum for tools, as if they were hung there to be admired rather than used. The floor was spotless. There were no dust balls in the corner or cobwebs in the rafters or oil spots left on the floor. Dad swept the garage out regularly and wiped up oil spots at the end of each day. Items like nails, nuts, bolts, and screws were neatly arranged in drawers of the workbench. Machinery like the lawnmower and air compressor were kept immaculate and in their appropriate places around the perimeter of the work floor.

The Oldsmobile, whose green body contained not a speck of dust, was partially disassembled, the parts arranged neatly on tarps around the car. Every sight and smell in that garage brought back my brother, David—the bulky old car with its elaborate grille and big fenders, the familiar smell of oil and gasoline, the sight of the parts of work in progress scattered about on the floor. I expected him to walk through the door at any moment. I longed for him to appear. I wondered how Dad could stand to work out here with David's ghost hovering all around.

The walk-in door to the garage opened behind me, and Dad came in. He glanced at me for only a second, then looked away with a frown of annoyance. I was startled and must have shown it. I suppose I looked strange standing there by myself with a dazed expression. Dad had come in too soon, before I had time to chase the ghosts away. Neither of us spoke for a moment as he tinkered with something at the workbench.

Finally I said, "Is . . . what's his name? Is he still coming?"

"Bobby should be here any minute. He's supposed to come at seven, and he knows I don't like people to be late."

"No. Everybody knows that," I said. I meant this to sound light-hearted but feared it sounded petty instead. Quickly I added, "I see you keep the garage as neat and tidy as ever."

"Bobby keeps it up for me," Dad said. "That was a condition of him working on the car in here. I can't stand a messy garage."

As we spoke, Bobby walked in. He looked different from what I expected. I had thought—maybe even hoped—he'd be a guy with dirty hands and an oily T-shirt, a guy who looked as if he lived and breathed cars and garages. Bobby was dressed in jeans and a T-shirt, but the shirt looked new and was neatly tucked in. There was something almost military about his posture. The things that stood out about him most, though, were his almost impossibly perfect hair and teeth. He had a thick mountain of dark brown hair, combed back in a style that was supposed to look casual, I suppose, but when you looked at it closely, you realized not a hair was out of place. It was sculpted smooth as a mold. None of it moved.

And his teeth! A flawless row of them flashed out at you as if they were boasting their perfection. I imagined that Bobby aimed them toward me as a challenge, as if to say, "How could there be anything wrong with me when I can keep my teeth so absolutely white and per-fectly straight?" He immediately struck up a conversation with me, small talk about California and the beach and how insane I was to leave it and come back to Indiana. He was friendly, but in a salesman-like way. He seemed to be trying a little too hard to win me over, acting just a little happier to see me than he should be, considering he didn't know me. I knew I was forming a harsh and possibly unfair impression of him. I had no particular reason to be suspicious of him, but I was. I reacted to him with the same mistrust I carried toward all salesmen— suspecting they were trying to sell me something that looked good on the surface but underneath all the hype was flawed.

"So you sell insurance for Jim White?" I asked.

"No, financial planning, actually," he said. "Insurance is just a small part of it. There are other types of investments too."

"For people planning retirement or something?"

"Many of our clients are investing for retirement, yes." He ex-plained some of the kinds of investments he dealt with and said he would be happy to show me what the company offered if I was interested.

"Right now," I said, "the only type of financial planning I'm interested in is how to keep my bills paid until the end of the summer." I asked him if he knew Bill, and he said he had met him.

"It seems that half the people at that church sell insurance," said Bobby.

I wanted to ask about the questionable investments Bill had mentioned at dinner the night before, but I didn't think this would be the right time.

Bobby asked, "Are you going to help us with the car?"

"Well, I thought I'd watch, if I'm not in the way."

"Not at all."

"It looks like you're doing fine on it without me. It's a beautiful old car. It was nice of you to help Dad restore it."

"Well, actually, it's nice of *him* to help *me*," Bobby said.

Dad turned from the workbench and explained, "This is Bobby's car. I told him I'd give it to him if he would help me restore it."

"Oh!" I said, too surprised to give any other response. Dad had not mentioned that detail the night before. He had never *given* a car to anybody, not even to David. He had never even let us *drive* his cars. Who *was* this guy?

"Well, that's enough chitchat," said Dad. "Let's get to work."

JACK

I wanted to get that clutch assembly installed sometime before the end of the century, but I could hardly get my two chatterboxes, Chris and Bobby, to shut up long enough to get any work done. I don't know why Chris wanted to be out there with us anyway. He couldn't change the oil in a car to save his life, and he's never shown the least bit of interest in restoring cars. But there he was, out to the garage before I was. He looked guilty when I walked in, or afraid or something, but I don't know why. He wasn't touching anything. Just standing there in the middle of the garage, staring around like he had wandered in by mistake.

Bobby's pretty easy to work with when it's just the two of us. He's good with cars and, for someone his age, knows a lot about the old ones. But get somebody else out there and he really turns on the gab. I guess he thought he had to entertain Chris, but it was getting on my nerves. Chris didn't like it when he heard I had given Bobby that car. He had such a look of horror you would have thought I had disinherited him and signed over all my worldly possessions to Bobby. I guess I can give my cars to anybody I like. Why would Chris care anyway? He wouldn't want one if I paid him to take it!

But Mr. Big Mouth Bobby kept making it worse by saying things like, "Chris, did you know that when your dad had his first '38 Olds in high school, he took out his first girlfriend in it?" Of course Chris didn't know that or the hundred other tidbits Bobby saw fit to share with him. You don't tell your kids about the girls you went out with before their mother. At least I don't. Chris looked like he had been hit in the gut every time Bobby popped out with one of those things. I don't even remember telling Bobby all that stuff, but I must have, because he was blabbing away about it half the evening. That Olds I had in high school was an important car for me, I guess, and when I work on one just like it, it all comes back. I hadn't thought about that girl, Laura, for years, until I started working on this thing.

That car ended up being nothing but trouble for me, but when I bought it, I thought Oldsmobile was the best car around. The summer before my senior year, these two neighbors down the road, Don and Dick Wilson—they were brothers—bought a pair of Oldsmobiles. Don bought a '48 with an automatic transmission—a hydromatic transmission, which was quite a rarity at that time, especially in our neighborhood. Anyhow, when I found that '38 Olds four-door sedan in a car lot near our house, I said, "That car is going to be mine." Dad tried to keep me from buying it, but finally he gave in. I should've listened to him. That car leaked oil like no other I've ever had. It was two quarts low when I bought it, so I put some more in, and it was a quart low the next day! A friend of mine looked at it and said it had a leaking pan gasket or maybe a bad main bearing, neither of which I had the money to fix. So I lived with it. I had to add a quart of oil every day, whether I drove it or not. It used even more if I went a long distance. I didn't want Dad to find out, but he did, of course. That car had a flat-head, eight-cylinder engine that never got more than ten miles a gallon, so that was costing me too.

I was little more than a slave that summer anyway. My sister June had contracted an old man to build a cement-block house on a lot she owned west of town. Don't ask me why she wanted a cement-block house. Ugliest thing you ever saw. Probably wouldn't even be legal to build nowadays. But I got hired to be this old man's helper. I was supposed to carry the blocks to him and keep him supplied with mortar. The mortar was basically mud. Now, you can imagine how exciting that job would be for a seventeen-year-old full of energy. The work was hard, but the worst thing was not being able to see or talk to anybody. The old man didn't speak an entire paragraph to me that whole summer. The only words I can remember coming from his mouth were "more blocks" and "more mud."

Anyhow, Bobby kept piping up with one thing after another that I had apparently told him, and Chris drank it all in like he was studying for one of his college exams. Finally I had to break in and say, "Are we planning on working on the car tonight, or are we here to gab?"

So Bobby shut up, and we got some work done. Chris stayed out there awhile, but pretty soon he got tired of watching and walked away without saying a word.

CHRIS

Bobby knows so much about my dad, you'd think he was writing his biography or something. He knew things Dad had never told me, like his first girlfriend! It was humiliating to listen to this guy I had never seen tell me my dad's life story. Bobby tried to coax more information out of Dad, but Dad acted pretty annoyed at both of us for even being in the room, so Bobby ended up telling what he knew of it himself. They were both at the workbench most of this time putting something together. I was curious to know exactly what they were working on, but I didn't want to show my ignorance by asking.

Finally Bobby said, "Ready to go," and he carried whatever it was over to the car. Then he lowered himself down onto his creeper, which is a board on wheels that you lie on to slide underneath the car. Dad had a creeper, too, and eased himself onto it, pushing himself under the car.

"I'm getting too old for this," Dad said, groaning as he went.

"Be careful," Bobby cautioned him.

They continued their work without any other conversation between them. They both seemed to know what they were supposed to do and didn't need superfluous words to distract them. Dad and David had worked the same way, almost seeming to read each other's minds as their hands moved deftly over the engine. When they did speak, it was rarely in full sentences, but short little requests for a certain wrench or part or for the light to be moved. When I had tried to work on the cars, I usually had a million questions I wanted to ask, which exasperated my father. *"We're not working on that now!"* he would say when my questioning strayed beyond the specific task at hand. But I often didn't know what we were working on. I would try to follow his instructions, but even when I succeeded, I rarely knew exactly what I was doing. The car was like a gigantic puzzle, but I could only see the pieces of it. David could envision the whole puzzle, and I could tell Bobby was the same way.

I was tempted to ask my dad more about the car he had in high school, about my grandfather, and why Aunt June would want to build a cement-block house and many other things. But I knew such questions would only annoy him. I looked at the four feet sticking out from under the car, then peered into the engine but couldn't really see what they were working on. So much for my helping Dad and Bobby. I was extraneous now, and if I said or did anything else, I would become a nuisance. This exact scene could have taken place ten years ago, and those feet sticking out across from Dad's could have been David's.

I had the strong urge to flee to California. I pictured my apartment—my bookshelves, the recliner, my computer, the balcony where my friends and I had barbecues on warm summer evenings. I pictured all of us on the beach playing volleyball.

I left the garage so quietly they probably didn't realize I was gone.

Going inside, I found Mom in the formal living room, which we rarely used unless we had a bunch of people over. My parents redecorated the house every few years with new furniture, carpet, wall hangings, and so on, but this room was an exception. Because it was such a superfluous room, where the sofa and carpet had seen little use, they had kept the ugly green-and-white sofa and matching love seat and the hideous maple coffee table and end tables for probably twenty years. Mom was sitting on the floor, which, because of her weight, I had rarely seen her do. In front of her was a cardboard box about the size of a filing cabinet drawer. It overflowed with photographs. Mom had arranged some of the photos in rows along the floor, and she was pulling out even more stacks of pictures.

"What are you doing in here?" I asked.

"Two things," she said. "We're having the fiftieth anniversary of the founding of our church this summer, and Pastor Jennings asked me to put together photo boards to show some memorable happenings from each decade. He's planning to collect pictures from different people in the church, so I thought I'd look through our box and see what we had. While I'm at it, I thought I'd go ahead and put our pictures in some kind of order. I've wanted to do that for years, and this is the easiest place to spread them out."

My family had never arranged photographs in albums. Despite my mother's fanatical neatness in most areas, she had never given much thought to photos. They were stacked in boxes in no particular order and put away in a closet. Maybe once a year or so, if somebody felt nostalgic, they were taken out and looked at.

Mom filed through a package of photos and stopped at one that caught her eye. "Who is this little green man?"

She held up a picture of a stuffed creature—something like a man or a dwarf or a science fiction creature about the size of a baby—that had a green body and big eyes and stringy hair made of yarn.

Mom said, "I remember that thing but don't remember whose it was."

"It was mine," I said. "His name was Meep."

"Meep! That's right," Mom said as if Meep were her long-lost friend. She didn't care a thing about Meep when I was little, believe me.

"You used to carry him around with you day and night. I remember now! If we tried to go anywhere without Meep, you'd scream your head off. You were just a little guy. Then suddenly you didn't carry him around anymore. Whatever happened to Meep? Do you still have him?"

"No, Mom! I was a little boy. I was only three or four."

"Well, what happened to him?" she asked.

"David killed him."

"What?"

"David got mad at me one time and threatened to kill Meep if I didn't stop bugging him. I kept pestering him until he got so mad he grabbed Meep out of my hands and ran into the bathroom and threw him in the toilet. He tried to flush him down, but he wouldn't go."

Mom sat back against the wall and stared off for a second, smiling. "That's right!" she said. "I remember now. It was hours before we got you calmed down."

"And then you made me throw Meep away. He was ruined."

"Yes," she said, and for a moment her red cheeks, which could be deceiving in terms of the emotions they were expressing, made me think she was close to tears. "You loved that thing."

"Mom, are you really going to arrange every one of those hundreds of pictures into albums? It'll take all summer. You've let those pictures sit in the closet for years without hardly touching them."

Then, in a singsong voice that signaled she knew more than she was telling, she said, "Well, we're going to have to get things organized."

"Why?" I asked. "You and Dad are the most organized people I know."

"Your dad and I have some ideas about some things we're going to do that will mean we need to get all this stuff straightened out."

"What are you talking about?"

"Your dad told me not to say anything to you yet. Not until things are more definite."

"What?"

"Well, don't tell him I told you. Let him tell you himself when the time comes."

"Mom, please, spit it out."

"We're moving."

"Moving! You're selling the house?"

"Yes, probably. That's what we've been talking about."

"Where would you go?"

"We've been looking at the condominiums they're building over by the high school."

"You can't move! This is your home!"

"Well, we could be in there as soon as summer, if they get it finished."

I was too surprised to know how to react to this news. My parents had lived in this house since I was four years old. Never in all those years had I heard them mention the possibility of moving. I could not imagine them anywhere but in this house, and I could not imagine strangers living here.

"Are you thinking of moving because of Dad's heart attack?"

"Partly," she said. "We had talked about it even before that. We planned to wait until he retired, but after his heart attack, we figured we might as well go ahead."

"Have you already bought the new place?"

"No, but we've looked at the model and talked to the builder about it. We'll probably decide within the next couple weeks. Your dad wanted to talk to a real estate agent first about what we could get for this house."

We sat silently for a moment while Mom shuffled absently through the photos in her hands. "So what do you think?" she asked.

"I'm amazed."

"Don't you see why it makes sense for us?"

"No, not at the moment. Look at all the work you've put into this house over the years. You've got it fixed up like you want it. It's in great shape. It's spotless. It's remodeled. What more could you want?"

"*Less* is what we want. We don't need a place this big anymore. You and David are gone, Robin will move out one of these days, I'm sure. Why do we need four bedrooms, two garages, an extra living room, and a yard to mow?"

"How big is the condominium?"

"Two bedrooms. A nice big living room. A two-car garage. It's just the size we want."

"Where will you put all your stuff? It'll never fit in there."

"We're going to get rid of a lot of things. We don't need all this. And we won't have to do yard work, which your dad can't keep up with anymore. The doctor told him not to do it."

"Can't he have one of the neighbor kids do the yard? Wasn't Greg going to do it?"

"Your dad doesn't like the way Greg does it. He doesn't trim very well around the fence and the bushes."

"Well, that's no reason to move," I scoffed. "What about the antique cars? Where will Dad put them?"

"He's going to sell them."

"I can't believe he'd do that!"

"He's not so interested in them anymore. Not since David died. Things change, Chris. Don't you realize that?"

"That's what people keep telling me. But this seems too sudden, too unnecessary. You two are still fairly young, fairly healthy. You don't have to sell off and move to some dinky place like you're ancient."

"Your father almost died of a heart attack last month! Do you call that healthy?"

"You said yourself he's been brooding. What's going to happen to him if he sells this house, where he's invested so much of himself, where he's lived so much of his life? And if he sells those cars that have been his main interest for so long, what is he going to do with himself?"

"Well, I don't think he's as attached to this house as it appears you are. Which seems odd, since you haven't been here for the last two years."

"I know, but with all the moving around I've done, this house has always been the one place that was familiar."

"Well, I'm glad you feel that way," she said. "But you can't leave and go on with your life and expect everything here to stay exactly the same. We're changing. We're getting older. We're even going to die one of these days. That's why when you ignore us for two years, you can't just dip back into our lives and pretend nothing's been lost. That precious time is gone forever. You're young, and for you a year here or there doesn't make much difference. But for your dad and me, every moment counts. Time is precious, and we don't have any to waste."

"I don't like this one-foot-in-the-grave talk," I said.

"You don't like to face reality. You never have."

"You and Dad still have many years ahead of you."

"We don't know that, and neither do you. You take too much for granted."

"Well, I didn't know we were talking about you *dying*. I thought we were talking about you *moving*."

"That's right," she said. "That's all we're doing. Moving. People do it all the time, so you don't need to make a big deal of it. And I don't want you giving your dad a rough time about it."

"I'm going to talk him out of it," I said.

"No, you're not! I don't even want you telling him you know about it yet. Let him tell you his own way when he's ready."

"When will that be?"

"When we've made a final decision."

"Does Robin know about this?"

"I told her it was a possibility."

"What did she say?"

"Not much. Unfortunately, she's got other things on her mind."

"Like what?"

"I'm not getting into that right now. I want to concentrate on these pictures. I've told you too much already."

———

This night had not yet revealed all its secrets.

At a little after ten, Bill called. "Time to play racquetball, man," he said as a substitute for hello.

"All right. When?"

"Right now. I can pick you up."

"Tonight? It's past ten o'clock."

"So what? Has Jack got you on a curfew over there?"

"Can we get a court somewhere this late at night?"

"It's all taken care of," he said. "I have a court reserved at eleven at my health club. It's the last reservation for the night."

This was the usual way Bill made plans with me. No polite invitation a couple days ahead. Simply a last-minute phone call and a demand that I be there.

"Don't you have to work tomorrow?" I asked with a sigh, thinking maybe I had had enough entertainment for one day.

"Of course I have to work," he said.

"Don't you need to sleep a little first? Personally, I'm wiped out."

"Chris, please tell me you have not become a fussy old man who has to have his warm milk and be in bed by the stroke of ten."

"Okay, no problem. I can kick your butt at racquetball any time of the day or night. Let's go."

"That's the spirit! I'll be right over to pick you up. Afterward we'll go get something to eat. I have some information you might be interested in. Be ready." He hung up before I had a chance to ask about his "information."

I was low on cash, and my last ten-dollar bill was in the glove compartment of my car. I decided to go out and get it before Bill arrived. I heard Dad shuffling around in the kitchen, so I knew he and Bobby must be finished working on the car. I glanced out the window and saw the light was still on in the garage. Apparently Bobby was given the job of cleanup, which made me smile. I went out the front door and intended to go around the house to my car.

When I walked around the front corner of the house and headed down the driveway toward the back, I was in the darkest, most secluded part of our property. As it turned out, it was the perfect place for Robin and Bobby to have a secret rendezvous before he left for the night. It was so dark that I almost ran into them. All three of us were startled. Bobby was leaning against the wall, and Robin was facing him, kissing him and holding his shoulders just lightly enough so that none of the dirt or oil he had picked up from the car got on her. She let out a little yelp when I swooped down on them, and my shoes made a skidding sound as I stopped.

For a moment, all of us stood silent.

"Chris! What are you doing here?" Robin said.

"Going to my car," I replied, not moving an inch. "What are you two doing here?"

"We were just talking," she lied. "Bobby is just leaving. He was saying good-bye."

"Oh," I said. "Friendly."

"I've got to go," Bobby said. He squeezed Robin's hand and stepped away from us toward the front of the house, where his car was parked.

"I have to go too," I said, making my feet move again toward my car. I was too stunned to know what to say. What could I say? Robin could kiss whomever she liked. What could I do? Beat him up? And for what? Robin was old enough to choose her own boyfriend without her big brother telling her who she could or couldn't see. But my instincts told me the guy was a jerk who would do nothing but hurt her.

Robin stood by the wall alone for a moment, as if she couldn't decide which of us she most needed to follow. After some hesitation, she picked me.

Robin caught up to me as I was fishing through my glove box searching for my money.

"What you think you saw was not what was happening," she said.

"Oh, really?" I asked. "What did I think I saw?"

"Come on, Chris."

"Don't tell me," I said. "He had something lodged in his teeth, and you were helping him pry it out."

"Chris, I shouldn't have to feel guilty. I shouldn't have to explain myself to you."

"I didn't ask for an explanation, did I? I was just walking to my car."

"Why did you come around that way instead of using the back door? Did you want to spy on us?"

"I didn't know there was an 'us,' and if I had known that the side of the house was where 'us' took place, I certainly would have chosen another path to my car. But ever since I was old enough to walk, I have preferred using the front door to the back. You know that."

"Well," she said, "the important thing is, I need you to promise not to tell Mom and Dad what you saw."

"I thought I didn't see what I saw."

"Don't be a creep."

"I know I have a ten-dollar bill in here, but I can't seem to find it," I said, shuffling through the mess. "Maybe I should blackmail you for my silence. Ten bucks or I squeal."

"I'd be willing to pay," she said.

I stood up and leaned against the car. "Who is this guy?" I asked. "What are you doing with him?"

"I'm not doing anything with him. We were just . . ."

"You're asking me to do you the favor of helping you conceal something from our parents, so don't treat me like a fool."

"I'm a grown-up now, Chris. What I do shouldn't be any of your business—or theirs either."

"Well, then, it shouldn't matter whether I tell them or not. You can always tell them it's none of their business."

"You know it's not that easy."

"Then talk to me. I'm your brother. I don't want to tattle to Mom and Dad. But I'm concerned about you."

"You don't like Bobby, do you?"

"I barely know him. I only talked to him once in the garage."

"But you don't like him."

"No, I don't."

"Why?"

"I don't trust him."

"Why not?"

"He seems like a schemer to me. A user. Like he's trying to charm you into doing what he wants."

She was silent for a moment; then she said softly, "He's not like that at all."

"How serious is this relationship?"

"I don't know."

"Robin . . ."

"It won't do any good to try to pressure me into giving an answer. I honestly don't know. I can't give you quick answers to explain the relationship. It's not that simple."

"Don't you see a problem when you have to hide it from everybody? What about Bobby? Has he told you not to tell Mom and Dad?"

"We just sort of decided not to."

"Don't you think it'll get harder to explain the longer you hide it? There's Bobby, working with Dad almost every day on that car while at the same time he's secretly seducing his daughter."

"He's not *seducing* me."

"Is Bobby afraid if Dad finds out, he won't give him that old car?"

"No," she scoffed.

"How did he get Dad to agree to that, anyway? Doesn't it seem strange to you, considering Dad never gave either of his own sons a car?"

"Dad's different now. You've been gone a long time, Chris, and Dad has changed. Bobby and I will work everything out. I'm sorry you saw us together. You have to trust me, trust that I know what I'm doing. You have to promise not to tell and let me do this my own way."

"I'm not going to tell, but I don't like it. Secrets like this only end up hurting people, and I don't trust a guy who would put you in that position."

"Haven't you ever kept secrets from Mom and Dad, Chris?"

I hesitated, not wanting to appear to dodge the question, but not wanting to let her change the subject either. "Yes, I have."

"So, sometimes there are reasons for it."

"I hope this isn't the last time we're going to talk about this. I wish you'd be more open with me."

"I will," she said. "Just not right now. I trust you, but I have to do things my own way."

"All right."

"What are you doing out here, anyway?"

"Looking for money so I can go out with Bill."

"At this time of night?"

"Yes, *Mom*, at this time of night. I'm a grown-up too."

"Well, good. At least maybe that will keep them off my case and onto yours instead."

"Thanks, sis."

————

Bill drove fast and liked the music loud. Some of the best times of our friendship have been spent shouting over the music in his car. Bill is the one friend I can always completely let loose with. When we're in his car, soaring in the rhythm of its motion and music, we feel free to say anything, shout anything, sing anything, joke about anything, no matter how rude or irreverent. But whatever "information" Bill was going to tell me was not likely to come out now. It would have to wait till after racquetball, while we sit in some dive, eating junk food.

In his heyday Bill had driven a sporty red two-seat Fiero, with stereo speakers built into the back of the seat, making it sound like the whole car was pumping out music. Now he drove a less flashy car, a plum-colored Saturn, the backseat of which was filled with the three-ring binders and briefcase of the insurance salesman he had become.

Bill was still pretty good at racquetball, but I noticed a few subtle ways in which time and the difficulties of life had taken a toll on my old friend. He had gained weight around the middle and his face had a slightly puffy look, totally uncharacteristic of the old, sharply featured Bill. He had told me he expected to lose thirty pounds over the summer, and he expected me to help him do it by playing a lot of racquetball, basketball, and whatever other sport we could think of.

My best strategy in competing against Bill was to wear him out. After winning the first two games, he was finally tired enough that I beat him easily the next two. By then the health club was closing, so we showered and headed off to Bailey's.

The only thing Bailey's has going for it is that it's open all night. It is a restaurant of wood-paneled booths, brass rails, green-shaded lamps, and greasy appetizers. Bill ordered onion rings and a chocolate milk shake.

"So much for that thirty pounds you wanted to lose," I said.

"Shut up!" he protested. "We just played an hour of racquetball. I'm starving."

I ordered vanilla ice cream and coffee.

"You're a wimp," he said and then got down to business. "Bad news, I'm afraid. I asked my boss about Premiere Financial Services—Jim White's company—where your dad's friend Bobby works. You need to tell your dad to stay away from it if he hasn't already invested with them. It's rumored they're being investigated and may even get indicted by the U.S. Attorney's office for fraud."

"Is Bobby part of it?"

"I don't know, but probably. The whole company's involved in some really bad investment scams. Ponzi schemes and things like that."

"What is that?"

Bill explained that a Ponzi scheme is an unscrupulous plan to lure clients into investing in something that is usually guaranteed to bring huge returns. But instead of investing the money into something legitimate, the con man uses it for his own purposes and continues to draw new investors into the scheme. He keeps the old investors happy by paying them with money from newer investors. For a while everybody's happy, but he can't keep luring new investors forever, so eventually the whole thing collapses, and everybody is wiped out.

"I can't believe Jim White would be involved in something like that," I said. "I've always known him to be a very honest man. His family is one of the most influential families in our church! He's on the church board and teaches Sunday school."

"I doubt if it started out as his idea," said Bill. "I always thought he was an honest guy too. I almost went to work for him. But his firm was known to be in some financial trouble a few years ago, so he teamed up with a partner who apparently got him into this shady stuff. Now he'll be pretty much shut down until they resolve this, if the rumors are true. They'll freeze his assets. He could face lawsuits and even go to jail. Do you know where a lot of Jim White's investors come from?"

"Our church."

"Right. A lot of people stand to lose their retirement, their life savings."

"How sure are you about all this?"

"I don't know many details about it yet. It's hard to get people to talk. But my boss knows a number of people connected to Jim's firm, so I have no doubt it's true. Do your parents have any money invested with them?"

"I don't know. Dad doesn't talk to me about his finances."

"Well, I hope your dad doesn't get burned by this. If you could ask him what he has invested in, I could try to find out whether it's part of the investigation."

"I'll try, but he's pretty touchy about that kind of stuff. I'll have to catch him at just the right time. Let me know if you find out anything else."

"Sure. So did you work on the car with your dad?"

"Sort of. I stood in the garage and watched."

"Doesn't your dad ever let you actually do anything to the cars?"

"He would, but I could never seem to get the feel for it. He tried to teach me a few times when I was younger, but my mind would wander. He'd be explaining something and suddenly I realized I didn't remember what he'd been saying for the last five minutes. So when it came time to do the same job on another car, I had no idea what to do. I'd start working, and he'd immediately jump all over me. Treated me like an idiot. I never could do anything mechanical with him watching— can't hammer a nail right or cut anything straight. I always tense up, waiting for him to tell me I'm doing something wrong. I couldn't even stand to drive if he was in the car with me. No matter how careful I was, I could tell he thought I was doing it all wrong. He didn't need to say anything. I could tell just by the way he frowned and shifted around in his seat."

As Bill slurped his milk shake and dipped his onion rings into a pool of ketchup, I changed the subject by asking him about the woman from his office he had started dating. Even though he had gone out with her only once before he came to California, he had spent half our drive back to Indiana praising her, telling me how beautiful she was, how easy she was to talk to, and on and on.

Now he slid his shake away from him and said, "I don't know why I want to get involved with a woman again. Women have ruined my life."

I laughed. "Do you really think so?"

"Don't you? Look at me. I'm a wreck."

"You've always been a wreck. You can't blame that on women."

"It's easy for you to laugh," he said. "There you are lying on the beach in California, teaching a few classes, surfing every weekend, worrying about whether your tan stays dark enough, taking your pick of any girl who walks by. You've got it made. Can you ever picture yourself moving back here for good?"

"No. I'm already starting to feel all tangled up, and I've only been here two days. Maybe I should forget this whole thing and drive back tomorrow."

"Oh no. You can't do that," Bill said. "The fun is just beginning."

ROBIN

I may be in some real trouble this time, and it has to do with Bobby. I pray to God I'm wrong. Everything about our relationship has been a surprise, but this is one shock I don't need.

My involvement with Bobby began pretty much by accident. When he came along, I was seeing someone else, Brandon, from the band I play in. In fact, Mom and Dad still think I'm seeing Brandon. Only Chris knows I'm seeing Bobby, and he only knows because we were stupid enough to get caught kissing right there by the side of the house. From the first time we went out, we thought it would be smart to keep quiet about it. For one thing, we weren't really sure at first there was going to *be* a relationship. We just sort of . . . eased into things. Bobby had just started working with Dad on the car, and Dad was also trying to get him a job with Jim White. Bobby didn't want to give Dad the wrong impression about the kind of guy he is, so we just kept it to ourselves to make things easier.

Bobby showed up in our church one day from out of nowhere. He was the cutest guy you ever saw. Gorgeous thick brown hair, the brightest smile, a perfect face. He looked like a model out of a fashion ad. Nice body too. Slender but fit, like there were muscles hidden under his shirt that he wasn't bothering to show off. I didn't meet him the first few weeks, though I kept seeing him at church and finally asked somebody who he was. Nobody really knew, except that his name was Bobby. Next thing you know, I look out our back window one night, and there he is with my dad in the garage, taking a car engine apart! I asked Mom about him. She was real casual about it, said Dad had met him at church, found out he was interested in restoring cars, and wanted to give him a chance to see what he could do. That was before Dad's heart attack, before the car they're working on now. Mom said Bobby had had a hard life and had recently become a Christian. Some of the men of the church were trying to help him out, get him a job, get him established and everything. He didn't *look* as though he had had a hard life. He looked like he had lived the life of a movie star.

Dad always stops working in the garage around nine o'clock at night. I don't know what's so magical about nine, but he never varies from that by more than fifteen minutes. So a little before nine that night I just *happened* to need to get my car, which Bobby's car was blocking, out of the driveway. I went out to the garage and asked if he could move his car. Dad said they were about done anyway and Bobby could go and Dad would clean up. Bobby washed off his hands and arms—nicely tanned, muscular arms, I might add—and walked with me to the front of the house, where we were both parked.

I could tell he wanted to talk, so I didn't rush things. He asked me about my car at first, which didn't impress me much. But then he asked me why he hadn't met me at church. I told him I had seen him there but guessed he hadn't gotten around to me yet. He asked where I was going. I told him I was going to see a friend. I was actually going to see Brandon, but for some reason I didn't want to tell him that just then. He said he was really hungry and asked if I wanted to stop somewhere with him to get a sandwich. Now, what would *you* do if the cutest guy in the universe suddenly asked if he could take you out to dinner? "All right," I said casually, even though inside I could hardly contain my excitement. That night we drove separate cars and spent an hour together at dinner, but from then on we talked on the phone or saw each other almost every day.

He seemed so genuine that first night. That's what I loved about him. He seemed so *interested* in me, as though I were the first woman he had ever gone out with. He has this conceited look to him, like a lot of good-looking guys do, but he didn't act that way. Just very caring. He was restless, though. Couldn't seem to sit still. Acted like he was afraid he was going to get caught or something. His eyes darted around every once in a while, as if searching for a quick exit. He still gets that look sometimes, and my biggest fear has been that he'll fly off and never be seen again.

I felt guilty going behind Brandon's back, but not as guilty as you might think, because Brandon and I are barely dating. I think deep down he really thinks of me as just his favorite female band member. And one who is not that great a musician. I do all right, but the band is not a part of my identity. For Brandon, it's everything he is. I got in the band because I love music, and it's kind of fun. But I don't really care if we play or not. Once every six months would be often enough for me. But Brandon is Mr. Perfection. He thinks he's a much better musician than the rest of us. And he probably is. But whenever a song goes wrong, he acts like it's a big deal, because we're not up to his standards.

But he is sweet. I don't mean to give a bad impression of him. I like him and care about him, especially away from the band. But I'm just saying that going out with Bobby wasn't as bad as it sounds because Brandon and I aren't really *tied* to each other or anything. Mom and Dad don't like Brandon particularly, but I think that's mainly because he has long hair and looks a little grungy and talks like a musician instead of like one of the Young Republican types they prefer. Brandon is sort of grungy cute. He has big brown eyes, very innocent looking, with his hair kind of surrounding his face. Anyway, Mom and Dad don't trust him, and I'm sure if what I think has happened really *has* happened, he will be the one they blame.

Which brings me to my problem.

As I said earlier, I may have gotten myself into trouble. My relationship with Bobby got a little carried away for a while. It's against my beliefs, but in the heat of the moment I felt pressure to—no, I don't want to say pressure. I don't want to blame him. I don't want to blame anyone but myself. I don't even want to blame myself. Maybe I'm wrong. Maybe everything's all right.

To tell you the truth, I got carried away. I'm afraid I may be pregnant.

I sit and wonder how this could be happening to me. How could I have let it?

But maybe it isn't really happening.

I try not to panic. I try to think about other things.

But if I am pregnant, that will be like a death sentence right now. I mean it. I would rather die than tell my parents.

I need to get away and think. It feels like someone is squeezing my brain. Oh, God, I know I have done wrong, but please, please don't let this be happening to me.

CHRIS

Aunt Dayle did not disappoint us with her chili on Saturday night. I could smell the extraordinary spicy sauce even before we got to her front porch. Aunt Dayle and her husband, Ray, live in Clermont, a few miles west of Indianapolis, in a subdivision of homes that is fifty to sixty years old. Their home, like most of those around it, is surrounded by a big lawn and a wide front porch with stone columns, but inside, the rooms of the house are tiny. Aunt Dayle is a pack rat, so when she bought new furniture, instead of getting rid of all the old stuff as my mother would have done, she tried to find a place to keep the old pieces—an end table tucked away in that corner, an old recliner wedged in next to the new one. The result is that when she also fills her house with relatives, there is almost no place to move. We have to work our way through the tiny paths that lead from the living room through what is supposed to be the dining room (but is actually filled with two mismatched coffee tables, a sofa, and two rocking chairs) back to the kitchen, which is where Monopoly will be played and chili served.

Uncle Ray met us at the front door. Ray is a quiet, sweet-natured man in his late sixties whose smile is like that of a jack-o'-lantern, just a few jagged teeth scattered haphazardly throughout his mouth. Ray has the largest belly I have ever seen. The round enormity of it filled the doorway as we walked up the porch steps and greeted him. He shook hands with Dad and Mom, kissed Robin on the cheek, and grabbed me by the shoulders and shook me.

"Where in the world have you been?" he asked me. "I was about to drive out there to California and haul you back here myself."

"You should have come out to visit me," I said.

"You teach me to surf?"

"Sure! Go deep-sea fishing too."

"That's more like it." Ray turned toward the kitchen and yelled, "Dayle, get out here! Some California hippie here to see you."

As I stood barely two feet inside the house, Dayle and Ray's second oldest child, Jeff, and his wife, Shelly, who were about my age, came up and hugged me, and right behind them were Aunt Jackie and Uncle Don. Grandma and Grandpa were seated in their favorite chairs on opposite sides of the room from each other, from where they would not move all evening except to go to the bathroom once or twice. Food and drink would be brought to them on trays, and whenever Grandpa wanted something, he would bellow to Grandma to bring it to him, but someone else would get it for him instead.

When Aunt Dayle appeared in the room, she held out her hands as if she were about to scoop up a big bouquet of flowers out of a vase. As she got closer, her high-pitched scream of excitement swelled, clearing everyone out of her path. Her short gray hair was combed back in an unstylish frizz, and her white apron was covered with spots of chili. She took my face in her hands and squeezed it hard, the same greeting she had given me ever since I was a little boy.

"I'm gonna get chili spatter all over you," she said as she hugged me. "Just look at your suntan. You must spend every day at the beach out there."

"He's gonna teach me to surf," Uncle Ray told her.

"What are you talkin' about?" Aunt Dayle asked. "You'd cause a tidal wave."

Uncle Ray put his hand up to his mouth as if to shield his comment from Aunt Dayle and growled, "This is a real special occasion, Chris. She put her teeth in."

"Don't start on me tonight," she said.

It was true, though, that she wore her false teeth, which was unusual. I had only seen her wear them at more formal occasions like graduations, weddings, and funerals. And she put them in for Sunday morning church, of course. But I expected she would have them out before the evening was over. She always said they hurt her gums.

I eased through the obstacle course of sofas, chairs, and TV trays to shake hands with Grandpa, who looked no more ancient, wrinkled, or feeble than he had two years earlier. "How you doin', boy" was all he said, but I knew that if I had a chance to sit with him and let him get warmed up, he would tell stories all night.

Grandma summoned me over to her chair the moment it looked like I was going to spend time with Grandpa instead of her. She looked the same as always, crumpled up and withered, as if she were slowly collapsing into a ball that would eventually blow away in the wind. Only her eyes and her smile still looked young, and they lit up lovingly as I walked over to her. She gave me a raspy kiss on the cheek.

"How's my little darlin'?"

"Fine, Grandma. How's mine?"

"I'm fallin' apart, honey. This'll prob'ly be the last family get-together for your old grandma."

"She's been predictin' that for the last twenty years," Aunt Dayle put in.

"Well, it's gonna happen pretty soon," Grandma said, "and then you'll be sorry you said that."

"Mom, you'll probably outlast half of us in this room."

Grandma looked at me. "Nobody in this family has compassion or respect for an old woman."

"Oh no," Dayle groaned, "don't let her get started down that track, Chris. Come in here and help me stir the chili."

Grandma grabbed my hand and said, "You're not gonna let them make you play that silly game tonight, are you, honey?"

"Yes, Grandma. I was planning to play."

"You been gone so long," she said. "Every day I used to look in the mailbox and hope you would have written me. But none of my grandchildren ever write."

"Sorry, Grandma. I've never been good at keeping in touch that way." As I said this, Aunt Dayle came by and put her arm around my shoulder to push me toward the kitchen.

Grandpa, who assumed everyone was as hard of hearing as he, yelled at Grandma, "Let him go, Grace!"

"Dad, don't start fussin' at her," Dayle scolded, and we retreated toward the kitchen, which was permeated with the aroma of the chili cooking in the familiar metal pot on the stove. Dayle said, "They just pick at each other all the time now."

"What do they argue about?"

"Oh, you name it. When I picked them up today, they were arguing about whose leg hurt the most."

"Whose leg hurt the most? That's a weird thing to argue about."

"I know."

"I don't think I'd even want to win that argument."

We walked over to the huge pot of chili, and Aunt Dayle stirred the bubbling meat and sauce and macaroni. "Are you hungry?" she asked.

"I am now. This chili is one of the things I miss most about living in Indiana."

"Well, honey, if I'd known that was all it took to keep you here, I would have made it every week."

"Is anybody else coming?"

Aunt Dayle looked over at me sternly, as if she were peering over imaginary eyeglasses, and whispered, "Nobody else is coming. Don't tell your mom, but your aunt Shirley said she just couldn't deal with your mother for a whole evening. Said they were sure to get into a fight if she came. They act more childish now than when they were girls."

I shook my head and started stirring the chili with the wooden spoon. "Well, Dayle, nobody can say you haven't done your best to be a peacemaker."

"It ain't easy," she said. "It's getting harder and harder to keep the family together. People just don't care about it as much anymore. They've all got their own lives they're taken up with and don't wanna be bothered with extended family. It wasn't like that when I grew up. You stuck with your family no matter what. Jeff's the only one of my knuckleheads who would come tonight."

She pulled a stack of bowls and plates down from the cabinet. Giving me a couple boxes of saltine crackers, she said, "Spread those packages around out there so everybody can get ahold of some. We might as well go ahead and eat. If you'll help me serve, we'll just let everybody stay where they are."

Robin sat on the arm of Grandma's recliner as I walked in with the crackers. Grandma tugged on Robin's skirt and said, "They would have thrown me in jail for wearing a skimpy little thing like this when I was your age."

"Well, times have changed," Robin said.

"Humph," growled Grandma.

As I served the first of the bowls of chili, Dayle came out and asked my dad to pray for the food. His prayer was short and to the point, thanking God for the food and the fellowship, amen. Grandma's head was still bowed as I set the bowl of chili on the TV tray in front of her. I didn't know if she was praying or if she had fallen asleep. In a few seconds she opened her eyes and scowled in silent disapproval at my father's perfunctory prayer.

Mom set up TV trays for everyone as they staked out their precious few feet of space. After everyone was served their chili and crackers and drinks, I found a place for myself in the middle of the living room floor where I could set my food on the end of a coffee table. My location put me in the midst of three conversations, though if I had closed my eyes, I would have thought that every person in the room was talking at the same time. Grandpa seemed to need an audience the most right at that moment, since only Jeff was listening to him, and even Jeff occasionally got pulled away from the conversation to answer one of Shelly's questions. Grandpa didn't seem to mind the lack of an attentive audience. He only needed one person listening to keep his story going. If the chaos in the room got so bad that he lost all of us for a moment, he would simply sit quietly and frown until we came back, and then take up where he had left off. When I sat down, Grandpa was saying, "This guy I knew had two sons who worked trimming trees. One son was up in a tree sitting on a limb, and he sawed it right off from underneath himself."

"He sawed off the limb he was sitting on?" asked Jeff.

"Yes! I'm not kidding. Just *zip zip zip* and down he came."

"What was he thinking?"

"He was up pretty high too. Broke his leg and I don't know what all. Lucky it didn't kill him."

This story was interrupted by Grandma's yelling to Grandpa, "What was the name of that cat Effie had?"

"Effie!" barked Grandpa. "What are you talkin' about her for?"

"What was her cat's name?" Grandma repeated. This search for a name was a common trait of their storytelling. Neither of them could remember names very well, but no matter how irrelevant to a story the name might be, they would not continue until they agonized over it.

"I can't remember," Grandpa said. "Seems like it was . . . oh, let's see." We waited patiently for the cat's name to emerge. I didn't know who Effie was, let alone her cat, but I was not about to complicate the story by asking for an explanation. "Seems like its name was Charlie," Grandpa finally said.

"No, no," Grandma protested.

"I think that's what it was," he insisted. "Charlie."

"No, Charlie was her husband's name," she said, and we all laughed.

"Well, that's what I remember. Maybe she named the cat after her husband."

"Well, anyway," Grandma said, "Effie could practically have conversations with that cat. I mean it! When you'd talk to her on the phone, you could hear the cat in the background, and it seemed to understand everything she said."

As Grandma finished her story, my attention was drawn to Ray's corner of the room, where he was laughing at something my dad was telling him. Ray's laugh was both fascinating and frightening. He would start out innocently enough, nothing more than a smile and a slightly perceptible shaking of his body. As the belly-shaking increased, his raspy voice finally broke through with a high-pitched *hee hee hee* that soon became nothing more than a frightening wheeze, which collapsed into a cough that turned his face red and cut off the laugh. Eventually he leaned his head back in his recliner, catching his breath and murmuring, "Oh mercy."

After a couple of these episodes, Robin turned to me and whispered, "I wish they'd stop making him laugh. I expect a heart attack every time."

Grandpa, feeling ignored, pushed himself forward in his chair so that he would be heard above the noise and declared, "I take two pills every morning. They cost a dollar apiece." Then he leaned back into his comfortable position again, as if content that nothing further need be said on that topic.

Not to be outdone, Grandma sounded off from her perch in the opposite corner. "I take *four* pills every morning, and every one of them costs over a dollar apiece."

After everyone had their say on the high cost of medicine, Grandma told how high her blood pressure was, and Grandpa, of course, topped it. Then everyone in the room who knew their blood pressure had to share it. I, unfortunately, had no idea what mine was so had to sit silently and eat my chili. Grandpa tried to get the same discussion going on blood sugar, since he knew no one would be able to match his high numbers, but the rumble of other conversations drowned him out.

I did not hear Mom comment on Aunt Shirley's absence until we were at the kitchen table playing Monopoly after the first round of chili was over. There would be seconds on chili, along with pie, later in the evening. All of us had played Monopoly so many times that the mechanics of the game took little of our concentration and left plenty of time for conversation. We had two games going side by side, but the discussion flowed freely between the tables. Only Ray and the grandparents opted out of playing, preferring an after-dinner nap in their comfortable chairs.

As the games flowed, Mom told how Aunt Shirley had snubbed her at the recent graduation party for my cousin Candace, Roger's daughter.

"They had an open house from two to four in the afternoon that Sunday. We arrived about three, and the first thing we see when we walk in is Shirley standing at the serving table picking vegetables from the relish tray. She glanced up at us and then turned her head back to that tray without saying a word. She stayed there till we got all the way past her and went into the family room. You would've thought that cauliflower was the most interesting thing in the world to her! She picked up each piece so carefully and poked at that broccoli like she was doin' brain surgery on it. She doesn't want to work things out. That's just how she is."

Robin said, "Maybe you should have spoken to her first."

"No!" Mom declared, "I'm not gonna talk if she won't even bother to look up at us. Forget it. I've already gone the extra mile."

"Well," Aunt Dayle said decisively, "we've got the whole summer ahead of us. We're gonna have picnics and burgers on the grill and watermelon and homemade ice cream, and people are gonna come whether they like it or not! I'm tired of all this. And, Jack, if I land on one of your hotels one more time, I'm gonna pour the rest of that chili right on top of your head."

Before the night was over, I went through the obligatory grilling about my love life, with several relatives offering the unsolicited advice that I get back with Beth. And I answered the typical California questions about earthquakes, the weather, the beaches, the prices, and how long it would take me to come to my senses and move back to Indiana for good.

"I was afraid when I heard you went out there," Aunt Jackie put in. "I figured you'd come back with pink hair or something. Or earrings or nose rings or who knows what. I wouldn't live out there for nothing in the world."

The game, with several coffee breaks, went on until after midnight, and for the first time since I had come back to Indiana, I felt truly relaxed and at home, content in the comfort of being with the people I had known all my life. Dad was at his best that night, making everyone laugh, and Aunt Jackie's appreciative high-pitched cackle was just the catalyst he needed to bring him out of his brooding and put him center stage, where he had traditionally been in earlier days.

Uncle Ray came to the kitchen for food a couple times, but otherwise he preferred the company of Grandma and Grandpa because, as he once told me, "They're the only people I know who are more tired than I am."

When the games broke up and we walked back into the living room, the three of them were asleep, their mouths hanging open. The rumbling sounds resonating from them were so loud you would think they were having a contest to see who could create the most deafening snore.

"It's like a symphony in here!" cried Aunt Dayle, startling them all awake.

"You leavin' already?" Uncle Ray asked groggily.

"It's four o'clock in the morning!" Aunt Jackie teased.

"Oh, is it?" Ray responded. "Let's have a little breakfast, then."

"You'll be havin' leftover chili for breakfast," Aunt Dayle said.

We said our good-byes and promised to get together again soon. Robin had been quiet during the Monopoly game. She looked preoccupied, worried, as if she didn't hear the conversation around her. In the car on the way home I asked her what was wrong. She brushed this off with a quick "Nothing," but her foot was anxiously tapping.

Mom said, "She's gotten awful moody lately."

Robin sighed. "It's late. Do you have to start this? Can't anybody sit and think in this family without being chewed out?"

Mom curtly replied, "We'll try not to bother you."

Nobody said a word for the rest of the way home.

CHRIS

$\mathcal{B}$ill served as a kind of bodyguard for me the next day when I went back to church for the first time. The two people I most wanted to avoid were the "ex-fiancées," Beth and Cheryl. I had no idea what kind of reception to expect from my own ex, Beth, and I dreaded seeing David's fiancée because my sister had told me Cheryl was looking to dig up some more of the "truth" about David. Even though we had gotten home late from Aunt Dayle's the night before, I could hardly get to sleep as I imagined those two swooping down on me at the same time. So Bill, the former football player, accompanied me from the parking lot, through the foyer, and toward the sanctuary that morning. His job was to find an excuse to yank me away from any unpleasant situation that might arise.

I considered skipping church altogether, but that idea did not last long. Stonybrook Church of the Nazarene was home, for better or worse. It was here I had made my closest friends. It was here I had met the girls I dated before I moved to California, and it was here I had become a Christian and found spiritual mentors. I had known the Lord's Spirit intensely in this place and had struggled through deep spiritual battles, fighting many doubts and temptations. Church was an unavoidable part of my life. I would have to face whoever showed up, no matter how uncomfortable the encounter might be.

Though I dreaded seeing Cheryl, the prospect of running into Beth brought far more complex emotions. I had replayed the possible scenarios endlessly in my mind. The Angry Scene, when Beth walks up and makes snide, accusatory comments, then storms off. The Cold Scene, in which she sees me across the foyer but turns away without a word. The Loving Scene, in which she embraces me, welcomes me home, tells me how much she missed me.

Stonybrook is not the kind of church where you can sneak inside and quietly take your seat. I was greeted by a dozen or more people—not merely with polite hellos, but with hugs and handshakes and conversations. I talked to Mrs. Barrows, who had been my fourth-grade Sunday school teacher and a friend of my parents for years. I saw Glenn Frist, whom everyone referred to as "Brother Frist." One of the oldest men in the church and one of the most loved, he had told me countless times as I grew up that he was praying for me and believing God would do something great in my life. I saw Ron White, an old friend from my teenage days, who was married now with a child. We had never been particularly close—not in the sense of having serious talks or getting involved in the direction of each other's lives—but he was part of almost every teenage memory I had when there was a crowd of us laughing, yelling, playing hard, driving too fast, staying up late, or doing something that would have shocked or worried our parents.

Ron now suggested, "Let's get everybody together again while you're home! Most of the old group is still here—Mark, Jeremy, Ruth, Rachel. We haven't been out for ages. Everybody's acting too old."

"We *are* too old," I said. "Besides, most of you are raising children now. You can't stay out half the night like we did in the old days."

"You sound just like the rest of them," he said. Then his wife pulled him away toward the sanctuary.

Many of the people who greeted us said they were glad to see Bill again because he hadn't been to church much lately. I asked him about this as we crossed the foyer, and before quickly changing the subject, he admitted that he had been skipping a lot of services because he didn't feel as close to the people as he used to.

When we heard the worship team singing choruses, we knew it was time to sit down. The sanctuary had been remodeled with new carpet, pews, and a new pulpit. The worship style had also been revised. The piano and organ used to be the only instruments used, but now a few guitars, trombones, trumpets—even drums!—had been added. Instead of an old man standing behind the pulpit leading hymns, a group of men and women sang a strange combination of newer choruses and old hymns—a compromise, I suspected, between those who thought the old style of worship was just fine and the younger people who either wanted to throw out the old hymns entirely or modernize them so much they would be nearly unrecognizable to the old folks.

There were just enough changes in the church that I felt stiff and disoriented as the service began. It was not like the old days, when I had lost myself in worship and felt the Lord's Spirit sweeping through me. As song after song spread through the sanctuary, I closed my eyes and sang, praying to God to draw me close to Him, as I once had been. I longed for the faith, for the certitude I had known as a teenager. My spirit had burned for the Lord in those days. My faith now was a quiet, hesitant thing, drifting, rocked by losses.

Pastor Jennings preached the sermon that morning. He had been our minister for more than twenty years, the only pastor I had ever known. Even though he was now in his fifties, the most striking aspect of his appearance was still the look of youthful eagerness in his face. His expression had a boyish, wide-eyed quality that made him look as though he was expecting something amazing to happen at any moment. His hair had thinned to almost nothing, and his tanned face had wrinkled and sagged a bit during the twenty years I had known him, but he had never lost that hopeful look or the energy that went with it.

Chuck Jennings had seemed larger than life to me when I was a kid. To me he was the very embodiment of Christianity, the ultimate authority on all spiritual issues. No one but my parents had exerted such a strong influence on my life. It was under his preaching, during a Vacation Bible School service when I was eight years old, that I became a Christian. His explanation of the Gospel was as clear on that day as any I have ever heard since.

When I was in high school and we started playing tennis together, I came to know a more human side of him. I remember the shock of seeing the great man in tennis shorts, reaching for a difficult shot, sweating, chugging a bottle of water. I think he believed, as did many people in the church at that time, that I might be ready to follow in his footsteps and become a pastor someday. He spent many hours with me, discussing my endless spiritual questions.

On this day Pastor Jennings preached about the fire of the Holy Spirit. "It is a fire that burns away that which is old and dead," said the pastor, "a fire that refines. The prophet Malachi said, 'But who can endure the day of his coming? Who can stand when he appears? For he will be like a refiner's fire. . . .' "

He moved around the platform, more than I remembered him doing in the past, as he read the words of John the Baptist from Luke. " 'I baptize you with water. But one more powerful than I will come, the thongs of whose sandals I am not worthy to untie. He will baptize you with the Holy Spirit and with fire.' "

He continued to read Scripture passages about the Holy Spirit, and I was feeling worse by the minute.

" 'They saw what seemed to be tongues of fire that separated and came to rest on each of them. All of them were filled with the Holy Spirit . . .' "

I could not look at him while he read this verse because my own soul was raging inside, and I felt as if he were looking right at me. I ached with regret for how far I had drifted. I was lost in reflection for a time, and when I picked up the sermon again near the end, the pastor was saying, ". . . the Spirit will fill you as it filled Jeremiah, who said, 'His word is in my heart like a burning fire, a fire shut up in my bones. I am weary of holding it in; indeed, I cannot.' The Spirit can burn in you as it burned in Abraham, as it burned in Paul, in Peter, in John. As it burned in our own singing a while ago."

I wondered whether I would ever know that burning again for myself. My soul prayed in wordless longing.

When the service was over, I wanted to slink quietly out of the sanctuary and go off somewhere alone to think. But that was not to be.

I had not spotted Beth or Cheryl during the service, and each step I took from my pew toward the foyer and the parking lot felt like one step closer to freedom. It was impossible to get through the crowd very quickly, and I had to greet old friends along the way. I made it through the sanctuary and halfway across the foyer when I saw Cheryl. She was standing alone by the door we would exit from to get to my car. There was no escape. Faced with the inevitable, I made no attempt to avoid her and walked up boldly, as if glad to see her.

Cheryl's looks had changed considerably in two years. Her blond hair, which had hung loose and wavy past her shoulders before, was now much shorter and stiffer. She wore heavier makeup, giving her a harder, more wary appearance. She had always been athletic, spending lots of time skiing, hiking, and doing aerobics, and she had kept her lean figure. But she wore a dark blue dress, which gave her a more serious, businesslike look, very different from the colorful image she had preferred before. She did not take a single step toward me as I approached, and she did not hug me or shake hands, which were common greetings even among casual friends in our church. The hesitancy of her smile was somehow a relief to me, since it indicated that she did not want an unpleasant confrontation any more than I did. We said a few pleasantries about how good each other looked, and then I said good-bye and moved to walk away.

"I'd like to talk to you sometime," she said, and my heart sank, thinking how close I had been to escaping. "I've thought about calling you so many times."

"Sure," I said. "I'd be glad to get together and talk. Give me a call sometime."

"How about having a cup of coffee tomorrow morning? I have to be at work by eight-thirty, but . . ."

"Oh, I don't know about tomorrow. I have to start back to work at the magazine."

"Oh, I see," she said stiffly. "Well, maybe we can work something out later."

"We will," I said. "I'll talk to you soon."

Bill and I walked out the door, and I thought I had probably bought myself at least a week's reprieve.

But Cheryl kidnapped me at the magazine the next day. That's the only way I can describe it.

This would be the third summer I had worked at *Shooter's World* magazine, where I wrote about the sport of trapshooting. One could hardly choose a magazine less suited to my background and interests, but after a couple summers of studying and writing about gun enthusiasts and their sport, I could now write as fast and securely about trapshooting as anyone on staff. I had first applied for the job out of desperation during a summer break from college several years before. I had been working as a temporary employee at a landscaping company, planting trees and flowers and shrubs around office buildings in downtown Indianapolis. The job ended midsummer, and I had no other prospects. Roxanne Martin, a college friend who had graduated earlier that year with a degree in journalism, was working at *Shooter's World* and told me of a staff writer position that was open during the busy trapshooting season. Several weeks earlier, I had given her a clip file of articles I had published in the student newspaper and asked her to keep me in mind if she heard of any job openings. I never expected to hear from her, certainly not for a job at a gun magazine.

"You mean I'd have to write about trapshooting?" I asked.

"Yes."

"I don't even know what trapshooting *is*," I said.

She laughed. "Yes, you do—a red clay target flies up in the air, and a guy shoots and tries to hit it. Whoever shoots down the most wins."

"Oh yeah. I've seen that on TV. But there's no way I would know what to write about it. I've only shot a gun a few times, just some target practice with a rifle."

"They can train you," she said. "I write about it every day. Do I look like Miss National Rifle Association to you? The magazine needs a good writer. Just come in for an interview. I told Frank you'd be really good at it." Frank Berkey was the managing editor.

I went in the next day, and Frank's first question was the one I dreaded the most: "How much experience do you have with trapshooting?"

I could think of none of those clever interview responses you're supposed to give that turn your weaknesses into strengths and make the employer want to hire you. I just laughed and said, "To tell you the truth, I don't know a thing about it."

He leaned forward in his chair, smiled, and said, "I didn't know anything about it either, and they made me editor!" After a few more questions, he told me that they liked my clips and I could start the next day. They gave me plenty of time those first few weeks for research on guns, trapshooting, and the magazine's writing style. My stories were heavily edited at first, but I learned from each one of them, and by the end of the summer Frank offered me a job for the following year.

My job this summer was to be the same as it had always been. I would cover the state shoots, which were the biggest events held each year, sponsored by the trapshooting association of each state. Those involved in the shoots sent our magazine extensive reports of all the scores and highlights, and I took their raw material and wove it into a story. Sometimes I supplemented the information with phone interviews, and two or three times a summer Frank would send me to cover a shoot live. The work was dull, but I treated it like a game, the object being to get each article through the editing mill with as few marks as possible.

Our office was a cluster of cubicles on the ground floor of a downtown publishing company. For me it had always been a quiet refuge from the chaos of my family. All day I heard nothing but the click of computer keyboards and an occasional conversation. No one in my family had ever been to the office, and even Beth, when we were engaged, had only come in a few times and had rarely called me there. I sat at my computer all day and strung together sentences, whose content was mercifully as far removed from my own life as could possibly be.

That is why I was shocked that Monday morning when Roxanne stepped into my cubicle and said, "Someone's here to see you." A second later Cheryl appeared.

"I came to take you to lunch," she said, and Roxanne, standing slightly behind her now, raised her eyebrows, smiled at me, and walked away.

After stammering around and failing to think of an excuse not to go, I found myself following her out the door.

Cheryl worked at a bank a few blocks away and was dressed in a business suit similar to the one she had worn to church. She also wore dark sunglasses, making her eyes as inscrutable as her motives. There were plenty of good restaurants within walking distance of my office, but Cheryl insisted on driving somewhere else. At first, she wouldn't tell me where we were going. "It's a place that has more sentimental value than anywhere around here," she said.

She drove fast and didn't say much. I regretted going with her. She headed away from downtown toward the west side of town where we lived.

"I have to be back in an hour," I warned her.

"So do I," she said. "Don't worry. We're going to Denny's. They're pretty fast at lunch."

"The Denny's over by my house?"

"Yes. Where you and David and your buddies used to hang out."

"Do they still have the same nasty waitresses there?" I asked.

"Yes. I go there quite often."

"Even that ugly one who always hated my guts?"

"She's still there," said Cheryl. "I'm sure she'll be thrilled to renew the acquaintance. I'll never forget when she practically threw that dish of coleslaw at you."

"She was brutal. Why did she hate us so much?"

"Maybe because you and David and your stupid friends tended to disrupt the whole restaurant. And you were probably lousy tippers too."

If Cheryl thought that sitting in the old Denny's would somehow bring David to my mind so vividly that I would be willing to spill a bunch of secrets about him, she was mistaken. I had no intention of having such a discussion with her or anyone else. I had hoped that everyone would treat the past the way I wanted to—put it behind us, put the best face on things, and not stir the emotional waters.

The mean waitresses were not there. The woman who came to our table was new, a pleasant, efficient server who took our order quickly. I tried to make the conversation as pleasant as possible by asking Cheryl about a safe topic—her work.

"Do you still have the same job at the bank?" I asked.

"Of course," she said.

"How do you like it?"

"Boring." Her eyes darted about restlessly, as if she wanted to cut the small talk and get down to business.

"So beyond all the politeness, Cheryl, how are you really doing?"

"I'm falling apart," she said.

"Really? You certainly don't appear to be."

She sighed. "No, I'm not falling apart, exactly. The first year after David died was impossible. The second year was bearable. But overall, I'm afraid I just haven't dealt with David's death very well. He left too many loose ends when he died, too many secrets. I can't get past that, no matter how hard I try. People say, 'Don't dwell on the past.' But I have no choice. The past won't leave me alone. So I've changed tactics. I'm searching for the truth. I think if I just knew everything about him, I'd finally be able to accept it and go on."

The waitress came back with our drinks, giving me a chance to figure out how to respond.

After we were alone again, I gave Cheryl the chance to pick up where she left off, but she only gazed at me intently. It was my turn.

"Everybody leaves loose ends, Cheryl. You can never just wrap somebody's life up all neatly. Not when they die so young and in the middle of things like David did."

She kept her eyes on me. "I have to know everything there is to know. David told you everything. You know which rumors are true. You could clear things up for me and ease my mind."

I sipped my water and looked out across the other tables for a moment. "David is the kind of person you can never get to the bottom of. The more you find out about him, the more curious it makes you. If you keep pushing for information and explanations, it will drive you crazy."

"So you just tell yourself to forget about him? Is that how you've handled his death?"

"I don't know how to get over him either. I think about him every day. But I've given up trying to understand all his motivations and actions. I'm grateful for the time I had him, and now, hard as it is, I try to let him go. That's what I think you should do too."

"I can't."

I paused for a moment. "What do you want from me, Cheryl?"

"I told you. I want to know everything you know about David."

"I can't tell you that."

"Why not?"

"He's my brother."

"He's dead."

"Is he? Then why do I still feel bound to him?"

She looked away, lifting her head toward the lights. I couldn't tell whether she was angry or just trying to keep from crying. She didn't strike me as someone who would burst into tears very easily.

Finally she said, "Maybe the answer for both of us is to talk this whole thing out as openly and honestly as we can. Take the mystery out of David, and then maybe we can let him rest."

"I don't want to take the mystery out of him. I want to leave him just as he is."

She looked down at the table and ran her finger around the rim of the water glass and scowled. I was determined not to break the silence. I had said all I wanted to say about David. I knew that anything I added would be a mistake.

When Cheryl finally spoke again, she had changed tactics. "You know," she said, "David told me quite a few things about your personal life that weren't too flattering."

I laughed. "You can't blackmail me, Cheryl. What are you going to do? Tattle to my parents? To Beth? Go ahead. I still won't betray David to you."

"He betrayed you often enough."

"Yes, he did. And if he were still alive, I would confront him about that. But he isn't. He's dead."

"Well, I'm still alive," she said. "I have a right to know certain things."

"Then you'll have to find out from someone other than me. You're wasting your time."

She looked utterly defeated throughout the rest of our meal together. She sulked silently awhile, and then we drifted into a polite discussion of our families, our work, the people we knew at church. We ate quickly and left.

When she dropped me off in front of my building, she said, "We'll talk again." She spoke in the courteous tone we had adopted for the latter part of our conversation, but I couldn't help hearing in it the hint of a threat.

ROBIN

*C*hris scared the daylights out of me when I got home from work Monday night. Mom usually leaves a light on in the living room at night so the house doesn't look all dark from the street, but nobody ever actually sits in there. I jumped half out of my skin when I saw somebody sitting slumped over on the floor, looking at something. It was Chris, shuffling through Mom's new pile of pictures.

"Boo," he said, once I had already made an idiot of myself by lurching halfway across the entryway. I went in and plopped down beside him, happy to have a chance to talk. I hated that things had gotten off to such a bad start since he had come home, with him catching me kissing Bobby and all. Not that we were doing anything wrong. But still, if it turns out that I'm pregnant—

If I'm pregnant.

It's hard for me to continue past that thought. Of all the things I have to deal with right now, why would I have to be pregnant?

Maybe I'm wrong. I keep telling myself that. It's early. In a few days maybe I'll be laughing this whole thing off.

But if I am in that particular condition, I'm going to need Chris to help me deal with Mom and Dad. I just wish he liked Bobby more. That would make it much easier for me. But he can't stand Bobby, I can tell. There's no good reason for it either. Bobby is sweet, he's honest, he's trying to overcome his past and live a Christian life. I guess what has happened between us doesn't make him look too good on the Christian part. But still . . .

I can tell you what Chris's problem boils down to, but he would never listen to me. Chris sees Bobby as one more slap in the face from Dad. That isn't true, of course. Dad didn't even know Chris was coming home when he started working with Bobby, but you could never tell Chris that. Dad used to throw David in Chris's face. Now Dad can throw Bobby in his face. I see it all clearly. Dad and Bobby speak the same language—carburetors and transmissions and all that—but Dad and Chris just stare at each other like they're aliens from separate planets, each one waiting for the other to make some hostile move so he can fight back.

I could straighten out the problem between Dad and Chris right now if they'd listen to me. I would tell Dad to accept Chris as he is and stop trying to make him into his ideal image of a son. The time for molding him is over. It's time to love him. I would tell Chris to stop searching for Dad's approval. Just love him as a father and realize they're never going to be buddies. Now, doesn't that sound like good advice? But I'm just little Robin. They wouldn't imagine that I'd say anything worth paying attention to.

Chris was holding a photo of himself and David playing with a ball in Grandma and Grandpa's yard.

I asked, "Did you and David stay with Grandma and Grandpa a lot when you were little?"

"Yeah. Quite a bit in the summer. We'd go for three or four days at a time. We loved it. They had that big old yard that was so much fun to play in."

"Look at all those flowers," I said.

"Grandma used to take us out every morning and let us help her water them. She tried to teach us the names of them, and sometimes she would let us cut some. Then she'd take them inside and put them in a vase."

"They don't have hardly any flowers at their house anymore."

"No. They're too old to take care of them. Did you stay with them when you were a little girl? I can't remember."

"Not that often. Every once in a while when I was like three or four years old. But then they started getting too sick to have me, I guess. Grandma never took me out to water the flowers, though. Not that I remember. The main thing I remember is Listerine."

"Listerine?"

"Yeah, that yellow stuff. Brown stuff. Whatever color it is. Grandma used to gargle it every morning. Don't you remember? It seemed like she did it for about twenty minutes. And she taught me how to do it. I thought it was so much fun, so weird. We never gargled at home. That stuff tasted so nasty, but I kind of liked doing it. It seemed like some bizarre ritual Grandma had dreamed up. I don't think I even understood why she did it. I guess I thought it was just a game of hers."

"That's a funny thing to remember, out of all the things you did there."

"I know," she said. "But I can almost taste that stuff right now just thinking about it. And Grandma's stockings. I remember those too."

"What?" asked Chris. "Grandma would flip if she knew these were your memories of staying with her."

"Well, you know, when you're a kid old people seem kind of bizarre to you. On Sundays, I used to like to watch Grandma put on her stockings. They looked like hose, you know, but they were old-fashioned, and she put them on separately, not like panty hose."

"I remember."

"She would put them on out in the family room right before we left for church. She was so old and her feet were so bad she could hardly maneuver those things over her feet. She would make this sound real deep in her throat, like *Aaawwwhh*, and keep trying till she got them on. She'd always be running late, and Grandpa would tell her we had to get going. It was always the big crisis of the morning. But I sat quietly and watched, enjoying every minute of it! I didn't think it was funny or anything. I had just never seen anything like it."

Chris laughed and said, "Don't ever tell Grandma we had this conversation."

"I don't blame them for not wanting to move out of their house and go to a nursing home or whatever," I said. "I mean, they've lived there since the Civil War or something."

"Did you know Mom and Dad are thinking about selling this house?" Chris asked.

"Yeah. Mom told me you were upset about it."

"I think it's a horrible idea," he said. "Can you imagine Dad selling his old cars and moving into some dinky little town house? Assuming he doesn't *give* away all his cars first."

We both knew that was a slap at Bobby, and I sat there tapping a picture on my knee about a hundred miles an hour until I saw Chris watching me. Then I stopped. He's always accused me of being fidgety. He put the pictures down and looked me straight in the face, and I thought, *Oh no, here it comes.*

"So, how are things with your boyfriend, Bobby?" he asked.

"I thought we covered this the other night," I said. "I know you don't like him, Chris, but you don't know him. He's a sweet guy, and I think you should give him a chance."

"Does he ever tell you about his work?"

"He works for Jim White from church."

"I know that. But Bill told me Jim's company might be in trouble for cheating people in some investments."

"I don't believe that," I said. "You shouldn't accuse people without any facts. I don't want to talk about Bobby."

"You've been awfully jumpy ever since I got home," he said.

Unfortunately, I was sitting so that my foot was tapping against the edge of the sofa.

"That's usually a sign you're hiding something."

"Everybody hides things. Even you," I snapped.

"Robin, we used to be able to talk."

I stood up and headed out of the living room. "We'll talk," I said. "But I'm hungry right now, and things have gotten complicated."

CHRIS

As reluctant as I was to try to stick my nose into Dad's finances, I felt compelled to warn him about the scams Bobby might have been pulling at Premiere Financial Services. If Dad was willing to trust this guy with one of his most treasured automobiles, it made sense that he might be persuaded to invest money with him. Dad was cautious financially, so I hoped he hadn't invested yet and I could save him from making a catastrophic mistake. Or if he had invested, maybe it was still early enough to pull out before he lost everything.

I thought it would be less touchy to approach Mom for information first instead of Dad. On Tuesday after dinner, I found her alone on the floor of the living room in the midst of her photos. Each day they slowly spread over a larger surface of the room, like a fungus threatening to overwhelm the entire house. The pictures now covered the sofa, the coffee table, the brick floor in front of the fireplace, and about a third of the rest of the floor.

"Why are you spreading them over the whole room like that?" I asked.

"I haven't decided yet how I'm going to organize them. Those for the anniversary at church I have to organize by decades. But the family pictures—I don't know. Should I do it by years, by people, or some other way? I wish I could organize them without looking at them. I get all caught up in remembering what was happening in the pictures, and if I don't speed it up, I'll never get this done."

"Mom, I have to ask you about something. It's about this friend of Dad's. Bobby."

"What about him?" she asked, her hands continuing to shuffle through her photos.

"Bill says Bobby could be in big trouble with the business he's involved in. Some illegal stuff. Do you and Dad have any investments with him?"

"I don't know, Chris. Your dad takes care of all that. We've had our insurance through Jim White for years. Isn't that who Bobby works for?"

"Yes. Could you find out from Dad? If he's involved with this guy, he needs to be careful. Maybe he could get out before it's too late."

She put the pictures in her lap. "Have you ever known your father to do anything risky financially?"

"No, but these are investments that maybe wouldn't *look* risky. I don't know."

Mom kept her gaze on me for a moment and then said, "Chris, I know you're upset because your dad gave Bobby that car."

"Mom, this has nothing to do with—"

She held up her hand to shush me and continued. "But you know as well as I do that you never wanted one of those cars and wouldn't know what to do with it if he gave it to you. So I will not talk to your father about Bobby, and I would advise you not to either. Your dad knows what he's doing. He doesn't need us to give him advice about money."

"All right, forget it," I huffed and started to stand up.

"Tell me about this picture," she said and handed me a snapshot of myself sitting on a ratty brown sofa in a dim living room with two posters on the wall behind me, one of the *Wizard of Oz* and the other of Ghandi.

"That was my first weekend in Chicago, when I lived with David." A couple years before he was killed, David had been offered a job as a mechanic in a garage near downtown Chicago. He moved into a tiny apartment in the city and invited me to stay with him during the summer between my years of graduate school at Purdue.

"How do you know it was the first weekend?"

"Because you can tell the apartment isn't torn up yet. Eventually David's idiot friends pretty much trashed the place."

"Is that why you left early?" she asked.

"Partly." I had infuriated David by suddenly deciding one morning to pack up and spend the final month of that summer at home in Indianapolis instead of in the appalling conditions of his apartment. A few months later, David quit his job and came back also.

"Things never seemed the same between you two after that. I was never clear exactly what happened."

"The whole thing was a big mistake," I said. "For both of us."

My eye caught another photo, this one of a happier time. I picked it up and showed Mom. "See if you can identify this one." It was a photo of David, me, and another boy standing in our swimming trunks in a boat on a lake.

"That's you, David, and Scotty Beeler. You were in high school, and the Beelers invited you to spend a month with them at their house on Marshall Lake."

"Right!"

"That was another mistake if you ask me," she said. "The Beelers almost came home early because you boys kept getting into so much trouble. Sneaking out late at night, and I don't know what all."

"I wouldn't trade that summer for anything," I said.

The Beelers let us boys take the boat out by ourselves a few times. One time Scotty actually let David drive it, as long as he promised he wouldn't go too fast. David kept it slow at first, but after a few minutes he pushed it a little faster, then faster and faster, until the boat was practically airborne, water spraying everywhere. Scotty screamed at David to slow down. David yelled unintelligibly and laughed his head off as I hung on to a railing, praying that I would not be thrown over-board. David drove closer to the bank, where he bellowed at the people in the nearby houses. Then he yanked off his shirt and twirled it around at them like a flag before he let it fly to the back of the boat. He kicked off his shoes. Then he leaned down and, to our amazement, took off his shorts, all the while maneuvering the boat ever closer to the shore. Naked now, he shouted "Whoo! Whoo! Whoo!" to the rich folks loung-ing at their umbrella-covered tables.

To those watching, the incident must have looked very different from the way it did to David. They could not feel the exhilarating speed as the waves tossed the boat up and down, hurtling him through sky and water, naked, free. They could not feel the boat detach itself from the physical world and lift itself to a more intense level of reality. To those on the shore, David was simply pulling a prank.

One of them called Mrs. Beeler, who threatened to call our mother. I talked her out of it, telling her I would save her the embarrassment by telling Mom myself, and that I would personally see to it that David never again drove the boat. I never told Mom, of course. David and I had long before cemented our unspoken brotherly code of loyalty to each other. We would never tell anything about the other that would make him look bad or put him in an awkward position. This was a bond that, as the years went by, worked more to David's advantage than to mine, since he increasingly had more to hide than I. By the end of his life, I believe I was the only person he trusted.

I thought of Cheryl, who was now trying to crack the bond she knew was even stronger in some important ways than the one that had existed between her and David. But I was not about to shatter that loyalty over a cup of coffee at Denny's. I confirmed that again as I stared down at the picture of him in the boat.

Cheryl's tone of voice had convinced me that she had finally turned against him. Whatever amnesty she had granted him at the time of his death had been revoked, and her old suspicions about him were once again in control. For Cheryl, the two years since his death had been enough time to wear away the glow that we had wrapped him in when we said good-bye.

For me, time had moved my emotions in the opposite direction. My anger against him had cooled, just as it had so many times when he was alive. I would get so angry with him that I never wanted to speak to him again, but within a few days, he would have smoothed things over with me and we'd be friends again. Now, like then, I was ready to let him off the hook. The things I loved about him outweighed the things I hated.

"Well, good luck sorting this all out," I said to Mom as I stood up again to leave.

"You ought to go see some of the neighbors. They've been asking about you."

"Not today, Mom. I've had enough of talking about the old days for right now."

"Talking about the old days? You've barely said two words!"

"I feel as if I haven't stopped talking about the past since the minute I got home."

Mom shook her head. "You're just like your dad."

ROBIN

I felt embarrassed going to the drugstore and buying a pregnancy test. What if some nosy clerk would start asking me questions about it? What if someone I knew saw me there with it and told my parents? What if the clerk would refuse to sell it to me because I was too young?

But none of that happened. Buying it turned out to be the easy part. I went to a drugstore far from my house. I put the pregnancy test in with four or five other things—candy, a couple magazines, some pencils, and paper—hoping it wouldn't draw attention to itself. But I probably didn't need to do any of that. The lady didn't even look at me or anything I bought. She just slid each thing through the scanner till the cash register beeped, then read me the total, took my money, and gave me the change. I could have been buying a gun or porno magazines, and she wouldn't have noticed.

When I got home, I was nervous and shaking so much I could hardly even do the test. But then I calmed down enough to read the directions and figure the thing out. I prayed to God like I've never prayed before that I would not be pregnant. I told Him if I'm not, I would never fail again, and the next man I would even think about would be my husband. *Please, God*, I pleaded, *if I'm allowed just one request in my life, let it be this.*

The directions said that two lines will show up on the strip if I'm pregnant, one line if I'm not. It seemed like it took an hour for it to come up, but it was really only a few minutes. I couldn't sit still the whole time. I was bouncing all over the room, picking things up, putting them down, straightening things, biting my nails, flicking my fingers through my hair.

Then I looked.

Two lines!

I am pregnant.

My life is over.

I was calmer than you might have expected after I saw this. My hands were the only things that gave me away. They were shaking so bad I had to sit on them to keep them still.

At first I couldn't accept the reality of it. *Pregnant. Pregnant. Pregnant.* I thought the word so many times that it lost its meaning. I know it sounds stupid, but I just couldn't connect myself with the idea of having a baby.

Maybe I read the test wrong, I thought. *Is it one line that means I'm pregnant, and two that I'm not?* My heart leapt with hope. But no. I knew I had read it right. *Maybe the whole stupid test is messed up. It's only some little package I bought in a drugstore. How could it possibly know whether I'm going to have a baby? These people should be sued for scaring young women half to death!*

But no. I couldn't deny this away, and slowly it became real to me, one thought at a time. *I have a baby growing inside of me. The baby will get bigger, and my stomach will get bigger. Everybody will see that I am pregnant. In nine months a baby will be born. The baby will be a real human being who will belong to me. And I will have to take care of it for years and years and years.*

That's when I started to cry.

I cried as hard and as long as I have ever cried in my life, as much as when David died. I couldn't think straight. I raged around my bedroom like a crazy woman.

When I finally wore myself out, my first instinct—the one I have always resorted to whenever I've been in trouble—was to figure out a way I could cover this up and wiggle out of it without anybody knowing. It's insane, I know, but that's the direction my mind went. The more I thought about it, the more frantic and depressed I became because I realized there was no way to hide it. I couldn't secretly have a baby. I couldn't move away for nine months and then pretend nothing happened. Everyone is going to know.

Telling people is the part I dread most. And the people I fear the most are Mom and Dad. I can't imagine going up to them and saying,

"Mom and Dad, I am going to have a baby." I'm going to need help telling them. I can't do it.

I also can't stand the thought of telling Brandon. I know we're not officially going together, but still it's going to hurt him. And people right off will think he's the father.

Oh, I can't believe this is true!

Then, of course, I'll have to tell Bobby, who has been acting distant toward me and ignoring me lately. He's the one I blame, besides myself. But I blame him even more. In the back of my mind I hold on to this tiny hope that when he finds out he'll want to marry me and everything will turn out all right.

But something inside me says that when he finds out, he will want to escape from me even more. He'll leave and I'll never hear from him again. The creep.

But I've got to give him a chance. I've got to tell him first and see what he thinks I should do. I've got to get him to see that this is *our* problem, not just mine.

Right now I can't say anything to anybody. I need time to think. Time to sit and think and wait for some kind of answer. I wish that I could fall asleep and wake up to find it's all over, that some magical solution has been found. But I know that won't happen. When I wake up, the only thing different will be that the baby is a little bigger, and I'll have less time before I'm forced to confess what I have done.

CHRIS

$\mathcal{B}$obby did not show up to work on his car with my dad for three nights in a row. Every evening Dad hung out in the garage awhile, polishing the car and piddling around at the workbench until he finally gave up, turned the lights off, locked the garage, and came inside. When I asked him where he thought Bobby was, he said, "I don't know. He didn't even bother to call. He should know I'm not going to put up with this kind of behavior."

"Have you tried calling him?"

"It's not up to me to call him!" Dad said, his voice quavering with that irritation so familiar to me. "I'm tempted to just sell that car and be done with it. I'm tired of this." He looked drawn and frail, his tattered blue T-shirt making him look thinner than he did in the collared, button-down shirts he wore during the day. He shambled off down the hall without another word to any of us for the rest of the evening.

On Saturday evening Bobby showed up. Unfortunately, I was the only one home. It was almost seven-thirty. Mom and Dad had gone to some dinner with their Sunday school class, and Robin was at work. When I answered the door, there he stood with his salesman smile, perfect hair, and spotless work clothes—a polo shirt and new jeans.

"Who are you here for, Robin or Dad?" I asked. The question dimmed his smile a little bit.

"Jack," he said. "I'm here to work on the car."

"Dad's not here. He's been expecting you for the last three nights."

"I know. I'm sorry. Some unavoidable things came up."

"Lawsuits and things?"

"Oh," he said, backing away a couple steps. "You've heard about our troubles at Premiere. It's not me who's involved in that stuff. It's another guy in our company."

"So you're not being investigated?"

"I'm really not allowed to talk about it. Just tell Jack I came by. I'll call him." He turned to walk away.

"Does my dad have any investments with you?"

Bobby turned around again and faced me. He didn't say anything for a moment. "I'm not allowed to discuss my clients or their investments," he said, then added, "but I'd like to ask you something."

"Go ahead."

"You've made it pretty clear you don't like me. I was just wondering if it's because of my friendship with your dad or because you saw your sister kissing me?"

"When I hear that some guy my family is involved with is facing the possibility of lawsuits and federal indictments and jail time, I get a little suspicious. Especially when I don't know how deeply my dad and sister are involved with him or how he talked them into it."

Bobby shook his head. "I know you've had trouble with your father, but you can't blame me. I helped him with his cars because he asked me to. I didn't even know you existed the first few weeks we worked together. I haven't tried to undermine you in any way. If you want that Oldsmobile your Dad gave me, take it. If you want to be the one in there helping him, do it. *He* told me you weren't interested. And as for Robin, I think she's old enough to decide for herself who she wants to kiss. The protective big-brother routine seems a little out of place."

I stepped out onto the porch. "All right, then, you tell me this. If there's no problem with your relationship with Robin, why all the sneaking around with her in dark corners? Why do you have to hide from your friend the fact that you're seducing his daughter?"

"I'm not seducing anybody," he scoffed. "It's a waste of time to talk to you about this. I'm leaving."

As he walked away, I said, "Robin told me you didn't want my dad to know about you and her. If your motives are so pure, why don't we just get it all out in the open?"

"It's none of your business," Bobby said. "But if you're determined to tell him, then do it. I hate to think what you've told him about our firm being investigated. You've probably painted me as some criminal mastermind."

"I wouldn't say 'mastermind,' from what I've heard about it. But the truth is, I haven't told him about that. If he made the mistake of investing money with you, I suggest you tell him yourself."

Bobby waved his hand dismissively and left. I had little doubt now that Dad had some money tied up with this guy. The question was how much, and how much he stood to lose.

ROBIN

I need to practice my confession.

This thing is sure to be a disaster no matter how I handle it, but it will be even worse if I go to Mom and Dad and Chris without knowing how I'm going to tell them. But first, should I tell them together or separately?

I think together. That way not all their emotion will be centered on me. Chris will worry about how Mom and Dad are reacting, and Mom will focus on Dad, trying to keep him from throwing a fit.

So let's say I have them together in a room—the family room. Mom and Dad act more human there than anywhere else.

They look at me, waiting for me to speak. I say, "I'm pregnant."

What reaction will this bring? Mom will start crying and won't be able to talk at first. Chris will be silent for a minute, contemplating. Dad will probably sit there and look wounded, trying to make me disintegrate with guilt. But first I'll have to repeat it several times in several different ways before he is willing to accept it. He'll want *clarification.* "What do you mean, pregnant? How do you know? Are you sure? Have you been to the doctor?" He will try to deal with the facts first, so he can avoid dealing with the emotion.

The next issue will be "Who is the father?"

Mom and Dad's first assumption will be that it is Brandon, who would actually be more acceptable to them than Bobby. With Brandon, at least, they would see us as a couple of kids whose hormones got out of control, who forgot their Christian values, and made a big mistake. But with Bobby it will seem like a betrayal of trust, especially to Dad.

It's possible that Chris will immediately identify Bobby as the father and save me all the trouble. Still, Chris said he wouldn't blab about seeing us kissing, so my guess is he'll sit there and let me tell it myself.

Should I reveal it slowly, giving little clues until Dad guesses and says the name himself?

Or should I take a more direct approach, blurt out the name immediately and do all the explaining later?

I think the direct approach is probably best. Get the shock over with first, so maybe the rest of the discussion can be more rational once they have calmed down.

Okay then, here we go.

"The father is Bobby McMahon."

Pause for emotional earthquakes and fireworks of various kinds.

Expect to have to repeat the name several times to overcome disbelief.

"Bobby. Bobby. Bobby.

"Yes, that's the one. Your whiz kid. The son you never had. The one you gave the car to. The one Chris hates."

Leave time for the "I can't believe he would do this" and "That jerk" comments.

Then give the details. Before they try to kill Bobby or try to have him arrested or something, they'll want to know details. "How on earth did you ever get involved that way with Bobby? When did you see him? Did he force you into this? Why did you hide this? How did you hide it?" Their knowing these things, of course, will not make me any less pregnant, but focusing on little facts will make Dad feel less powerless about the big fact over which he has no control: There is a baby growing inside of me.

My real answer to the question of how I got involved with Bobby is "I don't know. It just happened." But as you can imagine, that answer would not take me very far with my parents.

How about, "I fell in love with him from the first moment I saw him. Once I got to know him, I realized I loved him more than any man I've ever met. He's everything I could ever dream of for a husband. He's beautiful and funny and exciting and genuine. I would do anything for him. I think about him all the time. It was inevitable that we would get together."

I can't tell my parents all that stuff, though. Not about how Bobby is gorgeous and genuine and all that. They'd either laugh at it or it would make them so mad they'd bust wide open. I'll have to stick to facts. "We went out one night after Bobby helped Dad with the car. One thing led to another."

That doesn't sound so good either. I'll have to tell it somewhere in between—mostly the facts plus a little explanation.

The truth is, at first Bobby and I just wanted to talk and have dinner. We even spent a lot of time discussing Dad. Bobby is so in awe of him. I don't think Bobby would have gotten involved with me at all if he had thought it would end up hurting his friendship with Dad. I think he thought he could just get to know me a little bit, get in good with his buddy's daughter, go out a few times, keep it all quiet, and that would be the end of it. He's adventurous, a risk taker. He thought I was cute, that we could have some fun. But there was this attraction between us.

Why do people get together? I don't know. You can't just give it a simple explanation. It's not always logical.

But Dad will want a simple explanation. I have to think of how to word the reason in a few clear sentences. Dad will say, "He's older than you. He's my friend. You were going behind my back, so you must have known it wasn't right." And Mom will sit there beside him, nodding and occasionally shaking her head sadly as if to say, "Kids these days!"

How can I explain it? Since we couldn't get any privacy at my house, Bobby invited me over to his place. We weren't hiding it from Mom and Dad because we were doing anything wrong. Not at first. It was just easier not to tell them and avoid ending up in an argument. We both knew my dad. We did have that in common.

For a couple weeks we never touched each other. I swear that. We did not kiss. We did not hold hands. Nothing. It was kind of fun, this secret friendship. Then, as we started getting closer, it just seemed natural to—to get closer! I know nobody will believe me now, but I'm opposed to premarital sex. Philosophically, I mean. I believe what the church teaches, that sex should be reserved for marriage. We really didn't talk about it or plan it. It just seemed like we were really getting to know each other, so why shouldn't we sit on the couch together? Why shouldn't we hug each other, or hold hands? Who is it going to hurt? We know what our relationship is about. This is the way I thought about it, anyway. And I think Bobby felt the same. There was this big attraction between us, I have to admit, even though we didn't admit it to each other for the longest time. But when we started kissing and all, it was kind of hard to deny it. We never intended to go beyond that. It just kind of—

This is sounding really bad! I can never say all this to Mom and Dad. I'm going to have to work on this, or they'll eat me alive.

The point I'm trying to make is that it isn't a situation where we met and then suddenly went behind everybody's backs to have this secret passionate affair. Things happened that we didn't expect. Only a couple times did we . . .

Oh, this is horrible! I know it sounds worse the more I try to explain. Maybe the key is to give just a short little explanation and then refuse to say another word. I'm glad I'm practicing this ahead of time and not telling them cold turkey.

And if telling my parents isn't bad enough, first I have to tell Bobby.

Maybe I should run off and never be heard from again. Believe me, if I thought I could get away with it, I would.

CHRIS

We sang in church that Sunday with a fervency I had rarely heard. It was as if the entire congregation could sense the impending storm about to envelop the church and wanted to do everything possible to hold it off, to invite God's Spirit to take the place of it.

I paid close attention to the faces of my family. My dad was pale and haggard, a shrunken imitation of his old self, now seeming too small for his rich gray suit and white dress shirt that gapped at the neck. He hung on to the dignity of his appearance in every way he could, his hair perfectly combed back, his tie precisely knotted, his shoes gleaming. Mom sat next to him, her soft smile not quite concealing the wariness in her eyes, which darted almost imperceptibly in various directions, as though waiting for disaster but hoping to outsmart it by being ready to fight when it came. Robin sat with her legs crossed, her foot silently tapping in the air. She would bite her fingernails for a moment, then catch herself and stop, her restless fingers moving instead to her shoulder, where they twisted a strand of her hair. Who could tell what crisis lurked beneath those jitters?

A few rows behind my parents sat Jim White, wearing the same conservative brown suit he seemed to have been wearing for the last twenty years, his face broad and unrevealing, looking no more like a con artist than Ward Cleaver or any other 1950s television father you could think of.

Across the aisle and a few rows back was his protégé, Bobby, dressed in a blue suit, his teeth sparkling, his hair perfectly sculpted, looking as eager and confident as if he were a new college graduate preparing for the big job interview.

As my eyes swept to the far edge of the sanctuary, I saw her. Beth. I suddenly stopped singing because I had no breath. It was all I could do to stay standing and keep the hymnal from falling out of my hands. Not that there was anything shocking about how she looked; she hadn't changed a bit. Long dark hair hung around her shoulders. The same fair skin, shy smile, warm blue eyes. She sang each word with concentration. The only surprise was that this woman who had existed as an image in my head for so long was actually standing in the flesh across the room from me. She was so far in the corner that I had to stand at an obvious and awkward angle in the pew to keep looking at her. I stopped staring to avoid drawing attention to what I was doing, but I imagined as I forced myself to face the front again that I caught her eye for an instant.

When the service ended, I looked back, and she was gone. Despite my earlier apprehension about confronting her, I made my way as quickly as I could through the throng of people in the aisles. When I finally broke through to the foyer, she was nowhere in sight.

I lingered for almost twenty minutes, greeting people and scanning the crowd for her. She never appeared. Finally Pastor Jennings came through and shook my hand. "We need to play some tennis," he said. "I need to talk to you about some things."

"Just name the time," I said. "I can still beat you any day of the week."

"You asked for it now, pal," he said and promised to call me to set a time.

———————

When I got home Monday night, Dad was standing at the kitchen table, gripping the back of one of the kitchen chairs. I immediately sensed trouble. The kitchen was not a normal stopping place for my dad. He kept his cold unblinking eyes on me as I walked in, and the rest of his face was motionless, without a hint of a smile or frown or any expression whatsoever. It was a look I knew well. It meant criticism. It was the same look he had given me when he watched me as a teenager trying to paint the garage door or fix my bike or change the oil in the car. It was an expression that said, "You are doing it wrong, and I am about to point out in detail why it is wrong, but first I want to stare at you long enough to make you feel the wrongness of it, to make you squirm in shame and humiliation at the enormity of your incompetence."

"Hi, Dad," I said. "What's up?"

"I got a call from Bobby today." He paused, his fingers tapping once on the back of the chair, as if that sentence were enough to explain his anger and make me apologize or flee or disintegrate into a pile of ashes.

"What did he say?" I asked.

"You didn't tell me he came by Saturday night."

"No. I didn't really feel like getting into it."

"Well, we need to get into it now. I don't know what your problem is with Bobby, but I don't appreciate your trying to chase him off. I guess you're mad that I gave him that car, but it's my car, and it's none of your business. With the work he's done, he's earned it."

"Would you mind telling me exactly what he told you?"

"That you jumped all over him about the car and you practically accused him of being a crook and all kinds of other things. He told me he's not coming over here anymore. He's not going to put up with having his integrity questioned and his reputation smeared. Can't say I blame him."

"Dad, do you have any investments with him at Premiere Financial Services?"

"That's not for you to worry about. I've handled my finances just fine since long before you were born."

"But the company is being investigated for fraud!"

"How do you know so much about it?"

"Bill told me. He works in the investment business, and he knows the people involved. He believes people are going to lose their retirement funds—their whole life savings. He said the operation is going to be shut down, and some people could end up going to jail."

Dad paused for a moment, looked as if he were about to ask another question, but then said stiffly, "Bill works for the competition. What would you expect him to say?"

"Well, Bill wouldn't lie about that!"

"Neither would Bobby. You're ready to accuse everybody and see the worst in everyone. Do you think Jim White would let his clients be defrauded?"

"Jim may not have meant to do anything wrong, but Premiere has been having money problems the last few years, and Jim went into business with partners who aren't as honest as he is. He may have slid into this thing unknowingly."

"Well, Bill doesn't know everything, and neither do you."

"Neither do you, Dad, believe me!"

Dad leaned forward slightly, gripping the chair tightly, squeezing the wood as if to keep from rushing over and squeezing my throat. In an unnaturally calm, quiet voice, a tone achieved by willfully suppressing his frustration, Dad said, "Chris, I know things haven't been very good between us these last few years. I'm glad you're home this summer so we can work on it." These sentences surprised me, since Dad had rarely referred directly to our difficult relationship, preferring most of the time to simply ignore it. He continued. "But trying to undermine Bobby and turn me against him is not going to make me think more highly of you."

"That's not what I'm doing. You don't know the whole truth about him."

"Bobby is no more the cause of the trouble between you and me than David was."

As he said this, Mom walked into the room, and I took it as an opportunity to step out of the line of attack and walk to the refrigerator to get a drink.

Realizing she had walked in on an argument, Mom stopped abruptly and glanced back and forth at the two of us. Dad released the chair, walked out of the kitchen, and headed toward the garage without another word.

JACK

I would like a little peace.

I believe that home is the place to get *away* from bickering and chaos. But Chris *invites* it. Why does he want to get things all stirred up with Bobby? Chris seems to think that because *he* can't get along with me, he doesn't want anyone else to get along with me either.

Bobby's a good kid. Chris might even like him if he gave him a chance. But no, Chris would rather get caught up in jealousy and spite.

I don't have the energy for this anymore. Right now I don't care whether we finish that Olds or not. I'd like to sell the cars, sell the house, move into that condominium, and be done with it.

That sounds like a bitter old man, and I don't want to be that way either. I've never given in to that sort of thing, and I don't want to start now. Helen keeps asking me, "What's wrong? Why are you so quiet and moody?" I don't know how to answer her. I feel things are falling apart. Nothing is following the pattern I've always planned and hoped for. You try to live your life a certain way, treat people fairly, raise your family, follow the Lord, pour your best effort into your work, and think all that should bring you a measure of smooth sailing.

Instead, what matters most starts to fall away. I expected to see David develop and prosper and make me proud. Instead, he died. I expected to work until I felt like retiring, then leave with a sense that I had accomplished something at the company in which I invested almost forty years of my life. Instead, I had a heart attack, and the guys who are now running the place would probably be as happy to see me die as they would to see me come back to work.

Helen doesn't see our decline the same way I do. She has been just as devastated as I have by the individual incidents, like David's death, but she doesn't see the *pattern*. The strange thing is, it's right there in front of her, spread out amongst those hundreds of pictures covering the living room like pieces of a puzzle. How can she look at those old photos and not think *loss, loss, loss*? Those were the days when we were building and gaining, not shedding everything that's important to us.

I ran across a picture of Helen when she was pregnant with David. It's startling to see how young she looks. She's standing in the living room of our first house, the tiny little brick two-bedroom house on Gateway Drive, holding her enormous belly and smiling into the camera, surrounded by that awful natty gray sofa and the cheap pine furniture that was all we could afford then. But we were building then. We were starting a family. We had finally bought our own house. I was working at Maximilian Webber, laying the groundwork for deals with General Motors and other companies that would benefit our corporation for a generation.

When Helen was pregnant with David, it seemed like a miracle to me, as if all my life up to that point had just been playing around, and now here was adulthood and responsibility. I took dozens of rolls of photographs during those first couple years of David's life, believing I was witnessing events so amazing that every moment should be recorded.

David was a happy kid, always dancing around, always exploring. I have stacks of photos where he is twirling around, playing cowboy, trying to bounce a basketball, climbing over the furniture. He was always in motion.

We moved to this house when the kids were little, and the pictures from that time make the house look more full, even cluttered—filled with our children and their friends and all the toys and clothes and stereos and stuffed animals and posters and school books and who knows what.

Now look at this place. Until Chris came back, his room was a sterile guest room, so empty of life we left the door closed. David's room is too painful to go into, so we keep that door closed also. Robin's door stays shut most of the time because she likes her privacy. This is a house of closed doors. We have shriveled up so much that we're happy to move to a condominium half the size of this place. We're tired of rattling around like a couple of loose screws in a machine. Helen talks about the convenience, the reduction of maintenance work that the move will bring, but we can't deny that it's a sign of loss. We are adjusting the size of our home to fit the size of our lives. Smaller.

I know Chris thinks our move is a mistake, just as he thinks almost everything I do is a mistake, but I can't explain it to him. Chris is one more person I care about who is moving inexorably away from me while I stand by powerless to stop it. David left me suddenly, violently, but Chris has been leaving me just as certainly. Only it's taking him longer.

Chris has been pushing away from me for as long as I can remember. Even when he was a little kid, he never wanted my help. He always wanted to do it himself. David was different. He would ask me to show him how to do things or to do them with him. I remember walking into the garage one day when David and Chris were kids, maybe ten or twelve years old, and both of them had their bicycles upside down and were working on them. As soon as Chris saw me, he threw down the wrench and ran off somewhere to play. David called me over and asked me to help him. When I asked David why Chris had left, he said, "He doesn't like you to tell him he's doing it wrong."

If Chris had been the one who died instead of David, I honestly believe David would have drawn closer to me, would have wanted me to share in his grief and help him through it. Chris is the opposite. Even though he was jealous of David and saw him as a barrier between us, when David was gone, Chris made no attempt to move closer to me. Every strain that had built up between us snapped, and Chris flew off into oblivion. Smashing into my car wasn't what ended things between us that summer. If David had been the one to hit my car, he would have kept apologizing and talking to me and doing whatever it took until things were right between us again. Chris didn't even give me a chance. Of course I was upset at him for hitting my Chevy, especially when it was sitting there in the garage where it had been hundreds of other times when he had pulled in. I could have gotten over that, but Chris just assumed that it was the final blow and acted in such a way that *made* it final.

He always thought I didn't like him, but the truth is I felt I couldn't reach him. It seemed he was never paying attention. Always daydreaming. Not focused. Didn't take me seriously. Finally I withdrew. Maybe these are just the excuses of a father who has failed his son, but I really believe I did my best.

Now, Robin, she is like a stranger in our house. Sometimes we end up in the same room, and you would think I was some frightening intruder who had wandered in by mistake. She acts wary, talks fast, tries to end the encounter as quickly as possible and send me back on my way. But she has her moments, unlike Chris, of real affection toward me, when she is my loving little girl again the way she was for so many years. At least she seems to be moving out of the rebellious phase she went through in high school, when she spent so much time with her friends in that band and dressed like something out of a horror movie. There is no more colored hair and black fingernails, which they wouldn't allow in the store she works at anyway. But something is bothering her lately, making her jumpy and guilty looking. This is serious, I'm sure, but whatever it is, she's keeping it to herself. Another closed door.

I pray to God for guidance, I really do. But for the last two years I haven't known where I'm headed. The heart attack didn't surprise me at all—it fit the pattern perfectly. I'm only surprised I didn't die from it, and I don't mean that in any morbid sense. David's death just about did me in, and I don't believe I will ever recover from it. The grief comes in waves. If I'm busy for several hours at a time doing yard work or working in the garage, I can go for maybe half a day without any real sadness.

But the crushing grief always comes back, a feeling so desolate I sometimes literally bend over in pain trying to absorb it. It hits me at strange times, the worst being early evening, especially if I go out to the garage after supper. That's when David would have been out there with me, when we had our best talks and did our best work together. One evening a few months after he died, I went out there at sunset and stood at the workbench as the garage turned dark. The pain of the emptiness of that garage as the light faded was indescribable. I was paralyzed. I stood there for nearly two hours and let the waves of grief pour over me.

Working with Bobby eased the pain, but now it looks as though he'll be a loss too. I'm not going to try to talk him into coming back to work on the Oldsmobile. I'm selling it all anyway.

There's one further thing that worries me. Even though I didn't want to get into this with Chris, the fact is that I do have money, quite a lot of it, invested with Premiere Financial Services.

CHRIS

$\mathcal{B}$ill squatted like a blond Buddha on the floor of our living room, his legs covered with photos from my mother's ever growing collection. I found him there Wednesday evening when I got home from work. He sat there with my mother, sipping a glass of iced tea and laughing at the way we had looked as kids. Bill and I were supposed to go play softball after dinner, but he had come early.

"Mom has quite a popular photo gallery going here, doesn't she?" I said.

"These really bring back memories," Bill commented.

"Billy's in some of these pictures," Mom said to me. "Look at that one he's holding."

Bill gave me the photo. He is in the center of it, a tall, blond twelve-year-old in jeans and a T-shirt, holding on with all his might to a football that David and I, one on either side of him, are trying to wrest away. The struggle takes place in our backyard, the scene of many ferocious football games.

"Do you remember those great football games in your yard? I wish we could go back to those days. Things were simple then."

"No, they weren't," I said.

In the photo, Bill is laughing and looks carefree, almost as if someone were tickling him rather than trying to steal the ball from him, but David and I are not smiling. Our jaws are set in identical expressions of passionate determination as we try to force the ball out of his hands.

Football was one of the earliest and most bloodthirsty arenas of competition between David and me. We were determined to win at any cost. Defeat or signs of weakness were crushing. No matter how cold it was or how tired our friends got, David and I were always the last to stop those backyard games. I can still feel the crisp air, can picture the steamy breath of four or five boys ready to spring toward us, can feel my body smacked hard against the frozen earth, can hear David's voice as we argued over some play or some disputed touchdown.

"I thought you and David were going to kill each other out there a few times," Bill said.

"We wanted to."

"Chris! Don't talk that way," Mom chided. She took the picture out of my hand. "Billy is staying for dinner."

"Yeah. I know the best time to show up at the LaRue house, don't I?"

"You're welcome anytime," Mom assured him. "It's just like the good old days having you boys back in this house."

Bill and I went out on the porch to talk before dinner.

"Bad news," he said. "There are definitely indictments coming against Premiere Financial Services. And I heard Jim White is going to fire Bobby McMahon. It was Bobby doing most of the illegal stuff, I guess. At least that's what Jim is claiming. Bobby was promising large rates of return on investments, but they were nothing but pyramid schemes, using money from new investors to pay off old ones. Now it has all come crashing down. Did you find out whether your dad invested with him?"

"He wouldn't tell me directly, but I suspect he has. He didn't deny it. Is there anything he can do?"

"I don't know. By now it's probably too late."

ROBIN

Why does Bobby have to choose this particular moment to turn weird on me? I'm having the biggest crisis of my life, I'm trying to work up the courage to tell him I'm having his child, and suddenly he's avoiding me. I tried calling him at home about a million times, but he's either not there or he doesn't answer. I leave messages telling him it's really, really important that I talk to him, but he doesn't call back. He probably thinks "really, really important" means I want to tell him about a new pair of shoes I bought or a new CD that's out or something. I even tried calling him at his office, which he doesn't like me to do for some reason, but the secretaries always say he's out on an appointment and ask if I want to leave a message. After Chris caught us, Bobby said maybe I shouldn't go over to his place anymore until my parents know we're seeing each other. He said Dad would really be upset if he knew not only that we were dating, but that I was sneaking over to his place all the time when I had told them I was somewhere else. I don't really see the logic in that. When Mom and Dad find out we've been dating, I think they'll assume I've been going to Bobby's apartment. What difference will that little detail make anyway? I suggested we go ahead and tell them about us, get everything out in the open, but he said the timing was not good right now. Then Bobby and Chris had some kind of argument, and Bobby stopped coming over and calling.

After three days of leaving messages and not hearing from him, I decided to drive over to his apartment late one night after I got home from work. Right as I was getting ready to leave, he called. I picked up the phone in my room before anyone else answered.

"Bobby!" I screamed. "I've been trying to get ahold of you for three days! Why don't you answer my messages?"

"Sorry. I haven't had a single minute. We've had real problems at work, and I've had to help deal with them. It's been keeping me working until late at night. Has anyone told you about it?"

"No. I need to see you. Now. Tomorrow."

"I can't do it this week. What is this about? Why don't you tell me now?"

"I don't want to talk about it on the phone. It's too important."

"Robin—"

"Don't 'Robin' me, Bobby. It really is important. I want to drive over tomorrow night after you get home from work. I don't care how late it is."

"No. Listen, if it's something important, then you'll want me to be alert and awake and paying attention. I just can't do that this week. Not with all that's going on at the office. How about this weekend? I'll call you Saturday."

I knew that meant "Don't call me back before Saturday, and when Saturday does roll around, *maybe* I'll call you, unless I've thought up a new excuse by then."

I said, "All right. Saturday. But it has to be for sure. Saturday I'm coming over, one way or another, whether I have your permission or not. Whether you come up with another lame excuse or not."

He gave me a disgusted sigh. "Please don't get this way. This is exactly the kind of thing that will ruin our relationship."

"What's left of it."

"Why are you suddenly acting so paranoid?"

"What do you mean? This is the first time I've *talked* to you in almost a week!"

"But all these phone calls, these hysterical messages, all this pouting and saying things like, 'What's left of it.' You've never been like that. You're worse than a wife!"

At that moment I felt as though I couldn't breathe. What he said, and the way he said it, made me feel almost as bad as finding out I was pregnant. I had to just sit for a minute and let my brain unscramble. He had never acted that way.

"Are you pouting now?" he asked.

"I have to go," I whispered, because that was all I could manage. I hung up the phone and sat without moving for probably an hour. In the back of my mind I hoped he would call me back so I could hang up on him again for being so mean. But he didn't call. He was probably glad to be rid of me for now.

JACK

I went rummaging through all the paper work on my investments with Bobby—the statements, the prospectuses, the letters. Everything looked legitimate and in order. But I guess it would, even if it's a scam. In fact, they probably try even harder to make it look honest.

What Chris said about Premiere worried me, but I chalked a lot of it up to his animosity toward Bobby. A few days ago I called Bobby and asked directly about the rumors, and he claimed that if anything, he was a victim of the situation, not a perpetrator. He said there was another guy in the firm, somebody I had never heard of, who had gone out on a limb with some questionable deals. That guy had caused the whole firm to be investigated, and now this guy was trying to make Bobby the scapegoat. He assured me that my investments were completely safe and not part of the investigation.

"Look at your statements," he said. "You can see the kinds of returns you've been getting."

But today I got a call from Lanny Craig, a man I know from church, another one of Bobby's clients. He said Bobby is the one under investigation. Lanny put money in some of the very same things I did. He's looking into how we can pull out our money and what legal action we can take, but he's not at all optimistic. I tried to call Jim White after I talked to Lanny, but he wasn't in. I keep trying him at home, but all I get is his answering machine. I've tried Bobby at the office and at home too, but he also seems to have disappeared.

A wave of sweaty panic washed over me after about a dozen failed attempts to reach them. What if I've lost all that money? It's almost everything I have except for the little bit of retirement funds that are out of my reach. Thank God some of it was beyond my power to squander.

I have been a fool—maybe. I'm still not willing to believe this situation can't be salvaged. I'll get my money out somehow. I'll get Jim on the phone to reassure me. I'll get a lawyer if I have to.

I simply cannot imagine telling Helen that our money is gone.

I've been second-guessing myself all day, trying to figure out how I could have gotten myself into such a mess. Originally I invested a lot of money in my company stock plan, but I pulled it out and put it into another fund in preparation for retirement. My heart was giving me trouble, and I knew I would have to retire earlier than I had planned, so when Bobby came along with those higher rates of return, it appeared to be a good way to make up the money that would be lost by my retiring early. I let my guard down with him. I acted rashly, invested too much at once, didn't ask enough questions or do enough research. But I was feeling horrible at the time, still grieving, distracted.

Excuses won't bring my money back, though, will they? I have to fight this. Some days I feel I don't have an ounce of fight left in me, but still—for Helen's sake, if nothing else—I have to hold on to that money.

ROBIN

Seeing Bobby was a disaster from the very first minute. He was annoyed at me for insisting on meeting him at his apartment. He wanted to go out somewhere instead—probably so it would be easier for him to get away from me. When I got there, he had this kind of tired expression on his face, his mouth twisted in a little sneer as though he was trying hard to be patient, but could we please get this over with.

He told me to have a seat and pointed to the couch, then he sat a few feet away in his recliner.

"So," he said, "what is it you've been dying to tell me?"

"Wow. You just jump right in, don't you? Don't offer me something to drink or ask me how I'm doing or anything. It's just 'Sit down and tell me your story, so I can get on to the next thing.'"

He stood up slowly and heavily, as if I had asked him to lift the couch over his head. "What can I get you to drink?" he asked.

"Forget the drink," I said. "Just sit down and we'll talk. I'll try not to take up much of your time. I know you're anxious to get rid of me."

He sighed. "Robin, you just got here. Give me a chance. You've been sounding like you'll explode if we didn't get together and talk, so I thought you'd want to talk before we did anything else."

"I do."

"Then talk. I'm listening."

"It's your attitude that hurts me."

He theatrically looked toward heaven and threw his hands up in the air, the true martyr.

"All right," I said. "The fact is, I am pregnant with your child."

He stared for a moment, as if surprised that he could think of no clever comeback to this. "You're kidding," he said, his tone flat, detached.

"No. I am pregnant."

He started firing questions. "Are you sure? How do you know? Could the test be wrong? Did you see a doctor?"

I answered all these things, knowing that he was feeling the same kind of denial I first felt. Trying to prove it isn't true is easier than trying to figure out how to react to it.

He put his head in his hands and groaned. He got up and walked toward his front window. He put his hands on the sides of his head and growled, "No! No! No!" Then he took his hands down and bent over a little, putting his hands to his head again and saying, "No! No!" as if trying to escape the blows of someone hitting him. He did not look at me the whole time. I might as well not have been there.

Finally he fled to his bedroom without another word to me. For all I knew, he was finished with our conversation and was going to leave me sitting there until I got tired and went home.

But a few minutes later he came back and sat in his recliner. He shook his head. "How could you—how could it have happened?" he asked.

Maybe I'm just being paranoid, but the way he started to ask his question with "how could you" made me think he was trying to find a way to blame me.

He began, "Only once or twice did we . . ."

I laughed. "Only once or twice. Once or twice."

"I know," he said. "I'm trying to think. What should we do? What do we do now?"

"Well, we have to tell my parents, for one thing."

"No, no, no!" he said, as if this was an outrageous suggestion.

"Well, Bobby, obviously I'm going to have to tell. They'll eventually wonder what this thing is that looks like a basketball under my shirt."

"You can't tell them right now," he said. "Please. You've got to give me some time to think this through. We have to decide what's the best thing to do . . . the best way to handle it."

"I don't know what you're saying," I said. "What choices do we have?"

"Not very good ones," he said, looking away from me again, lost in his own thoughts.

I sat forward on the couch, trying to get him to look at me. "I think the real question is, what does this do to our relationship? Do you still want to be with me? Do you want to raise this child? Do you love me?"

He didn't answer, just kept staring off, as though looking for some hidden message up there in the corner of his ceiling. Finally it seemed my words suddenly reached him, and he said, "Don't you see there's more to it than that? You've got to give me time to think. Your father will be furious! It's hard to tell what he'll do. He could get me in more trouble than I'm already in at work. Your dad got me hired there. Don't you see that this could ruin both our lives?"

"If we don't tell them right now, what are we going to do in the meantime? What do you need time to do?"

"Think. Arrange things."

"Arrange things for *us*? I wish you would tell me what you're thinking. I have a right to know your intentions."

"I don't have any intentions, Robin!" he yelled. "What do you expect from me? I just found this out. How am I supposed to have a plan already? What are *your* intentions? What do you think we should do?"

"Well," I began as calmly as possible. "For example, if you are planning to stay with me and marry me, we could 'arrange' for when we're going to do that and where we're going to live, and—"

"Robin, we have never discussed marriage."

"So you don't intend to marry me."

"I didn't say that."

"Do you love me?"

"Of course I love you. We've had a beautiful relationship. But marriage is another whole category. If we did get married, we would want to know that we didn't do it just because you accidentally got pregnant. That would be a terrible reason to get married. Later on we would always wonder whether it was the *only* reason."

I sat back and thought for a moment. Suddenly I felt like crying and fought to suppress it. "I think we should go ahead and tell my parents and get it over with. If you're going to dump me anyway, then there's no need—"

"I'm not going to dump you!" he bellowed. Then he became quiet. "Robin, please, for your sake and mine and your father's, too, you've got to wait a little bit. This would not be a good time for your parents to hear something like this. Think of what they have already been through. Your dad had a terrible heart attack. He can't stand that kind of pressure right now. Let's hold off a few days and then decide what to do from there."

"All right," I said. "I just wish I could believe you're putting this off to do what's best for *us*. I'm afraid you're asking for time so you can arrange things for yourself and be finished with me for good."

"You'll have to have a little faith in me," he said.

CHRIS

I had imagined a dozen or more scenarios for how I would encounter Beth for the first time that summer. Most of them involved seeing her at church, since that was the most likely place I would run into her. Most of these imaginary scenes also involved some advance warning. I would see her walking toward me from the other side of the foyer, or I would follow her to her car in the church parking lot, and so on. In any case, I would have a few moments to prepare what I was going to say.

Our eventual encounter, however, did not happen that way. Instead, she appeared unannounced at my doorstep at nine-thirty on a Thursday night. I was sitting at the kitchen table that evening working on my dissertation. When the doorbell rang, I was reading a book that didn't make much sense to me on twentieth-century American fiction. I walked to the door, still preoccupied with what I was reading, and opened the door absently, expecting one of Robin's friends.

I was so stunned to see Beth that it took me a moment to respond. I had spent so much time thinking about her over the past two years that she seemed like a private creation of my mind, no longer a breathing human being. I could not recall a single one of those clever opening lines I had thought of to say to her at our first meeting.

"Do I look that shocking?" she asked with a laugh.

"You look great," I said. She was dressed casually, in white shorts and a blue cotton top. She was slightly tanned, and her figure was as trim and attractive as ever. Her hair was dark and wavy and spread beautifully around her shoulders. I had feared she might have changed in the way Cheryl had, whose heavier makeup, shorter hairstyle, and severe clothes had given her an older and harder look. But Beth appeared even younger and much less tense than she had two years before, when all our arguing had taken its toll.

From behind me I heard Robin say, "Let her in, Chris. Don't keep her out there like she's a salesman or something."

"We were talking," I said, embarrassed. Beth squeezed my arm kindly as she stepped into the foyer.

By this time both Mom and Robin were standing at the edge of the tile of the foyer. Beth greeted them and then turned her attention back to me. "I'm sorry to surprise you," she said. "Robin invited me over. We're going out for some girl talk."

I was both relieved and disappointed. Relieved that I wouldn't have to face an emotional scene unprepared, disappointed that her visit had nothing to do with me.

Everyone was watching me. Surprises did not bring out the best in me. When caught off guard, I often fall silent, with so many thoughts scrambling around in my head that I am unable to articulate any of them.

Finally I managed to say, "You haven't changed a bit. You look as good as ever."

Robin said, "Did you expect her to turn all ugly and shriveled without you?"

"I was kind of hoping so," I joked.

Beth smiled. "Well, you've held up pretty well yourself."

The first room people see when they come into our house is the living room. Like everyone else, Beth was immediately drawn to Mom's photos, which covered the floor like tiles in a mosaic. Beth stood at the edge of the sea of pictures and stared at them until Mom said, "Go on in there, honey. Everybody takes a look. There's some pictures of you in there. Let me show you."

To the rest of us the organization of the pictures was still a mystery, but Mom knew right where the photos of Beth were—in a stack on the center cushion of the sofa. I saw the photos over Beth's shoulder. Most of them were of the two of us, holding hands, clowning around, tickling each other, even kissing. There wasn't much open space on the living room floor, so I had to stand quite close to Beth in order to see the pictures. She flipped through them without hesitation, as if they evoked no particular emotion, but each one stabbed me with the old ache, the loneliness for her that I had tried so hard to suppress. I had contradictory impulses. I wanted to turn around and leave the room, as if to prove she was of no more consequence to me than any other of Robin's friends. But I also wanted to reach forward, put my hands on her shoulders, and draw her close.

Robin stood behind me, slyly nudging me in the ribs and contorting her face into ridiculous suggestive expressions when I turned around to look at her.

Beth asked Mom, "Are you organizing your pictures according to the different people who are in them?"

"Well, some of these will be used in a photo history display for the church's fiftieth anniversary in August. Those I arrange by decades. But I don't know what to do with the family pictures. I started off with a stack for Chris, a stack for David, one for Robin, and so on, but then I thought it might be more interesting to arrange them by years. A lot of the pictures don't have dates on them, so that was hard to do. Now I'm kind of stuck. I thought I'd get them spread out and just see what hits me."

"That sounds like a good plan," Beth said.

"It's no plan at all," Mom contradicted her, "but I like looking at the pictures anyway. Knowing me, I'll probably give up and throw them all back in the boxes where they were to begin with!"

"We'd better get going, Beth," Robin said.

As they left, Mom told Beth, "We should have you over for dinner one of these days."

"I'd like that," Beth replied.

She said nothing else to me, just smiled and gave me a little wave as she stepped onto the porch.

"Doesn't she look nice?" Mom asked after they had gone.

"Yes."

"Are you going to see her while you're home?"

"No, Mom. We broke up."

"She's been a good friend to Robin. I like her better than some of those other people Robin runs around with. You shouldn't snub her, Chris. Can't you see she still likes you?"

"No, I don't see that at all. And I'm not snubbing her. I'm just not dating her."

"I never really understood why you two split."

"It's too complicated to go into, Mom."

"Do you think you'll ever tell me any of your secrets?"

"What secrets?"

"Give me credit for some brains, Chris."

"I do."

She looked at me for a moment, shook her head, waited.

"Mom, I didn't come home this summer to dig up a bunch of stuff."

Mom let out a short laugh. "Well . . ." Then she fluttered her hand in dismissal, turned from me, and walked back into the family room.

———————

I didn't have to go visit most of the neighbors that summer. They came to us. On most evenings when they weren't busy with something else, Mom and Dad sat on our porch after dinner, and a few of the neighbors usually spotted them and came over to talk. I joined them as often as I could, including the Saturday following Beth's surprise visit. The porch was my favorite part of our house. It had been added to the front of the house at the same time the garage in the backyard had been built. Dad wanted the garage and Mom wanted the porch, so they built them both. It was furnished with padded wooden rocking chairs and a redwood swing. Fifteen people could fit on it if we brought out extra chairs and some of the kids sat on the floor. When I was growing up, our porch was the social center of the neighborhood. The neighbors gathered there almost every evening in the summer to tell stories, gossip, drink coffee, and watch the children play. I used to love to sit on the porch after an exhausting day of baseball or basketball or cutting grass. I'd sprawl out in one of the rocking chairs, enjoy a cool drink, and listen to the neighbors talk, drifting in and out of their conversations, as their laughter cut through the night air.

Now many of the old neighbors had moved away, but Trudy and Jim still came over regularly. They had lived across the street from us for almost twenty years, their house having been built not long after ours. I had grown up with their two girls, who were a few years younger than me. Trudy and Jim were in their fifties now; Trudy, graying and thin and frazzled, and Jim, slower and more potbellied than in his younger days. I knew them as well as I knew my own aunts and uncles, and when I was little, their house and yard had been almost as familiar as my own. Back then, most of our street seemed like one big extension of our own property, and the kids came and went freely from one another's homes. Trudy had always been a familiar figure in our kitchen, where she and Mom used to get together for coffee several mornings a week on Trudy's days off.

"Where is everybody this summer?" Jim asked as darkness descended and we slapped mosquitoes off our arms and legs. "This porch used to fill up with people every night."

"Yeah, we used to sit and watch the kids play kickball out in the street," Trudy added.

"And they would argue, argue, argue," Mom reminded us.

"Kids don't play kickball out there anymore," Trudy said. "Wonder why not?"

"They've all grown up."

"No, there're new kids around, but I guess they play different games now."

"Well, this neighborhood sure isn't what it used to be," Mom said. "The new people hardly ever come out of their houses."

"Wonder what made it change like that?" Trudy asked.

"Two things," my father answered.

"Oh, here we have it," joked Trudy. "The authoritative answer. Let's hear it, Jack."

"Let's see if you can guess what they are."

"Oh, Jack—" my mother started to say.

"That's all right," Trudy interrupted. "I know how Jack's mind works by now. Let me think. The two reasons the neighborhood changed. Is that the question?"

"Isn't as friendly as it used to be," Mom put in quickly. "Neighbors keep to themselves."

"All right," Trudy said to all of us, "you guys help me out now. Reason number one. People put in longer hours at work, don't have time for their neighbors."

My dad rejected this answer with a loud imitation of a game-show buzzer.

"Television," Jim said.

"Correct," Dad said, applauding him.

Trudy cheered and clapped him on the back.

"Why?" Dad asked.

"Why what?" Jim said.

"Why would television keep people from sitting on the porch with their neighbors?"

"Because they're sitting in their houses watching television instead of sitting out here talking."

"Right," Dad said. "But that's because when we first started sitting out here thirty years ago, there was no cable, and we had only three good channels to choose from. In the summer it was mostly reruns anyway, and most of our TVs were black-and-white. So that's the easy one. What's the other reason?"

All of us made numerous guesses, from computer games to the early stages of global warming that made it too hot to sit out. None of these satisfied my father. Finally Trudy said, "All right, Jack, we give up. You're about to wear me out. What's the answer?"

"Air conditioning," he said and took a sip of his coffee, as if it were so obvious no further explanation was necessary.

Trudy and Jim laughed, my mother scowled.

"Air conditioning?" Trudy cried. "You made me work up a sweat for half an hour, and that's the answer you came up with?"

"I'll probably regret this," Jim said, "but I'm going to have to ask you for an explanation of that."

"Don't you remember when we first moved here that none of the houses around here had air conditioning? We had fans all over the house, and all they did was blow the hot air around. Those humid summer evenings were unbearable. We would sit in the house and sweat, especially if the oven was on. So what did everybody do? After dinner, we all came outside to sit where it was cooler and to watch the kids play. First thing you know, we're all sitting together on one porch having cold drinks with ice in them to keep cool."

"Seems like the heat did push people outside more," Trudy agreed.

"I remember that first air conditioner we put in your house," Jim said. "That was the heaviest air conditioner I've ever seen."

I remembered it too. Dad bought a window air conditioner supposedly big enough to cool the entire house. It was as big as a small refrigerator. Installing it was a neighborhood project. Dad built wooden supports to hold up the part that extended several feet out the window. Then three or four of the neighborhood men helped lift it into place. I watched them struggle with it, too small myself to be of any help.

Mom said, "That old window unit never worked right. We had it in the kitchen, so that room was always freezing, but then in the back bedrooms you could barely feel it. That thing was loud too."

"That's exactly what I'm saying. Like everybody else in the neighborhood, we eventually replaced it with central air, which was quiet and kept every room in the house at the same temperature. So you see where that left us? Who wanted to sit out on a humid porch with the mosquitoes chewing away at us, when we could sit in our temperature-controlled family rooms in privacy and enjoy dozens of television shows on our big-screen color TVs?"

"Makes me want to run home right now!" Trudy joked.

"The only ones who refused to get air conditioning were the Rices," Jim said.

"Have you heard from them?" I asked. The Rices had been one of my favorite families in the neighborhood, even though my parents and most of the other neighbors considered them too eccentric. They had five children, and their middle daughter, Annie, was the first girl I ever had a crush on. To this day I have kept that secret from my family. The controlling obsession of the Rices' lives was Colorado. They talked about it endlessly, as if it were paradise, even though they had only been there once, before most of the kids were born. They had books and magazines about Colorado, calendars, maps, scenic mountain place mats. All their future plans centered on going there, first for a vacation, eventually to move there permanently.

They bought an old school bus, painted it red and white, and made a camper out of it. They bought a Wurlitzer organ for Mrs. Rice to play during the drive out there. It took two years to fix up their bus and save money for the trip. I helped them paint the bus and install the beds in it, all the while listening to their stories of the glorious mountains, streams, trees, and vistas of Colorado. I secretly hoped Annie would talk them into inviting me to go with them, because I was thoroughly captivated by their dream. I tried to talk Mom and Dad into taking us there. We always went to the same old places for vacation—Florida and Gatlinburg, Tennessee. I enjoyed those states, but once I learned of the glories of Colorado, I couldn't imagine wasting my time going anywhere else!

Mom and Dad were not enthralled with the vision of Colorado. Their eyes were closed to its magnificence. My dad's only comment on the Rices' trip was, "That old junker of a bus will never make it past St. Louis."

As it turned out, Dad was right. The Rices left at five on a Sunday morning in June and planned to return one month later. I got up early to see them off. I gave them fifteen dollars—my entire savings—and asked them to bring me back souvenirs. I was distraught to be left behind. To me, their bus was a masterpiece, even though they finally decided to leave the Wurlitzer behind because it took up too much room. I stood in the middle of the street and waved good-bye as the bus lumbered out of our neighborhood toward paradise.

Three days later they returned. The bus had broken down three times before St. Louis, and they were lucky they got the thing back at all. They parked it at the side of the house, where it sat rusting for two more years before they finally sold it to the junkyard. We heard no more about Colorado for a long time.

"The Rices finally made it to Colorado," Trudy said.

"Really?" I said. "All of them?"

"They're all living there except Lisa and Steve. Those two stayed in Indiana, I think. The kids are mostly grown now, of course."

"I really miss them," Mom said.

"You always thought they were strange," I said.

"I liked them, though. They were the most neighborly people you'd ever want to meet."

"That's because they never got air conditioning," Dad said.

"Oh, for pete's sake," Trudy said, "here we go with that again."

ROBIN

The day after I made my announcement to Bobby, Chris came to my room before church to ask if I had heard that Bobby was going to be fired from Premiere. I told him that couldn't be true because I had just seen Bobby the night before and he hadn't said anything about it. But then on Monday Bobby called me at work in the middle of the afternoon and summoned me to his apartment. His voice was businesslike, as if he were calling someone to come over and fix his toilet. I imagined that this was the voice he used at the office when he ordered the secretaries around. It certainly was not the voice that made me fall in love with him, the voice that was as soft as somebody sliding his fingers through your hair. But Bobby and I were far beyond the point where I could complain to him about his tone of voice. If I had brought it up, he would have switched to the annoyed tone, the tone that sighed and rolled its eyes and said, "What kind of weird stupidity are you bringing up now? Go ahead and say it, get it over with so I can dismiss it with a little huff and make you feel like a moron."

Anyway, all I said was "I'll be over as soon as I get off work." I thought about telling him I didn't want to come over until he changed his attitude, but I figured since it was so hard to get to see him, I'd better take advantage of the invitation and find out what was on his mind. I didn't ask whether he had been fired. I figured it was easier to let him tell it his own way.

He was nice to me when I got there. He tried to give me the old smile I loved so much, and he brought me some iced tea, then asked me how I was and tried to appear happy to see me. But he couldn't smile away the tension on his face. I kept thinking, *This is just a setup. This is his way of making me receptive to whatever scheme he has dreamed up for handling our situation. I am nothing more than a problem to him now. He is handling me the way he would handle an adversary or a reluctant client.* I played along with the scene he was setting, though, accepting the tea, slouching comfortably on the couch, and laughing at things that weren't funny.

He finally sat down in the chair across from me, but he sat forward in it, like he was about to lurch out of it. I knew he was ready to begin his little talk. His whole posture said, "Go along with what I say! Do it my way, or I'll leap out of this chair and grab you and force you to cooperate!"

He began. "Robin, this pregnancy is about the worst thing that could happen to either of us right now."

He stopped, waiting, I knew, to see if I agreed with this.

"I know it is," I said.

"For you, you're young. You're not married. You've got your whole life ahead of you. You have a family who will be very upset by this."

"You're really cheering me up."

Ignoring me, he continued. "As for me, I'm having a very tough time at work, and I may even have to leave there and find another job. Also, I am a friend of your father, and he will consider this a terrible betrayal. And for the two us, even though we've had a very special relationship, we were nowhere close to deciding to get married when we found out about this."

I had not been so far away from contemplating marriage, but apparently Bobby had a different idea about our "very special relationship."

"I heard you got fired," I said.

"That's a lie!" he insisted. "Who told you that?"

"It's a rumor going around."

"Well, it isn't true. If anything, I'm planning to quit if they don't start backing me up and stop trying to blame me for things that are beyond my control."

I didn't respond to this. My interruption had thrown him off the stride of his prepared speech, and it took him a few seconds to get going again.

"So . . . anyway," he continued, less slickly than before, "now we've got this set of circumstances, and we have to figure out how to handle

it. We have to decide what would be the best and fairest thing for everyone concerned."

"What do you think that is?" I asked, wanting him to get to the
point.

"What were you thinking?" he responded. He was stalling. I knew
he was not interested in any plan I would come up with.

I wasn't in a mood to make it easy for him, so I said, "I think we
should get married, give this child a good home, and keep building our
own relationship."

He sat back in the chair a little bit and looked away. Once again I
had broken his rhythm. Now he had to decide whether to respond to
my proposal or just ignore it and go ahead and say what he had planned
to say.

"Robin, I think it is never a good idea for two people to get married
just because the girl gets pregnant. That's a terrible basis for marriage.
We talked about this already."

"I know, Bobby. I'm not stupid. I know you have no intention of
marrying me. You've made your feelings for me quite clear."

"I don't know what that means," he said. "I'm doing the best I can.
Why do you bring up marriage if you know it's a bad option?"

"Because you asked me what I thought would be the best way to
deal with this. To me, in an ideal world, you would love me enough to
marry me and be this baby's father."

"In an ideal world, you would not be pregnant, and we could let
our relationship grow more naturally and worry about marriage later."

"Right. So marriage is out. Fine. Now, you obviously have some
plan already worked out, so why don't you just spit it out and quit all
this stalling around?"

His eyes could not stay focused on any one thing. He was obviously
nervous and didn't want to tell me his plan. He took our glasses out to
the kitchen and poured more tea in them. He came back and asked if
there was enough ice in mine. The glass was filled with ice, as both of
us could plainly see. For some reason, I took satisfaction in his squirming. I told him I would like a little more ice. He trudged back into the
kitchen and got me some.

When he came back out, he sat down again. "I have to go back to
New York tomorrow, where my family lives. I have connections there.
I know people . . . I mean . . . Let me just say this, but do me a favor
and think about this first before you react." He paused and took a deep
breath before quickly saying, "I think it would be best for everyone
concerned if you had an abortion."

"An abortion!"

"Please. Just let me explain the whole thing. You are very early in your pregnancy. It is much different now than if you would decide to do it later. I could arrange it very easily at home. No one would know. Not a soul would ever have to know you were pregnant. We could—"

"I won't do it!"

"Robin! Think. This thing could destroy both our lives."

"This *thing*?"

"The pregnancy! It could ruin us both. You admitted it yourself. And the child would be brought into a very difficult situation."

"Why would I go all the way to New York for an abortion? I could do it right here in Indiana."

"Someone would be more likely to find out if you did it here. I could arrange it so it would be very confidential. You could go there with me, say you are visiting a friend or something—we could easily find an excuse—then you could have it, recover, come back, and no one would know."

"I don't like the idea of abortion, and you know it. I don't even like to kill animals. I'm a vegetarian."

"Robin, please. What are those shoes you're wearing made of?"

"Leather. Okay, so I'm not completely consistent. But a baby is not a cow."

"And a fetus is not a baby. Especially not this early in your pregnancy."

"You're such a hypocrite! Aren't you in the pro-life group at church? You marched at that rally!"

"Okay," he mocked, "so I'm not completely consistent. Just like you. I do think abortion is not a good choice. I think it should be avoided if at all possible. But if it's a choice between destroying two lives or stopping what is not yet a human being, then I think abortion is the only option. For us I think it's the only option."

His suggestion of abortion had truly surprised me. Up to that moment, I was mostly afraid he would dump me and leave me to handle the baby alone, but I never dreamed he would want to abort the child. "Maybe we could put the baby up for adoption. The church works with those agencies—"

"No. The problem is not just raising the baby. The problem is your parents and everybody else at church knowing that you're pregnant. When they find that out, the real damage will be done."

I swirled the ice around in my glass. I was so angry and hurt I couldn't sit still. My foot was tapping so fast against his coffee table that his little ceramic planter almost rattled off the edge. "You're so different from what I thought," I said. "You seemed so loving before, so concerned about me, so interested. It was all fake."

"It was not fake, Robin," he said, his voice taking on the soothing, deeper tone that had once helped convince me that he cared about me. "I am concerned and interested. I love you. I still hope we can get through this together and that our relationship will survive. But we can't have a pregnancy hanging over us. We've got to get that out of the way before we can get back to working on *us*. I'm suggesting this for you as much as for me. I'm asking you to give me a chance. Let me go to New York, see what I can work out. Then I'll come back and get you, and you won't have to worry about this anymore."

I have to admit that, in a way, it seemed very appealing to sit back and let Bobby take responsibility for dealing with our problem. I could avoid all the embarrassment, the explanations, the ugly confrontational scenes with Mom and Dad. I could use it as a learning experience, ask forgiveness from God, and never let it happen again. Still, the thought of having an abortion, of actually agreeing to do it and then carrying that secret around with me for the rest of my life—I wasn't sure I could follow through with something like that.

Bobby said, "Just promise me you'll think this over seriously, and you won't tell your parents or anyone else that you're pregnant until after I get back."

"I've already told someone."

"Robin! Who?"

"Beth."

"Beth? Who's that?"

"You know Beth at church. My friend. Chris's former fiancée." I had told Beth a few days before, when she had come over after work. I felt I would lose my mind if I didn't talk about it with somebody, and I didn't want to go to my family yet.

"Oh, great," he said. "And how many people has Beth told?"

"Not a soul. I trust her completely."

"Have you told anyone else?"

"No."

"Well, don't. This kind of thing is too hard for people to keep to themselves. What if Beth tells your brother? And he tells your parents? Then it's all over."

"That might be the way *you* think, but Beth isn't like that."

Bobby rolled his eyes, as if he couldn't believe he was having a conversation with anybody so stupid.

"So will you give me some time to arrange things?" he asked.

"How long will you be gone?"

"Just a couple days. That's all I can afford away from work."

"Are you sure you're coming back?"

"Robin! Of course! Why would I go to all this trouble if I was going to take off for good? Don't get paranoid."

"All right," I said. "I won't say anything until you get back. But I'm not making any other promises. I'm not saying I'll go along with the abortion."

"Fair enough. Think it over. See if you don't agree that it's best for all of us. Real life isn't ideal. Sometimes we have to make tough decisions and do things we would rather not do."

CHRIS

$\mathcal{P}$astor Jennings glided across the tennis court with the speed and grace of a much younger man. He had stayed trim and athletic, jogging every day and playing tennis with any member of the church willing to take him on. I played him at the high school courts a few days after news of the Premiere scandal had begun to trickle out among the congregation. Jim White and Bobby McMahon had not shown up at church that Sunday, and some people wondered whether they ever would again.

We played hard and with very little conversation for over an hour, then took a break at the bench next to the court, drinking water from a cooler. It didn't take long for the conversation to turn to Premiere.

"How bad is it?" I asked.

"I know of at least seven families who stand to lose everything they've got," he said. "And those are only the people I've been told about. There may be even more. It's a disaster, no doubt about it. It's the worst thing to hit our church the whole time I've been pastor. It could tear us apart."

"It's unbelievable that Jim White could be involved in such a thing. Of anyone in the church, nobody embodies solidness and stability more than Jim."

"I know."

"I mean, everything about him is conventional. He wears the same dark suit every time you see him. Drives a respectable blue Buick, not too flashy but not too cheap. Has that nice house in the suburbs where they used to have us over on Sunday nights when we were teenagers. Basketball goal on the garage. He sings in the choir, teaches Sunday school, serves on the board. But he doesn't stand out too much, doesn't try to show himself off. . . ."

"You're exactly right," Pastor Jennings said. "And all those things are what made people trust him. There didn't seem to be one thing extraordinary about him. People thought, 'This guy is a rock. Surely *this* man would never take undue risks with my money.' "

"So you think he was just fooling everybody all this time?"

"Oh no," he insisted. "I don't believe that. Jim is horrified by what has happened. Some of his best friends and some of the most prominent people in the church have lost what it took them a lifetime to earn, and Jim knows it's his fault. He never set out to do that, I'm certain."

"How did it happen, then?"

Pastor took a sip of water and thought about it. "I don't think Jim ever intended to defraud people. Maybe I'm naïve, but that's how I feel. I think at first he himself was a victim of the scam. He brought new people into his business a few years ago when he was struggling. They started it. Then once it dawned on Jim what was happening, he was so far in that—I don't know—I guess he just tried to keep the thing going. I'm not excusing him in any way. I'm not sure I know his motivation completely. Maybe he was denying reality or trying to put off the pain he knew was coming."

"But to involve so many people in the church—his own friends!"

Pastor Jennings nodded. "Well, you know how it goes. Jim promised people big returns on their money, and apparently at first they were getting it. Or at least the statements they got from the salesmen made them *think* they were reaping big returns. Word of that spread to other people in the church, and before you know it, half a dozen families were investing in these fraudulent schemes."

"There's no way any of the money can be recovered?" I asked.

"I doubt it. From what I've heard, most of it is already gone. Jim told me he is promising to make restitution, even if it takes him the rest of his life, which I'm sure it will, if not longer. He's already decided to resign from the church board, quit the choir, quit as a Sunday school teacher. I'm afraid he and Leah will leave the church altogether."

"Some people will probably think he should."

Pastor leaned forward and answered, "They may, but we've got to fight that with all our might. It's bad enough that catastrophes like this happen, but if it forces people out of the church, even to the point of giving up their faith, then it becomes a true tragedy. Even an eternal one. You've got to help me prevent that, Chris."

I let out a quick laugh of surprise. "I really don't think there's much I can do," I said. "I'm just here for a few months, working at the magazine; then I'm on my way back to California."

"No way," he said. "I need your help here. You can't exempt yourself from this. This is your family—your church family."

"What are you asking me to do?"

"For starters, you've got to help me with your father. He's going to be one of the people hurt most by this financially."

"Oh, really?" I asked, a wave of dread washing over me.

"Yes. Hasn't he told you?"

"My father doesn't confide in me about his finances."

"Well, unfortunately, it will all come out into the open soon. There will be no more secrecy about it. Your father invested a considerable sum of his retirement money with Bobby McMahon, one of Jim's salesmen."

"Oh yes," I said with a scowl. "I know Bobby."

"Your father and Jim have been friends for many years. Everybody in the church likes and respects your dad, and they're going to be watching him. If he and Jim could somehow find healing and forgiveness in their relationship, it would be an example to the whole church. You've got to persuade your father to do that."

I laughed again. "Pastor, I have zero influence on my father."

"That's not true, Chris. Your father admires and respects you very much."

I shook my head. "Why do you think I left here two years ago?"

"I know all about the strain that you and your dad were under when your brother died. But I also know he loves you and is proud of you. We don't have time for you two to continue any kind of standoff. You've got to talk to him. Our church could be facing a split that will never heal. You could be the key in holding us together. I don't think it's any accident that the Lord brought you home this summer."

I sat silent for a moment, too startled to say anything. I was surprised, not only by how Pastor Jennings thought my father felt about me, but also by how adamant he was that I should play a role in reconciling the people of the church.

I sat quietly and sipped water. I wondered how badly Dad would be hurt by his loss in the scandal. The thought of it filled me with rage against Bobby. I said, "Sounds like the church was really suckered by Bobby McMahon. I know Dad sure fell for him. I couldn't believe it."

Pastor shook his head sadly. "The men of the church took a deep interest in Bobby, tried to help him out, get him established not only spiritually but also with a job. They helped him find an apartment and all the rest. They did exactly the kinds of things the church community should do when someone needing help comes to us. Bobby seemed so appreciative, seemed to be growing spiritually and adding to the life of the church. His betrayal is going to be hard to take. Restoring Jim White is one thing. Restoring Bobby will be much more difficult."

"I'm not sure he wants to be restored," I said. "I don't expect him to stick around."

"You may be right," said Pastor. "That's what makes this kind of situation difficult to deal with these days. In today's church, when things get rough, people leave. They strike out for something better. In the old days, there was more of a sense that we were family. We were stuck with each other and had to work out our problems."

I wondered if he had me in mind when he talked about people who leave when things get rough. Is that how he interpreted what I had done in moving away?

"When I sit in your services, I'm embarrassed to realize how cold my spirit feels. I've drifted so much in the last few years," I confessed.

"This is the summer of homecoming," he said. "For you and for the church. If this crisis doesn't split us down the middle, it's possible that God will use it to draw us closer to each other and to Him."

"You're an optimist."

He smiled. "I never would have made it this long in the ministry if I weren't. But I need your help, Chris. Your vacation is over."

"Well," I said, standing up, "your water break is over. I demand the chance to annihilate you in one more set."

ROBIN

I wasn't lying when I told Bobby I was a vegetarian. I don't believe in killing animals. In biology class my junior year we were supposed to cut up a pig, but I told the teacher I didn't want to do it. I offered to do something else to meet the assignment, but he said I had to dissect the pig or flunk the class. I finally stayed while my classmates did the work, but I didn't touch the thing myself. It was so stupid. I didn't learn anything from it anyway. It was just this blob of guts sitting there.

The only problem is I have this serious attachment to a couple pairs of leather shoes and one leather jacket I bought. But still. I don't eat meat.

The point is, knowing I feel guilty just cutting up a dead pig or eating a hamburger, how can Bobby seriously expect me to kill a human baby that's growing inside me? If it is a baby yet. Which I really believe it must be, even though I've tried to think about it different ways.

Our church has a pro-life group called Citizens for Life. My parents are in it, and so is Bobby, which is a laugh. They use a little room at church for an office and a library. They have it filled with antiabortion books, videos, brochures, and all the rest of it. I always called it the "abortion room," which my dad didn't like me to say, and which doesn't seem funny to me anymore under the circumstances. Anyone can go in there to read the stuff, so when Bobby left for New York, I went to church and asked the secretary to let me in.

I picked up the first brochure on the shelf and sat down and read it. It had a picture of a man's hand holding two tiny human feet between his thumb and forefinger. They were the feet of an aborted baby at ten weeks. Another picture showed a pile of limbs and blood and tissue from the body of an aborted baby. At this point I had to close the brochure because I thought I was going to get sick. My own stomach tightened, and I put my head down on my knees to keep from vomiting. I had seen pictures like this a few times before, but they had never had much effect on me. They hadn't seemed real before, nothing more than gross pictures that some brochure writer had used to prove a point. But now the reality sank in. My baby would look like this if I went through an abortion.

I decided not to look at any more pictures, but a few minutes later I found myself drawn to another booklet. This one showed a living baby so tiny it almost fit in the palm of the hand of the person holding it. The baby had been born premature, at only twenty-one weeks. Underneath that photo was another baby twenty-one weeks old, but this one was bloody and dead, having been aborted. It literally made me sick. I could not look at any more. I decided I wanted information only in words, so I read about the methods of abortion. I wondered which method Bobby wanted to arrange for them to use with me. What difference did it make? It was too horrible to think about. I paced around the room, trying to quell the nauseous feeling in my stomach.

It was Tuesday. Bobby was in New York and might have already started making arrangements for my abortion.

I had to stop him. I would not have an abortion. Maybe Bobby could cut himself off from the reality of what abortion really is, but I could not. If a baby was alive inside me, then it would just have to be born.

I needed to call Bobby while I still felt strong enough to say no without letting him talk me out of it. I had to work a few hours that day, but then I went home and worked up the courage to call him at about ten-thirty. It was an hour later in New York, and he was already in bed.

"What's wrong?" he said, his tone telling me right off that it had better be important for me to wake him up like this.

"I just wanted you to know I have made a definite decision not to have an abortion," I said.

"Why?" he asked in a disgusted tone, but before I had a chance to answer, he fired off a few more questions. "What happened? Have you been talking to someone? Did you tell somebody else?"

"I haven't told anyone," I said. "Your secret is still safe. But I've been reading about abortion. It's too horrible. I just can't do it."

"You promised me you'd wait until I got back before you made any decision."

"I know, but tonight after I read those things and saw some pictures, I knew I'd never be able to go through with it, no matter what you said to try to convince me. I thought I might as well call to save you from going to any trouble."

"I've already gone to trouble," he said. "Lots of it. What have you been reading, anyway?"

I told him about the antiabortion photos and booklets.

"Robin, think!" he yelled. "You're reading all the stuff that Citizens for Life uses to raise money! It's propaganda. They try to make it sound worse than it is. They show only the rarest, worst cases—like abortions from women in their third trimester, which are hardly ever done. That's not your case at all. You're barely pregnant! For you, it won't be like it is in those pictures."

"Barely pregnant," I said with a laugh. "That's a nice phrase. That could almost be funny if I didn't feel like puking right now."

"Robin, there is other information on abortion than what they have in that office," he pleaded. "Just do me the favor of waiting till you look at more objective information. More scientific information. You're making a rash decision based on emotion because you saw some gory photographs."

"No amount of information is going to convince me that I can do to this baby inside me the things that were done to the babies in those pictures."

"What is inside of you doesn't look like those pictures. Not yet. That's why we should take care of it right away. That's why I came out here so quickly. Robin, abortion is a safe, legal, quick, common medical operation. Millions of women do it."

"Yes, I know. One and a half million a year. I've read the statistics."

"And it's been debated for generations and fought in the legislatures and courts for decades. Even the Supreme Court said there is nothing wrong with it. You have a *right* to do it. Morally and legally and ethically nobody can stand in your way."

"But what if they're wrong? They're not the ones who are going to have to live with it. I am. And I don't think I can."

"Think of what you're going to have to live with if you *don't* do it," he said. "Quit looking at propaganda pictures and think about your own life for a minute. Having this baby will change the entire rest of your life. An abortion is over in minutes. Women have them all the time. They're hesitant at first, they're afraid, just like you, but they work up their courage and realize that overall it's the right decision. They do it. They recover. They go on and have successful, happy lives. That's the part you're not going to read about in the Citizens for Life office. You have a bright future. You have the rest of your life ahead of you to do whatever you want. To have a career. To go to college. To get married. To have kids when you're ready, not when it will shatter your life and devastate your parents, who are at the end of their rope already. Not to mention destroying my life and career. Not to mention bringing a baby into the world that you don't really want yet, that you would end up resenting for taking away your future. You've got to think this through. Please wait till I come home."

"When do you get back?"

"Thursday night."

"That's too long."

"What do you mean? It's only the day after tomorrow!"

"Well, I'm losing my mind over this. I need to talk about it with somebody right now. I'm tempted to tell Mom and Dad and get it over with."

"Robin, don't!" he begged. "You have to be strong. If you tell them, then this has all been a waste of time. If you need to talk to somebody, talk to me. I'll stay on the phone with you all night if I have to. Don't tell anybody else."

"I don't want to talk to you."

"Why not?"

"You don't fool me, Bobby. You're just trying to save your own neck. I want to talk to somebody who cares about me."

He was silent for a moment. "I do care about you, Robin," he said, his voice calmer. "I'm not doing this just for me. I'm doing this for both of us. Don't freak out on me and do something stupid. This is the biggest crisis of your life. You're bound to go through moments when you're scared and have doubts. Promise me you'll keep an open mind and won't do or say anything until I get back."

"No. I'm not making any more promises to you," I said. "Good night."

I hung up the phone with Bobby still protesting in my ear.

CHRIS

After two exhausting hours of tennis, Pastor Jennings asked me if I would come back to his office for a few minutes. He had a favor to ask of me and wanted to give me something.

He slapped a file on the desk as I sat across from him, sweaty, in his armchair.

"What is this?" I asked, picking it up.

"It's a story I'm hoping you'll write for us. You know how your mother is putting together photo boards that will give a pictorial history of the church for the fiftieth anniversary later this summer?"

"Yes, the pictures are covering half our house."

"Well, to accompany that, I'd like to have a book we could give everyone that would be filled with pictures and stories of the people who built this church over the decades. I think you're the man to put it together."

"Oh, Pastor," I groaned, thinking about how little progress I was currently making on my dissertation and how tired I was of writing after doing it all day at the magazine.

"I've already written about several people to give you an idea of the types of stories I want included." He opened the file and pulled out a page. "Did you know that this church started in Hazel Calvert's living room fifty years ago?"

"In her living room?"

"Yes, the same living room she has today, where she still entertains people from the church and still occasionally lets people stay if they need her help. There were only fifteen in the group back then. Four are still alive and in our church today. We need to tell their stories before they are gone."

I smiled and said, "You're not going to give me the chance to say no to this, are you?"

"No," he said. "This is too important. I want our celebration to be more than nostalgia. Our people need to understand how the current generation is connected to the past generations—as well as to future ones. They need to see how the Lord has held us together all this time and the amazing things He's done among us."

I picked up the file and glanced through some of the summaries of people's lives he had written. "It seems we're not as spiritually strong as those people were back then."

"Not at all!" he insisted. "Do you think those earlier generations thought it was all smooth sailing when they were going through their troubles? This church had a fire in the old building, a tornado in this one, and a scandal or two for each generation. The past only appears calmer because we can look back on it and see a pattern. We can see how the Lord brought us through each of the difficult times. But I guarantee they couldn't see the pattern back then. Hazel told me she never thought the church would get off the ground, never thought they'd get it together enough to grow a congregation, hire a pastor, and build a church building. Now look at us. Almost seven hundred people!"

I kept reading, hoping I could come up with a good excuse to say no to this project.

"You'll have a good budget. We want to do it right. I really appreciate your doing this, Chris."

ROBIN

$\mathcal{I}$ didn't sleep at all the night I talked to Bobby in New York. After I hung up on him, I went back to reading the abortion material I had borrowed from the Citizens for Life library at church. I got so tired that I finally leaned back in the chair and tried to sleep, but I couldn't. I felt sick. My stomach was churning. My head felt heavy and my temples were throbbing.

I had tried to sound firm with Bobby about not having the abortion, but the truth was I was still tempted to go along with him. I had to admit it was appealing to think that this whole nightmare could end with a simple procedure.

I was tempted to go talk to Chris but decided not to. He's so hostile toward Bobby that I can't have a rational conversation with him. When Chris heard Bobby was going to New York, he told me, "You need to come to grips with the fact that you'll probably never see him again." He made it sound like Bobby had done something so horrible at Premiere Financial Services that they were going to execute him or something. I don't know how much is true and how much is Chris exaggerating. Either way, I decided not to confide in him.

Instead, I did what I always do when I'm facing a big decision: I rehearsed each alternative in my mind, not just in concepts but in pictures, as if I were writing a movie that dramatized each scenario. Then I asked myself if this is the movie I want to make, or can bear to make, in real life. I tried to picture what would happen if I went along with

Bobby's idea of finding some excuse to go to New York and secretly have an abortion. In one scene I see myself standing in front of Mom and Dad as they sit in the family room, Dad reading the newspaper and Mom watching TV. I am trying to explain to them why I suddenly need to go to New York for a week or two to visit a friend. My friend Sherry.

"Sherry?" Mom asks. "I've never heard of her. How do you know somebody named Sherry in New York?"

"I used to go to school with her. Then her family moved. She went to our church awhile. Don't you remember her? Tall, kind of reddish hair?"

Dad puts the paper down on the table. He takes off his reading glasses and sets them on the paper. He looks skeptical. He can feel the untruthfulness in what I'm saying.

"What's this all about?" he says.

My story begins to unravel.

I picture another scene.

Bobby holds my hand as we walk across a parking lot toward the abortion clinic. It is a dumpy little building in a dirty part of town. I smell exhaust fumes from the buses, greasy odors from the open door of a tiny restaurant, a putrid stench emanating from the rotting garbage in a nearby dumpster. No one else seems aware of these city smells, but to me they are overwhelming, and I'm afraid I'll vomit before I make it inside.

As if the smells were not enough to hold me back, I see about twenty protesters with their signs standing between me and the clinic. One sign reads, *Don't kill your baby.* Bobby holds my hand tighter and says, "Ignore them. We'll walk right through them and go inside. They have no right to stop you. Don't look at them or listen to them or speak to them."

As I get close, one woman's voice drowns out all the others. She pleads with me, "Don't kill your baby. You don't have to do this. We will adopt your baby. We'll take care of it. Don't let them slaughter it. You don't have to do this. You don't have to do this."

Without realizing it, I have stopped and am listening to her. Bobby yanks my arm and pulls me inside the clinic, the door slamming shut behind us. Through the glass I see the woman still pleading.

In another scene I am lying on a table in a room that seems white, very white, unnaturally white. A doctor approaches me with some kind of instrument in his hand. The metal glints in the brightness of the light. *"You don't have to do this,"* the woman protester's voice sings my mind. *"You don't have to do this."*

I cannot do it. I cannot even play this scene all the way through in my mind, let alone live it. I don't care what Bobby says. The answer is no, no, no.

I hear Bobby's voice saying, "If your answer was really no, you wouldn't have to keep repeating it. You would only have to say it once. You keep repeating it because you're trying to convince yourself."

I will not argue with Bobby, not even in my head.

This is how I spent all of Tuesday night, creating and then suppressing horrible scenes, trying not to have arguments with my imaginary Bobby.

I went down to the kitchen at about five o'clock and ate some cereal and drank a little coffee. Then I went up to my bedroom and collapsed on the bed, finally falling asleep and not waking up until almost four in the afternoon.

On Wednesday night I worked, and by the time I got home, I had made a decision.

I had to tell Mom and Dad I was pregnant before Bobby got home.

I did not want to have an abortion, and right then my mind was firm that I would not do it. But I knew Bobby's power over me. I hate to admit this, but he could push me in directions I didn't want to go. If Bobby got home and our secret was still intact, and if he had all the arrangements made in New York, it would only be harder for me to say no to him. In a weak moment I might take the easy way out and go through with it. I'd like to think I'm stronger than that, but I know it could happen. But if my parents already knew by the time Bobby got back, then maybe he would stop pushing.

On Wednesday night my conviction was firm. On Thursday morning I had doubts, but I had to act fast. Bobby would be home that night. Mom and Dad said they were going out for most of the day to make some arrangements about selling their house and moving to the condo, so I decided I would tell them that afternoon as soon as they got home, a few hours before Bobby's plane would arrive.

There is a moment I can't get out of my head. The week before Bobby went to New York, I was pacing around the house, worrying about my dilemma, and I wandered into the living room to find Mom and Dad sitting on the couch, sorting through pictures. Mom is in there all the time, since those pictures are her new obsession, but I had never seen Dad pay much attention to them. I guess Mom had called him in there, because she was making him name all the people in an old picture from his side of the family. All those people are dead now, and I had never even heard of most of them.

Anyway, I sat there with them awhile and then Dad picked up an album that Mom had put together with pictures of David, Chris, and me as babies. Dad walked over to where I was sitting on the floor and squatted down on his knees beside me. "Look at these! Look at how much alike the three of you looked when you were babies. You can hardly tell you apart."

I glanced at it and expected him to take it away, but he held it there a moment longer, then turned the page to more of the same. I said, "By looking at these pictures, you would never imagine how different the three of us would turn out."

"That's for sure," he agreed. Then he said something completely unexpected, at least for Dad. "The happiest moments in my life and in your mother's life were when you three kids were born. Nothing compares to the thrill of that."

"Weren't you pretty used to it by the time I came around?"

"No!" he said. "We were overjoyed. We knew you were going to be our last child, so we wanted to enjoy every minute of those first hours of your life. I didn't want to put you down. I was so proud."

Those words may not sound like such a big deal, but I've almost never heard Dad say anything so sentimental. All I could think was *Before long I'm going to have to tell you about another baby who is on the way, and you're not going to be so proud of me then.* Sitting looking at those baby pictures and listening to Dad, all the pressure I had been feeling suddenly got to me, and I started crying. Mom and Dad sat there bewildered, because I almost never cry in front of them. But it came on so suddenly that I didn't have time to stop it. Dad scooted over and put his arm around me, which was also unusual and made me want to cry even more.

"What's wrong, honey?" he asked.

I couldn't answer him.

"Is it looking at pictures of David? Does it make you miss him?"

"Yes," I said, and by that time it had passed. I sat there and talked with them a little while longer so they wouldn't think I was totally weird. Then I got up and went to my room for the rest of the night.

The night I told Mom and Dad about my baby had to be the worst night of my life. They were supposed to be home in the afternoon, but after talking to the Realtor, they went out to dinner. All that did was give me time to stalk around the house for a few more hours and think of reasons why telling them would be a mistake. I was so frantic by the time they got home that I almost chickened out. I felt guilty telling them behind Bobby's back, since I promised him I wouldn't, but that was just too bad. To help make up for breaking my promise to him, I decided I would not tell them he was the baby's father no matter how hard they pushed me. Chris was over at Bill's that night, so when I went into the family room, only Mom and Dad were there. Mom sat on the couch reading the newspaper, and Dad was leaning back in his recliner, half asleep, watching TV.

At that point I put myself on autopilot. I let the words come out of me without thinking too much about them. "Mom and Dad, I have to talk to you about something."

Dad leaned forward and squinted at me with a look of concern— my wide-eyed gaze of horror must have frightened him. He hit the mute button on the TV. Mom dropped the newspaper on the coffee table. I tried my best not to cry. Beforehand I had told myself that the ultimate sign of handling this encounter successfully was that I get through it without crying.

I felt so lost and confused for a minute that I thought I would collapse.

Then I said it. "I think I'm pregnant."

My head felt hot, and for a moment the whole scene in front of me turned fuzzy and dark, as though I were viewing it through the faded screen of an old black-and-white television. I honestly can't remember the next few things that happened. Mom and Dad both stood up and came toward me. Both of them were talking. They flickered in front of me like characters in an old silent movie. I wasn't worried about not crying anymore. I was trying not to faint.

I don't even know the exact sequence of what was said, but I remember Dad asking, more than once, "What do you mean?" as if he had never heard the word *pregnant* before. Mom turned red-faced right away, then cried soon after that. Dad did most of the talking.

He fired off a bunch of questions, just as I imagined he would. I had made the mistake of saying "I *think* I'm pregnant," so he asked whether I was sure and whether I had gone to the doctor and all that.

Then Dad suddenly turned about as pale as Mom was red. He leaned against the bookshelf. His mouth was kind of hanging open, an expression you never see from him. I was afraid he was going to have another heart attack on the spot and thought, *Oh great, now killing Dad is another thing I'll have on my conscience.*

Without looking up, he murmured, "When?" but his voice was so low and distant I wasn't sure he was aware of what he was saying. Then he straightened himself up, looked at me directly with his glassy eyes, and again said, "When?"

"When what, Dad?"

"When did you go to the doctor?" he insisted, as if this were the heart of the issue. Besides, we had already covered the doctor questions.

"Last week," I said. "There's no doubt, if that's what you're wondering. I *am* going to have a baby."

"I believe you," he said. He looked at the bookshelf again. "It's just . . . how could this happen? How could you go to the doctor and find out you're going to have a baby and I don't even know it's going on? I don't even have any suspicion that it's going on? How could this happen?"

He looked over at Mom, who was crying too hard to talk, and then he started walking around the room with short, jerky steps, like he wanted to walk in a different direction but kept changing his mind at the last minute.

"Not this," he said, almost too low for us to hear. "Oh, God, don't let it be this."

Suddenly Dad stopped dead still, as if he had just thought of something profound; then he turned toward me and started firing another bunch of pointless questions at me about my trip to the doctor. Which doctor did I see and what did he say exactly and what kind of test did he give me? This avoidance of the reality of the pregnancy didn't surprise me. I had seen him do the same thing when David died. When the people at the hospital had come out to tell us that David had not survived the accident, he couldn't seem to accept the simple truth, so he kept going off on some tangent. What exactly had the doctors done to try to save him, what were his specific injuries, and how long past the wreck had he been conscious, and on and on.

I sat down on the couch to keep from passing out. Mom came over and put her arm around me. At least she seemed to be snapping back to reality.

Dad finally dropped the doctor line of questioning and asked, "Who did this to you?"

I should have known that would be next. He walked toward me, and I said, "Nobody 'did this' to me, Dad. Please. It's not like I was raped."

"Who is the father of the baby?"

"I don't want to get into that right now," I said. "I can't. This is hard enough for me as it is. Can't all these questions wait?"

"Is it that Brandon?"

"No," I said. "I can't talk about the father right now."

"But you can," he said. "Brandon is the only boy I've seen you with in the last several months. You're telling me it's not him?"

"None of that makes any difference," I said. "The fact is I am going to have a baby. I'm sorry. I'd almost rather die than to have to disappoint you this way. But there was nothing else I could do except just tell you. It's a fact, and I need help from both of you to get through this because I'm scared and don't know what to do. I can't stand you two hating me on top of everything else."

In a kind and soothing voice, Mom said, "We don't hate you, and you know it. How did you expect us to react to this? We love you, and we're shocked right now. We're going to work everything out, but you can't expect us not to be upset at first."

"That's right," Dad said, plopping down beside me on the couch and looking at me with clear eyes for the first time. He put his hand on mine.

For some reason, their kindness was even harder for me to bear than their resistance. My whole body felt like it was going to explode into a million pieces. Running out of the room was definitely not the ending I had envisioned, but I felt desperate to flee. I charged out of the family room and ran to my bedroom to pick up my car keys and purse. I escaped through the front door, with Mom yelling after me the whole way.

CHRIS

I spent half the night trying to calm down Mom and Dad. Mom's face was all red, her eyes puffy, her voice high-pitched and strained. Her condition was the worst I'd seen since David was killed. Dad looked drawn and haggard, as if the force of gravity around him had doubled, pulling him inevitably downward. I feared what the stress might do to him.

To make matters worse, Robin didn't come home that night. By two-thirty in the morning, Mom was ready to start calling around to Robin's friends to try to find her.

"We can't do that," I said. "We don't know where to begin to find her, and we can't go calling everybody she knows in the middle of the night. She'd be furious. What good will it do to find her anyway? She won't come home just because we get her on the phone."

"Well, at least it would relieve our minds to know where she is and that she's all right. Hasn't she put us through enough tonight? Does she need to disappear and make us frantic waiting for her?"

"I'm sure she's fine," I said. "She's an adult now, and she can take care of herself for one night. I'm sure she has gone over to a friend's house. Maybe that's best. Everybody can cool off a little bit and figure out how to deal with this."

"I bet she went over to that boy's house," Dad said.

"What boy?" I asked, immediately thinking of Bobby, who I secretly feared she had run to.

"That Brandon," he said. "I think he's the one responsible for this, even though she denied it."

I was almost certain Bobby was the one responsible, but I had no intention of telling Mom and Dad. Things were bad enough already. There would be plenty of time for the father to be revealed, and it was Robin's story to tell, not mine. I seethed with rage at him, so much so that my head was pounding, but I tried to smother my anger as much as possible so that my reaction wouldn't get Mom and Dad any more provoked than they already were. Wasn't it enough that he had shattered my parents' lives by swindling them out of their money? Was he going to get away with ruining my sister's life too?

I felt deep pain for Robin but also wondered why she hadn't told me herself. There was a time when I would have been the first person she would have come to about something like this. I longed to talk to her alone, to know what she was thinking.

I finally convinced Mom and Dad that they should go to bed, try to sleep, and let Robin come back when she was ready to face us the next day.

"I'll never sleep now," Mom said. "It feels just like . . ."

She didn't finish the sentence, and Dad and I didn't encourage her to. We both knew she intended to say it felt just like the day of David's crash—the sense of crisis, of helplessness, of disaster. Saying it out loud would only make things worse. Besides, the two situations were beyond compare. David's death was a tragedy for which there was no response but crushing grief. We were helpless to do anything. Robin was not dying; she was over at a friend's house, contemplating having a baby. Who could tell what depths of sacrifice and support she would need from us if she dared to let us in to help her?

––––––––

We did not hear from Robin the next day. That evening Mom called several of Robin's friends. She had not spent the night with any of them, and none of them had heard from her. Mom called the store where Robin worked. She was not scheduled to come in again until the next day, and no one there had talked to her. Finally Dad called Brandon, who said he didn't know where Robin was and didn't expect to hear from her since they had broken off their relationship and now worked together only professionally. Dad made no mention of Robin's pregnancy, and Brandon gave no indication that he was aware of it.

By ten o'clock that night Mom was ready to call the police and report Robin missing.

"You can't do that," I said. "She obviously wanted to get away, and you have no reason to expect her back at any certain time. What can the police do about it?"

"But we've called all her friends, and nobody knows where she is!" Mom insisted. "Where could she be?"

"We haven't contacted *all* her friends," I said. "We don't know who they all are." I thought of Bobby. By this time I was convinced she must have run to him. I was tempted to go ahead and tell all I knew about Robin's relationship with him, but something held me back. I still thought it was her story to tell, and I still thought she would show up at any moment.

The next morning as I wrote a boring story about the Delaware state trapshooting tournament, where Dale McInerney shattered 200 to win the singles tournament for the second year in a row, Beth called. Hearing her voice on the line startled me so much that I was unable to speak for a few seconds. Her voice did not fit in the world of guns and clay targets. Even when we had been together, she had rarely called me at work.

"I'm sorry to interrupt you there," she said. "But I need to talk to you. I was wondering if we could get together tonight."

This was the call I had been dreading and—if I were completely honest with myself—hoping for. The big surprise was that *she* was doing the asking, not me.

Before I answered, she broke in and said, "Don't worry, Chris. It's not about us. It's about Robin."

"What about her?" I asked, my emotions now thoroughly jumbled.

"I heard from her this morning."

"Is she home? What did she say?"

"She's not at home. She told me some things she wants me to tell you."

"What?"

"She made me promise I'd talk to you in person. I know this is all a little roundabout, but would you mind?"

"No, that's fine," I said. "But what can I tell Mom and Dad? They're frantic."

"Tell them she's all right. The rest I'll tell you tonight." We made arrangements to meet at Chili's restaurant at six.

I got to Chili's before Beth. Anticipating this meeting had already made me so nerve-racked that I didn't want to compound my apprehension by walking in and having to start talking to her immediately. I needed time to get used to the surroundings, to plan the attitude I would take, to anticipate what she might say and how I should respond. We had agreed that we were meeting to talk about Robin, not ourselves, but I knew that any conversation with Beth would also implicitly be about us.

If Beth felt any of the same anxiety, she certainly didn't show it. She walked in looking as carefree as if she were casually meeting a good friend for dinner. She wore khaki slacks and a simple blue and white top. Her hair was loose around her shoulders, and she was smiling. In the old days, her face had often carried a cautious expression, as if she were guarding herself in case the person she was talking to lashed out at her. That shield was gone from her face now, as it had been the night I saw her at home. That openness brought out her beauty so powerfully it startled me. I kept thinking, *This woman could cause me great heartache. It's dangerous for me to be here with her.*

I sat in a booth facing the door. She slid in across from me, reached out her hand, and squeezed my arm warmly. "Hi, Chris. Sorry I'm a little late. I got another call from Robin."

"So where is she?" I asked, grateful that we'd be able to avoid small talk for the moment and get right down to business.

"Here's the situation. She panicked after she told your parents. She went to Bobby's apartment that night, and he talked her into running off with him."

"Running off! Where?"

"Right now they're in Chicago at some hotel. She wouldn't say where exactly. She said she doesn't want you or your parents coming after her."

"I could kill that guy!" I fumed, my neck starting to ache with tension.

"She figured you would say something like that. She wanted me to stress to you that Bobby is not to blame for all that has happened. It was her choice to go off with him. She didn't want you or your parents acting like she was being kidnapped or something."

"So what's her plan? She didn't even take a suitcase with her."

Beth frowned and shook her head disapprovingly. "Oh, she didn't need a suitcase. Bobby took her on a shopping spree as soon as they got to Chicago. She has everything she needs."

"Oh, really? And where did he get the money? From all the people in our church that he ripped off?"

"Robin says that's all a misunderstanding. Bobby was just a salesman whose every action was legal and proper. Now Jim White is looking for a scapegoat, and Bobby's it."

"So Bobby's the victim!" I cried, barely able to control the anger in my voice as the waiter came to take our order. We ordered a plate of nachos to share, as we had done in the old days. When the waiter walked away, I said, "You realize, don't you, that even though Robin doesn't know it, this guy has conned dozens of people, including my own parents, out of their retirements, their life savings."

"I didn't know your parents were involved, but yes, I've heard that Jim White's firm is being investigated and that Jim has admitted his clients are going to lose a lot of money."

I sat back and took a deep breath. "So where do you stand on this?" I asked. "Do you think Bobby is guilty or innocent?"

"Guilty," she said. "Believe me, Chris, Robin is my friend, but I don't agree with the trust she has put in Bobby, and I've told her so. I thought she was starting to see through him, but then suddenly he became Prince Charming again."

"So what are they planning to do? Have a little vacation and then come back?"

"She won't really say. She was being a little vague with me, but I got the impression she's not planning to come back at all."

"That's insane!"

"I know. They have nowhere to go. They don't have jobs. She's pregnant. I don't know what they'll do. But I don't think she's dealing with reality right now. The bad thing is that Bobby has her convinced he needs her, that she's not running away from her own problems, but rather, she's helping him escape from people who are out to get him. She's acting like they're two innocent fugitives running from the angry mob."

"So what's Bobby's angle? What do you think he's up to?"

"I don't know. Maybe he's running just as frantically as she is. They boost each other's illusions."

"What does she want me to tell Mom and Dad? They don't know Bobby is the father of her baby."

"She said she wants you to tell them about Bobby. And she asks that you try to give him the benefit of the doubt and not hate him as much as she thinks you do. She also wants you to tell them she's all right, she knows what she's doing, she doesn't want anyone to come after her, and she'll keep in touch with them so they won't worry."

"I can't believe it," I said. "She's just throwing her life away."

"She is acting a little irrational right now," Beth admitted, "but I have faith in her. I think she'll come to her senses and do the right thing. She needs to know you're going to do everything you can to make having this baby work out for the best. You're her big brother, and she loves you."

"I want to help. So do Mom and Dad."

"She's not convinced of that. Otherwise she wouldn't have run away."

"She didn't leave a number where I could call her?"

"No. She wouldn't give me one."

A short time later the food came, and we sat silent awhile. I dreaded telling Mom and Dad about Bobby. Dad was looking frailer and thinner all the time, as if life was being slowly drained out of him. I didn't know if he could stand one more betrayal by the young man he had befriended.

After a short time I asked, "So why did Robin insist that you tell me all this in person instead of on the phone?"

Beth tilted her head back and laughed. "Do you really want me to answer that question?"

"Sure."

Her confident smile intact, she said, "She wanted us to get back together."

"Oh," I said, feeling my face redden with embarrassment. "Even with all the problems Robin's having, she's not too busy to meddle."

Beth took on a coy expression, her eyes narrow and slightly averted, her smile barely perceptible. "I've told her it was crazy to think you'd ever want to have anything to do with me again."

I shook my head and tried to smile despite the fact that my stomach was churning with—what?—dread and excitement.

Beth said, "The problem is the past. There's such a huge, dark cloud between us that I can barely see you through it."

I thought about this for a minute, then said, "The past isn't necessarily what you think it is."

"Oh, really? Does the past change?"

"In a way, yes. What we have the courage to reveal about it changes the conclusions we draw from it. Our past certainly looks different to me now than it did two years ago."

"I'm not surprised," she said. "You seem like a different person."

"A new haircut," I said. "That's about it."

We silently munched on the nachos for a time.

"Why did you come home, Chris?"

"To work at the magazine."

She sat forward, keeping her gaze downward, and asked, "Didn't you have any sense of coming home to settle things? Between you and your family? Maybe between you and me?"

"I thought things between you and me were settled," I said, knowing it was a lie. "You gave me that impression two years ago."

"Back then we were trying to outdo each other. Now maybe we can really talk. I know I told you we weren't going to talk about us tonight, and this is probably not the best time to do it, but I wonder if we could get together sometime and give it a try?"

"I could try to say no, but you know that conversation would be irresistible to me."

"Good," she said, leaning back again in the booth. "Let me know when you're ready."

ROBIN

*H*ave you ever felt every molecule of your body screaming out to do something, even though you know you'll regret it later?

That's what it was like deciding to go to Chicago with Bobby.

The first night on the road was one of the happiest I've had in ages. I was with the Bobby I had fallen in love with—funny, caring, exciting. I was alone with him. I had all his attention. He drove fast down Interstate 65, as if he just couldn't wait to get to our future together. We would move to a new town, we'd both get jobs, we'd get married, we'd have the baby. We'd start over with new friends who would accept us as we were and not make us feel like screw-ups.

Not all of these plans were spoken. I admit I was too scared to push Bobby very hard on his long-term intentions. We were taking life a day at a time. Anything was better than staying at home and letting the world cave in on us. We were taking action.

After I left home the night I talked to my parents, I went over to Bobby's apartment and waited outside until he got home from the airport. He was even more depressed than I was. I don't know what had happened that day, but he must have had a bad conversation with somebody on the phone, because he said he was never going back to his office and couldn't stay in Indianapolis. He didn't explain too clearly what the problem was at work, even though Beth and some other people told me the company has made people lose a lot of money. But Bobby said the people knew they were taking risks when they invested their money, and he didn't want to get into it much beyond that. He just said, "I can never go back there. Jim got the company into trouble with some things he had us do, and now he's trying to pin all the blame on me. I won't let him do it."

He didn't act mad that I had told Mom and Dad about the baby. He was too preoccupied with his own problems. We talked for a few hours, feeling more bummed all the time, and feeling more and more like there was nothing left for us in Indianapolis. Bobby was so sweet. I wish I could explain. He had lost that hard edge he had put on the whole time he was trying to talk me into an abortion. He was so sad, he reminded me of a little kid. I just wanted to hug him and tell him everything was going to be all right.

At first we just started joking about running off together and leaving everything behind. I don't know how we got started on it, but the more we talked about it, the less farfetched it seemed. After all, what did we have to keep us in Indianapolis? Bobby was out of a job, and I sure didn't have any great love for mine. We wouldn't be hassled by my family or by our friends from church.

Finally Bobby said, "Let's go to Chicago. That's one place where we could have lots of fun."

"Don't play those games with me," I said. "If you don't mean it, don't say it, because right now I wouldn't hesitate for one second."

"All right, then," he said, standing up. "I'm still packed. Let's go."

"Are you serious?"

"Yes. You said not to play games, and I'm not. Get up and let's go to Chicago. We'll have a blast."

"Tonight? I don't have any clothes or a toothbrush or anything!"

Bobby picked up his suitcase. "Chicago has plenty of stores. I'll buy you new clothes and a toothbrush and dental floss and tooth whiteners and toothpicks and anything else you need. You said you wouldn't hesitate for a moment. I'm walking out that door right now and driving to Chicago. If you're going with me, you'll have to get in the car without any more argument."

He walked out the door, leaving me sitting there on his sofa, dazed. I jumped up, turned off the light, locked the door behind me, and off we went. It was two o'clock in the morning.

It took us over four hours to get there. We kept talking to keep each other awake. I can't tell you how different Bobby was from the previous few weeks. He was singing to the songs on the radio and talking about normal stuff—different music he liked, things he did as a kid. He was nice to me and loving, holding my hand and even kissing me a few times. He was completely relaxed. It seemed that as soon as we walked out the door of his apartment, none of those problems we had known there existed for him anymore. He never mentioned Premiere Financial Services. By listening to our conversations you would never have known he had worked there. He never mentioned my pregnancy or the possibility that I would have an abortion. It was like he had forgotten I was pregnant.

I had a little more trouble putting our troubles out of my mind. I would be really happy with him for a few hours and hopeful that everything was going to work out all right. Then suddenly panic would grab me, and I'd get hot and nervous all over and think, *What are we going to do after this trip? Where are we going to get money to live on? Will they come after Bobby because of what he did at work? Will he want to marry me, or will he suddenly turn mean again and want me to get rid of the baby?* I didn't have these questions pop up one at a time like that, where I could work through each one separately. They came crashing down on me all at once, and I got so scared I wanted to scream at Bobby to turn the car around and take me home.

We stopped at a Days Inn in an ugly industrial area south of Chicago. By then I was so tired I could barely make myself get out of the car. Being pregnant has made me a lot more tired, and having stayed up all night didn't help. I went through a couple of bad hours there, looking at the gray morning sky, those smelly trucks, and those endless rows of broken-down warehouses. I thought this whole trip was a mistake. I would have given anything to be at home in my bed, willing to face whatever consequences came from Mom and Dad. Now there was one more transgression they could add to my long list—running off with Bobby. One other thing occurred to me. As soon as they found out who I was with, they would know he was the father. What a horrible way for them to find out. I thought about telling Bobby I wanted to get back in the car right away and go home, but both of us were too tired to make the return trip then.

One thing I insisted on was sleeping in a separate bed until we got married. Bobby sneered at this and said it was a little late to be worrying about that, but I was determined. He was too tired to argue, so we plopped down on the beds and tried to rest.

We slept for a few hours, and when we woke up, Bobby was as antsy as a little kid going to Disney World. He told me to hurry up and get ready so we could go on into Chicago. I felt scuzzy from traveling all night and wished I had some different clothes to change into after my shower, but Bobby said, "Don't worry about it. We're both going to buy new clothes today and anything else you need." He didn't say where we would get the money for all that, and I didn't ask.

One thing you have to say about Bobby, he knows how to have a good time. We parked downtown near State Street and went on a shopping spree in Marshall Field's, this great department store that has several levels and covers a whole city block. They have fabulous clothes. Bobby bought me three dresses, two pairs of slacks, four blouses, new underwear, makeup, shampoo, cologne, earrings, and a necklace. I kept telling him we shouldn't be buying all that stuff, but he insisted. Practically anything I saw and liked, he made me buy. We had to make a couple trips to the car just to be able to carry it all! After he bought me a bunch of stuff, we went to the men's section, where he bought himself three sport coats, several pairs of slacks, shirts, seven ties, socks, a couple pairs of shorts, some cologne, and a new wallet. "How can you afford all this?" I asked at one point, and he put his finger on my lips, looked at me seriously, and said, "I've got it covered. Don't ruin it with that question."

After we had bought half the store, we took everything back to the car except for one outfit apiece. Then he took me to this little Walgreen's drugstore with a diner attached to it, and before we ordered lunch, we went into the rest rooms and changed into new clothes. The other women stared at me like I was some weirdo as I took off the old clothes and put on my makeup, jewelry, and this fancy blue dress. But I didn't care what they thought, I was having too much fun. Bobby looked so handsome in his new sport coat and tie. He was happier than I've ever seen him. I brought my old clothes out in a shopping bag, but he made me throw them away.

"We could go to the Laundromat and wash them!" I said.

"This trip isn't about Laundromats," he insisted. "Throw them away."

After lunch we walked all over the city. We wandered down Michigan Avenue to shop, and he took me to the Art Institute, his favorite place in Chicago. It was fun to be all dressed up in such a fancy place with him. I wanted to walk slowly through each gallery, my arm cradled in his, gazing at and commenting on each painting. But Bobby was so hyper that we raced through that museum, stopping only seconds to look at each item. There were all these famous paintings, and he seemed really excited by them, but it was like every painting he saw made him want to rush on to the next one to see even more. He told me *American Gothic* was there, that picture with the farmer and his wife and the pitchfork. But it took us like half an hour to find it, and then we sped by it so fast it was like viewing it from the window of a rapidly moving train.

By early evening we were feeling tired again, so Bobby took me to the Fine Arts Theater across from the Art Institute, where we watched some foreign movie with subtitles. We walked in about fifteen minutes late, and I never did figure out exactly what the stupid thing was about. Two brothers were after the same woman or something like that. I fell asleep about halfway into it. The air conditioner felt good, and I liked the popcorn and the darkness and the feel of Bobby's arm across my shoulder.

Finally that night we walked to a Chinese restaurant for dinner, kind of a fancy one, with Oriental statues and fountains and black-suited waiters. I called Beth from there while we waited for our food to come. I called her during one of those flashes of reality that kept creeping up on me. Not once that day had Bobby and I talked about home or our problems. Even when I went to call Beth, I sensed that he wouldn't want to talk about it, so I just held my stomach like there was some kind of pregnancy problem and told him I'd be back in a few minutes. He didn't ask me what I was going to do. This baby thing does have its advantages.

After dinner we took a two-hour boat tour up and down the Chicago River through downtown and then out into Lake Michigan. The boat pulled close to the lakeshore, and we watched the water fountain show in Grant Park, the water spraying high in the air, changing colors and forming different shapes and designs. Bobby cuddled close to me the whole time and looked as content as I've ever seen him. Neither of us said hardly a single word during the entire boat tour, but I've never felt so close to him.

I know the whole trip may sound a little flaky and irresponsible, but it was the best day of my life. It almost makes all my suffering worth it. Beth and Chris and my parents would scream if they heard me say that, because I know everybody's going to be down on Bobby from now on, but he made me feel more alive that day than I've ever felt before. I was the center of the world for him. You would have thought it was our last day on earth, and we had to enjoy it to the hilt before it slipped away.

Bobby was sound asleep within ten minutes of our getting back to the motel. I couldn't sleep much. The worries started creeping over me again like tiny little spiders.

CHRIS

*Y*our demented women have invaded my life."

So said Bill a few nights after Robin's disappearance. We sat in the living room of his dungeon of an apartment late in the evening eating chili and crackers on TV trays. Bill's body sank so far down in his tattered sofa that he had to stretch to reach the tray. He lived on the ground floor of an old wood frame house with his landlord upstairs. The floors in Bill's one-bedroom place were creaky, the plumbing was old and in constant need of repair, the rooms were cramped, and the carpet was threadbare. The windows were covered with droopy dark drapes the owner of the building had discarded from his own apartment. Despite the dreariness of the place, Bill kept it spotless. Every dish was washed and put away. Every book and newspaper was in its proper place. Two walls in the living room were covered with shelves filled with alphabetized books, mostly spy novels and crime novels and a little science fiction. Most of another wall was taken up with Bill's collection of hundreds of record albums and CDs.

Bill's enigmatic statement about my "demented women" did not surprise me. Women were his favorite topics of conversation, and whenever he got turned down for a date, as he had been that day, his pronouncements usually veered toward the cynical. I thought at first the "demented women" must include Robin, since her running away was so much on my mind.

"What are you talking about?" I asked.

"That crazy girl your brother was engaged to."

"Cheryl?"

"That's right. She called me last night."

"Called you? Why?"

"Said she's on a quest for the truth."

"About what?" I asked, as if I didn't know.

"She has some pretty shocking ideas about some things that went on the summer David died. She says you refuse to talk to her."

Cheryl had called me three times after our conversation at Denny's, once at home and twice at the magazine. I told her I had said all I had to say about David and didn't see any point in getting together again.

"She's been bothering me ever since I got home," I admitted. I didn't want to think about Cheryl or let her tactics get to me, but I immediately felt the heat of anger rising in me.

"I would advise you not to tell that woman a thing. She's a dangerous one. I can hear it in her voice," Bill said.

"What did she say?"

"You won't like it," he said.

"Go ahead."

"Well, I don't remember all of it, but she said she suspects David was having some kind of affair when he died, and you knew about it and were covering up for him."

A wave of suffocating heat washed over me, and the apartment seemed as cramped as if we were stuffed into a tiny closet. I stood up and yanked open the drapes of the window closest to me. I wanted to lift the window higher to let in more air, but it was already up all the way. Bill's apartment had no air conditioning.

"What else did she say?" I asked as evenly as possible, trying to conceal my irritation from Bill.

"I don't think we should get into it," he said. "I know that girl has been a little off her rocker since your brother died. I didn't believe any of it."

"Just tell me, Bill."

"She said Beth might have been the one David was having an affair with."

"That's a lie!" I said.

"I know it is. She's trying to smoke you out by saying things so outrageous that you have no choice but to confront her and answer her questions. Don't let her get away with it."

"Anything else?" I asked.

"Not really. You might have to do something to stop her before she starts calling everyone you know. She's on the warpath."

I suspected that Cheryl might have told Bill even more lies, but I didn't feel like dragging them out of him. I was outraged enough already. I threw my napkin on the TV tray and stared out the window. "I should never have come back here."

"I tried to tell you that," he said. "Almost everybody you know is going off the deep end in one way or another, including me."

"You're not so bad off."

"Yes, I am. The only reason you like being my friend is that my life is more messed up than yours."

I laughed and shook my head. "You know that's not true."

"Yes, it is," he insisted. "It comforts you to think, 'Well, my life may be falling apart, but at least I'm not as big a loser as Bill.' "

"You're just feeling sorry for yourself because that woman turned you down for a date. How many times have we had this same conversation? All you need to do is get involved in church again, find a good woman, get married, and settle down. Simple."

"Oh, right. Nothing to it. I've already dated all the available women at church. That's one reason I can't go there as much as I used to."

"Well, your backsliding days are over," I said. "You're going to have perfect attendance this summer if I have to drag you there."

"Just don't try to fix me up with anybody."

"What kind of woman are you looking for, anyway?"

Bill looked toward the ceiling, thought for a moment, and replied, "I want a woman who, when you stare into the depths of her soul, stares right back."

"Would you care to explain that?" I asked.

"No. When I find her, you'll know what I mean."

———————

Mom called me at the magazine the following Monday and told me to come to the hospital right away. Dad had had another heart attack.

The strong, imposing father I had known all my life was replaced that day by an old man whose skin was pale gray, whose hair was thinly scattered over his head, whose eyes were dull and helpless. Oxygen tubes extended from his nose, around his ears, and up to the wall. Five other cords extended from his chest to a nearby monitor. A blood pressure cuff on one arm was also attached to the monitor, and two IVs were attached to his other arm. All the cords and tubes extending out of him only added to the impression of his weakness, as if he owed what little life he did exhibit to the workings of these contraptions.

This second heart attack should have come as no surprise. The day before, Dad had stayed home from church because he didn't feel well. It was the first time in ten years or more that Dad had missed church because of illness. I thought the real reason he was skipping church was to avoid having to talk to people about the troubles that enveloped him—Robin, Bobby, and the Premiere Financial scandal.

It had fallen to me a few days earlier to tell Dad that Bobby was the father of Robin's baby. He took the news much more stoically than I had expected. He nodded and looked away and asked no questions. Maybe he had already figured it out by then. Maybe he was numb to disappointment. Maybe I was simply not the person he wanted to discuss it with, since Bobby had been a point of contention between us.

I told him while the two of us were alone in the family room, he in his recliner and I across from him on the sofa. The room was silent, and it remained so for an uncomfortable fifteen minutes after I was finished. He stared out the window, and I kept my eyes on the coffee table.

Finally he said, "I don't see how I can face people at church. This whole thing is just too humiliating."

"They're your friends, and they have been for decades. They'll support you."

"They'll blame me," he said. "I did more than anybody to bring Bobby into the church, and he made fools of us all. He not only got my money, but he stole my daughter too. He did it right under my nose, and I didn't know it was happening. They will blame me for that. I can't even take care of my own family."

"They won't see it that way. What you did for Bobby was with the best of intentions," I said, surprising myself with my own sympathetic words toward how he had treated Bobby. "The church people are your family, and they'll stick by you in this. What good is it to have a church family if you can't go to them when things are bad?"

"There are limits," he said and refused to talk about it anymore. That was Saturday, and two days later he had a heart attack. During the day he looked bad, but by that evening he had stabilized.

That night I stayed with him until he went to sleep. When I drove home, my headlights flashed on something as I turned into the driveway. In our front yard stood a Realtor's sign that read *For Sale.*

JACK

$\mathcal{I}$ thought of the strangest things while lying there in that hospital bed. I was too groggy and hurting too bad to want to talk to anybody, but my mind kept wandering back the way it's been doing lately, and I kept thinking about right after I got back from Korea in the fifties. I don't know why that should come to mind except these hospitals kind of remind me of the military, with these regimented little meals on trays, the sound of heels on tile floors, and the discomfort of waking up in a bed that is not your own. When I got home from Korea in October of 1957, Indianapolis looked so beautiful to me after that wasteland that I literally thought I was going to cry the first night I went running around town with my friends. I had spent two years in Korea. We got there once the fighting had stopped and the thirty-eighth parallel had been designated the dividing line between north and south.

The war had taken such an immense toll on the place that Seoul was nothing but a bunch of bombed-out buildings. It was like going back in time. The road from Seoul to our camp was thirty miles of either choking dust or almost impenetrable mud, depending on the weather. The only electricity in practically the whole country was what we could get from the G.I. generators.

Korea could not have come at a worse time in my life. Before I got drafted, I was having the best time ever. I had gotten on at Maximilian Webber and was making good money. I had lots of friends. I had a '51 Ford two-door sedan to get around in. My friends and I took trips to

Florida and Myrtle Beach and weekend trips camping and fishing. I started dating a girl named Sheila, and it seemed like everything in my life had started to flow in a direction that finally made sense. The fifties had to be the greatest time in the history of this country to be a young person. I've never been one to get nostalgic about the past—I think it's usually best to just deal with what's in front of you now and make the best of it. But there was something special about that decade. There was an optimism present, a sense of fun and possibility. But then in October of '55 I got drafted. I had seen it coming. I had been checking with the local draft board every month or so to see how close I was getting to it. It was inevitable. I knew I was having too good a life for it to last. It's almost as if there's a law of nature that says you can only enjoy yourself for so long, and then there's a requirement that you be slammed back down to earth.

I stored my Ford in my parents' garage and headed off to basic training in Fort Leonard Wood, Missouri. Then I was stationed in Fort Monroe, Virginia, for a time, and finally they sent me to Seattle. From there I shipped out to Korea. Every day was a test of endurance, another slash on the calendar until my sentence would expire and I could go back to the real world.

There was only one thing that gave me any hope, even though this may sound strange to a lot of people. In the spring of '57 one of the guys in the barracks got a brochure advertising the new 1957 Chevrolet. People don't seem to care much nowadays when new cars are introduced, but back then people paid attention. This brochure had a color photo of a black 1957 two-door Bel Air hardtop. It was the most magnificent car I had ever seen. That guy got such a kick out of how much I loved the car that he gave me the brochure. I must have looked at it ten thousand times in those months before I got home. I had only two books by my bed—the Bible and that brochure. Many nights while I was walking out alone on guard duty, I would imagine myself in that '57 Chevy, driving around town with my friends and having as good a time as I did before Korea.

The brochure with its picture of that gorgeous car is what kept gripping my mind those first several hours in the hospital after my heart attack. One time I even found myself reaching to the side of my bed to find it, since that's where I had kept it in Korea, but the nurse pushed my hand back and told me I was messing up one of her tubes. When I came home from Korea in late October 1957, my one thought was to take the advertisement to the dealership and tell them I wanted to buy that hardtop. I was as nervous as a teenager on his first date when

I set out on my quest for that car. I went to every Chevrolet dealer within a hundred miles of Indianapolis. The dealers then were not as connected with each other as they are now, so they weren't aware of each other's inventory. I had to check out each place one at a time. That car was simply not to be found that late in the year. I found a few '57 Chevys, but they weren't the black two-door Bel Air hardtop in the picture. The '58s had come out in September, and the car I wanted had disappeared.

I have never owned a '57 Chevy. I have a plastic phone that's in the shape of one, and I have a radio that looks like the grille of one, and I guess that will have to do.

Things were not the same once I got back from Korea. A lot of my friends had scattered or gotten married, and the good times seemed harder to come by. I went back to my job at Maximilian Webber and finally gave up trying to find my dream car. I settled for a '58 Chevy Impala two-door hardtop with a blue bottom and a white top. It had a 348–cubic-inch displacement engine with an automatic transmission. It was a beautiful car to look at, but it was a piece of junk. On the way home from the dealer I made a stop, and when I started off again the transmission would not shift out of low range. I returned to the dealer, and it seemed like almost every week after that for the next two years I was taking that car back for something.

I don't know why all these things should come back to me now while I'm in this hospital bed dying. I do know I'm dying, by the way, despite all the reassurances they keep giving me. It's the strangest feeling, knowing my life is slipping away, just like David, just like my money, my daughter, and that beautiful black Chevy.

CHRIS

"I could just haul off and slap her," I heard Aunt Dayle tell my mother as I walked into the waiting room at the end of Dad's second day in the hospital. It was comforting to see her and Ray in the otherwise sterile room with its plastic furniture and its blaring television bolted to the wall. The chair Ray sat on was too small for him, his hips straining at the armrests. He had grown so large over the years that he now looked uncomfortable in anything but the enormous recliner in his own living room. He sat close to the TV, while Mom and Aunt Dayle stood in the center of the room, intent on excoriating whomever it was that Aunt Dayle said she could haul off and slap.

Ray waved at me as I walked in, and Dayle turned toward me and said, "It's your aunt Shirley again. You might as well know. She's refusing to come up to the hospital to see your dad, and your mom's upset about it."

"Did you talk to Shirley?" I asked Dayle.

"Yes, I called around to all the family to let them know about your dad, and I told Shirley she better get up here and see him. None of us know the future. We shouldn't be doing spiteful things we'll regret. But Shirley said with all this tension over Grandma and Grandpa and your mom, she didn't feel it would be appropriate to come."

"I don't care if she comes or not," Mom said, her flushed expression contradicting her words. "Things aren't ever gonna be the same. Too much has happened. Too many things have been said."

"Nonsense," Aunt Dayle protested. "Not enough has been said. That's the problem in this family. People want to walk off and be hurt and pout instead of facing each other and settling it. I told Shirley not to give me any guff about what she thought was appropriate. Her sister's husband is in the hospital, and she just better get over it and come."

"She's trying to spite me," Mom said. "Nothing new in that."

Aunt Dayle put her arm around Mom's shoulder and said, "Well, don't you worry, honey. I'm gonna knock some sense into this family if it's the last thing I do. Chris, the moment your dad is out of this hospital and well enough, I'm planning a family picnic, and everybody in this family is going to be required to be there. No excuses. No baloney."

This was Aunt Dayle in her glory, playing agitator and conciliator at the same time. Shirley's absence could have been explained away in a number of ways. Not *all* the relatives were able to visit Dad at the hospital, and for no one else was the failure to appear seen as a sign of disloyalty. But Dayle zoomed in on the conflict, and once its ugliness was bared, she immediately threw her energy into forcing reconciliation.

Mom said, "I'm not sure you can get people to come to family picnics anymore, Dayle. This family's not what it used to be. Everybody's interested in their individual lives now. They don't care much about family."

"I won't let that stand," Dayle said. Then she turned to me and demanded, "Now, what is this about your sister? Does your whole family have to go haywire all at the same time?"

"We still haven't heard from her to tell her about Dad," I said.

"Well, I could wring her neck too," Dayle said. "I've never seen such a family. I hate to say it, but I'm almost glad Grandma and Grandpa are too out of it to be completely aware of what's going on. They'd have a fit."

"They're not coming up to the hospital?" I asked.

"No," she said. "Right now they're barely able to walk to the bathroom. They'd never make it all the way up here. They're a mess. Between them, your dad, your sister, Shirley, and those clowns I raised, I can hardly keep up. My nerves are so ragged I'd like to crawl into one of those hospital beds myself and lay there for a week or so."

"Yeah," I said, "and Uncle Ray looks pretty stressed out too."

Ray sat sprawled in the chair, one hand lazily propping up his head, his eyes half closed. Without moving his body, he glanced up at me, smiled, and let out a wheezing laugh, which extinguished itself a few seconds later.

"He never worries about nothin'," Dayle said. "He lets me worry about everything. He just wants to know when it's time for dinner."

Ray raised himself up in his chair about an inch and said, "You can't control the way people live. That's what she's never understood. People are gonna do what they want, so there's no use getting yourself all riled up over it."

Dayle shot back, "If I took your attitude, we'd be even worse off than we are now."

Ray shook his head and turned back to *Wheel of Fortune* on television.

Despite the gloomy assessment of the state of our family, the hospital was full of relatives the next couple days. Aunt Dayle had done her job well and had told just about everybody about Dad's condition. Mom's other siblings, Jackie and Roger, came with their families, and so did Dad's sister Betty. Dayle's sons, Jim and Jeff, came, and Jeff brought his wife, Shelly. Grandma and Grandpa talked to Dad on the phone, sympathizing with him one minute and the next minute trying to convince him their aches and pains were worse than his heart attack.

Pastor Jennings came twice, and so did Bill. One time when I came out of Dad's room, I saw Pastor and Bill talking to each other in the waiting room. I was happy to see it, because I knew Bill had been on the fringes at church lately, and I hoped Pastor could help draw him back in. When I saw the pastor alone later that evening, I asked him how their discussion had gone.

"Bill is the new coach of the teens' softball team," he said.

"What?"

"Softball coach," Pastor Jennings said matter-of-factly. "He's a great softball player. Don't you remember that?"

"I know he's a good player, but I'm amazed you could talk him into doing it. I can barely get him to come with me on Sunday mornings."

"It's like I've been trying to tell you, Chris. None of us has the luxury of being able to sit on the sidelines. If Bill feels left out, the worst thing he can do is sit and wait for the church to come and embrace him. He has to jump right back in there and embrace them first. Bill doesn't need permission to come back. He's one of us. Dropping out should not be an option."

"You're determined to reconcile everybody, aren't you, Pastor?"

"What else is a pastor for but to reconcile people to God and to each other? What else is there? It's your dad and Jim White I want to work on next. I still think they're the keys to bringing healing to the church. I've been trying to get Jim to come up here, but so far he won't do it. He doesn't even show up at church anymore, and he's ashamed and afraid to face your dad. I wish you'd help me get them back together."

"Dad has been pretty silent about the whole thing," I said. "I'm not sure if he'd talk to him or not. What's happening with Jim right now, anyway?"

"He's probably going to be indicted by the U.S. Attorney's office, and he'll probably go on trial and go to jail. And he'll face several other lawsuits and be ruined financially. But if he goes to jail, I want him to go with the whole church surrounding him with love and support, ready to come and meet him when he gets out."

JACK

Last night I woke up sweaty with fear—something I haven't done since I was a child—thinking and worrying about the money I've been swindled out of. I was adding up the losses, sorting out the bad investments from the good, worrying about whether Helen will be able to make it if I die. What on earth have I done to her? Were *all* the investments scams? Can anything be saved? My brain spun out of my control, a blizzard of numbers flying in red splotches across my closed eyes.

Sometimes I get so mad at Bobby and Jim White I think I could kill them. Pastor Jennings asked me if I wanted him to set up a meeting with Jim, but I told him not right now because I'd probably have another heart attack right on the spot. Pastor's worried about Jim feeling too ashamed to ever come back to church. I'm going to have to forgive him eventually, I suppose, but right now I sure don't feel like talking to him or socializing with him or trusting him ever again. And I told Pastor I feel fully justified in doing everything in my power to get my money back. Pastor says we can't become a church of people who pass each other silently in the corridors and pretend nothing's wrong. But right now that's the least of my problems.

The money is not the only thing disturbing my sleep. Sometimes I wake in a state of half awareness, half nightmare about Robin. I imagine that she has not run off with Bobby, but that he has kidnapped her, that he is holding her hostage in a dark warehouse and I need to rescue her. In the nightmare I hear her cries from the darkened interior of the building, but my legs will not move. I am some distance away, in sight of the doorway, but I am trapped in a leaden body. One night I actually woke up from this nightmare with a horrible, strained groan, as if the breath were being crushed out of me, a sound I didn't realize at first was coming from me. The nurse came in and told me to lie still, I was pulling out the tubes.

Those are the kind of nights I've been having in this hospital, never sleeping more than a couple hours at a time. But sometimes my thoughts drift in calmer patterns, and I actually forget what year it is, and I float around in incidents long ago forgotten. I woke up last night with the strangest pains all over my body. In my confusion, I thought the tightness and aching in my arms must be from all the painting I had been doing to get the kitchen and living room ready to move into. That was impossible, of course, since I did that painting almost thirty years ago, but in my mind it might as well have happened yesterday. It was our first house, and Helen was pregnant with David, and we didn't have much time to get in there and get settled before she had him. The people we bought the house from just would not move out. They kept wanting another week, then three or four more days, just one excuse after another. It was getting down to a couple weeks before her due date, so finally I told them, "You have to go. You just have to move out."

Well, they did, but they left a big mess. Ketchup and syrup all over the kitchen cabinets, the walls all marked up, the bathrooms a mess. It was too filthy to move into, so we started cleaning it right up. Every day after work I went to the house and painted, painted, painted. Finally I got it done, but then the day before we were to move in, the water heater blew up when nobody was there. Those people had done something to it—I never did figure out what exactly—but there was too much pressure in it. The pop-off valve that was supposed to release the pressure blew off, and the hose that was supposed to drain the water away melted, and water poured out all over the floor. The steam filled the house and took that new paint right off the walls. When I walked in those rooms, the walls were a blobby mess, like the paint had just been flung up there instead of painted with my hundreds of careful strokes. I sat down on the floor, achy and tired to death, but then I got right up and started working again.

For three nights I got almost no sleep. I painted those rooms like a maniac. Finally we moved in, and a week later, David was born. I was sore and tired but thrilled to see my son come into the world. I had stamina for such things then. Helen and I were so excited by what was happening in our lives that we were able to absorb the disappointments and press on.

Now, three decades later, I wake up in a hospital feeling the same aches, tumbling into the same worries: Will we get the house ready before the baby comes, have we gotten in over our heads with this house, how can we possibly figure out how to raise this baby. Those days look fairly easy to me now, but only because I know how they turned out, how we got through them. I'm tempted to cling to the hope that someday I'll look back on this catastrophe and say it wasn't so bad after all, that the Lord brought us through once again as He has always done. But I'm not so sure. Thirty years ago I had stamina and inexhaustible energy. What keeps me going now? I can't even name it.

CHRIS

$\mathscr{I}$ talked with Dad mostly late at night after the other visitors had left. Someone usually took Mom home, and I stayed a few more hours until Dad was asleep. Once we were alone, he was more relaxed and more reflective than I've ever seen him. I told him not to feel any pressure to stay awake or to talk if he didn't want to. Sometimes he would drift off to sleep, then wake up and start talking in the midst of some imagined conversation or dream, and I'd have to catch up with him.

". . . reminds me of old Pete Cole," he said on his second night in the hospital after both of us had sat silently and dozed off awhile.

"What?" I asked.

"Old Pete Cole. He taught me everything I ever knew about cars. He was almost magical with them. Could stand next to a car and listen to it run and tell you exactly what was wrong with it. I used to go down to his garage and help him work for hours on end."

"I've never heard you mention him."

"Sure I have. He used to tune up my car right after I graduated from high school. Pete worked out of the garage at his house. He'd set a time when you were to bring the car in and a time when you were to pick it up, and he expected you to stick to it. There was no nonsense with that guy. I had a 1946 Chevy two-door sedan master deluxe. It looked good. Had two-tone blue paint. I added an in-dash push-button radio, an in-dash windup clock, chrome wheel trim rings, and white sidewall tires. Old Pete looked like a surgeon when he worked on it.

There was no part on a Chevrolet automobile that Pete didn't know.

"I always liked to watch Pete while he worked. He had this routine he followed. When he tuned the engine, he carried over a tray of tools, and he never had to go back to the bench to get more. He had a tray of tools he took underneath the car when he adjusted the clutch. Same thing with the brakes and every other part of the car. I never once saw him go back to the bench to get a tool he had forgotten. I started going over there even when I didn't need my car repaired, washing parts for him and helping him do simple repairs—just to learn from him. He was happy to teach me. I wish you could have met him. There aren't many guys around like that anymore."

Dad pulled himself up in his bed. He was fully awake now.

"You were always disappointed that I never learned much about restoring cars, weren't you, Dad?" I said.

"I don't know, Chris." He thought for a moment and added, "The world I grew up in was different from today. It was a factory world. You learned some skills, you got a job in the factory, you worked your way up, and you stayed there your whole life. I guess I expected you and David would follow the same path—it was the only one I knew.

"You and David were so different from each other. It's not that I didn't think you had good qualities. I just never thought you cared much about my opinion. I never thought you wanted to learn anything from me. David was more like me. He wanted to be like me. He wanted my advice and needed my approval. You never did. You were always on your own. Even when we were together, it seemed you were still in your own little world."

"... always on your own. Even when we were together ..." I was amazed to hear him say it, though I had always felt the same way. When we were growing up, I remember him taking David and me to car shows on Saturdays. Even though the three of us were together, it always felt to me that it was David and Dad together, and I was just tagging along.

"I tried to do right by you, send you to college—let you do things your own way, which was the main thing you wanted. I have to admit I didn't always think what you were doing made much sense. Just playing around in college and spending a lot of money was what it sometimes looked like. But I guess it's turning out all right, isn't it? Mr. College Professor. Magazine writer. But you sure seemed to get there the hard way."

"What do you mean?"

"When you were growing up, all the way till you were in college, you had a different passion every week. I was afraid you were never going to settle on anything. One week it was painting, then it was football, then it was singing, then you wanted to travel on some mission trip to South America. We never knew what you wanted. Just when we had spent a bundle buying you equipment to play football—shoulder pads and helmet and everything—you decided you were really interested in tennis or something else. I was afraid you'd end up like a lot of guys I've seen, kind of wandering around their whole life from one thing to another."

"But I was just a kid," I said, defending myself. "Kids are supposed to try things out, discover what their real interests are. A thirteen-year-old doesn't decide to settle down into a factory job for the rest of his life."

"I know," he agreed, nodding. "But look at David. It was simple with him. First it was sports, then it was cars, then it was girls. Then it was girls and cars together. End of story. But you were all over the map."

I laughed and said, "Dad, you know I never could have been like David even if I had tried."

"Oh, I know. I'm not criticizing you for that. Like I said, you turned out all right in the end. And now you're the only one here, the only one I've got left."

"No," I said. "You've got Robin too."

"If she ever comes back."

"She will. I know she'd be here right now if we could have gotten ahold of her."

Dad sighed, then took a drink from the cup on his nightstand. By his impatient shifting around in the bed, I could tell he was trying to tamp down his anger before it took control of him.

"How could she do this, Chris?" he fumed. "Throw her life away for this guy? Not that she's the only one at fault. How could I have brought him into our lives? Let him near my daughter. Invest money with him. Let him destroy in a few months what it took me years to build. I tell you, Chris, this may sound morbid, but I'm glad to be lying here right now. I deserve the punishment. If it's over for me, I have only myself to blame."

"Don't talk that way!" I insisted. "You had no way of knowing what Bobby was like. He'll be caught and convicted. Robin will come back. You've got Mom and Robin and me still counting on you. You've got to pull through for us. We'll work these things out one at a time."

"I thought I was doing all the right things," Dad said, "but I've made such a mess of it."

On Dad's last night in the hospital, I went out of his room not long after ten o'clock planning to go home, but what I saw in the hallway startled and disoriented me. There stood Beth and Cheryl, not three feet away from each other! I had always dreaded these two women getting together, comparing notes, swapping stories.

I must have stared at them for an uncomfortably long time as I stood in that waiting room doorway, and with a frightening expression, because they stared back at me with equally stunned looks of apprehension. Cheryl was dressed in a blue business suit, and her short, cropped hair, heavy makeup, and hard expression gave me the impression of a lawyer ready to rip someone to pieces on the witness stand. Beth looked nothing like that. She was dressed in shorts, sandals, and a light summer top, with her hair held back in a headband. As I walked toward her, though, I saw that her face was a little flushed and her neck had that red-and-white blotchy look I had long associated with anger or hurt.

"What are you two doing here?" I asked, without tact. After several days of working all day and spending each night at the hospital, I was dead tired and didn't have anything near the emotional control that it would have taken to get through this encounter gracefully.

Cheryl answered. "We came to see your father. What else?"

"You came together?"

"No," she answered with a sneer. "We both just happened to pick the same night. Lucky timing, I guess."

"He's getting ready to go to sleep, so if you want to see him . . ."

"I'll drop this little gift off and leave," said Beth, handing me what felt like a book wrapped in gift paper. She did not smile, and her lips were tightly pressed together—another familiar sign of anger.

Cheryl smiled stiffly and looked strangely triumphant and superior as she watched Beth hand me the gift and leave. She said, "Well, I think I'll just stick my head in your dad's door and tell him good night."

I ignored her and ran down the hall after Beth. I caught her at the elevator, but she didn't say a word as we rode down to the first floor, with a few strangers, raced through several corridors, and ended up in the slightly more comfortable semidarkness of the parking lot.

"I didn't mean to chase you away before you saw him," I said.

"Oh, it's not that," she said. "I'm sorry I came so late, but I had a meeting. I had no idea I'd run into Cheryl."

"What did she say?"

"Nothing. Why did you follow me out here?"

"Please, Beth. Don't be ridiculous. You're about to bust wide open because of what happened in there between you and Cheryl, so why don't you tell me? I'd like to get your version before I hear it from her."

"What kind of game are you two playing?"

"I'm not part of any game of hers, believe me. She's tormenting me as much as she is you."

"Is it true that you've been seeing her?" asked Beth.

"*Seeing* her?" I asked.

"Yes. Dating or whatever. You know what seeing means."

"No! Are you out of your mind? I've been doing everything in my power to avoid her."

"Oh, really? She told me you went to Denny's together to talk things over and—"

"We did, but—"

"And that you talk on the phone all the time."

"No," I said contemptuously. "She's called to bug me several times, but I try to get rid of her. I think there's something wrong with her! She practically kidnapped me that time we went to Denny's. She showed up at work unexpectedly. It's the same old story. She wanted to dig up some dirt on David. Don't be upset over that. I would never—"

"That's not what I'm upset over," insisted Beth. "You can go out or not go out with whoever you want."

"That's true," I said, although oddly enough that had not occurred to me until Beth mentioned it.

"It's what she's implying about me that bothers me."

"What?"

"She thinks David and I were having some kind of liaison before he died. She made it sound like you told her that."

"That's a lie! She's doing it to provoke me. She thinks if she spreads false stories to enough people, then I'll tell her all the dirt about David."

"Why don't you tell her what you know about him?" asked Beth. "She was engaged to him. She has a right to know."

"We've been through this before," I said. Ever since David's death, Beth has believed I should ease Cheryl's mind by revealing what I know about him. I refused to do this, and it added greatly to the strain between Beth and me in our final weeks together.

"I know we've been through it," said Beth. "But the longer you put off dealing honestly with her, the worse she'll get. You're carrying your loyalty to him too far, Chris. He's been gone for two years now. Consider the living. It's bizarre, like one of those Mafia movies where only blood ties matter, and you'll do anything to defend your brother no matter what he's done. Well, Cheryl is pretty tenacious too, and she will not stop until she gets what she wants, no matter how many people she hurts."

I knew she was right, and it outraged me. I knew now that I was not going to get off easy this summer, that I was not going to be able to glide alongside these people without being sucked into their obsessions, their questions, their accusations. How I longed for California, where I could get away with revealing only those parts of the past that I felt comfortable with. Here, in Indiana, no one seemed to share my preference for treating the past with delicacy and respect. Dad was the only other person I knew who wanted to leave the events of that time alone, but even he, as he came closer to what he thought to be his impending death, began dipping into his memories more often than ever before. The prospect of all these people calling me to account for what happened those weeks before David died made me want to pack my bags that very night and fly away.

"You can't exempt yourself," I could hear the pastor saying. *"Your vacation is over."*

I was not going to flee, but neither was I going to sit back without comment while Cheryl spewed her poison to everyone I knew. If avoiding her wouldn't work, I would have to devise a new tactic.

"I'll find a way to deal with Cheryl."

"Please do," said Beth, getting into her car. "I don't want her spreading lies about me to everybody we know."

She drove off and left me alone in the parking lot, bewildered. Now I would have to go back upstairs and face another fight with Cheryl. As I stood there figuring out what I would say to her, my whole body felt heavier and heavier with exhaustion. I was in no condition to even look at Cheryl, let alone argue with her. Instead, I hurried over to my car, avoiding all the hospital doors that Cheryl might emerge from, and drove away.

ROBIN

$\mathcal{B}$obby and I spent several days wandering around Chicago like
tourists. He insisted that we get dressed up every day and look our best.
He wore a new sport coat each day, with one of his expensive button-
down dress shirts underneath. He looked like a young millionaire out
on the town deciding where to spend his money. He stopped into a
barber shop on the second afternoon to get his hair trimmed. For some
reason it was important to him that we looked just a certain way. I don't
know why, since all we did was walk around a city where no one knew
us, drifting through stores and museums where most people were wearing shorts and T-shirts. But I was happy to play along. Each day he
chose the dress he wanted to see me in, and I wore it for him.

We went shopping again that second day, and Bobby insisted that
we buy a few more things, even though I didn't want to. I was worried
about having to eventually pay for all this stuff, but he acted really mad
when I said so. There was a perfume in Nieman Marcus he wanted me
to buy, but it cost over sixty dollars, and even though I liked it, I really
didn't need it. I said, "We've bought enough stuff already. I can do without the perfume. It costs too much."

"Am I asking you to pay for it?" he yelled, and I mean yelled, right
in front of the lady at the counter and all the other people shopping
around us. I was so embarrassed.

"You don't have to yell," I whispered, plopping the perfume back
down on the counter and walking away.

Big mistake. He came yelling after me and bellowed, "Why do you have to ruin everything by always talking about how much it costs? Who cares what it costs? You're not paying for it!"

"Quit screaming!" I begged.

"Why can't you let us enjoy ourselves for one minute without worrying about some tragedy that's going to result from it?"

I stopped and turned to him. "Just because I don't want to buy a bottle of overpriced perfume—"

"That's not the point! The point is you can't find pleasure in things the way they are *right now* without letting guilt and worry control you."

There were plenty of reasons I could have given for my worry, but what good would it have done? When Bobby gets all insistent and indignant like that, it only makes it worse if you try to argue with him. It's like you have to let that personality pass, and then when the good Bobby comes back, maybe you can reason with him. I don't think I'm all that much of a worrier. I know how to enjoy the moment and all that, but it happens to be a fact that you do have to pay for things. Eventually.

I said to him, "I'm about to collapse. I really need to go somewhere and sit down."

"Yeah, yeah," he said. Mr. Sympathy.

We found this coffee shop nearby, and I had a vanilla latté and a biscuit and felt a little better. Bobby pouted awhile and stayed quiet, but then his espresso apparently kicked in and he started talking nice again. He didn't apologize, though. He never does.

The day was pretty good again after the Nieman Marcus incident. We stayed away from shopping that afternoon and instead went to the planetarium. The show was so relaxing in the dome-ceilinged room with the lights turned off, making it look like the night sky. The stars swirled around up there on the ceiling, and a deep-voiced narrator explained what it was all about. Bobby kept his arm around me, and it was really romantic and fun, not all boring and scientific like I expected.

Bobby wanted to go to a fancy restaurant that night, but I had this incredible craving for pizza, so he took me to Gino's. It was more my kind of place—crowded, noisy, fun. In all the booths people had carved their names in the wood. They let you do it—it's kind of a tradition there. So I carved $B + R$ in our booth while we waited for the pizza, which was a thick slab of dough with cheese and green peppers and onions and black olives that made you feel like you weighed about thirty extra pounds afterward. We demolished that pizza without worrying about how fat it would make us. We were into not worrying about things that we normally would have cared about.

Bobby was in a good mood most of the night, talkative, telling me about the business trips he used to take to this city, the fancy hotels he stayed in, the friends he used to have here. Only after dinner did Bobby turn inward again, getting that guarded, faraway look that tells me he's thinking about something and doesn't want to be bothered. I've gotten good at recognizing that look and learned to leave him alone then, because if I say a word to him, no matter how innocent, he bites my head off or gives me some sarcastic answer that makes me feel like a moron. We sat there in Gino's for the last half hour saying nothing at all. David stared at the carvings in the booth. I sat slumped over a bit, exhausted and a little sick, wondering what on earth I was doing there.

A few mornings later Bobby left me alone at the motel. I intended to sleep in, since there was no reason in the world for us to get up early. We had nothing to do. "Don't get up," he told me when he started roaming around the room at some ridiculous hour—it must have been seven or eight o'clock. So I stayed put. He showered and dressed, and as he opened the door to leave the room, he said, "I'll be back after while."

I roused myself up to ask him where he was going and how long he'd be, but by the time I was with it enough to say anything, the door was shut.

At first I didn't mind him being gone. All the walking around the city the previous few days, along with the terrible exhaustion this pregnancy has brought on, made me want to lay there and not get up at all. Also, I felt a little nauseous. I didn't mind a few minutes alone to be able to think without having to tune myself in to Bobby's every little mood swing to know when I could say something and when I couldn't. I laid in bed for a couple more hours and tried to be happy. It wasn't easy. The only way I could do it was to pretend, kind of half sleeping and half awake, that I wasn't really here. Or, since I was here, pretend that this wasn't just a stupid trip that made no sense and that it couldn't change the fact that I was having a baby, that Bobby was a mess, and my family must be thinking I have lost my mind or worse.

Instead, I pretended that Bobby and I had just gotten married and this was our honeymoon. He loved me so much, and when we got home, our biggest problem would be getting all the gifts unwrapped that were probably covering our whole apartment—the sofa and chairs and floors, even our bed. In my imagination we had rented the apartment a few weeks before we got married and hadn't had time to set it up the way we wanted. But there would be plenty of time to do that once we got back from the honeymoon, and maybe one day Mom would come over and help me arrange things while Bobby was at work. In the meantime, I should enjoy the honeymoon, and if Bobby wanted to buy me all kinds of clothes and jewelry and perfume, I shouldn't worry about it. He must have plenty of money to cover it. Besides, think of all those envelopes filled with money we got at the wedding! I had no idea we would get so much!

This is the kind of fantasy I entertained myself with in that motel room in that grungy neighborhood on the outskirts of Chicago. Eventually I decided Bobby would be back pretty soon, and he'd be in a better mood if he found me dressed and ready to go, assuming he had thought of somewhere we should go. So I got up and got dressed, felt sick and had a headache, and was just as tired as if I'd never gone to bed. That's why when noon came and Bobby still wasn't back and hadn't called, and I had nothing to do but sit at the window and stare out at the parking lot waiting for him, I decided to just let myself go ahead and have a good cry.

I cried with my eyes focused on the parking lot, because if there's one thing Bobby can't stand, it's for me to cry when he doesn't think there's anything wrong. It frustrates him. He thinks I'm crying just to manipulate him or that I'm hiding something from him. He wants to know immediately why I'm crying and what I expect him to do about it. Nobody's allowed to just cry about things in general. Not around him. So I decided if his car pulled up, I would run in the bathroom real fast and fix my face so he wouldn't see the tears.

But he didn't come. He didn't come at twelve-thirty, and he didn't make it there by one o'clock. I turned on the TV and watched Sally Jessy Raphael, thinking surely Bobby would come back or call before her show was over. She had a really stupid show that day. It was one of those makeover shows, where they take these geeks with ugly clothes and ridiculous hairdos and try to make them look like normal human beings. At the beginning of the show you see how pathetic they look, and you hear their sad story. Then at the end they come out with their new look, and the audience screams and cheers like they're Cinderella or something. This new look is supposed to change their life, but half the time the makeover doesn't really help them that much—you can still see the loser they really are just underneath the surface. Besides, you know that as soon as they get home, they're going to revert back to their old way of dressing and doing their hair. It's not like Sally's going to be there to give them a makeover every day. So what's the point? Those makeover shows depress me for some reason. I must have looked at my watch about a million times during the program, wondering where Bobby was, but he didn't show.

I was starving to death, so I decided that instead of sitting there getting madder and madder at him for not coming back or calling or letting me know where he was going in the first place, I'd go out on my own and get something to eat. There wasn't much around this dumpy neighborhood, but I managed to find a Burger King a couple blocks away. Even though I'm a vegetarian ninety percent of the time, that day I broke down and ordered a cheeseburger, fries, and a Coke because—well, there wasn't that much to choose from, and I was incredibly hungry, and with all the turmoil in my life, what difference could one little cheeseburger really make?

Up to that point I had mainly felt anger with Bobby for leaving me stranded there all day without any word, but as I sat in that plastic booth at Burger King, my anger gave way to fear. What if Bobby wasn't coming back at all? What if his money had run out and he was too embarrassed or too cowardly to tell me? What if this was his way of getting rid of me and running off to solve his own problems? I tried to tell myself that couldn't be it. He wouldn't dump me without a word. It was too cruel, even for Bobby, who definitely had a cruel streak in him. Besides, he loved me. Hadn't he invited me on this trip? If he had intended to dump me, he could have done it in Indianapolis and saved himself a lot of trouble and expense.

Still, he was the most unpredictable person I had ever known, and I had to admit it was possible I wouldn't see him again. The thought of it threw me into a panic, and I jumped up and headed back toward the motel. I hadn't left a note in the room telling him where I had gone. That was my little revenge for him not telling me where he was. But what if he came back while I was at Burger King, saw that I wasn't there, and figured I had left him to go back home, which he had been accusing me of wanting to do? Would he come looking for me, or would he leave in a huff? But no, all my stuff was still in the room, so he would have to figure I was coming back. It was all stuff he bought me, though, and that I had griped about him spending the money on, so maybe he figured I left it there to spite him!

I had to stop playing these "what if" games. They always got me in trouble. I'd start thinking "what if" this or "what if" that, and I'd work myself up into such a frenzy you'd think the "what if" had really happened. I needed to talk to somebody. Not Bobby. Someone outside the situation who could help me sort out the difference between fantasy and reality. I decided that when I got back to the motel, I would call

Beth. Just for comfort, just to have somebody to talk to. Bobby had made me promise I wouldn't call home anymore, but since he was no longer there, I guess I wasn't obligated to keep that promise, was I?

What would I say to Beth, though? That Bobby had deserted me but I was going to wait around a little longer on him? That would make her and everybody else at home even more scared and mad at me. But what if Bobby didn't come back? How would I get home? I'd have to ask Beth or Chris or somebody to come and get me. The embarrassment would kill me! How would I explain my stupidity in taking this trip in the first place? Maybe now was not the best time for a phone call home. Better to wait till I knew something.

I stepped onto the motel parking lot, and thank God, there was his car. I was suddenly in a forgiving mood. I ran up to the room ready to hug him and forget about being mad at him, but as soon as I walked in, he said in his nasty tone, "Where have you been? Why did you take off and not leave a message or something?"

"Ha!" I said. "Look who's talking. I had no idea where you were or when you were coming back."

"I told you I'd be back after while."

"And I was starving so bad I finally decided to go down and get something to eat before I fainted. Where did you go?"

Then, out of the inside pocket of his sport coat, he pulls out the biggest wad of cash I ever saw. The bills were folded over and held together with a rubber band. He juggled it up and down in his hand like a baseball.

"Where did you get that!"

"We can't use the credit cards anymore," he said.

"You got all that from credit cards?" I asked.

"We've got to use cash from now on. Credit cards can be traced."

"What do you mean?"

"They can figure out where we are by where we use our credit cards. They could trace us to this motel."

"Who could?"

"The police. The FBI. Anyone who's looking."

I couldn't tell whether he was teasing me or whether he was serious. "Who would be looking for us?" I asked.

"Your parents maybe. They might have reported you missing, and the police might be searching. Who knows? We have to be careful. I can't stress how important it is for you not to call home. I hope you haven't broken your promise about that."

"No, but—"

"Good. Don't call. Under any circumstances." His tone was so solemn and conspiratorial that I almost wanted to laugh. I felt like we were in some kind of spy movie. I expected the CIA or the Russians or somebody sinister to come swooping into the room at any minute, crashing through the windows and breaking down the doors, with Bobby karate-chopping them one by one until we could make our escape.

"We're leaving here today," he said. "No more can be accomplished in Chicago."

As if we had accomplished anything in the first place! I could hardly keep from laughing.

"Where are we going?" I asked.

"Let me surprise you."

"No, Bobby."

"All I can say is this," he began, his tone lighthearted and friendly. "We are headed to a place where we can do exactly what you wanted us to do in the first place. Make a new start. Get jobs. Get our own place. Everything is going to be fine."

CHRIS

While I was at work one day not long after Dad got out of the hospital, Mom pulled one of the big armchairs from the family room into the living room. She lugged it in there herself, a physical exertion uncharacteristic of her. Sprawled out in that recliner, she looked as though she were floating on a raft in the middle of a lake of photos.

"Looks like those pictures are multiplying," I said as I joined her in the living room that evening.

"They are!" she said. "Your aunt Dayle brought over a couple boxes of pictures from Grandma and Grandpa's house. I don't remember ever seeing them before, and I don't know who most of the people are. But Dayle said Grandma insisted that I put her pictures in some kind of order, too, while I'm at it. She's afraid otherwise they'll just be forgotten and thrown away when she dies."

I stepped carefully into the room, looking for little spaces of empty carpet the way you look for rocks to step on as you cross a shallow creek. I had come to look for some photos of the people I would be writing about in the history book for church. Several families had loaned Mom their photos for the event.

"What are those you're looking at now?" I asked, looking over her shoulder.

"Your cousin Sandy's wedding. She got married two months before David died. I remember exactly what I was worried about when these pictures were taken. Isn't it strange, to remember your worries? I was worried about what I was going to wear to your wedding and to David's wedding. I don't really like the way I look in dresses anymore, and I was debating whether I'd wear that old green dress to your weddings or whether I'd just splurge and buy two new dresses that I might look halfway decent in. I kept picturing myself walking down the aisle of the church and having everybody whispering, 'She sure looks old' or 'She sure looks fat.' "

She continued to flip silently through Sandy's photos. I didn't say anything. I didn't want to talk about my own scuttled wedding or David's either. And I didn't want to do anything that would push Mom into a crying spell, which those topics sometimes did.

"It takes my breath away to think how fast it was all snatched away from us. One minute there were two weddings to plan for, with the biggest problem being what dress I was going to wear, and the next minute there were no weddings at all. One son dead. The other son gone away. Chris, if I let myself think about it, my chest feels like it is going to cave in with anguish. How could it have happened so fast? How much more do I have to lose?"

"I don't know, Mom." I had no idea what to tell her. Fortunately, she slapped those photos back down on the floor and picked up another pile.

These were old Christmas pictures, of which there seemed to be no end. She stopped at one of me with two gifts I had treasured—a cowboy hat and a toy guitar. I was about five years old, and in the photo I wore the hat and strummed the guitar while David made faces behind me.

"You wanted to play that silly guitar day and night," Mom said. "It made me wish we had bought you a real one, so at least it would have sounded good. That one was just a toy, and it made the awfullest little pinging sound you ever heard. But you didn't seem to realize that. You would hear the songs in your head, I guess, and think they were coming out of that guitar. You'd play like you were Johnny Cash one minute and Elvis Presley the next."

"I wish we still had all those toys," I said. "You shouldn't have gotten rid of them."

"What makes you think I got rid of them?" she said. "We have boxes of stuff up in the attic."

"Our toys? That guitar and cowboy hat and things like that?"

"Sure! It's probably all up there."

"I thought you sold everything in garage sales or gave it away to the Salvation Army."

"No. Some of it we did, but a lot of things we just packed up and stored in the attic."

"Why didn't I know that? Why have I never seen any of it?"

"You never asked. There's never been a reason to bring that stuff down."

"I want to see it!" I stood up and began to maneuver my way through the photo field.

"Tonight?" my Mother exclaimed. "You can't go up there now."

"Why not?"

"It's dark up there, for one thing!"

"Well, it's dark up there during the daytime too."

"But it's so dusty up there and deadly hot. It's dangerous too. If you step off one of those boards, you'll come right down through the ceiling!"

"I know all that, but it's cooler up there at night than during the day, and if I don't do it now, I'll put it off and never bother to do it."

"Well, I don't know what the big hurry is. Most of it's been there for twenty years, and you never cared about it before."

"Some things are more important to me now," I said.

I went to the family room and told Dad, still groggy from a nap, that I was going to bring some boxes down from the attic. After giving me the same warnings Mom had about why I shouldn't do it, he told me to watch where I walked up there and said, "Why don't you just leave the boxes in the garage when you're through with them. I was going to have to clear out that attic when we moved anyway, so there's no need putting them back up there." He offered to help, but I told him I could manage.

The hole that led to our so-called "attic" was in the ceiling of the garage. The attic itself was so tight you had to remain uncomfortably bent over the whole time you were up there. It had no real floor. Dad had simply placed several boards between the beams to provide a place for the boxes and to keep anyone from falling into the insulation and through the ceiling of the kitchen below. The humid Indiana summer air in that unventilated chamber was as suffocating as they had told me. Sweat dripped off my hair and into my eyes as I brought down one box after another—first the Christmas boxes, then boxes of old clothes, and then financial records. Finally I reached the ones I was interested in.

Mom came out into the garage to see what I had found, and each time I opened one of the boxes she squealed with delight. The first toy I pulled out had been one of my favorites—a red metal Tonka pickup truck. It was just a couple feet long, but it had been sturdy enough to sit on and ride down the driveway, which David and I preferred to do. I pulled out a few more Tonka trucks, including a long black oil tanker that I had loved, and then at the bottom of the box was a plastic wheel-shaped container for the little Hot Wheels cars that had run on the endless orange race tracks we had set up in the living room and in the backyard. Mom sucked in her breath with expectation as I opened the Hot Wheels container. You'd think I was opening a chest filled with jewels.

Another box held my precious cylinder of Lincoln logs, with the red trusses for the roofs and the green roof shingles. Mixed in with the logs were the little red and yellow plastic cowboys and Indians that had fit in and around the log cabins and forts and corrals I used to build. There was a chess set on which David had taught me how to play the game, a couple G.I. Joes with ripped shirts and a missing boot, and a whole big box of Robin's games and dolls and books. One box contained games that David and I had played with and then abandoned, like Bash and Barrel of Monkeys and Operation and Battleship. David and I had shared many of our toys, and so many of them had started out as his and then been passed down to me that I wasn't always sure whose things I was looking at. Mom didn't always know either.

Earlier in the summer Dad had told me that as a kid I was always changing my mind about what I was interested in, and I saw plenty of evidence of that in those boxes. There was a football uniform, a baseball uniform, baseball cards, a trumpet, a couple of unfinished landscape paintings, some bookends shaped like ducks that I had made out of wood, a how-to book on building a radio along with some of the abandoned electronic parts from that project, a book on writing a screenplay, a book on birds . . . and there were still several unopened boxes to go.

Mom said, "You had the shortest attention span of any child I have ever known. You were enthusiastic about everything you tried, but in no time you wanted to go on to something else. David was just the opposite. He'd find something and hunker down with it for hours, and he'd scream bloody murder when I finally made him put it away and go to bed."

"Did we get along when we played with this stuff? It's hard to remember."

"You did most of the time. You always wanted David to teach you everything. 'Show me how,' you'd say. 'Show me how.' Most of the time he did, but occasionally he'd get tired of you and try to swat you away. You'd go off by yourself awhile and then come back and start it all over again."

We slowly and silently examined the toys one by one, holding them reverently as if they embodied the past we had lost and were searching for again.

"I miss him," I said.

"So do I, honey," Mom said. "You looked up to David so much when you were little, up to about the time you were teenagers. Then things started to switch."

"What do you mean switch?"

"I think by the end he was looking up to you. He was jealous of you in a lot of ways."

"Do you think so? I never felt that way at all. I was always trying to catch up to him."

"I don't think he saw it that way," she said. "He would never tell you, of course. You two got very competitive those last few years. It hurt me to see it. There was no need for it. But I think deep down he was jealous of you for going off to college, especially those times when he'd get restless still living here."

"He could have gone off to college too," I said.

"I know, but he didn't have a vision for his life. And I think he was jealous of you and Beth, of your relationship."

"Why, Mom? He had Cheryl. Why wasn't that enough for him?"

"Cheryl was very volatile, and they argued all the time. You and Beth seemed so in love. You looked like the perfect couple to him. It ate at him. I don't know why."

"Did you ever talk to him about it?"

"No, neither of you ever wanted my advice, so I didn't try to give it. Neither of you thought I knew much of what was going on, but I knew a lot more than you thought."

"That worries me," I said.

"It should," she shot back.

As we sifted through the boxes, the phone rang, and Mom ran inside to get it. "It's Cheryl," she said as she stuck her head back into the garage. "What should I tell her?"

"Tell her I'm not home."

I was still more comfortable in the distant past than in more recent history. I would talk to Cheryl soon enough. Mom did not argue with me, as I expected she would. She simply retreated back into the house and shut the door. I heard no more about Cheryl that night.

ROBIN

I was hopeful again as we left the motel and set out for the mystery destination where our problems would be solved and we'd have jobs and new friends and plenty of everything. Hopeful, but skeptical too. I knew it wouldn't be as simple as Bobby said. Nothing with Bobby ever is. But at least we were doing something besides hiding out in a motel like bank robbers on the run. We were headed to a town about fifty miles south of Chicago where Bobby said he had good friends.

For Bobby, movement itself was a good substitute for solving problems. He didn't have to actually *get* the jobs and the home and the friends to feel that he had accomplished his goal. Once he got in the car and headed in that direction, it was as if all those things would naturally follow, and he could be as happy as if he had actually done them. So he was in a pretty good mood when we first started out, but then I had to open my big mouth and ask about a couple of *facts*, and that made him all sulky again.

He let me hold on to the cash wad when we first started out, treating me like a little kid who should be thrilled by holding money. I held it up and asked, "What happens when this runs out? If we're not allowed to use credit cards, where will we get more money?"

"Maybe we'll have jobs by then."

"But if we rent an apartment, don't we have to pay a couple months rent or a deposit or something up front, which would take a lot of this money, plus—"

"Don't start nagging me, please, Robin," he groaned, as if I had been droning away for hours.

"I'm not nagging. I think it's pretty reasonable to wonder—"

"Oh, shut up!" he yelled and yanked the money out of my hand. That's it. Take the toy away from the child, and maybe she'll forget about it and play with something else.

After letting out a few of those barely perceptible puffs of air that Bobby likes to spurt whenever he's extremely frustrated with me, he spoke in a slow and patronizing tone, as if he thought I was brain damaged and couldn't process words at the normal speed. "We're not getting an apartment right away. We're staying with my friends till we get jobs and get established. Then we will get an apartment and all the rest of it."

"Well, how long do you think we'll stay with them?"

He sighed like I had asked him to recite an entire book of the Bible by memory. "I don't know," he said. "I cannot predict the future."

"Well, won't it be a little awkward staying with people I don't even know—not just staying with them but *living* with them—for who knows how long? Do they want us to stay there? Do they have room for us?"

"Would we be going there if they didn't?" he snapped. "Kevin was my roommate in college. He shares a house with a few other people. He said a couple more wouldn't hurt anything. He's a very friendly and laid-back guy. It's temporary, Robin. I know it's not ideal, but our whole situation is not ideal. We can't just go to some town, pick a mansion we like along the river, and have the servants arrange everything for our arrival. You need to be a little more realistic."

"Ha!" I cried before I could stop myself. "Am I the one who's not realistic?"

He shook his head and refused to answer, refused to even breathe for a minute, as if to show he was the most patient man in the world and no matter how much senseless drivel poured out of me, he could not be provoked into losing his cool.

It took us a little over an hour to get to the town called Kankakee. The neighborhood we pulled into looked promising. It was a subdivision filled with boxy little houses that looked forty or fifty years old, set on quiet streets with big trees and kids on bicycles. When we pulled into the driveway of one of these houses, it reminded me of my own home, where, not for the first time that day, I wished to be.

The outside of the house may have looked like *Leave It To Beaver*, but inside was a different story. Bobby's friend Kevin met us at the door.

Bobby had told me he was some kind of salesman, and he looked it. All smiles, very friendly, but in control of the conversation, as if he was trying to sell us the house rather than just welcome us into it. He was Bobby's age, chubby but fairly good-looking, and well dressed. He still had part of his suit on from work—a starched white shirt, blue-and-red silk tie, cuffed blue trousers, and sparkling black dress shoes. When we got to his bedroom, I noticed the only neat area of the whole room was his open closet, which was full of good quality suits, sport coats, and dress shirts, each covered with a plastic bag from the dry cleaners.

Kevin gave us a tour of the house. A quick glance was enough to make it clear that this house belonged to a collection of individuals rather than a family. The living room, which was right inside the front door, was filled with furniture that didn't match—two old sofas, a couple recliners with quilts covering them, a bookshelf made of slats of wood separated by cement blocks, a television on a metal stand, a stereo, a couple framed posters on the wall. It looked like an apartment shared by college students forced to pack in a few too many roommates to cover the rent.

The tour quickly revealed there was no room in the house for us. We didn't see one of the three bedrooms because the door was shut, and loud music vibrated from a stereo inside. "Laura doesn't really like to be disturbed," explained Kevin. "You'll see her later."

Kevin talked nonstop as he guided us from room to room, but he didn't get around to telling us where we were going to sleep. I began to worry that Bobby had not made it clear to him why we had come. Maybe he thought we were only staying for the evening. Kevin was about to take us to see the backyard, which I was not the least bit interested in, when I finally broke in to ask, "So where should we put our things?"

Bobby shot me a hateful glance, but breezy Kevin didn't seem to mind the question. He said, "Oh, we're going to put you in the living room. One of those sofas folds out into a nice bed. Except you can kind of feel the metal pole in your back. Or you can sleep on the sofas themselves if you think it would be more comfortable. You can put your stuff wherever. Behind the sofa, I guess, or you can put your suitcases in my room if you want."

"We'll bring the stuff in later," Bobby said. "We didn't bring much anyway, and there's no hurry."

Then we took the grand tour of the backyard, which was a little square plot of grass surrounded by untrimmed hedges. A charcoal grill took up most of the tiny patio. The grill was thoroughly encrusted with charred black fragments of meat and grease. Kevin pointed to it and said, "I thought we'd barbecue some burgers for you tonight to celebrate."

"Celebrate *what*?" I wanted to ask but restrained myself. The words that came out of my mouth were "I feel a little wobbly from the heat. I think I need to sit down."

"Yes, well, a woman in your condition needs to take it easy," said Kevin.

———————

I got the job of scouring off the filthy grill while Kevin and Bobby went out to buy supplies for the barbecue. I worked alone with an SOS pad and a hose in the backyard. Laura, the one with the taste for loud music who didn't like to be disturbed, did not emerge from her room. As far as I know, she didn't come out until later that evening while we were eating out back. Even then, she didn't come out to say hello or good-bye. We heard a car door slam, and an engine start, and Kevin said, "That's Laura." That was as close to an introduction to her as I got that evening.

The other roommate, Tricia, who was about ten years older than the others, got home as I was finishing the grill. I looked up and she was staring at me from the back door.

When she saw me look up at her, she opened the door but did not come outside. "I assume you're one of Kevin's or Laura's friends," she said suspiciously, as if another possibility might be that I was a devious stranger who had walked in off the street to clean the muck off her grill.

"Kevin's friend," I said. "Actually, my boyfriend, Bobby, is Kevin's friend, and they went to the store to get some burgers and things for dinner. My name's Robin."

She nodded slowly, as if I had given her a great deal of information to process. "I'm Tricia," she finally said. "One of the roommates."

"Nice to meet you."

"I just got off work. I have to go change. That grill's a mess, isn't it? It's Kevin's grill. I never use it."

Not knowing how to respond to this, I smiled and kept scrubbing. Tricia let the door close and was gone. I finished the grill long before Bobby and Kevin got back, but I didn't feel like going inside to face Tricia or Laura or whoever else might be there. I leaned up against the house and looked out over the lawn and the scruffy bushes. Being here was a mistake. I had no doubt about that, but I also had no way of figuring out how to get Bobby to let us leave that night. He could tol-

erate a lot more discomfort than I could and was much more willing
to let a situation play itself out, even when he knew it wouldn't end
happily.

My only chance to talk to him alone was right after he got back
from the store, when Kevin was inside preparing the burgers.

"I don't want to stay here," I pleaded. "There's no room! It's too—"

"What's the matter? It's fine," he said. "Kevin has everything set for
us. What difference does it make sleeping on a couch for a few nights?"

"He's got roommates! I don't think he's even told them we're staying. We're going to be in their way. Why can't we take the money and
get a hotel room?"

"You're the one who never wants to waste money!" he said.

"I know, but if we get a job in the next few days, maybe the money
will hold out."

"No."

"Please, Bobby. Just do this one thing for me. I don't feel—"

"No," he insisted, and at that moment Kevin emerged with a plate
of hamburger patties, and everyone was all smiles.

I tried to psyche myself up for whatever lay ahead. I tried to determine to let everything wash over me, to become more of an observer
in the events and less a participant. I had tried this before in stressful
situations, and sometimes it kept me from freaking out. I would think,
*Look, there is Robin. Isn't it interesting to see what is happening to her. This
can be something she can look back on in ten years or so and find something
funny about it, or find something important she learned from it.*

That kind of distance is hard to sustain for very long, but I tried.

I also tried what I call living in the moment, another technique that
had proved useful at certain tense moments of my life. When I was
eating my cheeseburger, I tried to concentrate only on the taste of it,
only on the juiciness of the meat and the taste of the ketchup and the
texture of the tomato. In other words, I tried *not* to think of how much
I dreaded going back in that house and fixing the couch to sleep on,
when maybe one of the roommates would really rather stay up half the
night watching TV but couldn't because these deadbeat strangers were
there. I tried not to think about how hard it would be for Bobby and
me to find jobs in this town where we didn't know where anything was,
didn't know what kind of jobs to look for, didn't have a résumé or even
an address or a telephone. I tried not to think of how worried my family
must be by now and how unfair it was for me to not let them know I
was still alive. I tried not to think about the fact that Bobby had not
yet said he was committed to me and the baby for the long term. Or,

for that matter, that he was even committed just to me.

Living in the moment is a good theory, but when you have that many things screaming at you not to think about them, it's kind of hard to keep your focus on how gooey the cheese on the burger is. I was eating meat with reckless abandon now. I decided being a vegetarian would have to wait until I got my life a little more straightened out. After all, wouldn't meat be good for the baby? The protein and all?

I even tried praying, though I was afraid that God probably wasn't listening to me anymore. Yet in the back of my mind, I was pretty sure He *was*. No matter what messes I've been in all my life, I've never felt God completely abandoned me. That night I wanted to run back to Him and run back to my family and ask for forgiveness and accept whatever consequences might come. But I didn't. I kept thinking I could make everything work out all right if I tried harder, or if I learned to look at my desperate situation in a more positive light. After all, I was with the man I loved—or loved most of the time—meeting new friends, enjoying a barbecue on a beautiful summer evening, pursuing a daring adventure. Ha.

Tricia joined us for the barbecue—in a way. When the rest of us started to eat, she stood in the doorway again until Kevin waved her outside and invited her to have a burger. She took one but stood off to the side, as if watching a bizarre ritual she feared getting too close to. Most of us were wearing shorts and T-shirts, but Tricia, who had changed out of the dress she had worn earlier, was dressed in nice slacks, a silk blouse, gold bracelets, and a necklace. She kept looking at us like she wasn't quite sure what we were. But maybe I shouldn't blame her. I doubt if I'd like it if two people I didn't know suddenly showed up with plans to camp out in my living room. Her boyfriend pulled up in the driveway and took her away after she had nibbled her second cheeseburger.

Five or six of Kevin's friends came and went during the evening, and a couple of them had known Bobby in college. They talked about their good old days together, which left me nothing much to do except sit back and try to smile and fuel the fire of my own worries. The night got louder as it progressed, especially when Kevin pulled out the liquor after dark and his friends tried to top each other with stories of their pranks in college, which they found absolutely hilarious. One girl, who liked touching Bobby's arm whenever she talked, was especially annoying. She had one of those show-off laughs I've always hated. She'd stick her face way out and bellow so loud it could be heard blocks away.

These friends had a lot of Bobby's bad qualities but not too many of his good ones, or at least I thought so that night. They were flashy, shallow, and filled with secret criticisms that were covered with a smile. Some of their critical attitudes toward me, I have to admit, might have been my imagination. The truth is, pregnancy did not bring out the best in my looks, and I was sensitive to it. I felt puffy and fat and tired all the time and sometimes nauseous. I thought these friends of Bobby's probably saw me as a handicap, nothing more than a dependent kid following him around until he could find a convenient way to dump me. It was the opposite of the way I wanted them to see me—as his future wife, someone he adored, someone they would draw into their circle and become friends with. My mind, of course, carried this fantasy even further, imagining that we would buy a house like this one, fix it up, get those shrubs trimmed, invite these friends over for a barbecue, and they would love us and not look at me suspiciously, not stare at me with their secret insults, not care about the mistakes that had first led us here.

The truth is I didn't know what these people thought of me because they didn't bother to include me in their conversations. I didn't want to drink with them, so finally I went inside and laid down on the couch by myself. I could have slept for fifteen or twenty hours if they had let me. It was the only thing I enjoyed.

Bobby left me alone there the next day. He said he was going job hunting. I told him I wanted to go too, but he was adamant that he wanted to go alone. He told me this early in the morning while Kevin was in the bathroom getting ready for work and the other roommates were scurrying around the house—eating breakfast, ironing slacks, running the hair dryer—getting ready to leave.

"What am I supposed to do while you're gone?" I asked. "I can't leave if you have the car. I wouldn't have a key to get back in the house even if I did leave."

"It won't be too long," he said. "Watch TV."

"What am I supposed to do for food?"

"There's leftovers from last night. Can't you eat those? Come on. Help me out here. I'm trying to find a job. Isn't that what you want me to do?"

"I want one too. Why can't I go with you? Where are you going to look?"

"Kevin said he may have a couple leads on some sales jobs. You don't want to sit in the hot car while I go in for interviews, do you?"

"That would be better than sitting here alone in this house of strangers."

"They're not strangers," he said. "They're my friends."

I plopped down on the couch. "Bobby, don't leave me here all day. I feel lousy."

He shook his head, his jaw clenching in that familiar sign of frustration. "I'm trying to be nice about this, but we're never going to get anywhere if you keep complaining all the time and have to have everything perfect every minute of the day. All I'm asking you to do is wait here for a few hours while I go look for a job. I don't think that's so much of a sacrifice."

"How long are we going to stay here?"

"Depends on how things work out."

Then Kevin came out of the bathroom, and Bobby ran in to take a shower.

I finally met the mystery roommate, Laura, that morning before she went to work. She was about my age, a cute girl with long brown hair, incredibly thin in her tight-fitting dress. She was fairly friendly at first, but preoccupied, like she was in a hurry and had already dismissed me from her mind. She wasn't suspicious like Tricia. Laura didn't seem to care whether we were there or not. She didn't really act like she was in her own home. You'd think she was in a train station or something, just passing through—she didn't seem to really *see* anything.

Bobby kept close to Kevin the rest of the time before they left. He was joking and chatty with him so I wouldn't be able to get him alone to finish our conversation. Bobby had always been good at avoiding me when he wanted to.

When they left, I took advantage of being alone at first and enjoyed some time with my own thoughts. I sat staring for probably an hour before I ever moved a muscle. Then I took a shower and got dressed and microwaved a leftover cheeseburger for brunch. I was hungry for more than that, but I didn't want to ransack their kitchen. The pleasure of solitude wore off pretty quickly and gave way to a restlessness so powerful I couldn't sit still. I paced through the whole house, bouncing from room to room, being careful not to touch anything so they wouldn't know I had been there. The temptation I fought that whole day was to call home. I imagined myself calling my brother and saying, "This hasn't worked out. Can you come and get me?"

"I'll be there in three hours," he would say. I would leave a note for Bobby, and by late that afternoon I'd be in the car with Chris, headed down the highway toward home.

It's not like finding me gone would break Bobby's heart, I was beginning to think. What would he do if he came back to find me gone? Go out with Kevin to celebrate? It hurt me to think about it. Maybe I was wrong about him. Maybe he was more committed to me than I realized. After all, he had taken me with him all this way, which nobody forced him to do. He was looking for a job, which was part of the plan for our future. He had stopped talking about wanting me to have an abortion, though he hadn't yet gone so far as to say he wanted a baby.

Still, something inside me was growing heavier all the time, a feeling of impending disaster. It was a feeling—I know this is going to sound stupid—that I couldn't even stand to let myself think about unless I was in motion, walking fast around the house. A certainty that, in spite of his assurances, I had lost him, that it was just a matter of time now before he found a way to get rid of me.

The job hunt did not go well that day, so Bobby was pretty uncommunicative when he came back. Our conversation wasn't made any easier by the fact that the roommates could hear every word we said. Laura, at least, retreated to the cocoon of her room and drowned herself in music, but Tricia sat at the kitchen table paying bills in full view of us, and Kevin was bouncing around the house doing I don't know what. Bobby slouched on the couch, not even bothering to take off his coat and tie. It was almost six o'clock, and I was hungry, having eaten nothing since my breakfast cheeseburger.

"Why don't we go out and get something to eat?" I asked as pleasantly as I could, the way I do when I suggest things that might cheer him up.

He sighed and said, "Not now. I'd really like to just relax a little while. I had a late lunch anyway. I'm not all that hungry yet."

"I'm starved. I haven't eaten since this morning."

"Do you want the car?" he asked in his huffy tone of voice.

"I was really hoping we could go off and talk for a little bit. Do you want to take a walk?"

"I'm *resting*, Robin. Please."

I should have just left it alone. I know it's useless to talk to him when he gets that way. But I was tired of tiptoeing around. Having Tricia over there pretending not to glare at us was really bugging me. I had sat in that living room like a prisoner all day long, and I wasn't about to sit there silently all night like a blob, not knowing what he was thinking or planning. I hated the thought that I might have to repeat this humiliating experience the next day, and the next, while the roommates grew in their hatred of the freeloaders sprawled out in their living room.

So I said, "What's the plan now?"

"You just don't let up, do you, babe? You can drive down to McDonald's if you—"

"No, I mean the *overall* plan. Like what are we going to do tomorrow. What's the next step in the plan."

"I don't know," he said, his head back against the pillow and his eyes closed dismissively.

I couldn't sit still. I paced around the living room while we talked. "Why don't you let me go job hunting too?" I suggested. "I can find a job, and it's better than sitting around here."

"Who would want to hire a pregnant girl?"

"Lots of people! Is that why you didn't want me to go today? I could've stayed in my job at the store right up until the time I was going to have the baby. You can work when you're pregnant, Bobby."

"But will they *hire* you if you're pregnant?" he asked, lifting his head slightly off the pillow. "Take on an employee who is going to have to go on maternity leave in a few months? It definitely doesn't make you very marketable."

"Oh, well, excuse me for not being marketable."

"Don't start," he said.

"You'd think that I was the only one responsible for me having a baby."

"You are, in a way."

"Oh, really? You had nothing to do with it?"

"There's a difference between *getting* pregnant and *being* pregnant," he said. "If I were in your shoes, I wouldn't still *be* pregnant. You know that was your choice, not mine."

"Yes, and I have no intention of changing it."

"Then you'll just have to make the best of your situation and not blame me for the mess we're in."

"You blame me for the mess we're in?"

"Well, you certainly haven't helped things," Bobby said.

By that time I was whirling around that living room so fast I was almost dizzy. "Even if I had an abortion, that wouldn't solve all our problems!"

"No, but it would help. It would take a lot of pressure off. And there are other possibilities too. You could put the baby up for adoption—"

"Do you mind?" I suddenly screamed at Tricia, who had put her calculator down and wasn't even pretending to pay bills. She was staring at us like we were some kind of TV show being broadcast for her entertainment.

She ripped a check out of her checkbook and ignored me. I can't really blame her for staring, I guess. We were pretty hard to ignore. And it was her living room. But at that moment I could have ripped the tinted hair out of her head and enjoyed every minute of it.

To Bobby I pleaded, "Can't we go somewhere and talk alone? This is driving me crazy."

"No," he said. "It's pointless to go off and keep saying the same things over and over."

"Why did you bring me with you, then, if I'm going to be stuck here all day like some convict?"

"You wanted to come."

"Well, now I want to go home."

"Go, then. I'm tired of your whining."

Kevin wandered into the kitchen, which was visible to Tricia but was separated from us by a wall. Tricia said to him in her businesslike monotone, "Kevin, I need a conference with you."

Just like that. Not "Kevin, can I talk to you?" or "Can I ask you something?" or "Do you have a minute?" but "Kevin, I need a conference with you," like she was about to convene the United Nations or something. Kevin came out of the kitchen and headed down the hall toward his room. Tricia scampered after him.

As soon as they were out of sight, Bobby pointed at them with both his hands and then raised his arms in this dramatic shrug as if to say "Now look what you've done!"

My body felt as if it would pop right open any minute and my insides would spread all over that room. I wish it would have, just to give me some relief. I pointed at Bobby, and with my teeth clenched so tightly together the words could hardly come out, I said, "I am leaving here tomorrow, one way or another. If this Godforsaken town has a bus station or a train station, I am going to be there."

Bobby had fully emerged from his stupor by now and was sitting up, looking right at me. His voice was almost soothing as he said, "Don't make things worse than they already are. We're all under a big strain."

"I want out of here," I said. "I'm not staying in this house after tonight."

Bobby stood up and left the house. I went out to the backyard where it was easier to pace. Even prisoners are allowed time in the exercise yard.

After about ten minutes, I heard a car pull up out front, and when I peeked around the corner to see who it was, I saw Tricia walk down the driveway and get into the waiting car of her boyfriend. A few minutes after that, Bobby returned with McDonald's bags. *The inmates must be fed*, I thought and went inside to get my rations for the day, which he had thrown on the kitchen table on top of Tricia's bills. He went back to Kevin's room and ate the food alone, asking no questions. The fight might not have been over, but I didn't have the strength to continue it without a little nourishment.

Kevin and Bobby came out of the room later, all chummy and smiling, as if the previous hour had been nothing but some game between them and the women, and they had won. Bobby said, "Kevin and I are going out for a little bit. I'll be back later."

Then they were out the door before I even had time to respond. I could have gone after them, but right then the image of myself as a pregnant woman running barefoot out into the driveway screaming at two giggling men while the neighbors looked on didn't appeal to me. I kept my dignity and finished my French fries.

I stuck to my spot on the couch all evening and ignored the comings and goings of the roommates. No one said anything to me. I didn't read magazines or watch television. Instead, I planned my escape. The first thing I needed was money, which I would take from Bobby's wallet as soon as I knew he was asleep. I decided that by nine o'clock the next morning, I would be in a taxi on my way to the nearest bus or train station. I would buy a one-way ticket to Indianapolis, and as soon as I knew what time it was supposed to arrive, I would call Chris and ask him to pick me up. If Bobby wanted to go home too and try to work things out with me, he could do that. I wasn't necessarily trying to end it with him. That would have to be his choice. All I knew was this would be my last night in Kankakee. I comforted myself with that fact.

I played the departure scene over and over in my mind. In one version, Bobby begs me not to go when I announce the next morning that the taxi is on the way. He promises that we'll get our own place that day and get married and work things out the way he said we would.

In another version, he merely waves his hand to dismiss me when I tell him I'm leaving and says, "I should have known this wouldn't work anyway. You're nothing but a huge weight dragging me down."

Bobby's so unpredictable that I had no idea which reaction I would get, but it made me almost double over with pain to think that leaving tomorrow would mean I wouldn't see him again. I still loved him. I just wished he could be the real Bobby all the time. That's what I called him, the real Bobby, the one who could look at me and see all the way through, the one I felt safe with, the one I felt free to say anything to and know it would be all right, the one who was gorgeous and exciting and made me feel so alive. That man I would die for.

But this other one, who threw McDonald's bags at me and then took off, who was secretive and annoyed and shut me out, who treated me like a big fat blob he had to haul around—that Bobby hurt me too much to be around. Being without him would tear me apart, but being with him in this humiliating position was even worse.

When he and Kevin got back around midnight, I pretended I was asleep. Later I took a hundred dollars from the wad in his wallet. The next morning I got up early and took my shower and started to pack. Slowly. I was a little more tired and a little less angry than I had been the night before, and I wasn't sure I could handle a confrontation. Bobby took his shower and dressed.

I was working myself up to telling him I was leaving when he walked over to me, took both my hands in his, looked me right in the eyes, and said, "This is not working. This is not good for either of us. Get your things together. We're leaving here today."

CHRIS

The secrets and lies that Cheryl won't leave buried started the summer I lived with David in Chicago. Events were set in motion that I am still paying for today.

It began as a fabulous vacation. David had unexpectedly invited me to stay with him at the end of my first year of grad school at Purdue. His apartment was tiny and shabbily furnished, but it was in the heart of a city throbbing with energy. My own mind and body raged with a desire to escape from the near monastic life-style I had lived that school year in my eight-by-twelve-foot cell in the graduate residence hall. I was chained there most of the time by a heavy load of studying for exams, writing papers, reading endless books, preparing for freshman composition courses I taught, and suffering through hours of grading papers. When I was released from this cloistered life of discipline for a few months and allowed out into what we grad students called the "real world," I was like a convict pardoned from a life sentence. The lights of the city burned brighter than I had ever imagined they could. It was as if every light in every office building, bagel shop, department store, and restaurant in Chicago was wired directly into my bloodstream. I could not walk fast enough, be awake long enough, or laugh and talk often enough to release even a fraction of what burned inside me.

As I drove my little Chevette, its hatchback stuffed with all my possessions, through the streets of the great city and found David's apartment, I was optimistic that his invitation would be the start of a new relationship between us. Our teenage years were over, and it was time for the petty rivalries between us—in sports, girls, and the esteem of our parents—to end. We were adults, and this summer was a truce, a time for being together under a different roof as different young men.

While David worked as a mechanic, I got a job with a temporary service. Most of the jobs they gave me lasted three or four days and were as varied as loading boxes at a toy warehouse, entering billing information into the computer for a furniture company, and planting shrubs around downtown office buildings for a landscaping company. I often had a few free days between jobs, which gave me plenty of time to explore the bookshops, the parks, the lake, and the coffee shops, not to mention all the tourist spots like the museums and the Sears Tower. Friends from Indianapolis came up those first couple of weekends, and David and I showed them all over the city. It was the best time we had ever spent together.

I especially loved Chicago at night—the lights, the taxis swerving in and out, the endless noise, the preposterous height of the buildings. I loved the frenetic movement of the street we lived on, crowded and noisy with its Chinese restaurants, cleaners, tobacco shops, check-cashing stores, old hotels. Even the noise of the traffic, the honking, and the sirens at all hours pleased me, a sign that the city, like my own brain, was pulsing with hyperactive energy. I could barely get to sleep those first few weeks. When my friends were around, I wanted to stay out all night and talk, talk, talk.

David could not stand for either of us to have one contemplative moment the entire summer. One evening during my third week there, I sat down on his couch in the living room and started to read a book. You would have thought I had picked up a loaded gun! David ripped it from my hands disgustedly and said, "Come on! What are we gonna do tonight? You're not going to waste the summer reading."

Actually, I had planned to spend a great deal of time reading, since the list of books I needed to know for my graduate work had grown long. But David acted insulted every time I picked up a book. I took to reading only when he was out of the apartment.

I did not know David as well as I thought I did, so I did not guard myself against him as carefully as I should have. He had changed in ways I had never noticed. After all, we had spent most of the previous five years apart from each other. I was off at college most of the time, with only parts of my breaks spent with him at home. He had never lived away from home until now, and I knew that had frustrated him. He had been jealous of my opportunity to get away. He had visited me at college a few times, but those visits only increased his anger that I had found a separate world and he had not. He never gave much thought to going to college himself. He wasn't very academically inclined, and he didn't, I suspect, want to put himself in competition with me in that arena, which was one of the few areas in which I was almost certain to beat him.

Both of us were restless, but for David it was not a happy restlessness. It was desperation, as if this was his last chance to have a good time before he was trapped again and taken back to the way things used to be.

The trouble began a few weeks into my visit, when David started going out with a girl named Tracy. She was exactly the kind of woman I would have expected him to choose, one of the few people more hyper than he was. Even her looks reminded me of a cartoon cat whose tail had been plugged into a light socket, making her pulse with electricity. She had short blond hair, a little spiky in places, as if some of that electric current was leaking out. Her eyes were flashy and expressive, like a little animal studying its prey right before the attack. Her favorite sounds were loud, inappropriate bursts of laughter so jolting that everyone's head in a restaurant involuntarily turned toward her for a second, making her for a moment what she wished she could always be— the center of attention.

She was short, not much more than five feet tall, and her body was wiry, as if the energy coursing through her had whittled her away to nothing more than the bare necessities. She liked skimpy outfits, especially tight little dresses so simple they looked like she might have made them herself, except they were a little more elegant than that. Deceptively simple, as she was herself.

David set me up with Tracy's friend Linda, and we were to go out for the first time on a Thursday night. He didn't bother to announce his choice for me until the day before the planned date. I declined, saying Beth wouldn't like it.

"You're not tied to Beth anymore," he shot back.

That was true, but I hoped—or at least imagined—that things were improving between us and that this was the summer we would get back together for good. After dating in high school, we had broken up, but then when I started grad school, we cautiously started going out with each other whenever I came to Indianapolis for weekends. I loved Beth, even though she had kept me at a distance in many ways, and I didn't want to do anything to alienate her from me again. She had promised to visit me in Chicago the following weekend, so I told David I would wait until Beth came, and then we would go out with him and Tracy.

He scoffed at this. "Do you think I'm going to wait more than a week to go out with Tracy?"

"You two go by yourselves, then," I said.

"And what are you going to do in the meantime for the next week and a half? Sit here and *read a book*?" He asked this contemptuously, then added, "Do you think Beth's sitting at home all this time waiting for you?"

Yes, I thought, *that is exactly what I think*. But I didn't dare throw that answer into the shredder of David's sarcasm. I kept quiet, hoping he would accept my refusal as final and leave me alone.

He did not. He pressed his attack by saying, "Chris, you're here to experience the city, aren't you? You could have gone home or stayed at college if all you were going to do was mope around all summer and read books."

That was the theme of all of David's advice to me. Seize the day. Get out and have some fun. Accept no restraints. Don't be a book-reading freak.

"I don't think it's unreasonable to refuse to go out with a girl I've never met so that I can stay faithful to my girlfriend," I said.

"Faithful to your girlfriend who's probably going out with half the guys in Indi—"

"Shut up, David. You know that's not true."

"We don't have to tell Beth a thing about this," he said. "You don't have to account to her for every single minute of your life. Linda is just a friend. You don't have to marry her."

After a short pause, I said, "I don't like blind dates."

David ignored the words and listened to the pause. It was a hesitation that he interpreted as surrender, a two- or three-second lull that in his mind obliterated all the arguments I had raised.

He smiled and said, "Those girls will be waiting for us tomorrow night. If you want to embarrass me, ruin my chances with Tracy, and make a total fool of yourself, then don't go. Otherwise be ready by six-thirty."

I was ready by six-thirty. The fact is that David didn't have to shove too hard to push me over the cliff. I was already standing pretty close to the edge.

We started out at a little Thai restaurant just down the street from our apartment. The food was good, but the place, with its cracked up-holstery booths, faded Formica tabletops, and lots of shouting from the kitchen, looked a little run-down. I didn't think it was a good choice for a first date. My choice would have been a little better atmosphere, even if the food wasn't our favorite. What I did not know was that dinner was not the main event but just a prologue to the evening ahead, a fuel stop for Tracy the roadrunner, David the coyote, and me and Linda, the audience.

Tracy didn't like to stay in one place very long. Motion was half the fun. For her the night's success could be judged by how many places we were able to descend upon and how many people she could get to stare at her as she belted out her preposterous laugh and twisted her way between the tables coming and going.

The clubs and bars we went to got progressively louder, darker, and grungier as the night wore on. I was the driver that first night, and I tried to take on the aloofness of a hired chauffeur. I tried to simply let the evening pour over me and not think too much about it. I didn't care whether we ever went out with these girls again. There was not much romantic fire between Linda and me. She was several years older, not bad looking but nothing special either, with dark hair and dark eyes and what I thought of as a rather pouty or suspicious look on her face. She was the kind of person whose personality would have flourished in a much different setting—long walks through the park, a quiet dinner, and intimate conversation—but those were not the kind of dates we had. Linda assumed the role of the adult in our group, the one who finally had the nerve to say she was tired and called the evening to a halt, the one who tried to keep Tracy from carrying her antics too far, who shushed her when she got too loud. She and Tracy were nothing alike, but I think Tracy liked having her there because Linda's cautiousness and embarrassment only served to spotlight Tracy's behavior and keep her at the center of attention.

The evenings out with our foursome not only continued but became more frequent as the summer progressed, for reasons I cannot explain. It was as if in failing to find whatever vague fulfillment we were looking for on any given night, we simply flung ourselves into the action that much more the next time. David erupted in fury whenever I refused to go out with them. He and Tracy were trying to lure me into—it's hard to say what exactly—their attitude of abandonment toward pleasure, their rejection of moderation or thoughtfulness toward anything, from the way they drank and laughed and shouted and spent money to the carelessness they professed toward their future, their families, their careers. To care about something was a travesty, an insult. Sarcasm was the only acceptable tone.

Being with them was invigorating at first, a welcome release from my now seemingly colorless and bookish life-style at school. But being with them too long was like being forced to laugh long after the joke ceased to be funny. Soon we added another element to our social lives— parties at the homes of Tracy's friends. These were the most pointless evenings of all, little more than a bunch of losers sitting around an apartment getting drunk and smoking pot and making me feel disgusted with myself for being part of it.

Every attempt I made to back away from this life-style met with furious resistance from David. Nothing I did was ever enough for him. If I was willing to stay out until two in the morning, he pushed me to stay out until four. If I agreed to go out with him and the girls three nights a week, he would hound me until I went out every night. I was losing so much sleep that I was missing work a day or two a week, something I had never done before. I was also spending what little I made, saving none of the crucial money I would need when I went back to school in the fall.

After a few exhausting weeks, I escaped to Indianapolis for a weekend to rest up and to see Beth. I sat in church with her that Sunday with a dead, empty feeling. I was embarrassed by the songs, by the emotion of those around me as they raised their hands and sang praises to God. How could I stand here with Beth and pretend to be a Christian? I wanted to run out of the sanctuary in shame.

I didn't tell Beth about Linda or about my night life. Beth could tell I was tired and preoccupied, but she didn't push for details. She told me she knew of a couple summer jobs she could set up for me if I decided to come home for the rest of the summer, but that was as close as she came to asking me to leave Chicago.

I drove back that Sunday night determined to slow down and stop drifting from the values I deeply believed in, which, I had to remind myself, included things like staying sober, working hard, being loyal to people, paying my bills, and most importantly, following God with integrity. All those things were slipping away from me. David was offended and angry that I didn't want to take up where we had left off. He treated with derision the spiritual issues I raised. I realized that for him our faith was nothing more than one of those pesky constraints Mom and Dad had imposed on us at home, but we were now free to throw off. It outraged him that I would voluntarily hang on to those beliefs.

The problem for me was I was beginning to feel addicted to David's way of living, even though I was also disgusted by it. It was like eating one of those preposterous desserts they sell for birthday parties at restaurants, dishes with words like "monster" and "ultimate" and "super duper" in their titles, with seven kinds of ice cream and fudge and gooey piles of who knows what. There is a certain pleasure in eating it once you've abandoned yourself to the idea, but the fat, bloated feeling afterward makes you regret ever touching it.

What finally pushed me over the edge of what I could tolerate was when the late-night parties moved from the apartments of Tracy's brainless friends to David's place. It had been bad enough having to stay out longer than I wanted to, but at least after we got home I had been able to get a few hours sleep before going to work. But when her friends discovered our apartment was a great place to hang out, there were many nights when we did not get rid of them at all. Often when I woke up in the morning from an almost sleepless night, I would find one or two stragglers on the floor of the living room or in the kitchen.

Unfortunately, my bedroom was a sofa in the living room. The first few nights people were there, I tried to play the bad guy and kick them out about two in the morning, telling them I had to get up early. David would not hear of it. "I have to get up early too," he would say, which was true, though how he managed to repair cars all day on the little bit of sleep he got, I'll never understand. The biggest concession David would make was to offer me his bed—strewn with dirty clothes, magazines, and a few other surprises—until everybody left. That at least gave me the chance to lie down, but the noise made it almost impossible to sleep, and what sleep I got was often accompanied by nightmares induced by their howling music.

Finally, in a rare clear moment one morning in early July, I left Chicago for good. It was a Thursday, and the animals had camped out at our apartment for three nights in a row. That night I had slept—in those rare moments I could sleep—on blankets on the floor of David's room. I had to get up at seven and call into the temporary service to see if they had a job for me. I took a shower and then walked into the kitchen to grab a bowl of cereal and a cup of coffee. Amazingly, all our guests had left, but they had also eaten all my Cheerios and put the empty box back on the shelf. The milk bottle contained about a tablespoon of milk. There was a bowl of soggy Cheerios on the kitchen table, but I wasn't desperate enough to make a meal of it. I found the coffee, but the filters were not in their proper drawer, nor were they underneath the newspapers on the kitchen table, or in the sink stacked high with dirty dishes, or in the nearly empty cupboards, or in the garbage can, or anywhere else that I could see. I found a paper towel, origin unknown, and tried to form it into a coffee filter.

As the coffee brewed, I called the temp service. There were no jobs for me that day, and they didn't know about tomorrow either. Things were slow right now.

I poured a cup of coffee. It was chunky with grounds. Someone had been smoking in the living room, and the smell of it gave me a headache. I thought of Mom's sparkling kitchen, where dishes never stayed dirty for more than an hour after they were used and not a crumb was allowed to remain on the counter or in the sink. There were always at least two boxes of Cheerios, just in case one ran out. The milk supply was inexhaustible.

I thought of my bed at home. I thought of all the nights I had slept there for eight full hours in absolute silence, never appreciating the luxury of it.

I thought of Beth at home, just a phone call away. I considered the miracle that if I was home I could be in her presence after just a few minutes' drive, hugging her and hearing her laugh.

I didn't consciously make a *decision* to leave that morning, I just got up and started packing my things. Later, David accused me of having known I was leaving and sneaking away without bothering to tell him. One minute I was stuck there, chunky coffee and all, and the next minute the trip was over. I loaded the hatchback of my Chevette and headed out of the city down Highway 65, eager for sleep and food, confession and contrition, and a strict spiritual diet. I left David a note on his bed, apologizing for my abrupt departure and telling him I couldn't afford to stay there anymore.

I now believe David may have never forgiven me for leaving the way I did. He saw it as a rejection of him. The fact that he burned out of that life and came home himself two months later did not appease his anger with me for what he saw as my turning against him.

Even though I sensed David's hurt, I was glad the whole tawdry episode was over. If the Chicago story would have ended there, we could have treated it as a learning experience and put it behind us. That's what I wanted to do. I never contacted Linda or any of our other friends there again.

Crazy Tracy, however, continued to haunt us. I was already back at Purdue by the time David moved back home, and during the few times I talked to him that fall, he didn't mention her. When I came home for Christmas break, though, he told me he had driven up to Chicago a few times to see her. He had never invited her to Indianapolis.

"I have a feeling Mom wouldn't think she was the right girl for me," he said with a smile.

"I have a feeling you're right," I said. Tracy would have been Mom's worst nightmare for her son, and Dad wouldn't have been thrilled with her either.

In the meantime, David had met Cheryl at church and started dating her. "Does Cheryl know about Tracy?" I asked.

"Are you out of your mind?"

"Are you going to keep seeing Tracy?"

"I don't know," he said. "Cheryl doesn't have quite the iron grip on me that your girlfriend has on you."

"You realize that the quickest way to end a relationship is to go out with somebody else behind her back."

"Don't hand me that," he scoffed, as if fidelity were some bizarre concept that only an eccentric like me would espouse.

I didn't hear any more about Tracy until the end of that school year when I came home to work at the magazine. That was the summer before David died, and at first I thought he had begun to straighten out his life. He was going to church, dating Cheryl, restoring old cars with Dad, and displaying them at shows. He didn't show any hostility toward me, having dropped, I thought, the grudge he had held against me for moving out on him. We hung out together, played basketball, helped sponsor a couple camping trips for the teens at church. I had plenty of time to spend with him because Beth was gone for most of that summer teaching English in China through a mission organization. I missed her terribly, so much that I looked into buying a plane ticket and visiting her there, something I was never able to arrange. During the school year, Beth and I had seen each other almost every weekend, either at Purdue or in Indianapolis, where she was now a high school history teacher. We had talked about marriage in vague terms but had not yet become engaged, partly because I was living on next to nothing and partly because Beth still had a list of things like the China trip that she said she wanted to do before she got married.

In a strange way, Beth's absence improved my relationship with David. It muted the rivalry between us. Beth was always popular at church and in our house, particularly with Mom, and everyone expected us to get married someday. I think David felt pressure, whether real or imagined, to have the same kind of relationship with someone. It was an outgrowth of the competition we had always engaged in over girls, sports, and everything else in our lives. I hated that David continued to think of me as a rival rather than a brother, but nothing I tried had dampened that vying spirit of his. He put everything in our lives in the context of which one of us was better, and sometimes I caught myself competing with him in spite of my desire not to.

At first that summer I assumed he had ended his relationship with Tracy. I hadn't heard about her in months, and Cheryl seemed to be around him all the time. David soon told me otherwise, admitting that he had not yet managed to break it off with her. Why he told me I'm not sure, but he said it to me in a whispering, boastful way, as though I should be impressed that he could keep two girlfriends going at once.

Every few weekends, David drove up to Chicago to see Tracy and lied about it to Cheryl and our family. He said he was going there to earn some extra money by helping some of the buddies he used to work with restore an old car. After a couple of these trips, he told me the truth and made me promise not to tell anyone. It was a secret that I neither wanted to know nor wanted to keep. But I kept my mouth shut. Like the never ending rivalry between us, there was also a strong sense of brotherly loyalty. We had never told on each other, and we always did what we could to cover for each other when we were in trouble. I tried to get David to see that staying in touch with Tracy would lead to trouble, but my disapproval only made the whole affair seem more dangerous and exciting to him.

"Cheryl is not stupid. Sooner or later she's going to find out, and then you'll lose her," I told him.

"Maybe not," David said. "Chicago is pretty far from here. It's a different world. Neither girl knows about the other, and I don't see how they would find out."

"The real point isn't whether you can get away with this," I argued. "The point is that it's wrong."

"I'm not planning to keep seeing Tracy forever. Right now I just can't get rid of her."

"Why not?"

"I can't shake her!" he claimed. "Right now the best way to keep her under control is to keep her happy up there in Chicago rather than getting her so mad that she comes down here and messes everything up."

Can't shake her? I thought this was a flimsy excuse David was using to rationalize having two girlfriends. I was soon to find out that there was more truth to his story than I had suspected.

Beth came back from China at the end of that summer, and by Christmas we were engaged. We set the wedding date for the following Christmas break. I wanted to get married sooner than that, but Beth wanted to take one more trip to China the next summer and then have a few months to finalize plans for the wedding. We were showered with attention from our family and friends when we told them about our engagement. Pastor Jennings announced the news in church and in the newsletter. Aunt Dayle spread the word within twenty-four hours to even the most distant relatives, and she threw a New Year's Eve chili supper so that everyone could meet Beth. David was outwardly congratulatory, but I knew him well enough to sense that beneath his smiling exterior he was deeply disturbed. When we were alone, he was either strangely silent about my upcoming marriage, as if it were not even a reality worth discussing, or he asked about it in a dismissive, almost accusatory way. "So she finally talked you into marrying her, huh?"

I didn't challenge his attitude because I knew he would deny it. But I also knew how his mind worked, and I knew why our engagement bothered him. I had beaten him by getting engaged first. Even though I was younger, I had pulled ahead of him in one of the competitions of life. By doing so, I had drawn attention toward myself and away from him. Now the only thing our family and friends wanted to know from him was "Why haven't you gotten engaged too?" "When are we going to hear your announcement?"

At Aunt Dayle's chili supper and everywhere else, David insisted he had no interest in marriage and that I was foolish to get myself tangled up in it. He played the part of a staunchly independent bachelor too young and energetic to settle down, which was supposed to make me, by contrast, the dull conformist who trudged off and got married only because I was too uncreative to think of any other option.

Despite David's protestations against marriage, on Valentine's Day, just two months after my engagement, he proposed to Cheryl, and she accepted. They were to be married in November, a full month before my wedding. He had beaten me after all! He was delighted with the attention his engagement brought him at church, which he suddenly started attending more frequently, and he happily took part in the requisite celebratory get-together that Aunt Dayle threw. Mom had misgivings about this marriage, as did I, but she mostly kept quiet, apparently afraid that being happy about my engagement and upset about David's would be seen as a sign of favoritism.

Even in the worst of times, David had always confided in me, so I was surprised when he told Mom and Dad about his engagement before he told me. I found out first from them by phone while I was at Purdue.

When I came home the following weekend and got David alone, I said, "I assume this means you're going to end it with Tracy."

"Yes," he said, his eyes darting around. "I'm going up next weekend to tell her it's over."

"You're going up there?"

"This is the last time," he insisted.

"Why can't you just—"

"I have to tell her in person," he said in an almost pleading tone. "You don't know her. It's going to be hard enough as it is to deal with her reaction."

"Are you going to tell her you're engaged? Does she know about Cheryl yet?"

"I'm going to tell her it's over. She doesn't need to know every detail of my personal life."

I laughed in astonishment. "That's a pretty big detail to leave out! I can't believe you'd go all the way up there to break it off with her and not tell her the reason."

"She's a wild woman," he said. "I have to handle her my own way."

"But you are definitely breaking it off?"

"Yes," he said, annoyed. "Didn't I just say that? Why are you badgering me about this?"

"Because I know you well enough to know you're not telling me the whole truth."

"I don't know what you're talking about. I'll end it. Everything's fine. You just want to analyze everything to death until you find something wrong with it."

David's eyes were naturally narrow, but whenever he was hiding something or lying, they seemed to close even further, and the rest of his face took on a static, impenetrable expression. That was the look he had as he talked about Tracy. His eyes were slits. His expression was shut down. I knew there was more to the story than the fact that he would dump her, and it would all be settled, but I didn't know what it was. When he got this way, it was useless to press.

Tracy popped up again, of course, when I came home for what would be David's final, tumultuous summer. Mom, who didn't like to cook, nevertheless threw a big dinner for Beth and me and David and Cheryl on my first Sunday home from school.

Mom made meat loaf—her best dish—green bean casserole, mashed potatoes and gravy, rolls, and iced tea, and she bought apple and pumpkin pies for dessert. Dad and Robin were there and in good spirits. It should have been a happy occasion, but it wasn't. Cheryl spoke no more than two or three sentences during the whole meal, and even then it was only because someone asked her a direct question. She kept her eyes on her plate most of the time and chewed her food slowly and deliberately, like a child who has been told she has to clean her plate before she can have any dessert. She and David not only never spoke to each other during that dinner, but they didn't even look at each other or in any way acknowledge that the other existed.

In contrast to Cheryl, David was even more talkative than usual, as if to compensate for Cheryl's pouting. He chattered about the car he was restoring and the extra hours he had been putting in at work. The rest of us tried to follow his lead and deal with Cheryl's anger by ignoring it, but the atmosphere was tense and occasionally gave way to long uncomfortable pauses until finally someone mercifully filled them.

I didn't get to talk to David about it until later that night when he was working alone in the garage on his 1953 Chevrolet Bel Air. I found him with his head in the engine, his hands and arms smudged with oil.

David and I didn't bother with preliminary chitchat anymore. I simply asked, "So what was wrong with Cheryl today at lunch?"

"Nothing," he said, his gaze remaining on the engine.

"Come on, David. She looked ready to explode."

"Women get that way sometimes. Doesn't Beth?"

"No, actually, I've never seen her act that way at a dinner with other people."

"Well, I guess my fiancée is not as perfect as yours." He leaned over farther into the engine.

"What was she mad about?"

"I don't know. Nothing important."

I watched him work for a moment. He was having trouble loosening something. I had no idea what he was doing, and I didn't want to draw attention to my ignorance by asking. He strained with the wrench, his face turning red as he growled in frustration. Suddenly whatever it was broke loose, David's face coloring turned normal, and I worked up the courage to ask him the next question.

"So did you get everything resolved with Tracy?"

David raised himself up and stared straight at me, his eyebrows lifted in a defiant expression. "Of course I did," he said, but there was something about his tone of voice, the quietness of it, the lack of conviction, that told me in an instant Tracy had not been resolved.

I know that staring straight at me was supposed to discourage me from pursuing this line of questioning, but I went on. "Tell me what happened. How did she take it?"

"How do any of them take it?" he snapped. "How would you take it if somebody you cared about suddenly decided to drop you and marry someone else?"

"I'm not asking about me. I'm asking about Tracy."

"She took it fine!" he bellowed. "She laughed her head off!"

"Does Cheryl know about her?"

"No. She doesn't need to."

"Does she suspect?"

"Chris, I have to get this car done. Do you mind? Go torture somebody else. I don't feel like answering fifty million questions."

"All right. I didn't know you wanted to hide all this from me."

"Don't be a jerk, man." He leaned back over his car, and I left the garage.

———————

A few hours later, just before I went to bed, David came into my bedroom. I was leaning back against the wall in my desk chair reading a book. David, who had cleaned up by this time and was wearing a T-shirt and shorts, walked over to me, took the book out of my hands, closed it, and put it on the desk.

"She's driving me crazy," he said. "She's been dogging me for weeks, and I can't get rid of her. I need your help."

He didn't need to tell me who "she" was. He also didn't bother to admit that he'd been lying to me about Tracy. He knew I was aware of it.

"Tell me," I said.

He sat on the bed and said, "Right after Cheryl and I got engaged, I went up to Chicago for the last time—I wanted it to be the last time—and I told Tracy I couldn't see her anymore. I told her it wasn't working out, that things had changed between us."

"And that you were engaged?"

"Eventually, yes, I did have to get into that."

"Oh. Small details."

"Shut up. You don't know what a pain in the neck Tracy is."

"I think I have some idea," I said. "So up to that point Tracy had not known about Cheryl."

"No. Not really. She had accused me of seeing somebody else, and I think she pretty much knew, but she didn't *really* know. I mean I had never *told* her. So finally she got me so frustrated that I blurted out everything all at once. We were fighting, as usual, yelling at each other, and I told her the reason I wanted to break up with her was that I was engaged to be married to someone else. She went ballistic. Screamed her head off. Accused me of lying to her, ruining her life. Accused me of having promised to marry her, which I never did. Can you imagine me marrying Tracy?

"So I left and told her I was never coming back and that I didn't ever want to hear from her again. I should have known it wouldn't be that simple. She called me every day that following week, sometimes three times a day, and a couple times when Cheryl was here. I felt like such an idiot on the phone trying to pretend Tracy was a friend I was working on a car for, with Cheryl staring at me the whole time. I'd be talking all this car stuff into the phone while Tracy was ranting and raving so loud that I held the phone up next to my ear real tight so none of her yelling would leak out. Tracy said if I didn't come back up there and talk to her, she was going to come down here and find my fiancée and tell her the whole thing."

"So you went back up?"

"Yeah, that following weekend. I couldn't stand the thought of her coming down to Indianapolis and throwing one of her tantrums. She's demented enough to do it too. I decided I had to figure out how to get rid of her once and for all. I had to find out what she would settle for to leave me alone."

"And this whole time Cheryl is buying your story that you're going up there to work on a car?"

"She sort of half bought it. The lucky thing is I do have a friend up there who's working on a car, an old Cadillac, and even though he doesn't really need me and isn't paying me, he's always glad to have me come up and help him. It's a beautiful car. You should see it. So whenever I went up there, I'd tell Cheryl to call me at his garage at a time I knew I'd be there. He'd answer the phone, and I'd have him tell her how helpful I'd been to him. I had told him my girlfriend back home wasn't too thrilled about my being there. He doesn't know about Tracy either."

"You are one sneaky guy."

"Not sneaky enough, I guess, or I wouldn't be in this mess. So that weekend I sat Tracy down and tried to reason with her. Told her I was definitely getting married and nothing was going to stop me. I said we'd had some good times together, but now it was over, and we should get on with our lives and not do things to make each other miserable. She was calmer that weekend, but she still cried and still had this weird obsession with me. Then she started giving me this garbage about how I had deceived her and made her think I was going to marry her, that she had stayed faithful to me all this time and had given up good opportunities for other relationships, that I owed her for all the lies and pain I had caused."

"Owed her? You mean like money?"

"That's what it came down to. Then she got into the most insane thing of all. You should have seen her. She leaned forward like she was about to tell me this incredible secret. Her eyes were all teary and blood-shot, and she says, 'I assume you're still going to pay for my car like you promised.'

"I said, 'What car?' At this point I was beginning to wonder if she was having some kind of mental breakdown.

" 'You told me you would buy me that Probe,' she said, 'and you talked me into getting it. Now I'm going to be stuck paying for it while you leave me in the lurch.'

"I couldn't believe it! She was talking about her Ford Probe, a pretty nice one even though it had a zillion miles on it. A few months ago she had wanted to buy it and asked me if I would check it out for her and make sure they weren't trying to rip her off. I checked it over and drove it, and it seemed pretty good considering the miles on it. Then she asked me to deal with the guy to try to get a better price. So I got him down to three thousand, which was as low as he would go. Tracy thought that sounded pretty good, so she bought it. That was all that happened with the Probe. There was never any talk that I would buy it for her. Where would I get that kind of money? She knows how broke I am. I'm still paying off credit cards from when I lived in Chicago!"

It was true that despite the money David made as a mechanic, he had been not only broke but in debt for as long as I could remember.

He continued. "She insisted that I had promised her I would pay for that car, and here she had been waiting all this time for me to pay her, and now I was pulling this stunt just to get out of it. I almost died laughing! I said, 'You really think I would get married just to get out of paying for a car?'

" 'Just pay for it, then,' she said, like I already had admitted that I owed her for it.

" 'Forget it,' I said. 'Half the reason I'm so broke now is that I bought you so many things while I was living up here.' Saying that was a mistake, because it sent her off on a tirade about all that she had done for me and all the chances for happiness she had missed because of me. But it was all make-believe! Just incredible. I wanted to get out of that room as fast as I could and away from this freaky woman. I told her I wasn't paying for the car, and if that's what she was throwing these fits over, it wasn't going to work. Then I walked out and drove home and hoped that would be the end of it."

"But it wasn't," I said.

David sighed. "No, it just got worse after that. I've had to go up there one more time since then to calm her down. For whatever reason, she seems to have latched on to the idea that I owe her for her car, and she's not going to stop tormenting me until I pay her for it. Then right before you came home, she started calling the house again while Cheryl was here. Once an hour she would call. She's still threatening to come down. It's getting pretty hard to explain. That's why Cheryl's been mad at me. She knows something's going on, and I have to figure out something to tell her or some way to get rid of Tracy once and for all." David stopped, as if waiting for me to tell him what to do.

I said, "Well, first of all, I think you should tell Cheryl everything and ask for her forgiveness."

David leaned back against the wall and laughed. "Are you nuts? She'd kill me."

"She might. Or she might forgive you. Part of Tracy's power over you is that she can threaten to blab things to Cheryl. But if you tell Cheryl everything yourself, and Tracy knows it, then Tracy has nothing to threaten you with, and she'll fade away."

He shook his head slowly. "I doubt that. Besides, I saw Tracy even after Cheryl and I were engaged. How could I possibly admit to that?"

"It was a mistake to keep seeing Tracy, but now you've got to live with it. Forgiveness is a wonderful thing. I wholeheartedly believe in it."

He gazed out the window. "I believe in survival."

"Forgiveness could lead to that."

"I don't see how," he said. "I'm not like you, Chris. I can never seem to start from scratch. Everything I've done in the past always comes back to haunt me."

"That's because you don't let go of it."

"How can you say that? Look how hard I've tried to get rid of Tracy."

"She exploits you because you're hiding things and denying things. The only answer is to take her power away by confessing."

"How about you?" asked David. "Did you confess everything to Beth and ask for her forgiveness when you got back from Chicago?"

"No," I said, squirming in my chair. "But I asked God to forgive me for that whole mess up there."

"So you never told Beth about Linda."

"No. Maybe I should have. But Beth and I were barely dating at that point. And Linda was never my girlfriend. She was just some girl you made me go out with."

"Made you! *Made you!*" He laughed. "You're just making excuses. You don't follow your own advice. Confession and forgiveness."

"All right," I admitted. "Maybe I didn't handle it as well as I should have. But still, it's good advice. When I left Chicago, I turned my back on that whole life-style and begged God to restore my life spiritually. You can't fake your way out of this—a little lie here, a little truth there. You'll only end up caught in a nastier web."

David stood and folded his hands behind his neck as if trying to squeeze his head off, one of his gestures of frustration that was familiar to me. "You may be right," he said, "but there is one other thing I'd like to try first. If you help me with this and it doesn't work, I promise I'll try it your way."

I sighed in irritation. "You haven't listened to a word I've said, have you?"

"I will confess everything to Cheryl and ask forgiveness from her and God. Just promise to help me, man. We're brothers. You're the only one I can turn to."

"Name it," I said, wary of what solution he might have concocted, but also moved that we were close enough again that he would ask for my help. He hadn't spoken to me this way in a long time.

"I know I've said this in the past and been wrong, but I think I can get Tracy out of my life if I can remove this one final obsession of hers—that car I supposedly promised to buy for her. I think she has convinced herself I really did promise to pay for it."

"So you want to give her the money," I said.

"Right."

"Bad idea."

"Wait. My idea is she'll probably settle for half. If I could get her to agree to take half the money, then I could chalk it up as a fifteen-hundred-dollar mistake. At least that would end it."

"Would it end it, or would she keep coming back for more once she realizes you'd give in to something like that?"

"I honestly think she would take the money and run. She's looking for a way out of this too. We're both sick of each other."

"I don't like it," I said. "It's blackmail. It's paying her off to keep quiet. That's bound to lead to trouble."

"I know you don't like it," David said. "Neither do I. But I'm desperate. I have to give it a try."

"Where do I fit in?" I asked, afraid that I already knew the answer.

"Well," he began, hesitating. "The problem is I don't have a cent. I've been working hard, trying to save and get my debts paid off once and for all. But I've been stiffed a few times on these cars I've restored and . . . I don't know, money has never been my strong suit. I could pay you back within six months—I promise I will—but I need to borrow a thousand dollars. I can pull the rest of it together myself. I'm almost positive that will get Tracy out of our lives."

I laughed, shook my head, and said, "Of all the people you could turn to for money, I'm about the worst prospect you could choose."

"There is no one else for me to choose," he said.

"I have no money, David. I'm a poor graduate student, remember? It's all I can do to pay my rent."

"Please, Chris. I know you and Beth have been saving."

"But that's *our* money. That's not *my* money to give away. We're saving for the wedding, and to get an apartment."

"The wedding's not till December. I'll have paid you back before then."

"It's not mine to give."

"To loan, you mean."

"Do you want me to go to Beth and tell her this whole story about Tracy and ask her—"

"No! Please. You can never tell Beth about this. She talks to Cheryl. I never would have told you anything if I thought you were going to blab it to Beth."

"Then how am I going to explain a sudden withdrawal of a thousand dollars from our meager bank account? I'm not going to start lying to her. I think we've seen the trouble that can cause."

"Just tell her you're giving it to your brother to help him out. Tell her you can't explain all the circumstances, but it's a desperate situation that could affect the rest of his life. The money will be back in the account in just a few months, well before she needs it. I'll pay interest if you want."

I fidgeted in my chair. "It's not a matter of interest. There just has to be a better way."

"Please, Chris. I told you I'd try your way if this doesn't work. Confession and forgiveness."

"My way is certainly cheaper. Forgiveness costs nothing."

"It costs plenty," said David. "Now, how about it?"

"I don't think paying off Tracy is a good equivalent for restoring your life spiritually and resolving things honestly with Cheryl."

"I *will* restore my life spiritually. That's what I want to do. Cheryl and I both. Just as soon as we get past this. A thousand dollars, Chris. You don't know how hard it is to ask you for this. Help me out here, and I'll never forget it."

As much as I considered the loan a bad idea, I was flattered David thought I was the one who could help him, and I was encouraged that he was at least promising to turn his life around once this crisis was over. I could get the money. Our finances would be tight, and it wouldn't be easy, but the money was not the real obstacle. The question I wrestled with was whether I should hold firm and try to get him to resolve this problem in the way every instinct told me was best or give in to the almost irresistible temptation to go along with him and make him feel that I was a brother who loved him and would do anything to help him out of a jam.

"You couldn't get an advance on your credit card or something?" I asked weakly, my resolve crumbling.

"I'm maxed out," he said, suppressing a smile, knowing now that I would give in.

"All right," I said. "I'll take a look at the account, and if the money's there, I'll lend it to you, even though I have a bad feeling about how this is going to turn out."

"Thanks, brother," he said and hugged me so hard it knocked me off my chair.

I gave him the money the next day. I decided not to tell Beth what I had done, at least not for a while. If I told her, she would press me for the real reason he wanted the money, and I'd be forced either to break the confidence with David or lie. I kept the wedding money in my bank account, and I intended for it to be replaced before Beth ever realized it was gone. As I feared, my decision to do things David's way led to disaster, but in ways even more sinister than I had predicted.

———

Tracy settled for half the price of the car, as David thought she would, and that gave us a few weeks of peace. David said little to me about how this deal came about except to say, "It's over. She took the money, and we'll never hear from her again."

But we heard from her again, even louder this time. Less than three weeks after we were supposedly rid of her for good, the phone calls started up again. She called two or three times a day. This not only annoyed David, but Mom and Dad also. David could not adequately explain to them the identity of this frantic young woman who was not his fiancée but who demanded to speak to him even more often than

Cheryl did. He tried to pass her off as some girl he had known in Chicago that he had gotten into a bad car deal with, but Mom and Dad knew he was lying. They turned to me for an explanation, but I refused to get involved, referring them immediately back to David. The calls were most embarrassing when Cheryl was over. David tried to get Mom to tell Tracy he wasn't home, but she would do this only a few times. As had always been the case at our house, if we were home, we took our own phone calls. Whenever he had to talk to Tracy, David took the call alone in his room, and the conversation never lasted for more than ten minutes. If Cheryl was there, she would sulk for the rest of the night, making David angrier, which in turn made Cheryl even more pouty. When I got him alone, I asked him whether Tracy was after more money, but all he would say was "She's out of her mind. I don't know how to stop her." The open, confiding tone he had used the night he asked for the thousand dollars was gone. He had retreated back inside himself and shut me out.

After several days of the renewed phone calls, which sometimes came after Mom and Dad had gone to bed, Dad told David he didn't know what was going on, but he wanted the calls to stop. He said if they didn't, he would talk to the girl himself and see what was going on.

Almost miraculously, the calls did stop right after Dad issued his ultimatum. We had four days of silence from Tracy. Then the situation took a turn for the worse. It was a Thursday evening, and David and Cheryl were in the living room with Mom and Dad watching television. Beth was at a training meeting for her upcoming China trip, so I was alone in my room doing some reading. I heard a car pull into the driveway, and a moment later I heard a woman's voice in the foyer. It was Tracy, and she was talking to Mom.

Then I heard David's voice in the foyer. I was tempted to go out to see what was happening, but I didn't want to be put in the position of having to fit into whatever preposterous story he was probably making up right at that moment to explain Tracy's presence.

In a few minutes the voices stopped, and I heard the creak of the floorboards in the hallway as someone walked toward the bedrooms. I heard David's door slam shut. I put my ear up to my door, but the voices in David's room were too muffled for me to hear.

I heard his door fly open with a crash, and I backed away from my own door just in time for David to burst into my room. I was standing so close to the door that he charged right into me. Then he put his arms on my shoulders, pushed me against the wall, and in an intense whisper said, "She's here!"

"I heard."

"Can you believe it! And Cheryl's right there in the living room. You've got to help me get her out of here."

"Cheryl?"

"No, idiot. Tracy."

"How am I supposed to do that?"

"Listen, Chris, I'm going to ask you to do something, and I don't have time to debate it with you. Cheryl's already mad at me, and if she thinks Tracy is here to see me, I'm dead."

"What do I have to do?" I asked, dreading the prospect of getting sucked into another one of his schemes.

"Two things. One, she's demanding five hundred dollars right now, and she swears she'll leave me alone after that. She has calculated that that's how much I owe her for—"

"David! She's a liar! You can't give her more money."

He pushed me against the wall again and held me there. "My whole engagement with Cheryl is about to go down the drain. I'll pay you the five hundred with the rest I owe you. I guarantee this will be the last time I ask. I'll put a stop to her now one way or the other. Come on now. Cheryl could pop in here any second."

"What's the second thing?" I asked, stalling my decision on the first one.

"I need you to go into the living room with Tracy and act like she's with you."

"No way!"

"I have to introduce her somehow! It would seem suspicious not to. And Tracy wants to see Cheryl. That's her other demand, believe it or not. Her absolute final demand to end this thing. So you have to help me. She has agreed to pretend she came to see you."

"Well, I haven't agreed to it!" I protested. "I'm engaged too, remember? I shouldn't be having strange women visiting me here any more than you should."

"You can cover it easier than I can. Say she's a friend from grad school who was stopping by on her way home to somewhere. Terre Haute, maybe."

"You come up with these lies so easily," I said, which brought to his lips a quick, perverse grin of pride. "This is stupid, David. Nobody's going to believe Tracy's in grad school."

"Don't be a snob. I've seen a lot of your Purdue friends that are freakier than her. Now get your checkbook. Please."

"Do you remember the deal we made that if the thousand dollars didn't work, you would try things my way?"

"Don't start with that," he said. "My way hasn't failed yet. In fact, it's just about to succeed. If you ruin it now, I'll never forgive you."

What made me go along with these preposterous schemes of David's? All I can think of is that it has always been this way between us—we help each other out of jams, period. I can't bear to consider the other possibilities—that I lack the courage to stand against him in the moment of crisis, or that deep down I am just as corrupt as he is. As I wrote the check for five hundred dollars to Tracy, I said to David, "Never again, under any circumstances, will I give money for this."

"I already guaranteed you this would be the end of it," he said.

"I don't care if she threatens to destroy every marriage in the family and slaughter every one of us one by one, she's not getting any more of my money."

"What did I just say? It's finished," David said. "Now let's take her in the living room and get this over with."

"I feel like an idiot."

I had not laid eyes on Tracy since I had lived in Chicago. She hadn't changed much, maybe a little skinnier, more frenzied, her hair a little spikier. She was remarkably calm considering all the commotion she was causing. She actually tried to hug me, but I pushed her away.

"I don't like this game you're playing," I said.

"I'm the one who's been toyed with for the last year and a half," she said.

David gently pushed us both toward the door and said, "Let's not have a little debate here. Let's just go say our introductions so Tracy can hit the road."

"Thanks for your hospitality," Tracy said.

"Thanks for blackmailing us," I said.

"That's enough," David said.

I'm afraid I didn't give an award-winning performance in the living room that night. Mom, Dad, and Cheryl were silent as we paraded in. Tracy ended up between David and me as we stood in a row in front of the fireplace, our audience gaping at us. Tracy's looks were an attention grabber in any setting, with her blond shock of hair exploding out of her head and her wiry, catlike frame appearing ready to dart out at you at any moment. Dad was the least able of the three of them to conceal his skepticism about this stranger in our midst. His eyebrows were contorted in as much confusion as if we had found a space alien in the backyard and had brought it inside to examine it.

I opened my mouth to introduce her, but the words came out so croakingly soft at first that I had to begin again. "This is Penelope," I said, choosing the name only an instant before I said it, and bringing an insane smile to Tracy's face. "I know her from Purdue. She's passing through town, and she just stopped by to say hi. She's from Terre Haute. She's driving there tonight."

"Whereabouts in Terre Haute are you from?" Dad asked. I couldn't tell from his tone whether this was a serious question or whether it was an indication that he didn't believe our story.

Tracy looked at me and smiled. "Um . . . the west side," she said.

"You know a guy named Melvin Polk?" Dad asked.

"Um, the name sounds sort of familiar, but no, I can't place him. Maybe my dad knows him."

"Terre Haute is a big place," Mom put in weakly, apparently trying to put our guest at ease.

"Not so big," my father growled.

David rolled his eyes.

I said, "Well, Penelope wants to get home before it gets too late, so she's going to be leaving."

"You want a Coke or something?" Mom asked halfheartedly.

"No, thank you," Tracy answered, "I'd better run. Nice to meet you all."

Then she turned and headed for the door, making David and me have to practically run to catch up with her. On the front porch, out of hearing of the living room, David said to her, "Now, I want—" but she kept on walking, never looking at us, waving her hands in dismissal as she headed down the driveway. David made no attempt to stop her or to finish his sentence.

As she drove away, I said, "This still isn't over, is it?"

"It will be," he said. "I have to get back in there. It wouldn't hurt if you went back in there too."

"Why?"

"So they can see you acting normal, like her visit was no big deal."

"So they can ask me more questions about my friend Penelope, and I can make up more lies about her? No, thanks. I've had all I can take for one night."

David shrugged, squeezed my shoulder, and went inside. That was it. No word of thanks for the five hundred dollars or for participating in the whole pathetic episode.

I tried to put Tracy out of my mind. Fortunately, Mom and Dad asked no questions about "Penelope." Though I am sure they knew something was phony about the incident, I never knew how much of the truth they penetrated then or later.

David drove up to Chicago that weekend to see Tracy. When I asked him why he was going, all he would say was, "With her you can't take any chances. I have to find a way to make sure she never shows her face again. I don't think Cheryl bought the 'Penelope' routine, and if Tracy comes back and drops her disguise, it's all over for me and Cheryl."

When he got back Sunday night, he came to my room and said, "She's history."

"What did you do, kill her?" I asked, and for a second, it crossed my mind that this was a possibility.

He laughed and said, "No. How evil do you think I am?"

I did not answer that. Instead I asked, "What did you do?"

He was reluctant to tell me, but throughout the next hour he gradually made it clear that he had threatened her in various ways if she ever came to Indianapolis again. He threatened to turn her in at work for being a drug user, which may or may not have been true. He threatened to spread rumors about her among her friends, tell her landlord about supposedly illegal activities going on in her apartment, do harm to her car.

"How evil do you think I am?"

I got the impression David was hesitant to tell me about this only because he didn't want me to have any more damaging information about him, not because he felt guilty about it. He acted satisfied with himself that he had scared Tracy into submission. He boastfully declared that he had told her, "The minute I see your face in Indianapolis, life as you have known it is over."

Tracy did not come back, but the relationship between David and Cheryl did not improve. She could not let go of her suspicions about Tracy and other issues, and David either openly lied about these things or refused to discuss them.

CHRIS

*D*uring those last few weeks of his life, David worked furiously on the car that would kill him while the rest of his life continued to crumble. As his relationship with Cheryl slid further into suspicion and accusations, he grew more resentful of the harmonious relationship between Beth and me. Beth had to raise her own money for her planned trip to China, which was to last for seven weeks. As the trip grew closer, she realized she was two thousand dollars short of the amount she needed. She had sent out letters to family and friends asking for support, but people were more reluctant to give for her second trip than they were for her first. I told her she should take the balance out of our savings, but she didn't want to spend that money on anything except the things we would need once we were married. This filled me with pangs of guilt, considering what I had done with that money. As she reached the final payment deadline for China, she decided not to go. I was sorry she had to back out, but I was thrilled that we would have the whole summer together.

David, however, reacted with silence when I told him Beth was staying home. "I'm glad she'll be with me," I said, not knowing how to interpret his stony look. He finally responded with a few accusatory questions like "Why couldn't she borrow the money?" I couldn't understand why he'd be upset that Beth would be with me for the summer instead of thousands of miles away. Looking back, I believe he was simply worried that people would notice the stark contrast between the loving relationship Beth and I enjoyed and the increasingly nasty relationship he and Cheryl had going. Faced with the prospect that his own engagement was self-destructing, David decided his only choice, though I didn't realize it at the time, was to undermine my engagement with Beth. Then, at least, this absurd contest would be a draw. He would never have admitted that, of course. Articulating it, even to himself, would have revealed it as too preposterous for him to act on. But some of the signs emerged immediately, and some came to light only after his death, once the damage had been done.

One night not long after David had made his final, threat-filled visit to Chicago to resolve the Tracy situation, she called him, and they had an abrupt, unfriendly conversation. Fortunately, Cheryl was not there to witness it, but I was. I should have left David alone, because her call frustrated and angered him so much that he was slamming things around the kitchen, but I said, "I thought you had convinced her not to call you anymore."

He flashed me a stern, almost hateful look and said, "I've got it under control. You don't need to worry about it."

I was in the process of pouring myself a glass of milk, and I kept silent as I filled the glass, put the bottle back in the refrigerator, closed the door, and headed out of the room. I would venture no more conversation and was hoping for a clean getaway. David stood facing the sink, trying to get control of his anger, but the way he gripped the edge of the sink and leaned slightly over it gave me the momentary impression of someone who was about to vomit.

A few steps before I was safely out of the room, David spun around and fumed, "Don't think that Tracy gives you anything to hold over my head."

I walked back in and set my glass on the counter. "What are you talking about?" I asked.

"You heard me."

"I don't want anything to hold over your head."

"I know Cheryl talks to you sometimes."

"Well, I've never told her anything. You know I never would."

"Do I know that? You're not innocent, Chris. You've done things. I've seen you in situations that I'm sure Beth would not be too thrilled to know about."

"I'm sure you have," I said, trying to keep my voice soothing and reasonable. "So we're even. So let's leave the past where it belongs. Now Beth and I are engaged, we're faithful to each other, we're working to plan a good Christian marriage. Everything else is past and forgiven."

David scoffed and turned away.

"I know you're mad because Tracy called, but don't take it out on me. I told you what I thought you should do about this situation. I still think the only way to bring peace between you and Cheryl is to tell her what's going on and ask her to forgive—"

David spun around toward me again and said, "I'm not asking for your advice. Thanks anyway. I know how to handle Cheryl. She's not Miss Little-Innocent-Victim-of-David the way you try to make her out to be. You can't lay all the blame on me. Cheryl's probably cheated on me too."

I picked up my glass and started to walk out again.

"I've seen the way she looks at you. I wouldn't be surprised if you two have tried something behind my back."

"You're sick," I said. "The days of those kinds of games are over. I don't want to hear it, not even in joking."

"Why are you so riled?" he taunted. "I'm not jealous. Beth gives me a glance every once in a while too."

"Not even in joking, David. I mean it."

"Beth would come to me in a snap. In fact, I—"

His words shot a sudden surge of rage through me. Barely realizing what I was doing, I grabbed him by his shirt, pulled him forward, and slammed him against the refrigerator, breaking a few of Mom's magnets and sending most of the others flying. I think I was even more surprised by my actions than he was. I punched him twice in the face, and he was too stunned to react. We hadn't fought with our fists in years. Mom reached the kitchen almost immediately and screamed. David looked surprised but not angry. In fact, he appeared to be suppressing a smile. Mom scampered around on the floor, picking up the magnets.

David left the room. I helped Mom with the magnets and gave her some vague explanation for why we were fighting. She said, "You need to be helping him, Chris, not beating him up."

"I'd like to help him, Mom. I don't know what to do." I was embarrassed about losing my temper with him, especially so soon after talking about forgiveness.

"What's he involved in that has you and Cheryl so upset?"

"I don't know."

"Don't lie to me," she said. "You know more than you're telling. That's the way you two have always been. Covering up for each other. But some things need to be faced and dealt with."

"Why don't you tell that to David?"

"Do you think he listens to me anymore?" she asked.

"Do you think he listens to me?"

She shook her head. "Maybe I need to throw him up against the refrigerator myself." She looked at the fragments in her hand. "You guys broke my 'World's Greatest Mom' magnet. That was my favorite one."

David and I did not discuss the incident in the kitchen again. The next night he asked me to go play basketball with him, and we played for a couple hours without even mentioning any of our difficulties.

A few days later, though, as Beth and I sat on the porch after dinner, she started asking me questions about the time I lived with David in Chicago, which she had never been curious about before. Did I date anyone while I was there, she wanted to know. I cautiously told her that I had gone out with Linda several times, but only because David pushed me into it, and I said I was never very interested in her. I reminded Beth that she and I had been free to date other people back then.

"It's just funny that in all this time you've never mentioned any Linda," she said.

"I don't see anything funny about it. Do you really want me to talk about every girl I've gone out with? I wouldn't think that would make for a very good conversation."

She looked at me and started to say something, but then changed her mind and looked away again. Finally she asked, "Do you still keep in touch with . . . anybody . . . you knew in Chicago?"

"No. That was not a great time in my life, and I'd rather just put it behind me. Why are you suddenly asking about this?"

"I'm just curious."

"Has David been telling you things?"

"Why would you think that?"

"Has he?"

"No!"

Her tone of voice was wrong, just slightly too high-pitched. This was the first time I ever believed Beth was lying to me. I was certain she was asking about Chicago because David had planted some story in her mind.

"I don't want you talking to him anymore," I said.

"Why not? Does he know things you'd rather keep hidden?"

"No! But I wouldn't be surprised if he was telling some lies about me right now to cause trouble between you and me."

"Why would he do that?"

"That's just the way he is."

Beth dropped her questions for the moment, but she looked at me with an inscrutable expression, her true thoughts hidden deep within her.

I found David alone in the garage late that night polishing his old car. He looked up when I walked in but didn't speak.

"What have you been telling Beth about me?" I asked.

He kept the cloth moving on the car in swift, circular motions. In a lazy tone he asked, "Did she tell you I told her something about you?"

"I know from the questions she's asking that you did. I just want to know what lies you've been telling her."

"Maybe you have a guilty conscience."

I walked over and grabbed the rag out of his hand. He stood up straight and looked directly at me, his body tense, ready for a fight, his lips pressed into that devious half smile.

"I don't think you want to start a fight. Dad about flipped when he heard you threw me up against the refrigerator and broke Mom's stuff. You're on thin ice with him. You start messing around and damage one of these cars, you'll be on your way back to Purdue early."

"Why do you try to ruin everything for me and yourself and every-body else? Things don't have to be this way. You bring your own tragedy upon yourself."

"Leave me alone, then."

"I just came in here to tell you one thing," I said. "Don't go near Beth. I don't want you to ever talk to her again unless I'm there."

"Oh, is that what you're afraid of?" he asked, smiling.

"What?"

"I could get her to be with me instead of you anytime I wanted."

"Don't start this, David."

"I could get her with a snap," he said, snapping his fingers a fraction of an inch from my nose.

I pushed his hand away and shoved him up against his car. "I'm telling you to stay away from her. This goes way beyond the tricks you've played on me with girlfriends in the past. If I find out you've seen Beth, I'll tell Cheryl everything I know. You've always been able to trust me, but if you break my trust with Beth, I will tell the world about you and Tracy. Mom and Dad too."

I had not intended to make this threat. The possibility of betraying David had not even occurred to me until the moment he started taunt-ing me about Beth.

"I could get her in a snap," he repeated, pleased that this idiotic phrase annoyed me. "I did talk to her. I got her to see me then, and I could get her to see me now if I wanted. Any time I want. Any place. To do anything I want."

I shoved him away from me, and he slipped on a patch of oil and fell to his knees a few feet away, scattering his tools with a clatter across the garage.

"In a snap!" he yelled after me as I walked outside into the darkness.

David fell in love with the phrase "in a snap" and taunted me with it every time I saw him for the next several days. He would say only those three words, then walk away without waiting for a reaction. He and Cheryl were spending less time together, and he was spending more time alone or with Dad in the evenings, tinkering in the garage. Dad was perfunctory and distant with me. For all I knew, David was telling him lies about me too. I didn't have the strength or inclination to fight that battle. My real concern was keeping David from poisoning Beth against me.

When I was alone with her on the balcony of her apartment the next day, where she had served dinner for us, I warned her that whenever David was depressed or in trouble, he often lashed out at people, even those who cared about him, and that's what I believed he was doing now. I pleaded with her not to let him lure us into the same web of destruction that was ruining his engagement with Cheryl.

"What's he doing to make her so mad?" she asked.

"She suspects things about him."

"What does she suspect?"

"I don't know."

"But you *do* know," Beth said. "Why won't you tell me?"

"It's a brother thing," I said. "There are certain things you can't talk about."

"I never knew you to be so secretive," she said. "It worries me."

"I'm not secretive about *us*. But if something is told to me in confidence, then I can't go blabbing it."

"You can't even tell me?"

"No. Certain things—"

"Do the secret things about David also have something to do with you?"

"No. What did he tell you, Beth? I know he talked to you. He told me he did. You said he didn't, but I know he did."

She looked caught, her face tinged with embarrassment.

She said, "You want me to tell you everything, but you reserve the right to hide things from me."

"I'm not hiding things from you. I'm keeping a confidence."

She thought about this for a second and replied, "So am I." Then, as if to indicate the conversation was over, she picked up some of the plates, slid open the screen door with her foot, and walked inside, slamming the door behind her.

"You shouldn't have secrets with my brother," I shouted to her. I took up the rest of the dishes and went inside to continue the conversation. She was rinsing the dishes and placing them in the dishwasher. Her face was frozen, the way it gets when she has shut me off.

The open door of the dishwasher stood between us. I leaned on the counter, hoping to make eye contact with her, but she was now focused solely on the dishes. I said, "Someday maybe everything can be explained. But for now, just realize that he's desperate. He'll say anything. Whatever he's told you, you can't believe. All I ask is that right now you stay away from him. He's dangerous, Beth. Please stay away from him."

She turned off the faucet and placed a rinsed casserole dish on the counter. "You're the one who looks guilty, not David," she said without looking at me.

"Don't you see, Beth? This is exactly what he wants to happen between us. He wants to sow suspicion. Don't let him win. Don't let him undermine us."

Beth would not discuss it anymore that night, and I didn't know whether or not I had convinced her to stay away from David and his lies.

The next indication I had of David's scheming came the following week, the day before he died. I had avoided home as much as possible since my argument with David in the garage. After work, I spent most of each evening at Beth's or Bill's. The day before his accident, David found me in my room after work while I changed clothes to play racquetball with Bill. David stuck his head in the door and, without saying a word, reached his arm in and began snapping his fingers. I ignored him at first, but as he kept up the snapping, accompanied by his leering smile, I said, "Why are you doing this? Don't you see how stupid it is? Snapping your fingers over and over. You're a moron. What's the point?"

He stopped snapping and stepped into the room. He stared at me for a moment, then said, "I want to keep you from being so smug. So untouchable. So much better than the rest of us."

"It isn't like that. You don't need to turn everything into a competition. There's no reason why we can't both win, why we can't both be happy."

His face registered no sign that he heard these words. "You'll see," he said, snapping his fingers. "I want to do an experiment to show you I'm right. I'll prove it. You'll see."

"What do you mean an experiment?"

But he fled my room and slammed the door behind him. I finished changing clothes and left. I was tired of playing his games.

On the morning of David's death, I awoke later than usual, about nine o'clock. I had been out the night before, first with Bill and later with Beth. As I sat up in bed, I could see that someone had slipped a folded piece of notebook paper under my door. At first I thought it must be from Robin, since such a gesture was more characteristic of her than anyone else in the family.

I opened the paper and read, *Be back soon. Snap.*

These were the last words I ever received from my brother. Even though I didn't know exactly what the note meant, David's "snap" frustrated and infuriated me in exactly the way he must have intended. I wadded up the note and threw it away. I pulled on a robe and went looking for him. Mom was at the kitchen table drinking a cup of coffee and reading the newspaper.

"Where is he?" I demanded.

"Which one?" she asked.

"David."

"He took that old car out to test it. Said he just about has the engine right and wants to give it a whirl. What's wrong?"

"Is Dad with him?"

"No. He went alone. Was he supposed to take you with him?"

"No."

"Well, then, what are you all wild-eyed about? He should be back before long. Sit down and have some cereal. You haven't sat at this table for more than a week. Do you want some of that coffee before I turn it off?"

"Okay," I said and went to pour myself some. Maybe the note was only a hoax, I tried to tell myself. A stupid way for David to throw "snap" in my face and get me riled even before breakfast. Maybe the only answer to his strategy was to ignore him. I poured some coffee, got myself some Cheerios and milk, and sat at the table. Mom passed me part of the paper. She knew I was normally not too talkative at breakfast, so she didn't try a conversation. Like my father, I normally spent the first forty-five minutes of the day engrossed in breakfast, the newspaper, and coffee. Today, the newspaper was nothing more than incomprehensible blobs of ink that my eyes stared at blankly. If David's note did mean anything, I thought, "snap" was his way of saying he could get Beth to see him any time he wanted, and "be back soon" meant he had gone to see her.

I walked over to the phone and dialed her number.

"Aren't you going to finish your cereal?" Mom asked.

"Gotta call Beth."

Beth did not answer. Her machine came on, and I hung up. So what did that prove? She could be running errands, as she often did on Saturdays. She could be sleeping in and not answering. She could be in the shower.

Or she could be with him.

Whatever the truth was, David's little note had served its purpose. My stomach was tied in knots even before the Cheerios turned soggy.

After I finished eating, took a shower, and dressed, I tried Beth again. Still no answer. I went out to the garage. His car was still missing. The longer I went without being able to talk to Beth or David, the more convinced I became that they were together. What was he telling her? What was he trying to talk her into? Why did she see him against my wishes? I tried to not allow the possibility of a romantic relationship between them to enter my thoughts, but it crept into my mind anyway. That would be the ultimate triumph for David, and I wouldn't put it past him. But Beth? No way. Unless he found a way to trick her, lure her. Oh, why couldn't she just stay away from him?

I flung David's tools, one by one, against the inside of the garage door, barely aware of what I was doing. I stopped after a while and tried to reason with myself. David could drive up at any moment and laugh the whole thing off. Beth could call and say she had been at the store, and why don't I come over and have lunch with her?

I needed to get my mind on something else. I called Bill and asked if he wanted to play basketball. He did. I left for a couple of hours, and by the time I got back, my brother was dead and my family was paralyzed with grief.

The next several days were a haze of pain and mourning, with visits from family and friends, hugs, regrets, memories, the funeral, and the inescapable question: Why? I no longer had the inclination or the time to pursue the meaning of David's note, though I did retrieve it from the garbage can.

Beth was loving and supportive to me during those sad days. The suspicion and distance that had built up between us vanished for the moment, and we were as close as we had ever been. She stayed up half the night comforting me. She prayed with me. She bought me cards with words of comfort from the Bible. Spiritually, we were united in a way we had always longed for.

Beth was also a supportive friend to Cheryl, who was almost hysterical at times. Everyone spoke only good things about David. No one alluded to the rift between him and Cheryl that had been growing wider every day. No one hinted at the existence of Tracy, and no one called her to tell her David was dead.

My preference would have been to bury all the ugliness with David and never refer to Tracy or any of the rest of it again. To me, that made good sense. Why torture ourselves over things we can no longer do anything about? Learn from those bad experiences, but don't keep resurrecting them. Live in the present and work to make it as good as possible.

Beth didn't see it that way. She said my problem had always been that I would rather ignore things than deal with them.

David finally accomplished his purpose of bringing us all down with him, but he did it from the grave. The seeds of suspicion he had sown sprouted and grew rapidly after the shock of his death had worn off. Questions that lay dormant during his funeral sprang to life after the relatives had gone home and the phone calls tapered off and we had time to sit alone and ruminate over the past.

We wanted to know where David had been in the hours before his accident. He had never driven any of his antique cars for more than an hour at a time, so he must have stopped somewhere, but no one claimed to have seen him. I asked Beth whether she had seen him that day, and she said no, she had been shopping. Another mystery was that one of the items pulled from the wreck was my checkbook! I certainly had not given it to him, and I don't know when he had taken it or what he planned to do with it. He had not written any checks from it. I hadn't used it for three days before he died, so he could have come into my room and picked it up any time after that. I told no one about David's note, but I kept it in my desk and pulled it out and looked at it occasionally. His cocky *Be back soon. Snap,* which had so angered me before, now made me unbearably sad, since no power on earth could bring him back.

The truth spilled out several days after the funeral when Beth came over to see me and said she wanted to talk to me on behalf of Cheryl.

"What does she want?" I asked defensively, since Cheryl had already approached me again with suspicious questions that I did not want to answer. "I don't plan to help her dig up a bunch of dirt on David, if that's what she's after."

Beth said Cheryl only wanted to know the facts, so she could set her mind at ease. I didn't think the facts I knew would set anyone's mind at ease, and I told Beth so. Beth said Cheryl had the right to know the truth no matter how painful it might be. I disagreed, and we argued about it awhile.

In the tense silence that followed this disagreement, Beth's face took on a worried look, her eyes narrow and averted. Quietly she said, "Cheryl told me something you said to her that bothered me a lot. She said when you refused to tell her anything, you told her your mind was arranged in compartments, and David's death sealed off a whole huge chamber of secrets and memories that you would never open up again."

"I might have said something along those lines," I said. "I think my loyalty to David shouldn't end just because he's dead."

"That wasn't the part that bothered me," Beth said. "I'm more worried about all those separate compartments you keep in your mind, each with their little secrets that you won't allow to cross from one chamber to the other."

"Well, I wouldn't carry it too far—"

"It makes me wonder what you keep hidden from me in some of those compartments."

"You make it sound different than it really is," I said. "I've poured my soul out to you. There's a difference between hiding things from you and blabbing things that David told me in confidence."

"So you won't tell me the secrets about David that Cheryl wants to know?"

"Would you tell Cheryl?"

"I'd hate to hide things from her."

"Then, no, I guess I won't tell you."

Beth looked away, and an angry silence filled the room. After a few minutes she stood up and said she had to leave. She headed toward the door as I followed, practically running, after her.

"You barely got here!" I said. "Sit down and let's talk. Why are you so upset about this? Why are you so intent on finding things out about—"

"It's not that!" she shouted without looking back.

"What is it, then?"

"I can't talk about it right now."

She got in her car and drove away. Running off like that was completely uncharacteristic of Beth. I had never seen her do it. She had always been the one to sit and reason things through until they were resolved. I didn't know what was gnawing at her, but I was sure it was more than simply her concern that Cheryl find out David's secrets.

Beth refused to talk to me on the phone that night, which was also unlike her even when she was extremely upset with me. One of the things I had always loved about her was that she was not the kind of woman who stormed off and pouted or threw temper tantrums or slammed the phone down in your ear. Those were the kinds of girl-friends David ended up with. Beth had always been different. But that night she said she needed to work out some things for herself and would call me when she was ready to talk. I was baffled.

She called the next evening and said she was ready to talk. I told her I would be right over, but she said she would rather come to my house. I took that as a bad sign. Her place was much more private than mine, with Mom and Dad and Robin hanging around, so the only rea-son she would choose my house over hers was that she could make another quick getaway if she needed to.

———————

Once Beth and I were sequestered in my bedroom, she sat on the edge of my bed and I sat facing her on my desk chair. She looked afraid to begin, her eyes flitting about as if searching for the exit.

"What's wrong, honey?" I asked.

She looked me in the face and, with a strange reluctance in her posture and expression, said, "I think we need to postpone our wed-ding."

"What?" I whispered, my own body too amazed to allow me the breath to speak out loud.

"In fact," she said, looking down now and picking imaginary lint from her slacks, "I called the church today and canceled the date."

"What's going on?"

"I don't think our relationship is based on openness and honesty right now. I don't think you're ready for marriage until we work some things out."

"Don't tell me what I'm ready for. It's not me who's putting the wedding off."

"All right, I'm not ready. We're not ready. We've always said we wanted a strong, honest Christian marriage. I insisted on that."

"So did I. How have I violated that?"

She hesitated. Her skin looked very pale, and little red blotches, her telltale sign of stress, appeared on her neck. "Let me ask you something," she said. "Do we still have the money to pay for a wedding?"

A sweaty wave of dread washed over me. So here was the secret behind her bizarre behavior. She had found out about the money. "Of course," I answered. "Don't we? Unless you've spent—"

"I haven't spent anything," she said. "Have you spent any of the wedding money that was in your account?"

"I didn't spend any of the money, but I loaned some to David."

"How much?"

"Fifteen hundred dollars."

"Is that all?"

"Yes. How much did you think?"

"Did you loan it all to him?" she asked.

"Yes. He was in some trouble and I helped him out. I can get that money back, no problem. It's no reason to postpone the wedding."

"You didn't loan any of it—or give any of it—to someone else?"

"No."

"Someone named Tracy?"

"Oh!" I exclaimed, then stood up and paced involuntarily back and forth, the mysteries of the last week solving themselves one by one with little flashes in my brain. "I get it now! That's why David had my checkbook. He showed you the entry made out to Tracy. For five hundred dollars. What did he tell you about it?"

"Why don't *you* tell me."

"But *when* did he tell you? He must have seen you the morning of his accident. He wouldn't have risked carrying my checkbook around for more than a day, or even part of a day, because I might find it missing. Did you see him that morning?"

"Yes, I did," she admitted.

My surprise gave way to a flash of anger. "And you have the nerve to accuse me of not being honest? You lied and said you didn't see him that morning!"

"I know I did, and maybe that was wrong—"

"Maybe! *Maybe!*"

"But I didn't think David's funeral was the appropriate time to get into it."

"How could you see him when you knew it was the one thing I wanted you not to do? You promised me you wouldn't see him."

"I felt you were hiding things from me, and apparently I was right. The only reason you didn't want me to see him was you didn't want me to know the truth."

"No!" I insisted. "*This* is the reason I didn't want you to see him.

What's happening right this minute! David must be laughing himself silly in his grave! He—"

"Chris, don't talk like that."

"All he wanted to do was make everybody as unhappy as he was. I hate to say that about him now that he's dead, but I can't help it. He won! Don't you see? His whole goal was to plant dissension and suspicion between us, to see if he could bring us down the way he and Cheryl were falling apart. If he knew you had postponed our wedding, he would be ecstatic! Did you tell him you were going to?"

"No. Of course not."

"Too bad. He could have died a happy man."

Beth was rattled. Her eyes were narrow, her mouth closed tight in anger. She didn't want to have to say any more. She wanted me to suddenly break out into explanation, to cry, to beg for her forgiveness. I was outraged, both at her and at David. I was in no mood to budge. I stared her down.

Finally she said, "So do you mind telling me your version of who this Tracy is that you gave our wedding money to?"

"What did David tell you?"

"What difference does it make what he told me? I'm asking you. I shouldn't have had to hear it from David. You should have told me the minute you wrote that check. It's my money too!"

"How many times did you get together with him?"

"Who is Tracy?"

"I'm talking about you and David right now," I said. "Where did you hold these little rendezvous? In your apartment? At little out-of-the-way cafés where no one would recognize you? Did you wear disguises? All this time I was trusting you. You came to me after you had been with my brother, and you acted so innocent."

"It's not like we were having an affair! I saw him just a few times because he said you were in trouble and there were things you would never tell me but that I had to know if I was ever to help you."

"Help me!"

Beth stood up. "I know David's motivations may not have been pure, but I'm not going to let you turn this around and make me look like the one who's done something wrong. David and I did not have any type of relationship, and you know it. You're just trying to avoid telling me whatever relationship you might have had with this Tracy girl."

"Is that what he told you? That I had a relationship with her?"

"Yes, he did. Isn't it true?"

"No!"

"Then why did you give her five hundred dollars behind my back?"

"Tracy was David's problem."

"What do you mean?" she asked.

I hesitated. This story I had never wanted to tell. But David had betrayed me! Made it look like *I* was the one who had something going with Tracy. "If I tell you, do you promise not to tell Cheryl?"

Beth's gaze was still hard and distrustful. After a moment of hesitation she said, "I'm not in a position to make any promises. I think you owe me an explanation, and I don't want any strings attached to it."

"Then I'm afraid I can't go into it."

Beth grabbed her purse from the bed, gripping it with her fist as if she was about to turn it into a weapon and slug me with it. "I have nothing more to say until you're ready to explain why our wedding money ended up being given to some girlfriend of yours in Chicago."

She opened my door and walked out. I followed her down the hall. "That's not the way it was, Beth."

At the front door of the house, she turned to me and said, "I'll give you some time to figure out what you want to say to me, but don't insult me by trying to change the subject or come up with excuses or turn it around and make it look like I've done something wrong. This is about you and what you did. I won't discuss anything else."

She walked out and slammed the door behind her. My first impulse was to run after her and try to straighten everything out right then, but with my hand on the doorknob, I changed my mind. I needed time to think.

Four times that night I picked up the phone to call Beth, and four times I put it back down. I wanted to clear up the confusion about Tracy, but my insides churned with anger. In my agitated state that night, I believed that Beth's conspiring with David behind my back and lying to me about it was worse than anything I had done. I resented her final words that this was only about me and my actions.

The depth of David's betrayal overwhelmed me. I sat in my room and stared for hours, stewing over it, trying to piece together the totality of his evil scheme. It wasn't enough for him merely to lure Beth into meeting with him, which by itself would have infuriated me. It wasn't even enough for him to try to seduce her. David's plan was far more complex. He wanted not so much to win her away from me, though he may or may not have tried to do so, but to turn her against me by removing his own bad traits from himself and placing them squarely on me. He planned to undermine me by turning me into himself! I, not David, would be the errant brother, too weak or too duplicitous to get rid of my old girlfriend, stooping so low as to raid my own wedding fund to secretly pay this evil woman.

Then David would come across as the stronger and wiser older brother, the brother eaten up with concern over the way Chris was ruining his life, and worried sick over what Chris's deceitful behavior would do not only to himself, but also to Beth. I could picture him approaching Beth with his sad, reluctant, puppy-dog eyes, saying something like, "I don't know whether it's right for me to tell you what I've come here to say, but something has to be done before Chris damages himself and everyone else in ways that can never be repaired."

I got so angry thinking about it that I sprang off my bed and paced wildly around the room. Eventually I ended up exhausted in my chair, my hand nervously beating a rhythm on my desk so loud that Mom finally slipped out of her bedroom—it was about two in the morning—tapped on the door and asked, "Are you all right in there?"

"Sorry," I said. "I didn't realize . . ."

I wanted to put David away for the night, but he would not leave me. Beth must have been skeptical about his Tracy story, so he offered proof. My checkbook. With a thousand dollars written out to him and five hundred to Tracy. Why a thousand to him? Embarrassedly, he would admit, "Chris talked me into delivering the first payment for him to avoid getting caught. He disguised it as a loan to me. I tried to talk him out of it, but, well, when my brother begs for help, how can I say no? And Chris *promised* this would be the last time. But the next time he gave her money, he didn't even bother hiding it. He was becoming so reckless, he just wrote her the check. That's what had me worried. This is all so *unlike* him."

If Beth had needed even more proof, David could have told her about Tracy's visit to the house, when I introduced her as "Penelope" to Cheryl and Mom and Dad. Beth could even ask them about it if she wanted to confirm it!

What I couldn't piece together was David's ultimate goal in all this. Surely he realized I would eventually catch him at his game, and then what? Would he try to pass it off as some elaborate practical joke? One possibility that occurred to me kept me awake for the rest of that night, even though I tried to push it from my mind. Maybe David had no intention of seeing the scheme through to a conclusion. Maybe he intended to end his life that day on Culpepper Highway and let the rest of us sort out the mess as best we could. *Snap. Snap.* Maybe it was the best way he could think of to bring us all down with him.

This gruesome interpretation came to me at about three-thirty, and I spent the next several hours worrying over it as I sat in Dad's recliner, absently watching TV with the mute button on, the actions and motivations of the silent actors as inscrutable to me as those of my own dead brother.

At five o'clock I made a pot of coffee, drank three cups of it, ate a bowl of cereal, showered, dressed, and went to work at the magazine. It was my first day back since the funeral.

I was light-headed with fatigue when I saw Beth that night. I had decided to tell her everything, then afterward try to convince her not to spill it to Cheryl. She let me come to her apartment—she was not giving herself the option of running out this time. She was much calmer than she had been the night before. For her, making that first accusation had apparently been the hard part, and now she felt secure to handle whatever came.

She did not say a word as I told her about David and Tracy's relationship in Chicago, how he kept seeing her even after he was dating Cheryl, and how, even when he tried to break up with her, she kept calling him and making demands on him. I told her of his frequent trips to Chicago, which Beth had vaguely been aware of. I explained about the car that Tracy claimed he owed her for, and how David begged me to give him the money to get her off his back. I told of Tracy's unexpected visit, that I had pretended she was one of my friends and had paid her the final five hundred dollars.

When I finished, I experienced that good feeling of having revealed every detail so thoroughly that I could not be blamed for hiding anything or twisting it to my advantage. Beth was strangely quiet—surprised, I thought, or maybe skeptical.

She asked, "Why would he do it? Why would David make all that up about you?"

"It's hard to understand," I said. "He was a complicated person. His life was disintegrating. Cheryl was figuring things out. She didn't trust him anymore, and it was just a matter of time before she would figure out about Tracy and probably dump him."

"Why would he take that out on you?"

"For the same reason he got engaged. For the same reason he put his wedding date a month ahead of ours. There was always this weird, destructive rivalry between us. I tried to stop it. I tried to tell him it might have been fine when we were teenagers, but it was insane for us to continue competing as adults."

She sat quietly. Finding out the truth did not seem to wash away her grievances against me. I waited in vain for some kind of positive sign from her. She kept her preoccupied gaze away from me, staring off as if searching for something in the distance.

Finally she said, "I can't believe I've known you all this time and didn't pick up on what was happening."

"Not even my parents know what David was really like," I said. "And now I think it's too late to tell them. Just like it's too late to tell Cheryl. Let them hang on to the David they knew."

"Secrets like this only do harm in the end. Covering up for him wasn't loyalty. It was destructive."

"Beth, please don't tell Cheryl what I've told you. I beg you. Don't ruin everything about him that was good. Don't destroy whatever love Cheryl still has for him."

Beth thought for a moment and answered, "Thank you for finally telling me all this. I need some time to think things over. I'll call you soon." She stood up, dismissing me.

"Is that it?" I asked. "Don't you have any response to what I've said? Do you believe me?"

"Too many things have been said lately without thinking them through. I don't want to make that mistake again. I don't think it's unreasonable for me to ask for a few days to think things over."

I stood up and walked over to put my arm around her. She stepped away from me. I said, "I'll come over tomorrow, then."

"No," she said. "Let me call you."

She had considered me guilty for so long that she could not immediately declare me innocent. Her coldness left me hurt and depressed. I stood at the door for a minute, giving her a chance to ease her resolve and start talking to me again. She did not move.

"I love you," I said.

"I love you too," she answered in a rather mechanical tone.

I said a quick good-bye and left.

———

She took four days to call me. After the second day, I began to see her delay as a way to make me suffer, a way to punish me for the secrets I had kept from her. Many times I came close to calling her and demanding to know what she was thinking and what she planned to do. On the third day I did call her, but there was no answer, and I left no message.

The agony of waiting for Beth to call was deepened by the invisible cloud of gloom that suffused my parents' house in the aftermath of David's death. Mom was a mess. She would burst into tears at the most unexpected times, when she was opening the mail or putting bread in the toaster or opening the pages of a magazine. We were all on edge around her because we never knew when her calm demeanor would instantly disintegrate into uncontrollable sobs. Robin escaped the sadness of our house by spending as much time away from it as she could. She ran around with her friends and stayed at their homes as late in the evenings as our parents would allow. During this time her rebelliousness intensified. She got involved with her band and dressed weirdly, changed her hair color every other day, put on ugly black lipstick and black fingernail polish, and did everything else she could think of to push Dad and Mom away from her.

Dad was colder to me than he had ever been. His silence toward me was painful, but I could have put up with that. What was unbearable was the way he looked at me whenever I first walked into the house or appeared in a room where he was. His eyes would widen for an instant in shock or annoyance, as if he had expected it to be someone else, and then he would look away with no further expression, denying my presence in the room. This gesture was so subtle, and probably so involuntary, that I dared not bring it up with him. He would have accused me of being paranoid. But every time I saw him, I got the look—and I felt guilty. Guilty for not being David. Guilty for not being the one who had died. I had never wanted to move out of that house so much in my life.

It was during these days that the idea of taking a trip to California took hold in my mind. Three of my friends from Purdue had moved to Southern California the previous school year. Rachel DeSilva had been close to finishing her dissertation and had taken a job the previous fall at a community college near Los Angeles. Two of our other friends, Alan Peterson and Chad Hooper, had joined her there in the spring semester and gotten jobs teaching freshman composition part time. Right after David died, Rachel sent me a sympathy card and invited me to come out there to spend part of the summer if I wanted to get away awhile. She said Alan and Chad really wanted me to come, and they had room for me to stay with them. She said she could even set up some part-time teaching at her college in the fall if I was interested.

At first I set the invitation aside because I knew Beth wouldn't want me leaving, and we would be busy with wedding preparations during the fall. But if she really did plan to postpone the wedding, what would it hurt if I went out there for a few weeks? Frank, my boss at the magazine, had been very understanding about my brother's death and told me to take off as much time as I needed. I let the idea float around in my head. I didn't think I would really go, but even the *fantasy* of fleeing this tragic place and lying in the sand on a hot California beach, letting the rumble of the waves drown out my grief, was a comfort to me.

Beth was friendlier when I saw her next, but it was a friendliness I could not trust. There was a calculated, rehearsed quality to her attitude that night, as if she had decided ahead of time that she was going to deliver her message and let nothing rattle her. We met at a picnic area at Eagle Creek State Park near my house, one of our favorite places to hang out. I took it as a bad sign that she wanted to meet me there instead of letting me pick her up. It meant she could take off if things didn't go well. On the other hand, I took it as a good sign that she offered to bring some Kentucky Fried Chicken for dinner, since a meal meant she wanted to stay for a time. The signs being too difficult to interpret, I simply agreed to show up.

"With all that has happened," Beth said as she sat across from me at the picnic table after spreading out the chicken and baked beans and mashed potatoes, "I still think it would be best for us to postpone the wedding."

"Till when?" I asked, my heart sinking.

"Early next summer, after school's out."

"That's almost a year from now."

"I think we need time to heal, to build up trust again." She kept busy with the food, as if to minimize the significance of the change she was suggesting in our plans.

"We've been together for a long time, Beth. There comes a time when a relationship has to sink or swim."

She finally put her fork down on her plate and looked at me. "I've lost some trust in you, Chris. I need time to gain it back."

"Should I assume that you don't believe what I told you about Tracy?"

"Cheryl certainly doesn't believe it."

"You told Cheryl what I said?"

"I asked her whether she remembered the night Tracy came over. Penelope. Your 'friend from Purdue.' I asked her whether she thought Tracy might have really been there to see David."

I groaned.

"Cheryl said Tracy was definitely with you. She said it seemed pretty obvious you knew her. She said Tracy showed no sign of knowing David."

"Well, as many times as David almost got caught with Tracy—with her calling all the time and him going up to Chicago to see her—Cheryl would have to be purposely trying to blind herself to reality not to be suspicious of Tracy."

"She is suspicious that David had a girlfriend, but she doesn't think it's Tracy."

"What!"

"She thinks both of you had girlfriends on the side. She said David gave her that impression."

"Well, he gave you that impression too, didn't he? That was his little game. I explained all that."

"She thinks the reason you're so insistent on covering up for David is that you have your own secrets to conceal."

"I can get Tracy on the phone right now and prove to you that I had nothing to do with her!"

"Do you have her phone number?"

"I could get it."

"I tried," she said. "It's unlisted."

I shook my head in disbelief. "Why don't you hire a private investigator? Follow me around. Keep me under constant surveillance. Look, if you want to talk to Tracy, I can track her down, and we can settle this once and for all."

"If she pretended to be somebody else once, she could do it again, couldn't she?"

"I can't believe this! Beth, it's so absurd. If you would only see Tracy for one second, you would know that she's not the kind of girl I would ever be with."

"Cheryl said she's quite attractive."

"Give me a break."

"Actually, I'm inclined to believe you about Tracy, but even if everything you've told me is true, you've still shaken my faith in you. I mean, what a rotten trick that Tracy thing was to play on Cheryl. You're just as responsible as David. You helped him keep it going. You financed it! With our wedding money!"

"I'm sorry! From the bottom of my heart I am sorry I ever went along with it all. But the circumstances . . . I was trying to get David to do the right thing. I practically begged him to confess the whole thing to Cheryl and be done with it."

"Don't you see there are things for us to work out?" she asked.

I picked at my chicken in silence, feeling utterly defeated. Beth kept a wary eye on me. Finally I said, "Let me ask you one thing. Are you really talking about postponing the wedding several more months, or is this your way of telling me you don't want to marry me?"

"I love you, Chris. I've wanted nothing more than to marry you. But our marriage has to be based on honesty. You know I can't tolerate secrets and lies. Let's give things a chance. You've been through a horrible trauma. So has your family. So have we. Let's build our relationship again, let's pray together, let's make sure it's right. In the long run, what difference does a few months make if it helps us to know we're making the right decision?"

Her words did not convince me. "I never had any doubt we were making the right decision," I said. In spite of what she was saying about building our relationship and all that, I sensed that the postponement was an elaborate and careful way of walking away from me. "How did everything turn so bad?" I asked.

"It's not necessarily bad, if we'll use this time—"

"All right," I interrupted, not wanting to hear another let's-give-ourselves-time speech. "I won't fight you. I've never been so worn down in my life. We'll put off the wedding if that's what you want. But I think we should pick a definite date and stick to it."

"Fine," she said.

We sat quietly together at the picnic table, listening to the buzz of insects in the nearby woods, the occasional hum of a car on the road nearby. I sensed Beth had another item on her agenda. Her posture had not relaxed. She sat slightly forward toward me on the bench, as if ready to make another point. I dreaded what it might be. I was emotionally wrung out and would have preferred to let my thoughts drift.

"There is one more thing I want you to do."

"What?" I asked without enthusiasm as Beth's gaze bore down on me.

Having failed to bring my face to life to hear her new mandate, Beth plowed ahead anyway. "The only way you and I can work through this situation is to be honest and open with each other, to clear up any misunderstandings between us."

This was my cue to affirm what she was saying so that she could build toward her request. I refused to play along. I sat stone faced.

She continued. "I think you owe Cheryl the courtesy of telling her about Tracy and all the other secrets, to set her mind at ease."

"I thought you already did that."

"No. I just *asked* her about the night Tracy came to your house. I think it's your responsibility to tell her the truth."

"Well, I won't do it. You're wasting your time, Beth. We've been through all this. If that's one of your conditions, then I can't meet it."

"It's not a condition," she said. "But please, just think about it. It's the right thing to do, and I'm asking you to do it."

———————

A couple things happened over those next two days to clinch my decision to go to California for the rest of the summer. The same evening Beth postponed our wedding, my friend Rachel called from California as I sat in my room moping. Alan and Chad were hanging out at her apartment, so the three of them decided to call me to see how I was doing and to renew their invitation. Their voices were so lighthearted, so untainted by the sadness and seriousness that had hovered all around me for the last few weeks, that I was immediately drawn to them. At Purdue the four of us had grown close during our endless hours of complaining about our poverty, eating together at the cheapest places we could find, going to movies, studying for classes, writing papers together during coffee-drenched all-night sessions. I had lost touch with them once they had moved to California, but it was a friendship deep enough to renew itself almost immediately.

Each of them took turns telling me of the good life they could offer me. We would relax on the beach and watch the waves and women. We would play volleyball on the beach, surf, Rollerblade. We would visit Disneyland and Universal Studios. Take drives up and down the coast. They could get me jobs if I stayed long enough. They would let me live in Chad and Alan's apartment if I wanted to make this more than a vacation.

"I have no money," I protested.

"Just get here," they said. "We'll work out the rest."

I did not feel like telling them that my previous objection to the trip—my impending wedding—had vanished. I told them I would strongly consider coming, and they made me promise to get back to them by the end of the week.

After I hung up, I realized that those twenty minutes of talking to them had been my first moments of happiness since before David died. The worry and heaviness lifted just long enough to help me remember that life could also be about celebration and fun, not only grief and contention. I took this as a sign I should go.

Beth disagreed. She gave me a dozen sensible reasons why the trip was a bad idea when I told her about it the next evening. We couldn't afford it. My parents and Robin needed me right now. I had a good job at the magazine and shouldn't jeopardize it for that summer or for the future by suddenly taking off. Our relationship was at a crossroads, and this was no time to abandon our efforts to work things out. Who was this Rachel girl anyway, she wanted to know, and why was she so anxious for me to come visit her in California?

Beth's objections appeared solid and undeniable set up against my vaguely expressed need to escape, to get out from under the cloud of oppression that constantly hovered over me. As was becoming common, our evening ended in a tense standoff, with neither of us absolutely refusing to go along with what the other one said, but neither of us giving in either.

It was after ten that night when I left Beth's, but I didn't feel like going home. I drove over to Bill's instead. He thought I should go to California. He thought it would be a good way to lift my spirits and Beth should be more understanding. "You'll have the rest of your life to be married and tied down," he said. "Take this trip. You know you'll regret it if you don't."

That night, pulling into the garage at the precarious angle required in order to fit my car in there with the other two, I misjudged the distance and ran into my father's old Chevy. I stayed up all night surveying the damage, running my hand over and over the dent as if to heal it. I rehearsed how I would tell him what I had done. Even before I spoke a word to him, I believed firmly that this would sever the already tenuous bond between us. As dawn broke outside our garage, I decided to go to California.

I called in sick that morning. After enduring the humiliation of telling Dad what I had done and watching him walk around and around the car muttering incomprehensible phrases through clenched teeth while his face reddened and his body trembled with rage, I collapsed on my bed for a couple of hours and tried to sleep. It was no use. I was numb with physical and emotional exhaustion, but my brain would not sleep. Curiously, the numbness emboldened me. I was less afraid of the consequences of the actions I was about to take than I normally would have been.

I went to the phone book, looked up a travel agent, and ordered a plane ticket to Los Angeles for the following day. I left the return date open. I pulled two large suitcases out of the coat closet and packed them with enough clothes, books, and other necessities for a long trip. I called Rachel and told her I would be there the next day. She was shocked by my quick decision but said she and the guys would be waiting at the airport to pick me up. I called Frank at the magazine and resigned from my job. He told me to have a good time and call him when I was ready to work again. It was not quite eleven o'clock, and my plans were complete. The difficult decisions having been carried out, I went to my bedroom and slept soundly for the next five hours.

At dinner that night, I told Mom and Dad that I was leaving for California the next morning. Dad said nothing but sat silently, scowling at his mashed potatoes. Mom protested, saying that the accident with the car was no reason to storm off. She said that of course Dad was upset at first, but accidents happen and he would get over it. Dad made no attempt to confirm her optimistic prediction. "Cars can be fixed," she kept saying. I apologized to her and said I wasn't leaving only because of the car. I told her I needed more than anything to get away awhile.

"When are you coming back?" she asked.

"I don't know."

She burst into tears and ran into the kitchen. I left the house and drove over to Beth's apartment. She was as cold and unpleasant as I had ever seen her. There was a shrillness about her objections that, in normal circumstances, would have made me back down in order to pacify her. Once again, my numbness served to strengthen my resolve. There was no turning back.

Beth was unsympathetic about the unbearable strain that had emerged between me and my father over my plowing into his prized automobile. She considered it a minor incident and, like Mom, insisted Dad would get over it in a few days.

She was also angry about the high price I had paid for my ticket, almost two hundred dollars more than it normally would have cost if I had booked it further ahead. "Don't you care about saving money for us at all?" she demanded. "Don't I have any say in how we spend our money?" She was also furious when she found out Rachel was going to be one of the people to pick me up at the airport. She accused me of caring more about taking a vacation than working on rebuilding our relationship. She asked if I planned to make it my pattern to run away whenever problems arose.

I withstood her onslaught fairly quietly, not because I had no response but because I did not have the energy to mount a defense. My passiveness in the face of her passionate objections made her even more angry. I tried to explain my need to flee, but she cut me off.

"All right. Go, then. I'm tired of talking about it. Go. Send me a postcard sometime." She literally began pushing me toward the front door.

"Beth, I don't want to leave like this."

"Well, this is the way you're leaving. So go. It's a waste of time to talk about it. You decided all this without bothering to ask my opinion, so what difference does it make what I think? Good-bye. Be sure to use plenty of sun block."

"Please, let's sit down and—"

"No. It's over."

We were at the front door by then, where she had pushed me. She let go of me, turned around, walked into her bedroom and slammed the door, locking it behind her. I talked to her at the door for a few minutes, but she kept silent. Finally I left the apartment.

My flight left at seven-thirty the next morning. I called Beth from the airport. She was calmer but just as adamant as the night before in her belief that I was doing the wrong thing.

"I have to do this, Beth," I said. "Please try to understand. I love you with all my heart. Please allow me this one trip."

"I'm afraid this will lead to things that will end our engagement."

"Do you mean that as a threat?"

"No."

"How did we ever end up being so nasty with each other? I never thought it could happen."

"You undermined my trust, and then you refused to stay here and do what was necessary to fix it."

It was time to board my flight. In spite of my arguments with Beth, I felt relieved and optimistic as the plane took off that day. I didn't believe I was doing anything to hurt our relationship in the long run. I would go have a good time and then come back a better man, rested and healed and ready to approach my father and my fiancée in a more loving way. I was thrilled with the roar of that airplane as it hurled itself hundreds of miles through the air, giving me the sense of forward movement, of escape.

———————

Except for worrying over Beth, my first two weeks in California were paradise. At least one of my friends, and sometimes more, was off from work each day during that time, and they seemed intent on showing me as many places as possible and treating me like the ultimate tourist. We spent many days at the beach—my favorite place—where I could feel the hot sun and hear the soothing waves. I loved to stare at the water and listen and think—or not think—and let the worries and memories and grief and prayers wash over my brain like the waves. My friends had little patience for my inertia. They preferred beach volleyball or surfing, which I never quite caught on to.

We also went to many other places—Disneyland, Universal Studios, Las Vegas, San Diego. We spent nights in Old Town Pasadena or barbecuing at somebody's apartment. I called Beth every night. Thoughts of her gripped my mind all day, but our conversations at night were not happy. I tried to talk her into coming to California, but she refused. "I can't afford it," she said, leaving unspoken her underlying point that I couldn't afford it, either, and was wasting our savings on this frivolous trip. She also reminded me that she was committed to working in the summer program at her school and couldn't just take off, which brought to our minds the fact that I lacked such commitment and had run away from a solid job without even a day's warning.

When those two weeks were over, I reached a crisis. I could have considered I'd had a fun vacation and gone home—that's what Beth wanted me to do. On the other hand, August had arrived, and the start of school at Rachel's community college was only a month away. Rachel now was definite that her college could hire me to teach two sections of freshman composition. However, I was already scheduled to teach at Purdue, so if I was going to stay in California, I had to let Purdue know quickly so they could replace me. No matter at which school I taught, I planned to spend my nonteaching hours studying for the horrendously difficult qualifying exams that I would take the following spring, exams that were my final hurdle before tackling the dissertation. Since my coursework was finished, I didn't need to be on campus at Purdue to study for the exams. I could study any place that had a good library.

On a Friday morning at the end of the second week, I called the airline to book my flight back to Indianapolis. It is hard to explain what happened inside me during those few minutes I was talking to the clerk about the different times and dates and layovers available during the next several days. I pictured myself arriving on the front porch of my parents' house, opening the front door, and slicing through the dreary cloud of grief that engulfed the place. I saw my father's eyes piercing through me with blame and anger. The woman on the line had given me several good options for a return flight. Nearly any of them would do. I could leave at seven in the morning or take the red-eye at ten at night, with several other possibilities in between.

"Which one would you like, sir?" she asked, her voice taking on that computer-like tone of politeness and impatience.

"I can't do it," I said.

"Pardon?"

"I cannot go home and walk into that house. I want to, but I can't."

"You don't want the reservation, sir?"

"No, I'm sorry. I'll have to call you back."

I found Alan in his bedroom and talked him into going to the beach. I would have to work up the courage to make my next move. Going or staying. I couldn't stand to do either.

By the time I called Beth that night, I had decided to stay in California. Or as I explained it to her and myself, "I *can't* come home."

"You *can*," she protested. "Don't act as if you're being forced to stay out there with your friends, including this Rachel girl, your friend or girlfriend or whatever you call her. The one who wants you with her so bad she got you a job at her college."

"Please, Beth. Rachel is not the issue. You've met Rachel. You know there's no romantic interest there." This was true. Rachel, in looks and personality, frankly had no appeal for me as a girlfriend. Although I had fun with her in a group, when her more annoying personality traits were diluted by the presence of others, alone she could be tiresomely academic and pedantic, droning into long monologues about literary or other academic topics. As for her appearance, though I hated to say it this bluntly even to Beth, Rachel's long stringy hair and lumpy body were not a temptation for any of my romantic longings.

I tried to explain to Beth my dread of going back to the house where David's ghost hovered.

"You'd be living up at Purdue pretty soon," she answered. "You could move up there early. You wouldn't have to stay in your house even one night. Purdue is sixty miles away. How far from your family do you need to be?"

"Oh, two thousand miles seems pretty good right now."

This insensitive remark was answered with an angry silence. Though I felt that each word I spoke made me sink deeper into a quagmire, I went on to tell Beth how much I missed her, how I longed to be with her but needed her to come to me. I just couldn't go back to Indiana right now, and that's all there was to it.

"If you do this," said Beth after several more rounds of my pointless attempts to explain myself, "then it will show me you're not serious about working out the problems between us. It will show me that you're determined to dig yourself even further into this David-like weirdness that you've adopted lately. I will not reschedule the wedding under those conditions."

"You would call off our engagement just because I decided to teach here for a semester?"

"I can't handle these games of yours anymore, Chris. If you stay there and we schedule the wedding for next May or June, who knows what bizarre new thing you'll come up with that will make us have to postpone it again? I won't do it. I can't take this anymore."

"You're the one who wanted to postpone the wedding."

"And I think you know why. Do we have to go through all that again? The fifteen hundred dollars? Tracy? And those are only the things I've found out about."

"So you're giving me an ultimatum to come home now or our engagement's off."

"I don't know. I guess so. You're pushing me to the brink."

"I love you with all my heart, Beth. I know we're going to get married. I believe it's God's will. I really do. I just can't come home right now. I admit that I can't explain the reasons in a way that makes sense to you. But that's the way it is. I can promise to come back after the first semester, if that will help."

"How generous. No, I wouldn't dream of asking you to interrupt your vacation to appease me."

———————

The following week I accepted the position in California and told Purdue I wouldn't be back until spring semester at the earliest. I didn't believe Beth would really call off our wedding. We had broken up before but had always worked things out. For the first few weeks after I decided to stay, we kept up our daily arguments on the phone. After that, she started refusing to take my calls. I left long messages on her machine, and only occasionally did she call me back. A month into first semester, she changed her phone number and kept it unlisted. I was so desperate to talk to her I came close to quitting my job and flying back home.

But I didn't. Always, the need to be away ultimately beat out the urge to go back. In early October, she told me the wedding was definitely off. I still only half believed it. I could not afford to fly home that Christmas and decided, under the circumstances, to teach another semester in California. I joined a church, made new friends, got to know my students, put together something of a life out there. I continued to tell everyone I was engaged and did not date anyone.

In May, I went back to Purdue to take my exams. I did not go to my parents' house. I reserved a motel room in Lafayette for four nights, which was all I could afford. Beth refused to see me. I showed up at her apartment two nights in a row. The first night I caught her in the parking lot as she came home in the afternoon. She was coldly polite and did not invite me inside. The next night, I knocked on her door repeatedly, but she did not answer.

When I got back to California, I reluctantly decided, long after Beth had, that it was time to accept the fact that we were no longer engaged. I decided to move on, to consider her a part of the painful past, to put her in that forbidden part of my mind where David resided.

JACK

$\mathcal{I}$ barely got out of the hospital in time for Dayle's big shindig on Saturday of the week I was released. She said it was going to be the biggest family picnic of the summer and that everybody was required to attend. No excuses accepted.

"What's the occasion?" I asked her when she told me about it.

"You're the guest of honor," she said. "It's a welcome-home party."

"A farewell party, more likely. The last chance to see me alive."

"Jack! Don't you dare talk that way. You've got years ahead of you. The best years of your life. Get that surgery done, get good and retired from your company, then you and Helen can do the things you've always wanted to do."

The surgery she was talking about was an angioplasty, which the doctor had wanted me to have while I was in the hospital but I had put off. He let me go home on medication instead but said if the chest pains came back, he would do the angioplasty right away. He said that delaying it was very dangerous, but I told him there were things I had to take care of.

My prospects for coming through the Premiere Financial scandal unscathed got bleaker all the time. The day I got home from the hospital, I had a visit from Mitch Roth, a guy in our church who also stands to lose a lot of money in this fiasco. He's been unofficially representing the rest of us in finding out as many details as he can and then reporting back to us. He brought a briefcase filled with files of information about every investment, and we went over it for a couple hours. Finally I asked him to set all the paper work aside and just tell me very frankly how he thought all this was going to turn out.

He said I could fight it out with Jim White and fight it in the courts—that's what he would advise me to do—but in the end, it was almost certain that I would lose just about everything I had invested, and the only people who were going to walk away with any money were the lawyers.

Mitch said, "Be grateful you didn't invest *all* your money with Bobby McMahon. Some people lost everything. You're lucky."

"Some luck," I said. "Losing most of my life savings overnight."

Sometimes I think I could stand the loss of the money if it wasn't for the embarrassment of what has happened. I mean, I've always tried so hard, been so careful. The truth is I used to look down on people who end up getting ripped off the way I have been. I thought they were suckers to get involved in those schemes. It almost seemed like they deserved to get taken.

I, on the other hand, made only the most prudent investment decisions. At work I got into the plan where I bought stock every month and the company matched a percentage of it. I watched it grow year after year. Sure, it went up and down in the market, especially during a really bad spell in the eighties, but I wisely hung on, and it prospered. It fueled my fantasy of an easy and luxurious retirement. When the company ended the stock plan, I sold it off and invested in some other things, then eventually I invested it in Bobby's frauds, with the personal assurances of my good friend Jim White.

Helen wasn't much interested in the details of my investing. She told me to do whatever I thought was best. What captured Helen's attention were my elaborate plans for how we would use the money once I was no longer working. We weren't going to be tied down any longer. As soon as Robin was on her own, we were going to focus on Helen and all the things she had dreamed of doing. What she had always enjoyed most, during those few times in her life when she thought about her own happiness rather than the family's, was going to exotic places, staying in nice hotels, eating fancy meals, walking along the beach in the evening, sitting on a balcony somewhere and watching the people go by as the palm trees swayed in the breeze.

That's how I planned to spend retirement. Not every day, of course. I was no millionaire, even if I hadn't lost most of our money. But we were finally going to take the trips we had dreamed of—not the two- or three-day getaways we could manage while the kids were growing up and I was still working—but real vacations to Europe, to Hawaii, to a cabin somewhere in the mountains, wherever Helen wanted to go.

Now it was gone. Not just the money either. Even if I had made the brightest investments in the world and was loaded with cash, that wouldn't change the fact that I'm probably going to die pretty soon. What was the use now of all the careful plans I had made? All my adult life—at least since I've been a Christian—I wanted to protect myself and my family inside as safe a bubble as possible. The right job, the right neighborhood, the right church, the right life-style, the right investments.

How I had struggled to arrange my life so we could have absolute security. *Absolute security!* What a phrase! As if even the most foolproof retirement plan or any other kind of plan on earth could provide that. As if anything could prevent it from all being snatched away in an instant.

I am left to wonder why God let it happen to me. From the moment David died until now, my soul has screamed out that question. I ask myself if my faith has been just another one of those safe choices on my checklist, like picking a sound mutual fund or a dependable refrigerator.

Is God trying to get my attention? Was I too smug before, so caught up in my own clever little plans that I didn't really need Him, treating Him only as a respected old man I nodded to occasionally? I don't know why my older son died, my younger son fled from me, my unmarried daughter got pregnant and ran away from home, my health collapsed, and my money vanished at the hands of two men I thought were my friends. I'm hesitant to settle on too easy an answer. I am pursuing God like never before, so if it's my attention He wants, He's got it.

I know I've made mistakes. There was a long time when I drifted spiritually, especially when the kids were little and I was so caught up in building Maximilian Webber. When we first moved to this house, it took us a while to find a church we liked, so for those first few years we stopped going almost completely. Sometimes I was working seven days a week anyway. Those days I didn't think too much about it, but was I getting my family off on the wrong track even then? I just don't know. And then when David died, I have to admit I was pretty much useless to everybody.

There is one thing I have left, and that's my dignity. And I'm determined to do everything in my power not to throw it away. What I mean is, I don't want to end my life as a whiny victim, with everybody saying, "Poor Jack. Look how he lost it all at the end." I don't intend this in a prideful way. I know we all get battered and bruised. I suppose most people limp to the finish line. But I refuse to go to my grave whimpering and shaking my fist at God and bemoaning all that I've lost. One strange consequence of losing so much is an unexpected sense of freedom. I'm holding on less tightly to what I can't control—security, money, the actions of other people.

That is why Helen and I have made a decision, and we're going to announce it at Dayle's picnic. Instead of spending my final breath cursing fate for the money we've lost, Helen and I are going to start spending what we have left on things we always wanted to do. We no longer have the money for most of the trips we wanted to take, but we can scrape together enough money for at least one. Lord willing, we are going to Europe as soon as I recover from my surgery. That isn't the last expenditure we've planned either, but we'll save the next surprise for the appropriate time.

Helen has broken through the same barrier I have about money. In fact, taking the trip was her idea. She came up with it the night that I sat her down and went through all the details about how much we had lost through Premiere. I explained what she would have left to live on when I die. She took it more calmly than she has taken any of the other tragedies we've faced. She looked straight at me, no tears, an expression of strength on her face that was not quite a smile but seemed to say, "After all we've been through, there is nothing you can say to beat me. I'm getting good at this now."

Once we had gone through all the finances in exhaustive detail, we sat out on the porch in the dark and drank coffee. In the most hopeful voice I have heard from Helen in years, the same tone she had used when we had planned every significant event of our lives, from getting married to picking out our home to planning for our children, she said, "Let's show them we're not defeated. Let's take that trip to Europe."

"What!" I said. "Are you forgetting the conversation we had just a few minutes ago?"

"No, I'm not. We lost a bundle. I realize that. And everybody will find out about it before long. And everybody will expect us to mope around, to hold a grudge against Jim and Leah White, and cause commotion and bellow as loudly as we can. I don't want to do that. There's enough money for one trip."

"But that's money you'll need to live on if I die—"

"If you die, Jack, my only regret will be that we didn't spend more of our money together while we still could and that we didn't celebrate our life together the way we should have. I have no interest in hoarding it up for the future. There will be enough money. Let's take our trip."

I reached over and took her hand in mine. "Helen, if God has ever given me a gift greater than you, I don't know what it is. I love you so much."

"I take that as a yes," she said.

"Call the travel agent tomorrow."

That was one of our best nights in years. We stayed up for several more hours talking about our plans and feeling twenty years younger. None of this obliterated the burdens that weighed us down—Robin's disappearance, our financial problems, our never ending grief over David—but we were not going to spend the rest of our lives dwelling on our regrets. We were going to Europe.

CHRIS

*A*unt Dayle didn't manage to get all the relatives to show up for her picnic, but she did sweet-talk, cajole, or coerce seventeen of us to be there, including two of her own kids, several of her grandkids, her sister Jackie and family, Grandma and Grandpa, Mom and Dad, and me. It took no arm twisting to get me there. I have always loved Dayle's picnics. Her house may be cluttered and cramped, but the backyard has plenty of room, not only for the people and their tattered lawn chairs, but also room for a croquet game on one side and the sagging badminton net on the other. There was also a little plastic pool for the younger kids. We were among the first to arrive, and when I got to the backyard, carrying the big aluminum tray of baked beans that was our contribution to the meal, the apron-clad, teeth-wearing Dayle was tending to the two charcoal grills while her son Jeff was urging her to enter the modern world by buying a VCR. I set the beans down on the picnic table and received my one-armed hug of greeting from Dayle as the conversation continued.

Jeff was saying, "That movie *The Blob* is on tomorrow night at the same time as Dad's baseball game, and you know you two are going to fight over it."

"You want to watch *The Blob*?" I asked, surprised.

"I love that movie!" Dayle said.

"Well, if you had a VCR, you could tape it and watch it as many times as you want."

"I know," she said. "We're the only ones in the family who don't have one."

"It's the 1990s," he said. "Everybody has a VCR. I'm embarrassed to tell people."

"We don't have a dishwasher either. We do 'em by hand. Nobody understands that."

Uncle Ray, sprawled nearby on a lounge chair so overburdened that the plastic netting supporting him nearly touched the ground, added, "We don't even have a—whatcha call it?—phonograph."

We laughed. Jeff said, "They don't call 'em phonographs anymore, Dad. Stereo."

"Well, we don't have one of them."

"Wind up the old Victrola," Jeff said.

"Well, we did have one of those," Ray informed us.

"You did? You wound it up?"

"Yes! We was proud to have it. Wind it up. Play those 78s."

"Did you know they don't make record albums anymore? Just tapes and CDs?" Jeff asked.

"Of course I know it," Dayle answered. "But we don't have a tape player. No CD. We don't even have an answering machine on our phone."

"You're a low-tech family," Jeff said.

"No computer either," Dayle continued.

"Even I have an answering machine and a computer and a stereo. And you guys have tons more money than I do," Jeff said.

"Ha!" said Dayle.

Jeff asked, "Did you have a telephone when you were growing up?"

"No-o-o-h," Dayle replied. "We didn't have a telephone till we moved to Indianapolis."

"How old were you then?"

"I was twelve and a half years old when we got a telephone."

"What did you do before that?"

"Wrote letters."

Ray added, "Or somebody in the neighborhood would have a phone and we'd get them to give somebody a message. I remember in our neighborhood the McGuires had the only phone. They got the first TV, too, when that came along. Used to have twenty people stuffed in their living room just to watch that tiny little screen. Hardly anything on TV in them days. Only had shows at night. Wrestling is what I remember. It was real wrestling too. Not this stuff they have nowadays. But you could barely see it. We didn't care, though; we thought it was a miracle. You kids are spoiled today. You have no idea."

Jeff said to Dayle, "Well, are you going to tell Chris and Aunt Helen about the latest ruckus?"

"No," Dayle said in a conspiratorial whisper. "Keep quiet about it before Helen comes out here. No need to get her all upset."

I had no doubt "the latest ruckus" would emerge, but Dayle liked to reveal things her own way.

In the meantime, another surprise awaited my mother. As each family arrived, they brought boxes of various sizes and carefully presented them to Mom like wise men bearing their gifts to Jesus. When Aunt Jackie brought the first shoe box, Mom asked what it was and started to open the lid. Dayle sprang over and clamped down the lid before Mom could see what was inside. "Don't tell her yet!" Dayle cried. "Wait till they're all here."

Once Mom had five mystery boxes at her feet, Dayle stepped away from her sizzling hamburgers and hot dogs on the grills long enough to give Mom permission to open the boxes. Seven or eight of us gathered around for the opening, while the others played games in the yard or sat in their lawn chairs in the shade of the trees and talked.

"Pictures!" Mom cried as she peered into the first shoe box full of photographs. "As if half my house isn't covered with them already." But her intent gaze and delicate handling of each photo showed she was pleased with this present.

Dayle explained, "I've been telling everybody about that living room of yours and how every inch of it is covered with pictures. So we decided to make you the family's official historian before this family falls apart completely and nobody cares anymore."

Jeff's wife, Shelly, sitting on the far end of the picnic table and greeting the unveiling of the photos with a frown of boredom, said, "This family's falling apart already if the latest I hear about Shirley and Roger is true."

"What latest?" Mom asked, always eager to keep track of the strategies of her rival sister Shirley.

"We're not gonna get into that now," Dayle quickly interjected, furrowing her eyebrows at Shelly in disapproval. "Nobody's gonna ruin this day. These pictures are a way of keeping us together so we'll have good memories preserved for years to come. I told everybody to bring any pictures they could spare, so here they are."

Jackie's twenty-five-year-old daughter, Carrie, who was standing behind Mom and looking over her shoulder as Mom opened each box, said, "There's one Olan Mills picture of me in that awful green dress when I was six years old. Mom must have fifty copies of it! It's so ugly I'd be ashamed to have it in your album."

"I had thirteen copies of that picture," her mother said, "and I loved that little dress. It absolutely is going into the album."

Dad, who had been talking to Ray nearby, walked over when he saw the photos starting to spread out across the picnic table. He playfully complained, "I've already lost one room to pictures. Now I'll probably lose the family room too. These things'll be covering my recliner by tomorrow. If this keeps up, I won't even have a place to sleep! Whose bright idea was this?"

"It was my bright idea," Dayle admitted. "You got something to say about it?"

"Yeah. Let's keep this family history at your house."

Mom said, "You like to look at these too, Jack. I've caught you in the living room rifling through my pictures many times."

While we waited for the burgers to get done, we passed the photos around the table. Many of the first ones we saw were of Christmas, without a doubt the most thoroughly documented holiday in our family. As the Christmas photos reached Carrie, she said, "Boy, these sure show how the family has declined. Look at all the people who used to show up at our get-togethers."

Everyone expected cynicism from Carrie and no one answered her, but she had a point. The pictures, some of which had been taken at our house on Christmas Eve when I was little, showed dozens of relatives filling the rooms. Cousins galore, many of whom I hadn't seen in years, some scattered across the country, others I didn't know what had become of. Now some of their parents, like Shirley and Mom, were not even speaking to each other.

The photos showed joyous occasions, with presents everywhere, wrapping paper all over the floor, baking dishes filling the tables and counters. Christmas was the one time of year when my mother didn't mind the house being cluttered. Most of the clutter she brought into the house herself, adding new boxes of decorations each year. Dad could never manage to get enough lights on the Christmas tree to please her, and the boughs strained from the weight of countless ornaments. Mom loaded the fireplace mantle with ceramic Santas, ceramic Christmas trees that lit up, stockings, wreaths, and garland. Tins of candy and nuts sat on every tabletop. She covered the front door with wrapping paper and more stockings. Electric candles glowed from each windowsill, and outside, the house blazed with twinkling colored lights.

Growing up I had found this all so comforting, especially when I came home from college for Christmas break. I was always exhausted at the end of a semester after living in a cramped dormitory room with cold tile floors and fluorescent lights, swigging coffee all night to stay awake while I wrote papers and crammed for finals. To come home to a house stuffed with Christmas, the fireplace blazing, and Mom constantly pushing cookies and hot chocolate at me was like arriving in heaven. Those were the happiest family times. Were they really fading away?

I ended up next to Dad in the serving line. I was still thinking of the Christmas pictures and Carrie's comment about the decline of family. I said to Dad, "It's sad to see the family pulling apart like this. I never thought it would happen."

"That's because you haven't lived long enough to see one generation disperse and give way to the next. I have. When I was a kid, I was always around my cousins and aunts and uncles. Then they gradually faded away, and the family became my brothers and sisters and their kids and your mom's brothers and sisters and their kids. Now those kids—your cousins—are breaking off into their own families."

"When you're little, you think the relatives you have around you will always be there."

"Families are never as stable as they seem," he said. "One generation can never hang on to the next one. The older you get, the easier it is to see that."

Grandma and Grandpa had been instated upon the lawn chair version of thrones, the most plushly cushioned cedar patio chairs Aunt Dayle owned. They sat regally under a tree as plates of food and large plastic cups of iced tea were brought to them and placed on their TV trays. Both looked uncomfortable. Grandma was bent forward so far that it looked as if she were trying to roll herself into a ball. Her feet did not touch the ground but dangled helplessly beneath her TV tray. Grandpa looked as if he had been tossed into the chair from a passing car. He was crumpled toward the right side of the chair, leaning heavily on the armrest. Instead of putting his TV tray in front of him, Aunt Dayle put it on the side, since that's where most of his body was. A small entourage of their children and grandchildren had gathered around them, and Grandpa was seeking his wife's assistance to tell a story.

"What was the name of that lady we knew who was all bent over—"

"What?" Grandma cried.

"That lady who had that thing wrong with her that made her so bent over she was almost double."

"Oh," Grandma said. She stared ambiguously into the distance, making it unclear whether she was contemplating an answer or simply dismissing Grandpa's question. The rest of us waited silently.

"What was her name?" Grandpa prompted again.

"The real tall one?" Grandma asked.

"Yeah," he said as his hand tried desperately to rescue the hamburger that had fallen out of the bun and was rolling across his tray. "I mean, she would have been tall if she could have stood up."

"Well, I didn't think of her as all that bent over. I knew this girl when I was in school who was so tall that she had to have her clothes special ordered from—"

"Well, for heaven's sakes," Aunt Dayle grumbled and headed back toward her grills as Grandma launched into her story about the tall girl. The name of the bent-over woman never emerged, and Grandpa made no further attempts to resurrect the story.

Before long, Dayle attracted a small audience of her own, which included Jeff, Shelly, my mom, and Jackie, so on my way back for seconds I wandered by to listen in.

Dayle was telling of her shopping trip for Grandma the day before. "She wanted seven cinnamon rolls, two of those onion bagels, and some raisins."

"Does she eat all those cinnamon rolls?" Jackie asked.

"No, she hides them!"

"Why? Won't Grandpa let her have cinnamon rolls?"

"Yes! He couldn't care less. But she thinks she has to hide them. Thinks Grandpa would be afraid they'll make her fat."

"As if he's one to talk," Jackie said. "Where does she hide them?"

"All over that house! There's no tellin'. And she forgets about 'em. I've found stuff all over the place. I found Pop-Tarts in her underwear drawer once when I did her laundry. It's a wonder they don't have rats. They do get ants, though. I put out those little traps, but I can't get rid of 'em."

Mom said, "I bet if Shirley and Roger could hear some of this, they wouldn't be so hateful against us for thinking Mom and Dad shouldn't live on their own anymore."

"Is Uncle Roger mad at you now too?" I asked.

"Don't stir it up," Dayle warned.

But Mom couldn't leave it alone. "He's siding with Shirley. That's what everybody's been pussyfooting around about all day. I finally squeezed it out of Shelly. Roger refused to come if I was here. I guess I'm the bad guy of the family."

"No," Dayle said. "It's all a big misunderstanding. And if all of us could sit down together for five minutes like normal people, we could get it settled. But if people refuse to talk to one another and say things behind everybody else's back, what can you do?"

Jackie, who always avoided tension and didn't want to get drawn into this controversy, had begun to flip through the photos in one of the shoe boxes. She held up a photo and asked, "Is this Shirley's living room?"

"No, it's Dayle's," Mom replied.

Shelly said, "Seems like all your houses looked alike back in that era. What was it, the sixties or early seventies? I've seen that same sofa—"

Jackie interrupted, "Oh, everybody in this family had early American furniture back in those days. It seemed like that was all we were allowed to have for some reason. I don't think there was a member of this family who didn't have a ceramic eagle over the TV set. Don't ask me why. I thought it was hideous, but I had one too. I was the first one to get contemporary furniture—a simple leather couch and some modern wallpaper with red and black in it. You shoulda heard the uproar. Shirley said it looked like I was decorating a brothel. Nobody in this family ever had much imagination. But thank goodness we're past that early American furniture phase. Only Dayle has any of that stuff left. And Grandma and Grandpa too, I guess."

I spent most of the afternoon playing badminton and croquet with the kids. In our family, the "kids" were all those younger than my parents' generation, so I still fit the category. Dayle's picnics always included two meals, so around six in the evening most of us walked away from croquet and badminton or whatever we were doing and gathered in a ragged huddle near the picnic table. The evening was always my favorite part of these get-togethers. By then the awkwardness between relatives who had lived apart for so long had melted away, and we felt the comfort of being with family. Because people felt closer, the conversations turned more mellow and quieter.

During a lull in the conversation, with all the but the younger children within hearing distance, Dad said, "Well, all of you brought us pictures today, and Helen and I brought a few to show you."

As he spoke, Mom dug through her purse and pulled out a stack of brochures.

"Assuming I live through the surgery I'll be having in a couple weeks and I recover at the rate the doctor said I should, Helen and I are going to Europe."

"Oh my goodness!" Jackie cried, holding up a foldout brochure of a castle. The oohs and ahs from my relatives as the pamphlets made their way around would have made you think my parents were buying the castles rather than just visiting them. But it was the happiest, most hopeful news of the day.

I walked over to sit next to Mom and said, "I can't believe that now of all times you would plan this trip. With Dad's health, and with the money . . ."

"We've been putting this off our whole lives," she said. "This may be our one and only big trip, but we're going to take it. Your dad doesn't want to let that deal with Bobby defeat him, and neither do I. We are taking this trip."

"Good for you," I said.

"You realize there may not be much money left for you and Robin after your dad and I blow it all."

"Don't worry," I said. "You deserve every penny you spend and more. Robin and I are young. We'll get along. Besides, we don't plan to face that problem for a long time."

Dayle came over and put her arm around me. "One thing I'll say for you and your family," she said, "it's just one surprise after another. Now you, mister, had better surprise me by saying you're not going back to California."

"I have to go," I said. "I have a job."

"Then I'm going to pack a bag and go with you."

"I'd love to have you. Bring Ray too, and I'll show you all the fun places out there."

"You think Ray'd get off the couch long enough to go to Disneyland? If you could bring it to him, maybe he'd consider it. It's your grandpa who'd jump at a chance like that."

"Really? He can barely walk."

"Yeah, but he don't know it! At least twice a week he makes me go dig out a suitcase for him because he says he's going to go stay somewhere else."

"You really get it out for him?"

"Yes! He gripes and gripes and keeps telling me to get it out there for him, he's leaving, so finally I haul it out of the closet and set it there by his chair. When I come back to their house the next time, it's back in the closet, and we go through the same thing all over again."

"Where does he think he's going?"

"Oh, who knows. One time he told me he was going out to see you. He said you told him once he was welcome to visit, and he was going to take you up on it. He said he's always wanted to see the Pacific Ocean. I think he just gets tired of sitting there all day. And Grandma nags at him all the time. He was used to being so active when he was younger. He likes to imagine he could still get out if he wanted to. Putting the suitcase out there seems to calm him down, so I say, hey, do whatever keeps 'em happy."

Mom and I helped Dayle spread out the leftovers for dinner, and then it was time for the prayer. Dayle prayed it herself this time. "Heavenly Father, we thank you for this rare day together with the people we love and are closest to us. We pray for healing with those who are not here. We ask you to bring Jack through his surgery so he can tromp through Europe without a care in the world. We ask you to bring Robin back safely to us. Don't let any of us fall away from each other or from you. In Jesus' name we pray. Amen."

ROBIN

$\mathcal{B}$obby has amazing powers of persuasion over me. If I didn't love him so much and deep down *want* him to try to win me over, it would really make me mad that he can make me change my plans in an instant. It's not that he says much either. There's no long boring spiel. He just gives me a certain deep look, and suddenly I'm ready to go along with him. Like when he talked me into going to Chicago on a moment's notice without a suitcase or toothbrush or a word to anyone. There isn't another soul on this earth who could have talked me into that.

His idea for me to have an abortion was another story, of course. I had to draw the line there. But still, he had me *thinking* about it, which nobody else could have done.

Anyway, on the morning I was planning to leave Kankakee and get back home one way or another, I was as determined as I've ever been to follow through with it. But then Bobby waltzes in after being so nasty to me for the previous few days and plants those warm eyes on me and holds my hands and says, "This is not working. This is not good for either of us. Get your things together. We're leaving here today."

Now, what I should have said was "*I'm* leaving here today. And I'm going alone. You're right that this isn't working and isn't good for us. And you're not good for me either. This whole thing was a mistake. You've been nothing but bad news for me from the day I first set eyes on you, so go away and leave me alone."

But I did not say that.

What I did do was cry. I don't know where the tears came from. I don't even know what the tears meant, because I was tired and sad and happy and relieved and scared all at the same time. But anyway, I cried, and Bobby held me close, and the next thing you know, we had our stuff together and were headed out the door.

I've noticed that the best times with Bobby are always at the beginning of something—the first couple hours of a date, the first day of a trip, the first few weeks of a relationship. He starts everything with enthusiasm and hope and a beautiful loving energy that makes you want to draw as close to him as possible. But gradually, as the promising beginning turns into dull routine, he turns inward and his expression becomes hard and angry, like he's having some kind of argument with himself.

As we drove out of Kankakee and into the farm country east of town, the wind rushed in through the rolled-down windows and the music blared loud on the radio. Bobby stuck his head out the window and shouted, "Whoo!" to the cornfields passing by. "I sure am glad we're leaving there," he said.

"So am I." We were both relieved to free ourselves from the awkwardness of staying in Kevin's house, where no one wanted us. It felt good to be on the move, headed somewhere, even though only Bobby knew the destination. He was in a good mood, but I still didn't have the guts to ask him where we were going. Nothing could push him over the edge into meanness faster than being asked his intentions.

After about forty-five minutes, the road through the country led us to Interstate 65, which he took south toward Indianapolis! *We're finally headed home*, I thought, relieved that this pointless adventure was drawing to a close. By that point I finally missed my family more than I dreaded them. The question now would be how to explain to them what we had done. Would Bobby go with me and help me make them understand why I took off that night? Would he tell them we planned to get married and settle down and get our own place and go back to church and make this thing work out right?

I worked up the courage to ask what I thought was a noncommittal question that he could not construe as nagging. "How far is Indianapolis from here?"

"A couple hours," he said, and then returned to silence. The euphoria from the beginning of the day had dissipated, and he was already crawling back inside his cocoon. The windows of the car were closed now, the air conditioner blew artificial air, and the radio played loud enough to only *hear* the music, not *feel* it. Bobby stared ahead at the road and never bothered to glance at me. I dreaded his inward movement and tried to delay it by running my fingers through his hair and over his shoulders, but I could feel the slight tensing of his body as I touched him. He was lost to me again. All I could do now was sit quietly and try not to irritate him until he found his way back.

Neither of us said a word until we reached the exits for Lafayette, which is only about an hour away from home. I was getting so uptight about facing my family that I felt I had to get some kind of conversation going or I'd bust wide open. "This is near Purdue," I dared to say, "where Chris goes to school."

"Oh yeah," Bobby said, brightening. "I used to have some friends who went there." Then suddenly, as we were just about to pass the exit for State Road 26, he swerved over into the right lane, almost demolishing the car beside us, and took the exit. It was a congested area of gas stations, fast-food restaurants, and hotels.

"Are you stopping to get gas?" I asked, hoping we weren't going to have to endure a visit with more of Bobby's friends.

"I need to make a couple phone calls," he said. He pulled into a gas station and left me sitting in the car while he talked on the pay phone. I saw him make three different calls, but they were so short he apparently didn't find anyone home.

"Didn't get ahold of them?" I asked when he got back in the car.

"No. I called information. My friends don't live here anymore."

We crossed the road and had cheeseburgers at Wendy's. Bobby didn't look at me through the whole meal. He stared out the windows while he chewed, looking all around the restaurant like he was expecting to meet someone but wasn't sure which door they were coming through. We were only an hour from home, so I didn't want to get him riled by talking. *Let him act like a paranoid gangster on the run if he wants,* I thought. *This ordeal is almost over.*

When he was finished with his burger, he wadded up the wrapper, stood up, and stuffed the trash into the garbage slot nearby. I still had half a sandwich to finish, but he didn't bother to worry about that. He headed out the door, and I ran after him, clutching my Coke and unfinished meal.

What happened next made me want to open the door and bail out of the car right there on the highway. To get to Indianapolis we had to go south on 65. *South.* As we passed the sign that said *65 South Indianapolis,* I found myself leaning hard to the right as if to push the car in that direction. But Bobby went under the highway and instead took the on ramp that went north on 65. North toward Chicago and Kankakee! Toward pointlessness and confusion!

I couldn't keep quiet any longer.

"Where are you going?" I cried. "Indianapolis is the other way!"

"Who said we were going to Indianapolis?" he asked in his smug voice.

"Well, I figured that since we've been driving all day toward Indianapolis—"

"I can't go back there, Robin. It's ruined for me. Don't you realize what they're going to do to me if I go back there? Jim White's going to blame all his mistakes on me. I get to be the scapegoat. And he'll have the whole church behind him, including your dad. Can you imagine what they're saying about me now that I've taken you with me? They'll probably accuse me of kidnapping on top of everything else."

"That's ridiculous! I'll tell them I went on my own! I'm an adult, and I can go where I want. Kidnapping! That's so stupid!"

"Would you please explain to me why you're flipping out? I never once said I'd take you back there."

"You never told me *anything* you planned to do! And I was afraid to ask, because whenever I do, you jump all over me. I'm sick of this. What are we driving around for?"

"I can let you out at the next exit if that's what you want," he said. "I thought we were in this together. I thought you wanted to go with me. I didn't force you to come with me."

"We're not going back to Kankakee, are we?"

"No. Chicago."

"Why? What's the point? Why drive to Lafayette if you want to end up in Chicago, the exact opposite direction?"

"Because this morning I thought maybe it would be a good idea for us to settle in some town in Indiana. Maybe Bloomington or Vincennes or Evansville. But I've been thinking about it all day, and now I've decided I can probably do better in Chicago. Salaries are better there. There are more opportunities."

"Well, we were there once, remember?"

He huffed out a disgusted sigh. "Look, Robin, it's easy for you to sit back and nag and make your sarcastic comments, but you haven't contributed one thing to this trip. I've had to do all the thinking. I've had to come up with all the money. If you're not going to do or say anything productive, the least you can do is not undermine me at every turn."

"I can't cut myself off from my family forever," I said.

"It's your choice. There are lots of exits between here and Chicago.

I can drop you off at any one of them."

"Is that what you want? Why did you ask me to go with you this morning if you just want to dump me now?"

"What I really want is for you to shut up for a little while so I can figure out what we're going to do. I thought we'd stay in downtown Chicago this time. Closer to where I can look for jobs. You liked the Palmer House when we were walking around downtown. I thought we'd try to get a room there."

"How can we possibly afford that?" I asked.

"I bet I can land a job within two days," he boasted, trying his Mr. Salesman personality for a change. "We can afford it that long. There are lots of things we can do if you would change your attitude."

I turned away from him and slumped down in the seat to try to sleep. I wasn't feeling too great. Being pregnant made me tired all the time. I was hungry all the time too, but nothing I ate really satisfied me.

When I woke up, we were on the outskirts of Chicago. I remembered the first time we had driven this highway to the city, how excited I was, how much like tourists or newlyweds we felt. That seemed like a million years ago. Now we were like a worn-out Bonnie and Clyde duo. Bobby was still darting his head around and looking in all directions, as if expecting the final shoot-out at any moment.

I sat up and asked, "Why do you keep looking around like that?"

"Looking around like what? I'm driving."

He didn't even realize he was doing it. We were soon downtown, where we had spent the best part of this trip, but the tall buildings and the lake and the parks had lost their appeal for me. I had given up any illusion that this was going to have a happy ending. Bobby managed to get us a room at the Palmer House. When we got inside the room, I collapsed on the bed without even looking around too much. For some reason this made him mad.

"Well, here we are in the Palmer House!" he said, as though I had been in a coma for the last twenty minutes and didn't know where I was. "What do you think of it?"

"It's nice," I said.

"Don't strain yourself with all that excitement."

"I'm tired."

"You slept all the way up here!"

"Well."

"Look how nice this room is. Feel how thick this carpet is. Look at those drapes. It beats the Days Inn, doesn't it? And we're close to everything you liked. Marshall Field's. The good restaurants. Aren't you even going to look out the window?"

From the bed I could see that there was a building directly across from our window. All I could see was bricks and windows. "Why would I want to look out at that building?"

"You can see State Street if you stand over at the side of the window and look all the way to the left! What's the matter with you? When we were here before, I thought you loved this hotel."

"I liked this hotel *lobby*," I said. "I liked thinking about Chris hanging out here when he and David lived in Chicago. I liked everything those first few days. That's when I thought there was a point to what we were doing."

"You're impossible to satisfy, aren't you? I don't know why I've bothered with you. No matter what I try, you're going to ruin it, aren't you?"

I didn't answer him. I picked up the hotel book on the nightstand and found the room service menu. Bobby sat in the chair by the window and watched me. I called and ordered a pasta dish, chocolate chip cheesecake, and a Coke.

"I agree with you that this is better than Days Inn," I finally replied. "It has room service."

Those were the last words I ever said to him. He opened the suitcase, took my things out of it, and threw them on the bed. Then he closed the suitcase and took it out of the room with him without a glance in my direction.

CHRIS

*R*obin's first words were "Do you hate me?"

She called me at the magazine a few days after Aunt Dayle's picnic.

"Of course I don't hate you," I said. "But it's all I can do to keep Mom and Dad from calling out the FBI. Are you all right?"

"I guess so."

"Where are you?"

"Chicago."

"He hasn't hurt you, has he?"

"No. I'm fine. I'm not with him anymore. He took off and left me stranded in this hotel."

"Come home, Robin."

"I don't have any money." Like a fool, I had sneaked the hundred dollars back into his wallet in Kankakee so he wouldn't accuse me of stealing from him.

"Then I'll come and get you. Tell me where you are. I'll take off work and come today."

"Only on one condition," she said.

"What?"

"I want you to bring Beth with you."

"Robin! This is no time to be playing matchmaker between me and Beth. You're in a very serious situation."

"I'm not playing matchmaker. Beth is my friend. Next to you, she's the person I trust the most."

"I'm not sure she'd come with me," I said. "She's also working at the summer program in her school. I don't know if she'd take off work to come."

"She will," said Robin. "I know it's a lot to ask, but I know she'll do it for me. Please, Chris. I need to be around some normal people. I need the two of you to be standing with me when I walk in that front door and face Mom and Dad."

"All right. I'll ask Beth if she'll come. Now tell me where you are."

"I'll call you back in an hour," Robin said and hung up.

Beth agreed to come, but she couldn't leave until two-thirty that afternoon. When Robin called back, I told her we would be there later that evening. I had pictured her in some run-down bus station or truck stop, but when she told me she was at the Palmer House, I had to laugh. "At least you get dumped in style," I said.

"Believe me, Chris, I'd rather be locked in my own bedroom without any dinner right now."

"If Mom and Dad have anything to do with it, you might get your wish."

"I'm too old for that!"

"That's what you think."

"Just get up here."

I have to admit I was excited but also nervous to be sitting beside Beth and know that we'd be alone with each other for the next four hours. In many ways this trip was the least threatening way for us to be together. There was plenty of opportunity to talk as we rolled down that straight, flat highway through the cornfields, but there was no pressure to get into uncomfortable topics if we didn't want to. After all, we were on our way to rescue Robin, not to dissect the past or analyze our relationship. Beth looked beautiful, though she appeared to have made no special effort to dress up for this occasion. She wore the dress slacks and sandals and simple green blouse she had put on for work. Her hair was pulled back with a headband, and her feminine, perfumed scent brought back a thousand evenings we had spent together.

As we made the transition from Interstate 465 to 65 North out of the city, she got started on the dangerous subject of Cheryl.

"Since you came back from California, Cheryl's obsession with David's past has been reawakened. I thought she had gotten over it a year or more ago. She hadn't called me in months before you came home. Now she's making up all kinds of things. You probably know she even called Bill to try to pump him for information."

"I know she has. But please don't believe her. I was worried you were believing her that night I saw you two talking together at the hospital."

"At first I didn't know what to believe. But now I know she's unreliable. The problem is that not everyone knows she's making things up. Something needs to be done about her."

"Yeah," I said halfheartedly, wary of the "something" she might have in mind.

Beth looked out at the trees along the road and said nothing for a time. I would have been happy to have dropped Cheryl from our conversation, but a few minutes later Beth said, "The latest paranoid idea Cheryl is putting out is that I might have been having an affair with David right before he died. She thinks that because she knows I saw him the morning of the accident. She can't understand why I would have gone to see him."

"I'm not sure I ever understood that either."

"Well, it wasn't because we were having an affair!"

"I know. But you covered it up and didn't tell me about it at first. Like you felt guilty or had something to hide. That was so unlike you."

"I did feel guilty about talking to him behind your back. But David asked me to meet with him. He said he had information about you and that Tracy girl. I knew something weird had been going on, but I didn't know what. So I fell for it. I met with him, and he tricked me into believing Tracy was your girlfriend and not his."

"But you could have told me that right off."

"Just like you could have told me about Tracy right off," she said.

"I know that. I don't deny that I handled the whole thing stupidly. I was trying to be loyal to my brother, help him out of a mess."

"He was playing each of us against the other one," said Beth.

"He fooled us all, didn't he?"

"Yes, he did, and we're all still paying for it."

"I figured by now you would have broken down and told Cheryl all about David and Tracy."

"I've been tempted, but as I've always said, it's not my story to tell. It's yours."

The rest of our conversation on the road that day took place in fragments—sometimes many miles and many minutes apart—as we contemplated and tested each other and inched our way toward understanding.

"I wasn't sure you'd come to Chicago with me," I said, breaking one of the silences, "since in a way that city was the source of all our troubles—David's scheming, the dreaded Tracy . . ."

Beth shook her head. "Chicago wasn't the source of our troubles. Our trouble was that we weren't honest with each other, we covered things up, we did things behind each other's backs, we didn't trust each other completely."

I thought about that for a moment and said, "I regret all that now."

"So do I."

There was a stretch of silence as we both retreated to our own thoughts.

Then Beth said, "Robin told me you had planned to come here this summer and never even call me or see me."

"I didn't know if you'd want to see me after the way we left things."

"Did you really think you could come here and spend a whole summer avoiding me?"

"I don't know. Maybe deep down I didn't want to avoid you. We do seem to be sitting together right now."

"I can't resist asking you something," Beth said. "Why did you put up with so much from David for so long?"

"I didn't put up with it. I was going to put a stop to it, but then he died."

"But all the time before that he was lying to you and using you—"

"I can't explain why I put up with it. There was another side to him. A part of him that knew me like no one else did. There was a loyalty between us that was unquestioned, that went beyond circumstances. He was my brother. I loved him and I hated him. I can't explain it. I still miss him now, in spite of everything."

We fell silent again, and sadness washed over me as I thought about David and what he had done to all of us. It was so senseless, so unnecessary, and I had been so helpless to change things.

Beth broke into my thoughts and asked, "Do you remember that when you went to California you said you were just going for a quick vacation, maybe a week or two? Did you ever expect you'd still be living there two years later?"

"No. I never expected to go there at all."

"Why do you like it so much?"

"Oh, I don't know. The weather, I guess. And the job has been pretty good. And—"

"No, I mean why do you *really* like it? Don't tell me about the weather. What kept you there?"

I knew no easy answer to this. "I'm a different person in California.

Out there I was able to start over, be whatever I wanted to be, create a new identity."

"So I guess that old saying about how you can't run away from your problems isn't true," she said. "It looks like you managed it."

"No. I'm not saying the change was all good. There was a cost to it."

"Like what?"

"Loneliness. Missing people."

"Like who, for instance?"

"Like you, for instance."

"I'm flattered," she said with a coy smile.

"After a while, I had this longing to be with people who really knew me, who had known me for years. People who weren't still making up their minds about me. People I could be myself around, like you and Bill, without worrying what you were going to think of me. I know that contradicts everything I said about wanting a new identity, but it's true. I wanted both things at once. To create a new self and to be around people who loved the old self."

"That sounds like you," she said. "Do you remember when you used to talk about how your mind was divided into different chambers and David's death sealed off a whole huge chamber of secrets and memories that you would never open up again?"

"Yes, I remember."

"I always thought that idea of separating your mind into chambers sounded pretty coldhearted, like you could love me or love David in a particular chamber, and if things didn't work out, you could just seal that one off and open a new one. Get a new haircut, new address, new identity. Build a brick wall around the old things and forget them."

"You know it wasn't like that," I said. "I agonized over our breakup. I never wanted our engagement to end. You were the one who called it off."

"Well," she said, "maybe I had to seal off some chambers of my own."

We let that comment float around in the car while a few more mile markers whizzed by.

Then I said, "I think some of my chambers are breaking open again this summer."

"Is that why you came home?"

"Everybody asks me why I came home, but no one believes me when I say I came home to work at the magazine."

"You came back because you're stronger now."

"Stronger?"

"You're finally strong enough to face facts that you wanted to bury two years ago."

"Like what?"

"Facts about your father, for one thing. That he's more complex than you've ever given him credit for. That he doesn't love you or hate you as much as you needed him to in order to shove him into one of those little chambers and dismiss him. The fact that you're more like him than you thought. How's that for starters? And you're strong enough to face the fact—not just know it, but live with it, put the knowledge in its proper place—that David betrayed everyone he ever loved. You. Cheryl. Your parents. You were beginning to figure it out toward the end of his life, but then his death required you to make a saint of him and set aside the truth."

"Do you think God has a plan for the circumstances of our lives, or do you think it's all haphazard?" I asked.

"I think He has a plan."

"So do I."

Being next to Beth in that car felt so familiar that it was all I could do to keep from reaching out and holding her hand, which would have violated all the rules I had set for myself that summer and could have thrown this little rescue mission into turmoil. Beth didn't appear to share my dilemma. She sat there as calmly as if she were taking a bus ride to work.

Robin had been gone for so long and under such difficult circumstances that I expected her to look a little frazzled from her ordeal—maybe thinner from not eating well, a little dirty from wearing the same clothes for so long, haggard from so little sleep and from the lack of her usual makeup.

The Robin who opened the door to her smartly appointed room at the Palmer House looked nothing like the pitiful vagabond I had imagined. She wore a sleek new purple dress, a new gold necklace and matching earrings, perfect makeup, carefully coifed hair. Far from looking emaciated, the pregnancy had begun to plump her up a little bit.

As she hugged me close, I smelled the light sweet scent of a perfume I had never known her to wear.

"You should run away from home more often," I told her. "You look terrific."

"I wish I could afford such a luxurious vacation," Beth added.

"Neither of you would want to have gone through what I've endured," she said. "I'd trade all this in a second for the way things were before I ever met that creep."

"He bought you all these clothes?" Beth asked, running her fingers over the dresses, slacks, and blouses that hung nearby.

"Yes. We blew lots of money those first few days. Then it all turned sour. I'm so glad to see you guys I could scream."

"Well, sit down and tell us what happened," Beth said.

Robin sat on the bed and told us of their sudden decision to flee to Chicago, their shopping sprees, their arguments, the fiasco in Kankakee, her vain hopes that Bobby would marry her and settle down in a new life, his mood swings, his final disappearance. He had left her the day before, and she had spent a night here alone deciding what to do next. We told her what had happened at home since she left, including Dad's time in the hospital. She said she was sorry she had let us down and gone off on such a hopeless escapade. She vowed she would never be fooled by Bobby again, in the unlikely event that the creep ever showed up again.

When all the stories had been told, Robin said, "Now I'm starving. Let's go eat somewhere. I waited to have dinner till you came."

"Maybe we should eat it on the road since it's so late and we have such a long ride home," I said.

"Oh, we can't go back tonight!" she cried. "We have to stay here tonight, Chris, please. We have the room reserved for one more night."

"Robin, Mom and Dad have been frantic."

"I know, but there's no way I could face them in the middle of the night. I'm exhausted. Come on. Let's show Beth around Chicago, and then we'll go back tomorrow when we're fresh."

"We have to work tomorrow," I protested.

"Actually," Beth said, "tomorrow is my day off."

"How can you afford to keep staying in this room?" I asked Robin.

"Bobby's paying for it!" she said. "He gave them some kind of credit card for the room, but I don't know how he did it, because he told me before they were all maxed out and we couldn't use them anymore in case the CIA came swooping down on us or whatever. But we might as well enjoy a vacation on the little geek. We've sure earned it."

"I guess it's settled, then," Beth said with a smile. "Now, let's pick a place to eat before I faint."

"You two are relentless, aren't you?" I said, but I was pleased that Beth wanted to prolong our time together. "I'll have to call the magazine and leave a message that I won't be in tomorrow. And I'll have to call Mom and Dad. They're expecting us back tonight."

"I don't want to talk to them!" Robin insisted. "I'll wait to see them in person."

"You don't need to worry so much about your mom and dad," Beth assured her. "They're just going to be happy you're safe at home."

"They'll kill me," Robin said.

"No, they won't."

"You don't know my parents."

"Yes, I do. If you build up this big horrible scenario in your mind about how bad it's going to be to see them, it's only going to make the actual meeting more tense and awkward. Face them with open arms, say you're sorry for the pain you've caused them, say what's done is done, and ask where to go from there."

"Pay attention to her," I said, wondering if Beth would apply the same advice to our own relationship.

I made my phone calls, and then we headed out into the city. Robin was lighthearted and funny that night, having secured her one-day reprieve from Mom and Dad. Only occasionally, when the conversation turned to her future, did she grow quiet and apprehensive. She and Beth insisted that I take them to the old neighborhood where David and I had lived.

"I thought of you and David the whole time Bobby and I were in Chicago," Robin said. "Every time we went somewhere, I wondered if you had gone there too."

We went to my favorite Thai restaurant down the street from our apartment. Afterward we had coffee at the tiny coffeehouse where I used to go in the evenings to escape David's obnoxious friends.

None of us wanted the evening to end. We went to another coffeehouse just to keep talking. Between Beth and me, the seriousness and intensity that had filled our conversations on the drive up was replaced by the laughter and enjoyment in each other's presence that we had taken for granted in the old days.

The next day each one of us, for our own unspoken reasons, was reluctant to rush back home. Robin wanted to postpone her day of reckoning, and Beth and I enjoyed the luxury of being together without having to actually declare that we were "together." Each time I tried to play the responsible adult and say that it was time to head home, Robin would think of one more thing we just had to do before we left. She had to show Beth some shops in Water Tower Place, and of course we had to shop in Marshall Field's one more time and buy some Frango mints. Then after lunch she insisted this whole journey would have been a waste of time if we didn't spend just a few minutes walking along the lake. And Grant Park was so close it was a shame to not go there and rest in the shade awhile. At each change of venue there was usually some food to accompany it—ice cream for the lake walk, Mrs. Field's cookies for Grant Park. As we walked through the park, Beth reached out and held my hand as she had thousands of times in the past. It took both of us a moment to remember that the gesture was no longer appropriate to our relationship, and she pulled her hand away. A few seconds later I took her hand back in my own, and she kept it there.

———————

Robin squirmed around all over the backseat as we approached Indianapolis. Her bubbly mood had dissipated once we were in the car bound inevitably for home. She chewed her fingernails furiously, and her face took on a sulking, forlorn expression that I suspected must have been quite common during the bad days with Bobby. She slumped in the seat and declined to take part in most of the conversation. When she did speak, it was to express worry. What would her friends at work say? Was there a chance they'd ever let her come back to work? What would happen if she couldn't find another job? Were Mom and Dad going to be willing to help her once the baby came? The questions spilled out so rapidly that she was on the verge of making herself frantic.

Beth tried to calm her down. "You have to deal with one thing at a time, Robin. You can't expect to solve all your problems between Remington and Lafayette. Your mom and dad have always been there for you, and you know they won't abandon you now. Chris is here. I'm here. Your aunt Dayle. Your friends at church."

Still the questions sprang forth. Did all the relatives know about her predicament? (Yes.) Were they gossiping about her at Aunt Dayle's picnic? (Yes.) Did the fact that she ran off have anything to do with Dad having another heart attack? (Impossible to say.)

Next to what Mom and Dad would think of her, Robin worried most about the reaction of her friends at church. "I don't think I'll go back to church anymore, even though I'd like to."

"You've got to go back," Beth said. "You can't hide from people. They can't support you if you shut them out."

"I know, but they'll all think I'm some evil woman who's more lost than ever, who could never be a Christian."

"Robin, you told me yourself that you realized you made a mistake, that you wanted to ask forgiveness and hold on to your faith and live as a Christian."

"I do! I've prayed more these last few days than I've ever prayed in my life."

"You've also started making some good decisions. You got away from Bobby. You didn't let him coerce you into an abortion. You're coming home. You're coming back to the Lord. Right?"

"Right."

"Well, then, how can the church or anyone else expect more than that? That's all any of us can do. If the people of the church don't understand that, then they're the ones who are lost, not you. But I think they're ready to love you, so you're going back if I have to drag you there myself!"

"Miss Compassion," Robin said, but smiled for the first time in a hundred miles. I realized Robin needed Beth's kind of love from all of us—not merely quiet acceptance, but a love that held her close and drew her in and promised to be there no matter what.

By the time we pulled into the driveway, Robin was pale but calm and resolute. She wanted Beth and me on either side of her, and she held our hands as we approached the door. Her dramatic preparation was unnecessary, however. The house was dark. Mom and Dad were not home.

There was no note on the kitchen table, no sign that they had expected anyone to come. The light on the answering machine blinked. I hit the button, and Mom's frightened voice spoke out to us. She had taken Dad to the hospital. We'd better come quick. He wasn't doing too well.

ROBIN

$\mathcal{B}$y that time I was assuming just about everything wrong in the world was my fault, so I figured Dad had started having chest pains again because he was as nervous to see me as I was to see him. The weird thing was that his being in the hospital made it easier for me to face him again. I mean, the attention wasn't focused all on me and my problems. Dad was in a whole lot more danger than I was.

Chris and Beth walked into the hospital with me, one on each side like bodyguards, just as I asked them to. We saw Mom first. She was talking to a nurse at the desk close to Dad's room. She looked up and gave us a blank expression at first; then her face lit up with surprise, and she crushed me with a hug, her words choked out by tears before she could even say hello. After the hugging, she said, "I'm so glad you're all back! I didn't think I could go through this again by myself. You look good, honey. Are you all right?"

"I'm fine. How's Dad? What happened?"

"He woke up feeling bad this morning. Lots of pain in his chest and his arm. I thought he had been hurting the last couple days. He gets that stiff look in his face that makes you know he's in pain but doesn't want to say anything. So we called the doctor, and he said get him to the hospital right away."

"What does the doctor say?"

"He wants him to have that angioplasty right away. Says he should have had it before he left the hospital last time." As if reading my mind, she added, "The doctor said nothing short of surgery could have prevented this. It wasn't caused by stress or worry."

"Can I go see him?" I asked.

"Let me go tell him first, prepare him a little bit," Mom said. "He told me to send you in when you got here, but still, it won't hurt to have a couple minutes' warning."

A few minutes later she came out and told me to go on in. "Only one visitor is allowed in there at a time, so you'll have to go by yourself." I left Mom and my bodyguards behind and walked the white tile corridor alone like a frightened child on her first day of school.

Dad looked pale, and his hair stuck up like two little horns in the back where he had laid his head against the pillow. He had tubes going into his nose and arms, which made him look helpless and fragile.

"I'd stand up and hug you," he said, "but Nurse Nasty bawls me out if I so much as shift my weight from one hip to the other."

"I'll come to you, then," I said and hugged him lightly so that it wouldn't affect the machinery or alarm Nurse Nasty.

"You're all right, aren't you, kid? He didn't hurt you or anything?"

"No, Daddy, not any more than I was hurt already."

"Well, he hurt us all, I'm afraid."

"I'm sorry I took off like that. At the time it seemed like the only thing I could do. . . ."

Daddy tried to push himself up in his bed. "The important thing is that you're back now. The present is all we can deal with. That's one lesson I'm learning." He took a sip from a straw in the cup by his bed. I never saw my father drink from a straw except in the hospital. I wouldn't have thought anything about it with anyone else, but with Daddy, it made him look weaker, more dependent.

"So you got stranded in Chicago. Is that where you were the whole time?"

"No, we went a few more places than that."

"I want to hear all about it."

"There's not much to tell. Nothing that can't wait till you're out of here. I want you to know that I'm back now for good, and Bobby is gone. I'm going to have this baby and try to do what's right."

As I finished this, the nurse came in and fiddled with the tubes, checked the monitors, and took his temperature. Daddy kept silent while she did these things, but his eyes were sad, and his whole face had that distant, disconnected look that Mom calls "brooding."

When the nurse left the room, Daddy said, "I've been so paralyzed."

I had been concentrating so hard on the nurse and the tubes and the monitors that at first I thought he meant something physical. Like an idiot I said, "You mean it's not just your heart—"

"No, I mean for the last couple years, ever since David died, I've felt paralyzed." This was not so unusual anymore for Dad, totally switching topics and leaving a person floundering to catch his meaning. Eventually he would work his way around to making the connection. "Paralyzed is the only way I can describe it. It's like I couldn't break free from my mind and say or do or feel the things I wanted to. I was stuck inside myself. Everything I managed to do was automatic, like some person apart from me running my body. And I'm sorry, because I know you needed me then more than ever, but I couldn't work my way to the surface. I can't explain—"

"Don't apologize to me, Daddy," I said, afraid I would start crying if he continued. "You have nothing to be sorry for."

"But I've wondered if I had been more involved with you these last couple years whether this whole situation might have turned out differently. I should have seen . . . should have known what was happening. I never should have brought Bobby into our lives."

"No," I said. "I made my own choices. I'm not blaming you and Mom. Never would I blame you two."

"I've been looking at things differently lately," he said. "All these disasters have woken me up. I have so much to make up for. With you. With Chris. With your mother. I don't know if I'll have time."

This was different all right. I had never heard Dad admit he owed anybody anything. Trying to sound more hopeful than I felt, I said, "Things aren't so bad, are they? You and Chris are getting along better this summer. I'm starting to get straightened out. The doctor says you'll get out pretty soon—"

He ignored this and said, "Robin, I want you to know that your mom and I will do anything we can to help you. We're going to be with you every step of the way through this, and when that grandchild comes, we'll do everything we can for him. Or her. You don't need Bobby. You can raise that child as a Christian in a Christian home."

"That's what I want to do," I said. I stood up. "Now I better let you get some rest. I don't want Nurse Nasty after me."

"All right, honey. I'm glad you're home."

I stopped off at the rest room on the way back down the hall. I needed a couple minutes alone. I was so touched by Daddy's unusual supportiveness that I was on the verge of tears, but I still wasn't comfortable talking to him about Bobby. With Daddy and everybody else I tried to act all brave and determined about Bobby, calling him a creep and vowing that I wouldn't take him back even if he begged me. The truth is I wanted him to come back and plead with me. I longed for him to take hold of me and say he loved me so much he couldn't live without me. That's my punishment, I guess, at least part of it. I can't have him, and I can't stop loving him.

Chris stayed at the hospital longer than anyone else that night. He called it the "night shift" and said his late-night talks with Dad in the hospital had been the best they'd had all summer. After Beth and Chris had a private conversation that she wouldn't tell me about, Mom and I took Beth home. Once we got home, Mom went to bed, and I stayed up on the porch and waited for Chris. He was still talkative when he got home, so we drank iced tea and enjoyed the cool darkness of the porch.

"Dad's so different," I said. "I've never seen him so philosophical and emotional."

"He thinks he's going to die," Chris explained.

"Have you two worked out your problems?" I asked.

"In a way, I guess. Not officially."

"Which means no," I said.

"We're talking to each other. For us that's pretty good."

"But neither of you have actually said you're sorry for avoiding each other for two years."

"No."

"Even if you two did make up, probably nobody would know it because you wouldn't actually *say* anything to each other. You'd just punch each other in the arm or whatever it is guys do."

"You don't have a very high opinion of men, do you, Robin?"

"Not at the moment. But that's no excuse for you to ignore what I'm saying. The trouble with you and Dad is that neither of you want to be the first to give in."

"That's not true!"

"It's pride. He wanted you to come crawling back. You wanted him to beg you to come back. It was stupid and ugly, and it lasted for two years. Then you finally came back but only by saying, 'It's because of the magazine. The magazine can't survive without me.'"

"I'm amazed that you're saying this!"

Chris wasn't used to getting advice from his little sister. He was more comfortable helping me out of my messes.

"If I have to face facts about my life this summer," I said, "then you should also. And let's be honest, we may not have much more time with Dad."

"The doctor said—"

"I know what he said. But you don't keep having one heart attack after another without eventually dying."

Chris shook his head and looked away from me. I normally wasn't so blunt with him, but I was like Dad. Hitting rock bottom had jolted me out of my stupor.

After a moment he said, "I didn't plan to stay away for two years, and I didn't do it to spite Dad. There were reasons all along the way why I couldn't come back. Dad was mad at me. Beth broke up with me. Coming back only meant pain. It would only make things worse. Part of the time I couldn't even afford to come back. Things just worked out that way. Besides, Robin, don't forget that you ran away too."

"But not for two years. And tonight I went in to Dad and apologized."

"I'm glad. See, it wasn't so bad seeing them again, was it?"

"No. Making up with someone usually isn't as horrible as you think it's going to be. But somebody has to break the deadlock. It's just like this dumb argument between Mom and Aunt Shirley. They barely even know why they're mad at each other, but neither of them will get on the phone and apologize. You and Dad are circling each other like little boys in a playground brawl who really didn't want to fight but who would be too humiliated to back down."

"Why are you jumping all over me tonight?" he asked.

"Seeing Dad so sick scared me. I feel our whole family's on the verge of something. Either falling apart for good or finally getting our act together. And since I finally worked up the courage to say all this to you, I might as well tell you one more thing. Beth loves you, and she has waited a long time and put up with a lot. But she has her limits. If you don't get back with her soon, you're going to lose her forever. The world doesn't stand still while you fool around in California."

"Let's not forget that it was Beth, not me, who called off our engagement," Chris said, defensiveness in his voice.

"You can use that excuse if you want, but you'll end up sad and alone."

CHRIS

"Fate seems determined to throw us in each other's path," I said to Beth when I saw her the next night.

"I think it has more to do with our family and friends," she answered unromantically.

Beth had been appointed to the committee planning the anniversary service, and we sat next to each other at a meeting in the church boardroom.

"How did you get to be on this committee?" I asked her.

"Pastor Jennings demanded that I serve."

"Ah! Is he part of the conspiracy to reunite us?"

"He is cochair with Robin," she said.

"Those two are tough to fight against. If we're not careful, they'll succeed."

Beth pretended not to hear this, and the meeting began.

The celebration weekend, which Pastor had titled Homecoming, was a little more than a month away, and there were dozens of details to take care of. We were planning an all-church dinner, which was to be held in a huge rented tent following the morning service. We discussed arrangements for the food, the tables and chairs, the table centerpieces, and the best way to get everybody through the lines and finished with their meals before the afternoon service would begin. Beth and another woman were designing the bulletins for both services, my mom was arranging the photos on boards, which would be displayed throughout the church, and I had to get the church history book written and to the printer within a couple weeks. Several out-of-town guests needed places to stay, as well as transportation to and from the airport. There seemed to be no end to the details that still needed to be sorted out before the big day arrived. My history book was coming together, but Pastor Jennings and others had suggested that I include the stories of so many people that the manuscript was certain to be too long to fit the number of pages we could afford. I would have to delete at least two, maybe three, stories of people in the church. This was after I had already cut out many that were worth telling. Pastor said he would meet with me individually the next day to help me decide which ones to cut.

The meeting dragged on for almost three hours, and afterward Beth and I ended up talking to each other in the parking lot. I was on my way to the hospital to see Dad, who had come through his surgery quite well that morning, and I asked Beth if she wanted to go with me. To my surprise, she said yes. I took her in my car, and after a visit with Dad that was short because of the late hour, I brought her back to her car.

It felt so good to be with her that I wanted to hold her in my arms and kiss her good-bye as I would have in the old days. But these were not the old days, and despite our accidental meetings, we were still broken up. As we stood in the church parking lot at the door of Beth's car, I thought of what Robin had said to me and the advice she would give me now if she were here. She would tell me to *act*, to take hold of Beth now and to iron out the particulars of the relationship later. I thought of the playground fighters she described, circling each other, delaying the inevitable battle.

I playfully asked, "Do you think certain people are destined to end up together no matter how circumstances conspire against them?"

"No," she said. "I think people possess enormous powers to screw up even the most promising relationships."

I was at a loss as to how to respond to this.

Beth laughed, reached out and gave me a quick hug, then got in her car and drove away.

———

I don't know how long Jim White had been standing in the hospital corridor before we noticed him. He came on the night after the surgery, when Dad was starting to feel a little better. Robin was in the room with Dad, and Mom and I were in the waiting room talking to Aunt Dayle and Uncle Ray. When Mom and I stepped out into the corridor, there stood Jim, wearing a brown suit like the ones he wore to church, his hands folded humbly in front of him. His face had what I thought was a pained, embarrassed expression, and he stood close to the wall, as if hoping to escape notice or afraid we were going to toss him out.

Of all the people involved in the Premiere Financial scandal, Jim White was the hardest for me to understand. I could see how a slick operator like Bobby could come into a church and sucker people out of their life savings, and I could understand how my father and other trusting souls in the church could get sucked into the scheme. But Jim White as a swindler did not fit at all. With his conservative looks and his hangdog expression, he looked too shy to be any type of salesman. I wondered how he even got into sales. I knew little about the insurance business, but maybe it had been different in an earlier era when he entered it. Maybe the times had passed him by and now he was in over his head, victimized by crooks who were his own employees. Still, he was responsible for bringing financial ruin upon my family. If he didn't know what was going on in his own company, he should have.

I stood back and said nothing. Mom walked over to him and shook his hand. "Jim," she said. "It was nice of you to come."

"I didn't know," he said. "I didn't know if you or Jack would want to see me under the circumstances. But I felt so bad about his heart attacks that I wanted at least to wish him well. How is he doing?"

"This hasn't been his greatest day, but the doctor expects him to go home tomorrow or the next day if nothing else comes up."

I walked over and shook Jim's hand. In all the years I had known him, the only detail of his appearance that I had ever noticed a change in was the hairline that receded ever so slightly each year until now the top of his head sported just a few brown and gray strands.

"How long are you home for, Chris?" he asked.

"Just the summer."

Jim opened his mouth to say something but then immediately closed it again as if he had changed his mind. He took a step backward and looked at Mom and then me. His awkwardness was painful to all of us. Finally he tried speaking again. "Helen, I know the lawyers are still working through the details, and there are a lot of things I'm not supposed to talk about, but I just have to tell you I'm sorry for how things have worked out. I had no idea . . ."

Mom patted his arm and said, "I let Jack handle the financial things himself, and even now I only have a vague idea of what we owned and what we lost. I only know that you and Leah were our friends for twenty years, and when this is all over, I hope we can sit out in our backyard and have a barbecue like we used to and forget about all this. But I can't speak for Jack. He has taken this harder. He has lost what it took him his whole life to gain."

"I know. I was hesitant to come, but Pastor Jennings finally wore me down, and I promised I would."

"That sounds like Pastor," I said.

"Do you think Jack will see me?"

"I'll tell him you're here," Mom said. "We'll see how he's feeling."

A few minutes later she came out of Dad's room with Robin and pointed Jim toward the door. I had expected Dad to make an excuse not to see him. Pastor had been urging the two to sit down together ever since the scandal broke, but Dad had put him off.

While Jim was in Dad's room, Pastor Jennings showed up in the waiting room with the rest of us. He was delighted to hear that Dad and Jim were together. He told Robin he was also relieved to see her back, and he invited her to go down to the snack bar to get a Coke, which she did. When they came back about fifteen minutes later, Jim still had not come out of Dad's room.

"Now it's your turn for a little conference with me," Pastor Jennings said to me. "I think I have more meetings in that hospital snack bar than I do in my own office." He had asked me to bring the church history material to the hospital so we could talk about it after he visited Dad. I took my briefcase containing my notes and photos to the cafeteria and laid it out before him.

"I have to cut at least three people's stories," I said.

"I hate to hear that. Who are you thinking of cutting?"

"It isn't easy. I was thinking of Earl Pinckney. He—"

"Oh no!" Pastor said. "He became a Christian in prison. He's got an inspiring story. You can't cut that one."

"It's good, but it was a long time ago."

"Almost thirty years! And he's still walking with the Lord!"

"Well, there's Tim Branson's story. Tim was—"

"No, you've gotta keep that one. He's a third-generation Nazarene and is going to be a pastor like his father and grandfather. It shows what we're all about as a church, one generation connected to the past and future ones."

"How about Darrell Padgett? I know you won't want to cut it, but—"

"He has such a great ministry! He does martial arts, teaches it to kids. He's done so much as an athlete, and it's all intertwined with his faith. His athletic and spiritual disciplines fit so well together. People have to hear that story."

"Pastor, you're being no help at all. I have to cut."

"I know. Couldn't we just make the print smaller or something?"

"Not unless we want to distribute magnifying glasses along with the books."

"I'm sorry, Chris. You'd better decide for yourself which ones to cut. Just don't tell me which ones they were. Make them as representative as you can. People from each generation, each era of the church, people of different backgrounds who have been brought to the Lord and are serving Him in all different ways."

"All right. I'll make the cuts and get the manuscript together as soon as I can."

"The story I really wish I could tell is the one taking place right now in your dad's hospital room, two of the finest men in the church rocked by a scandal but practicing love and forgiveness in the name of the Lord. And your sister finding her way back home and to God. I wish we could tell that one. Talk about a Homecoming theme."

"I'm frankly surprised my family would be candidates for this book as messed up as we've been the last few years."

Pastor thought for a moment before answering. "Did the Prodigal Son consider himself a good candidate to go back to his father? We're all candidates for the book as long as we're coming home. Your family is finding its way back to the Lord, Chris, and you should thank God for it."

"I have to ask you something, my friend," I said. "I think I know the answer, but did you deliberately put Beth and me on that committee to get us together again?"

He smiled, which gave me the answer.

Then he said, "I don't know whether you two belong together or not. If not, then serving on a committee with a dozen other people won't make any difference. If you do end up together again—well, you can thank me later."

———————

By the time Pastor Jennings and I got back to the waiting room, Jim White was gone. Dayle and Ray had left too, and Robin was in with Dad. Mom was alone in the waiting room.

"How did it go with Dad and Jim?" I asked.

"I don't know," she said. "Jim slipped out without saying anything else to me. Do you want to see Jack now, Pastor?"

"No, it's late, and Chris still hasn't visited with him. Tell him I'll come back and talk to him tomorrow. He'd probably rather spend the rest of the evening with his family."

Robin came out of Dad's room shortly after Pastor left, and she took Mom home, leaving me alone with Dad for our "late shift."

"Well, at least you didn't kill Jim White," I said to Dad as I sat by his bed. "I hear he slinked out unharmed."

"There's not going to be any slinking," Dad said emphatically. "Not by me or Jim or anybody if I can help it."

"I thought you didn't want to talk to him."

"Well, I'm going through some big changes in my old age, Chris. I'm not going to let Jim White or Bobby McMahon determine my future. If the end is near for me, or even if it isn't, I'm not going to crawl away from my life as a bitter or pathetic old man."

"So you forgave him?"

"Yes, I did. But even forgiveness is not going to be enough. Too passive. I've lost a lot, so that means I'm going to have to be more creative with what's left."

"Like the trip to Europe?"

"Yes, that's one thing. But I have a few other ideas too. Your mother is way ahead of me on this. She's barely fazed by losing the money. She says we should simplify. Take care of you kids, give as much as we can to the church, and be done with it. Invest in things that will outlive us."

"I expected you to be even more careful with your money after all this, but you and Mom are going in the opposite direction."

"I lean on your mother's faith," he said. "It hasn't been as easy for me. But once that first bit of money was pried out of my hands and I knew I'd never get it back, I realized how quickly it can all fade away. Not only money, but life, everything. I worked my whole life to make us safe. That safety is an illusion. I don't mean to be morbid, but I know now that death can snatch it away from you in a moment, no matter how solid your investment is. There is no safety except in God. And He's concerned about other things."

CHRIS

*I*n the month leading up to the church's big Homecoming celebration, the Premiere scandal was like a poisonous cloud hovering over the congregation. Jim White stayed away from church, and nobody knew where Bobby was. The legal process moved so slowly that it appeared nothing was being done. Everyone, especially Pastor Jennings, hoped that the anniversary services would shake the gloom and bring about reconciliation.

The Homecoming committee worked hard that month to make the event a success. Mom finished the photo boards, though the living room was still flooded with pictures. I squeezed as many stories and photos into the history book as possible. Beth and I saw each other during the frequent committee meetings, and we also started secretly spending time alone together, the frequency of our dates—a word we avoided—increasing each week.

The church was packed on Homecoming Sunday with most of the regular congregation and a few hundred visitors in attendance. As I looked around the sanctuary, I noticed that Bill's softball team, which had gone undefeated for four weeks in a row, sat down front with their proud coach. Robin was a few rows behind them, sitting with friends, as she had done every Sunday since her return. In the back of the church I saw Cheryl sitting ominously alone. She had been strangely quiet for a few weeks, though I had no idea what venom she may have been spewing in secret.

Dad was to spring a few surprises on us that day. I didn't see him in his usual pew that morning as the service began, but I knew he was in the church somewhere and figured he might be helping Mom with the photo boards. He had been feeling better since being released from the hospital, and during the week leading up to Homecoming, he was more active and upbeat than I had seen him all summer.

Pastor Jennings beamed as he stood in front of the packed congregation listening to the loud and excited voices of friends greeting each other for the first time in years. After the welcome and announcements and the first hymn, "A Mighty Fortress Is Our God," he stood in front of us again and said, "We have found many ways of celebrating the great work that the Lord has done in this church during its first fifty years. One thing you need to do before you go home today is take a careful look at the photo history boards out in the foyer that Helen LaRue has put together. We're sorry for any embarrassment those pictures might cause some of you by showing receding hairlines, polyester leisure suits, and the gigantic hairstyles popular at the time for women.

"But those photo boards serve a serious purpose during this anniversary. They are our family album, reminding us of how we have lived our lives together from the beginning days of this church in Mrs. Calvert's home through the five decades that have followed it. You look at those photos and watch the kids in one picture become the adults on the next photo board and the grandparents in the final one, each generation giving way to the next, each church building giving way to another, as we grow and find our way to God through good times and bad. You can see the crisis moments—fires and financial difficulties and hurt feelings—and you can also remember the miracles and reconciliation and the redeeming love of our Savior.

"We're here this weekend to do more than be nostalgic. We're here not only to thank God for the past but also to seek where He wants to lead us in the future. He's teaching us how can we live with one another and love one another and forgive one another."

The pastor paused, came out from behind the pulpit, and stepped to the edge of the platform. "This has been a difficult summer for our church in many ways. Lives have been hurt. Relationships have been broken. What better day than this for healing and forgiveness to begin? We've changed the order of service a little bit from what is printed in your bulletin. I'd like to introduce a quartet that many of you will remember, and they will lead us in a time of praise to the Lord."

My dad walked onto the platform first, followed by Jim White, two other singers, and their pianist. The stillness in the room as my father and Jim stood side by side, getting ready to sing, was more dramatic than if the entire congregation had gasped in unison. It was the first time Jim had appeared on the platform since the scandal broke, and the first time he had been seen publicly anywhere with one of the victims of the scam.

The group had not sung together for several years. They launched into their songs without comment and as naturally as if they still sang together every Sunday. To hear their voices blending in a medley of songs like "Jesus Paid It All," "My Tribute," and "Bless His Holy Name" was a more vivid illustration of homecoming and reconciliation than anything our committee could have planned if we had had the biggest budget in the world. Forgiveness flooded the sanctuary. When they finished singing, they didn't say a word and didn't need to. As Dad smiled and sang with those friends, I knew he had succeeded in his determination not to slink away as a victim. He was not a dying man. He was a new man.

Pastor Jennings' sermon, "The Greatest Homecoming Story Ever Told," was Jesus' parable of the Prodigal Son. I couldn't help thinking Pastor might have had me in mind as he spoke of a son who flees from his father but eventually returns and reunites with him, receiving forgiveness and celebration at his arrival home. This is the happy ending Pastor had been dangling in front of me all summer. There is even a disagreeable older brother in that story who tries to undermine the younger one. The older brother is alive in that story, but I've found it's no easier to come to terms with a dead brother than with a live one.

ROBIN

My face got all hot and embarrassed when Pastor started in on the Prodigal Son. I was afraid everyone was looking at me and thinking, *Yeah, we know who he's talking about now, only in this church it's not a* son *who's prodigal, it's a* daughter. Any minute I expected him to drop the story and say, "Now, if you think this guy fouled up his life, take a look at Robin LaRue."

Not that Pastor would do anything that mean. In fact, it was only after talking to him at the hospital that I finally decided I would come back to church. I told him how bad I felt for all I had done and how scared I was to face everybody. He said that if I didn't feel I could come back, then he was a failure as a pastor and our church was a failure as a church. He said God doesn't love us because we're good or because we deserve it. God loves us because it pleases Him to do so. All we can do is acknowledge our neediness and come to God that way. And that's pretty much how the Prodigal Son's story turns out. The father accepts his son back and throws a party for him and loves him even though he's done nothing to deserve it.

So I decided that even if people did think Pastor was talking about me, maybe it would teach them that I'm exactly the kind of person God would throw a party for.

JACK

$\mathcal{P}$astor Jennings didn't tell me what he was planning to preach on after we sang, but in all the years he's been here, I've never felt so strongly that he was targeting me for a sermon as when he started in on the Prodigal Son. The only problem is I'm not sure which character he takes me for. I feel that I fit every one of them! I'm like the son who needed disaster to strike before he finally woke up and faced the facts about his life and then ran back to his father for forgiveness. I'm also like the older brother, who expected everybody to live up to a certain standard that he thinks he himself meets. And now, I'm even like the father, welcoming back Robin, welcoming back Chris and my old friend Jim, killing the fatted calf for them, restoring the bonds between us before it's too late.

Near the end of his sermon the pastor spoke of the long tradition in our church of coming to the altar at crucial times in our lives, whether seeking a miracle from the Lord or guidance or salvation. He said that God the Father stood ready to welcome us with open arms just as the father had welcomed the Prodigal Son. The pastor invited us to come to the altar to pray and to seek forgiveness from God or from other people. He said, "This is Homecoming Sunday. Why don't we come home to the Lord and to each other? Some of you need to ask for forgiveness, and some of you need to grant it. One simple prayer at the altar won't replace the work that some of you will have to do to bring healing in your relationships, but it is a step forward that God will honor."

Even though the whole service was saturated with forgiveness, I walked down to the altar to take part in it as thoroughly as I could. Pretty soon Jim White came down too, and so did Chris, and so did Robin. And so did a number of others, too many to count. We prayed on our own while the congregation sang a hymn and the pastor spoke, then others came down to join us in prayer. The entire front of the sanctuary was packed with people praying out loud, their hands on each other's shoulders. Once they had prayed for one person, they prayed for somebody else, until after a while there was such a jumble of us that no one knew who was praying for whom.

CHRIS

*D*ad surprised everybody by going down to the altar and praying. I haven't seen him down there in years. Almost none of the men of his generation go down to the altar when the pastor gives an invitation. They seem to think it's a sign of weakness, an admission that they've done something wrong or need help. He even came up and hugged me in front of everybody and said, "I'm sorry, son. I let you down. I'm so sorry." I was too stunned to give much of an answer. I told him I was sorry too, but what I really wanted to say was, "What is happening to you?" I knew that the answer would be beyond words, this profound filling of his life by the Holy Spirit. He spoke to Robin, too, and to Jim White, but I didn't hear what he said. I was too busy praying, "God, please don't pass me by. Whatever you are doing in my father, please don't let me miss it myself."

Dad pulled one more surprise that day, but he did it anonymously. After the first service, we had an enormous meal under the tent and then gathered back in the sanctuary for another celebration, which included songs from some of the best-loved soloists who had moved away over the years, and a reminiscence from one of the former pastors of the church. Then Pastor Jennings talked about the church history book I had put together, which had been distributed as people left the morning service. He said our history revealed that we were a ministering church that gave of itself. He mentioned several people in the book who had devoted themselves to ministry, including Glen Abel, who had directed a dozen Work and Witness teams to other countries, Tricia Peterson, who had worked in the children's church for almost forty years, Tom Berenson, who ran the buses, and Myrlie Stokes, who had started the Helping Hands ministry to the poor and homeless of Indianapolis. He said that the planning committee decided to make the offering that afternoon go to missions, both to other nations and to the mission work in our own community, as a sign that in our next fifty years we would continue to be a church that not only looked inward but also reached out to others.

Pastor said a first donation of ten thousand dollars had already been made, and the couple who gave it wished to remain anonymous. The Lord had recently taught them to put a different value on their possessions, and they wanted to invest in something that would live on after they were gone. I knew immediately that the gift was from Mom and Dad. I knew that Dad had spoken those words to the pastor. Dad kept his gaze forward and betrayed no emotion as Pastor spoke, but when I looked over at Mom, she beamed with a smile of childlike excitement that I had not seen since the day she announced her trip to Europe. I stared at Dad so long that he finally glanced over and gave the faintest hint of a smile. His plan was complete. It was his last Sunday on earth.

JACK

$\mathcal{L}$ife is full of things you never thought you'd do. That's what I was thinking the day after the Homecoming service as I sat alone on the porch at the end of a hot sunny day. I never thought I would lose most of my retirement and then give ten thousand dollars to the church and plan a trip to Europe. I never thought I would sell this house. I never thought I would speak to Jim White again. I never thought I would outlive any of my children.

I never thought I would die. The possibility was always sort of a vague notion in the back of my mind, I guess, but never until this summer did I contemplate it as an unavoidable event, something that would actually occur in a particular place and time, altering my reality forever. Death to me always seemed more like one of those remote contingencies you anticipate when you buy homeowner's insurance—the house *could* burn down or be destroyed by a tornado or be wiped out in some monumental flood. But if you were reasonably careful and had fairly decent luck, the chances were in your favor to squeak through without any of those catastrophes. As arrogant as this sounds, death seemed like one of those things that happen to weak people who didn't take care of themselves or use their head or plan very wisely. Kind of like the idiots who let themselves be bilked out of their life savings.

Chris had mowed the lawn when he got home from work that day, and I could smell that wonderful aroma of cut grass as I watched the last of the day's sunlight slant across my yard. How many hours, days, weeks of my life had I spent tending that lawn—planting, fertilizing, weeding, cutting, watering—and how many more hours had I spent teaching and badgering David to do it, and then Chris after him. The maple tree in the middle of the front yard was once so spindly that I had to secure it with little ropes attached to wooden stakes. Now its trunk is massive, its branches shade the entire lawn, and I am an old man.

I taught all three kids to ride their bikes on this street. I glance across this lawn and can picture David when he was a little guy standing with his baseball mitt playing catch with me. I see Chris just barely old enough to waddle along, waving his arms wildly the way he used to and trying to toss a football that was too big for him. I remember Robin as a little girl singing at the top of her lungs and spinning herself around in the yard until she fell down dizzy. When I picked her up, she'd laugh and flail around and sing some more. Pretty soon I'll have a grandson or granddaughter running across this lawn, squealing as if they were the first person ever to discover the joy of motion or the tickle of the grass between their toes.

I am not ready to leave.

Early evening, just after dinner, was always my favorite time in this house. When we first moved in, I remember that incredible feeling of success and well-being that would fill me those first few minutes as Helen and I sat down in our living room after a hard day of work. This was what we had worked for. We finally had it.

Chris could never understand that kind of satisfaction. Maybe most kids can't. He just wanted to get away. He always wanted us to move somewhere more exotic, someplace that had a beach. He thought Indiana was the most boring place in the world.

It's funny that he would get so upset now about us selling the house, when he never cared a thing about it before. He could never find any pleasure in something simple like setting up a garage, arranging the tools just the way you want them, painting the place to make it look nice. I know this house almost as well as I know the members of my family. That may sound strange, and I've never said it to another soul, but it's true that a house has its own personality. Its peculiar sounds. You could take me all over town blindfolded, and I would still know this house the minute I stepped in it. The click of the furnace. The way that each faucet in here sounds different from every other one. The chirping of the crickets in the garage. I wonder if my kids will ever see the value of being in a place and staying there, knowing it and being known in it. Not only in a house, but in a family, a church, a job, a community.

My biggest fear of dying was always what it would do to Helen. David's death hit her so hard that I wasn't sure she could take another blow like that. After he died, she was so wounded that I used to try to shield her from talk of death any way I could. If we were watching a TV show and the death of a child was mentioned, I would quickly change the channel. We never went to another funeral, not even to that of a close friend at church. Our conversations maneuvered delicately around David, this huge unspoken presence—or absence—in the room.

Now I'm not so worried about Helen. I know grief will weigh heavily on her, but something has changed in her that is hard to describe. It's as if she has broken through some kind of barrier—much the way I feel I have—and she is no longer afraid. She has the calm strength of one who has endured what she feared the most and knows that there is life on the other side of it. Her trust in God is beyond circumstances now. I don't protect her anymore. I lean on her.

CHRIS

$\mathcal{B}$y the time of Homecoming, Beth and I were seeing each other almost every day. We never talked about why we were keeping our dates a secret, we just did it automatically. For me, I guess I didn't want to have to deal with prying questions or face embarrassment if the relationship fizzled yet again. The dates escalated as the days went on. First we went out for coffee, then we went out for dinner, then Beth invited me over to her apartment for the evening.

Our first few times together were tense. I felt I had to be ready at any moment to defend myself for all that had happened in our past. Finally, on the night Beth had me over for dinner, she said, "The problem is that whenever we're together, we feel the need not only to resolve everything from long ago, but also to figure out our entire future. It puts too much pressure on us. Let's forget all that and enjoy being together right now."

"The danger is that one or both of us will end up hurt."

"That's the risk you take when you invite people into your life," she said.

The truth was that by then I felt compelled to see her. I was beyond intellectual arguments with myself about whether it made sense to renew the relationship and all that. She was the only woman I had ever truly loved, and I wanted to be with her no matter how things turned out.

As we ate carrot cake and drank coffee in her living room that night, she said, "Maybe we got all the bad stuff out of our relationship early in our lives, and it will be smooth sailing from now on."

"You're a romantic," I said.

"If I weren't," she said, "I would have run away from you long ago."

_____

On the Wednesday after Homecoming, Beth had a meeting at school in the evening, so we had a quick dinner together at a little fast-food Chinese restaurant, and then I went home. Dad was waiting for me on the porch.

"You remember when you first came home, you offered to help me clean up the old Chevy?"

"Yeah."

"Is that offer still good?"

"Of course! When?"

"How 'bout right now?"

"Sure. Do you feel up to it?"

"Absolutely. Cleaning a car is the most relaxing thing in the world."

I didn't bother to challenge this assertion. In California, I had never washed my own car. I had always run it through the car wash at the gas station.

"When we get done, I'll take you for a ride in it if you want."

"I'd love it!" The car had not moved from its cobwebby slab of driveway all summer.

We spent two hours polishing that car, longer than I had ever spent cleaning any other. We wiped away every spider web underneath the car, shined the heavy chrome on the grille and the hood ornament and the side panels that said *De Luxe*. I vacuumed the carpet and seats on the inside, cleaned the windows inside and out. I sat in the driver's seat and wiped off the enormous white steering wheel, built to maneuver these bulky cars in an era before power steering. We used Armor All on the whitewall tires until they were gleaming.

Robin came out for a minute to see what we were doing. Dad was working on one of the tires, and I was vacuuming the front seat. I stepped out of the car to speak to her, but she only smiled and shook her head as if to say, "It figures." I thought of her comment about Dad and I making up. *"Probably nobody would know it because you wouldn't actually say anything to each other. You'd just punch each other in the arm or whatever it is guys do."*

Robin waved and turned around and went back inside. Once we had cleaned every inch of the car, it was time for a ride. Even clean, the inside of the car had a peculiar musty smell that was not unpleasant but reminded you of its age and made you feel as if you were stepping back into that era. The car sat up higher than most modern cars, and people in the neighborhood stared in curiosity and admiration as we drove by. The sky was almost dark as we pulled out of the neighborhood and headed toward the lesser-traveled roads west of town that seemed most appropriate for this machine of an earlier generation.

"I should never have let this car deteriorate," Dad said. "There are so many things I've let go these past couple years. It's like I was in a daze. I can't explain it. I felt trapped inside myself."

Trapped inside himself! He didn't have to explain it. I had felt that way all my life.

JACK

I was trying not too successfully to explain a few things to Chris as we took our ride in the old Chevy. I know he thinks I hold a grudge against him for crashing into the car. His mother told me that. But I really don't. The car wasn't the point.

Failing to think of an eloquent way of getting this across to him, I finally came out with this: "I want you to know that I never wanted that accident with the car to make you move away."

"I know, Dad."

"I was devoted to the car, but almost anything would have set me off back then. I hated losing touch with you those two years. I thought about it every day. But something inside me collapsed that year, and it's taken me all this time to begin to crawl back to the surface."

"I know exactly what you mean," Chris said. "I felt the same way myself. Maybe that's why I stayed away so long. I guess we're just alike."

"Who would have thought that?" I said, and we laughed.

I felt I should say more, but Chris looked contented, as if I had said it all, so we just enjoyed the ride. It was one of the best times we had spent together. I finally felt he was really *sitting* there with me instead of just putting up with me until he could find a convenient time to escape, the way he used to.

"Next time we should take Mom and Robin too," Chris said when we pulled back into the driveway.

"That sounds good to me," I said. "Thanks for helping me clean this thing up."

CHRIS

I practiced softball with Bill and his team that Thursday. Their winning streak had kept morale high, so their practice was vigorous. I had never pictured Bill as a coach and had been skeptical of Pastor's decision to put him in that position. But Bill was a natural at it, blending just enough encouragement with authority to keep the boys working hard. Practice started right after I got off work and lasted for two hours at the church's softball field, so by the end of it I was worn out. Bill, however, was still filled with energy, clapping and yelling and joking with his team. After his final pep talk to them, Bill and I got cleaned up and went to O'Toole's for dinner.

It wasn't long before the conversation steered itself toward my renewed relationship with Beth.

"You did it, didn't you?" he complained in an indignant tone that I couldn't quite take seriously. "You let her get her hooks into you even though you vowed you wouldn't when you came back this year."

"Well, some loves never die."

"Oh, listen to yourself!" he bellowed in mock rage. "I drove two thousand miles across the country with you, listening to all the garbage about how it was over between you and you had learned your lesson."

I smiled and nodded, admitting what he said was true. "Well, I realized I still love her. And she loves me too."

Bill shook his head and sighed. "You are weak and pathetic. Both of you. You deserve each other."

"You're not half as cynical as you try to pretend."

"Yes, I am," he insisted. Then after a short pause, he burst out, "You're going back to California! This is no time to get entangled with a woman."

"Take it easy, Bill. Details can be worked out. I can teach here just as well as in California. I still have to finish at Purdue anyway. If I'm coming back to Indiana, this would be the right time."

"You can't leave California."

"Why not?"

"You love it there! The weather. The ocean. The girls on the beach. Don't let yourself be brainwashed into thinking this is what you want to do. Where will I go for vacations?"

"Bill . . ."

"Are you telling me that you two are going to get married?"

"Yes, as a matter of fact we are."

"But you've only been back together a few days!"

"It's been a little longer—"

"When did you decide this?"

"Probably within the first ten minutes that we were together again. We don't know when or where and all that, but we know it's right. I truly believe the Lord brought this woman into my life, and she feels the same way."

Bill looked down and sipped his Coke. "Don't get all sentimental about women with me," he said. "Women have ruined my life."

"No, they haven't," I said. "You haven't given them enough of a chance."

If there was any barrier that remained between Beth and me, it was the trouble with Cheryl. With all the confession and forgiveness that had taken place during Homecoming, I was finding it harder to justify shutting Cheryl out. Reluctantly, I agreed to Beth's suggestion that we invite Cheryl over, and I would tell her as much as I could bring myself to.

I dreaded this meeting, but I finally believed it was inevitable. Cheryl would not stop her quest for the truth no matter how many lies she had to spread to provoke me to reveal it. I had to come to terms with her one way or another.

Beth invited her over to her apartment on Friday night. Cheryl wore a dress with a gold necklace and earrings, in sharp contrast to our more casual look of shorts and T-shirts. Her heavy makeup made her look as if she were hiding behind a mask. As she sat across from us at Beth's kitchen table, she looked like a judge preparing to deliver the death sentence. My stomach churned.

Beth had invited her for dinner, but she had declined. She wouldn't even drink a cup of coffee.

"Cheryl," I began, "I know you've recently become interested in getting to the bottom of David's strange behavior in those months before he died."

"I've always been interested in it," she corrected me.

"Yes, well, I've always been reluctant to talk about it because of loyalty to my brother. But Beth, and just about everyone else, thinks that the fair thing to do would be to tell you everything I know. To ease your mind, I guess. So I'll answer whatever questions you have."

"I don't want to ask questions," she said. "I want to know everything that was going on with him. You know what I want to know."

Now that we faced each other, both of us hesitated to speak the words that put the man we both loved in a bad light. I didn't know how to proceed.

Finally Cheryl blurted out, "Was David having an affair with another woman?"

"Yes, he was. Her name was Tracy."

After that, telling the rest of the story was easier. I told her how David's relationship with Tracy had started in Chicago and how she kept pestering him even after he had tried to get rid of her. I apologized for the part I had played in his schemes. Cheryl asked only a few questions and did not express much surprise at anything I said. She sat with her arms folded in front of her and her head slightly bowed, as if each word I spoke was a blow that she had to absorb.

When my story was over, she leaned back in her chair, her body losing its rigidness. We all sat quiet for a moment. I had been prepared for her to cry or lash out at me in anger, but she did neither. She looked into the distance, barely aware of us.

"Can I get you something to drink?" Beth asked her.

"No, thanks," she said. "I have to be going." She stood and headed for the door. As she stepped out she turned to me and said, "Thanks for telling me this. I know you didn't want to do it, but it helps."

After Cheryl was gone, Beth said, "That went pretty well, didn't it?"

"Yes. Much better than I feared."

"That's the way it is with confession," she said. "The anticipation of it is worse than the actual telling. People aren't always as shocked by things as you think they'll be. Think how scared Robin was to face your parents and her friends at church. The agony of avoiding them was ten times worse than the pain of confronting them."

We avoided any more mention of Cheryl that evening. A burden had been lifted from us, and we were more content in each other's presence than we had ever been.

————————

Beth's parents had moved to Kokomo, about an hour's drive north of Indianapolis, the year after I went to California. On the day after our talk with Cheryl, Beth and I drove up to see them. We thought it was time to let our family and friends know that we were together again. We were too apprehensive to discuss marriage with them yet after the fiasco of two years earlier. We thought we would ease them into the idea gradually over several weeks as they got used to seeing us together. We made plans for lunch with them and supper with my parents.

The time we spent with Beth's parents was extremely polite, and everyone carefully avoided touchy topics about the past so that an outsider listening in would not have deduced that Beth and I had ever been engaged.

"It's a start," Beth said noncommittally as we headed back to Indianapolis. On the way home we stopped at Eagle Creek Park to walk around the lake and enjoy the warm afternoon. Then we went back to Beth's, and I waited while she got cleaned up for dinner. We were supposed to meet my parents at our house by six, and we were running late. It was ten till six when we pulled into our driveway, and I still had to take a shower and change clothes. I could do that in less than half an hour, but when Dad made plans for six, he did not mean six-twenty.

Before we even got to the porch, old Mrs. Lawrence from next door came running across the lawn toward us faster than I had ever seen her run, and I knew something must be terribly wrong.

"Your dad," she puffed, out of breath. "The ambulance took him to the hospital. Your mom said to get over there right away."

"How long ago?" I asked.

"Couple hours."

By the time we got to the hospital, Dad was dead.

Pastor Jennings was already there, and so were Mom and Robin. They took me in to see his body, which was still in the hospital room. The sight of his lifeless gray face was almost too much for me to bear. Pastor stayed with us the whole evening and helped us make arrangements and call our family and friends. Beth also helped, calling many of the people in the church and Dad's co-workers.

The next few days were a blur of funeral preparations and a steady stream of visitors, both at our house and at the funeral home, where we had visitation for two nights leading up to the funeral. Aunt Dayle and Uncle Ray were at our house from morning till night every day and were a great help in greeting people and fixing meals and answering the telephone. Mom had not moved her photos from the living room, and people who visited liked sifting through them and reminiscing about Dad.

Mom held up pretty well, going for several hours at a time without crying, then collapsing into someone's arms when a comment sparked a memory or when the reality of Dad's death hit her particularly hard.

One of the most difficult moments for me was when my cousin Jeff came by the house on Sunday and wandered out back to take a look at Dad's old Chevy. I told him I would show it to him, so I got the keys— the first time I had ever held them—opened the doors, and sat on the driver's side. Every detail of that car, from the gleaming black fenders to the shiny chrome hood ornament, the round clock in the dashboard, and the massive white steering wheel, brought Dad alive to me and filled me with the hollow dread of his absence. I gripped the steering wheel with both hands and rocked slowly back and forth as waves of grief poured over me.

The funeral was at our church, and I was surprised at how many people came that I had never met. A few dozen men and women Dad had worked with at Maximilian Webber came. Many of them introduced themselves to me and told me how much they had admired Dad. While I didn't know most of them by sight, I had heard many of their names over the years in the stories Dad told at the dinner table in the evenings. Jim White was there, as were Bill, Cheryl, and more people from church than I could count. Most of the neighbors from our street came. Even Aunt Shirley was there, and at the visitation the night before the funeral she and Mom hugged and talked and, at least for the moment, buried their differences.

One person who talked to me not long before the funeral was Mrs. Calvert, who was known for having founded our church in her living room. She told me of the death of her husband many years before. She said that during the years when he was working, she used to sit at home in the evenings and wait for him to come home from work. He always parked out front and walked around to the back of the house to take his dirty shoes off at the back door. On his way back there, he would tap on the window of the room where she sat. "It was a friendly little hello," Mrs. Calvert said, "and it let me know he was home so I wouldn't be startled by his noise in the back of the house."

"On the day he died," she said, "I had just been up to see him at the hospital, where he'd been for several days. He was fine when I left him, and when I got home, I sat down in that chair where I used to wait for him to come home from work. All of a sudden I heard his tap on the window. I didn't think anything of it at first because I was so used to hearing it. But then I thought, no, it couldn't be him. Ten minutes later, the phone rang, and I was told he had died.

"I've always believed that tap on the window that night was his sign to me that he was home. Home with the Lord. And I know your father is home now too."

Pastor Jennings presented the funeral message, and one portion of his message was particularly memorable to me. He said, "Some people die unprepared, as if the very concept of death had never occurred to them. Others, like Jack, leave with a sense that, even though they have not finished everything they had hoped to do, they have taken care of the essential things. Those of you who have been with Jack LaRue over the past several weeks know that he left with a sense of grace, a sense of resolution. None of us could ask for more than that."

After the funeral, we had a big dinner at our house for the relatives and some of the people from church. Beth and I made no secret that we were together and intended to stay that way. Robin was thrilled, and several times throughout the day when she saw us together she would come up behind us and give us a hug.

Aunt Dayle told everyone she was planning a baby shower for Robin, and as the afternoon faded, I heard someone asked Robin whether she hoped for a boy or girl.

"I have a feeling it's a boy," she said. "And if it is, I intend to name him Jack."